The Tale of the Outcasts

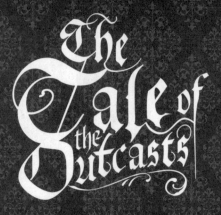

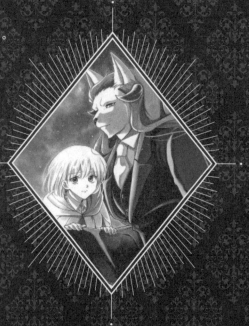

1

story & art by

Makoto Hoshino

The tale of outcasts

1

Contents

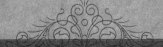

⚜Night 1⚜ Let's Be Alone Together

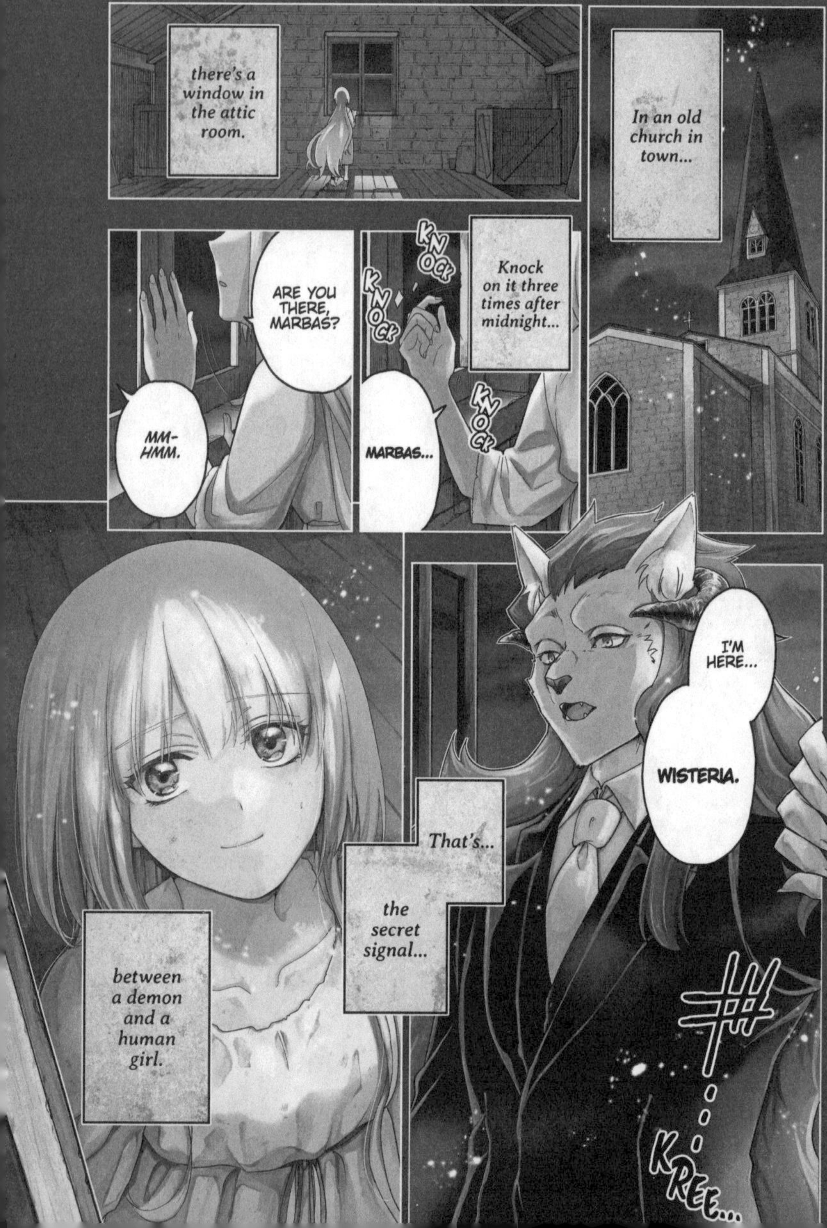
In an old church in town...
there's a window in the attic room.
Knock on it three times after midnight...
KNOCK
KNOCK
KNOCK
MARBAS...
ARE YOU THERE, MARBAS?
MM-HMM.
I'M HERE...
WISTERIA.
#...KREE...
That's...
the secret signal...
between a demon and a human girl.

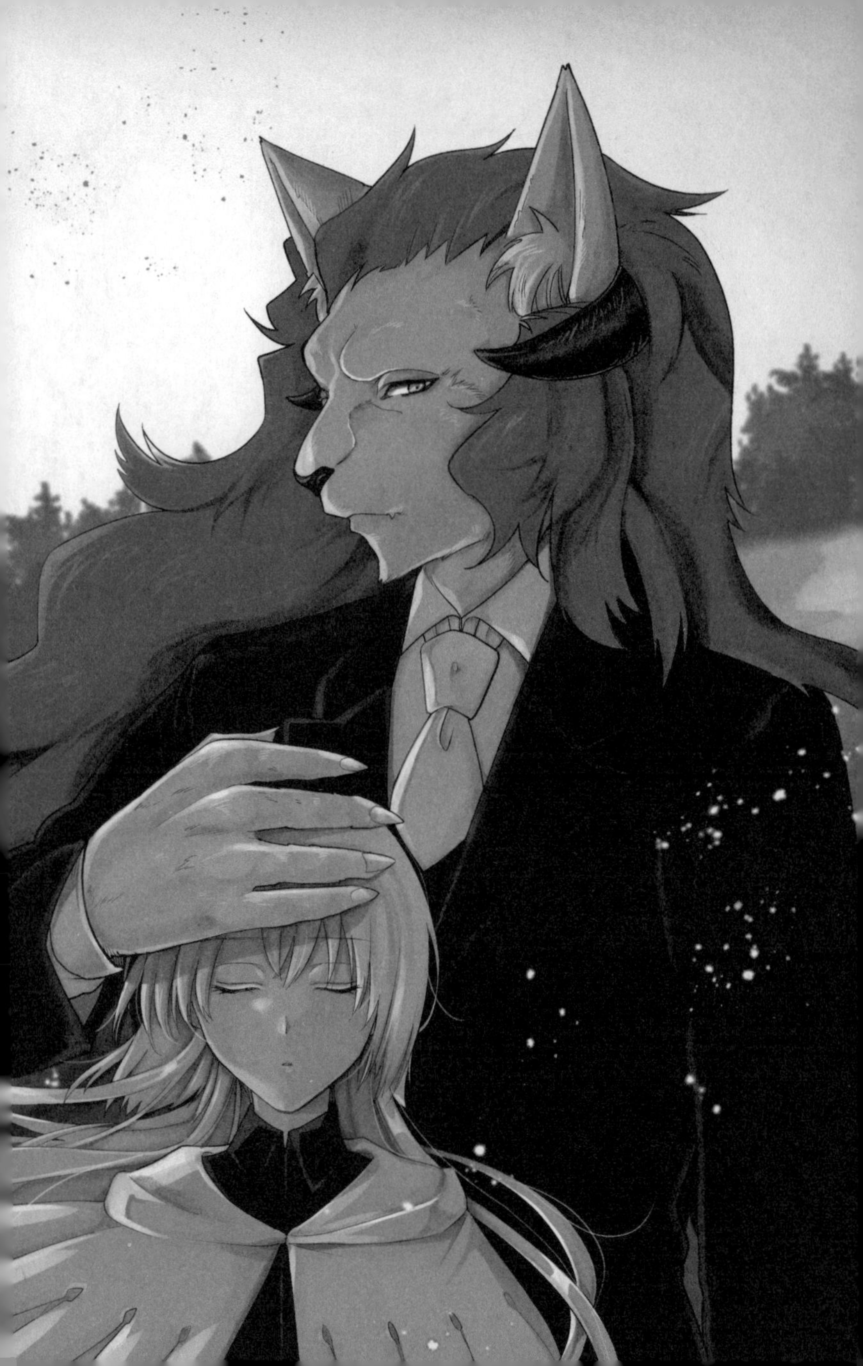

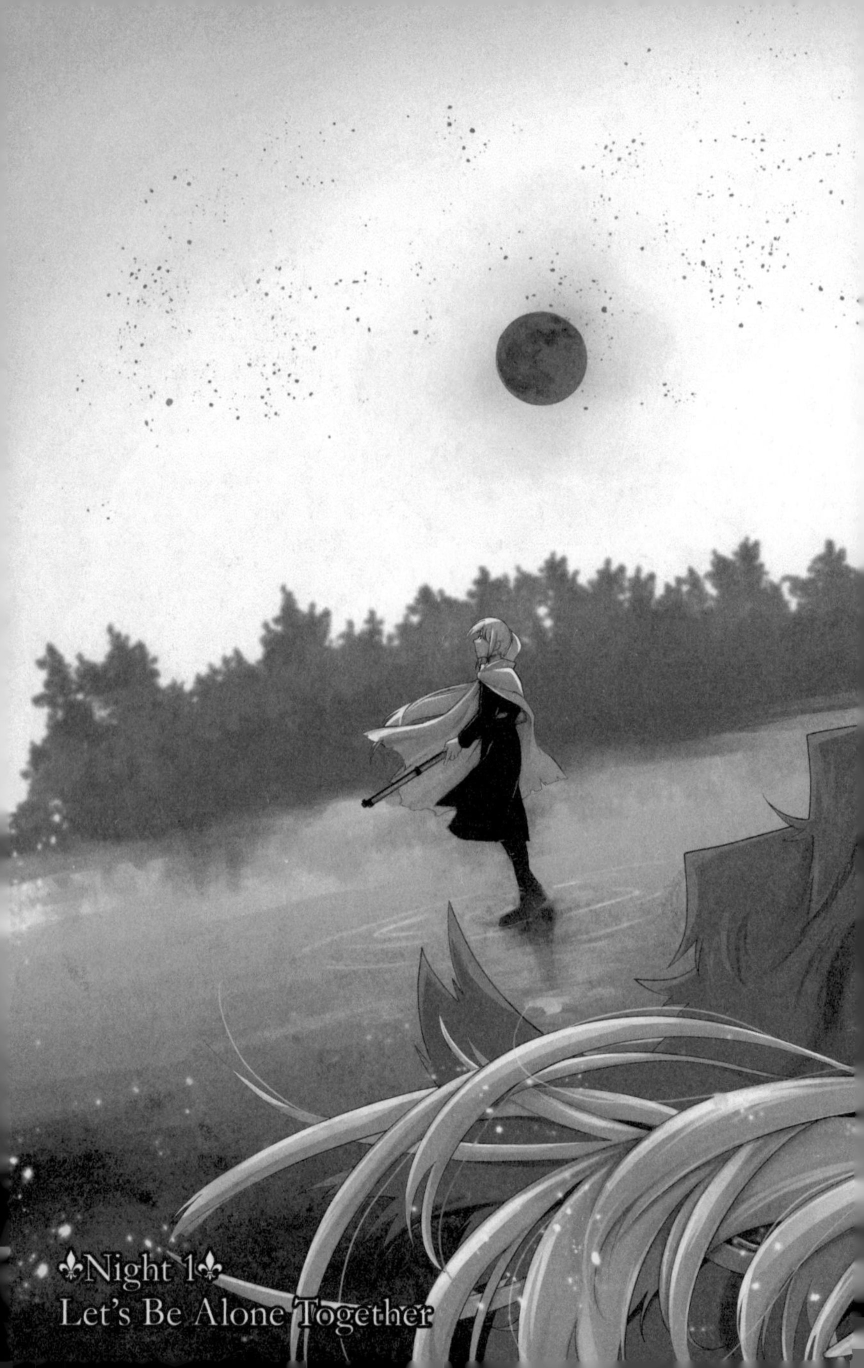
⚜Night 1⚜
Let's Be Alone Together

The Tale of the Outcasts

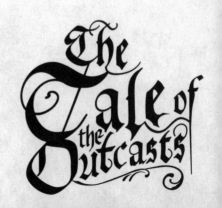

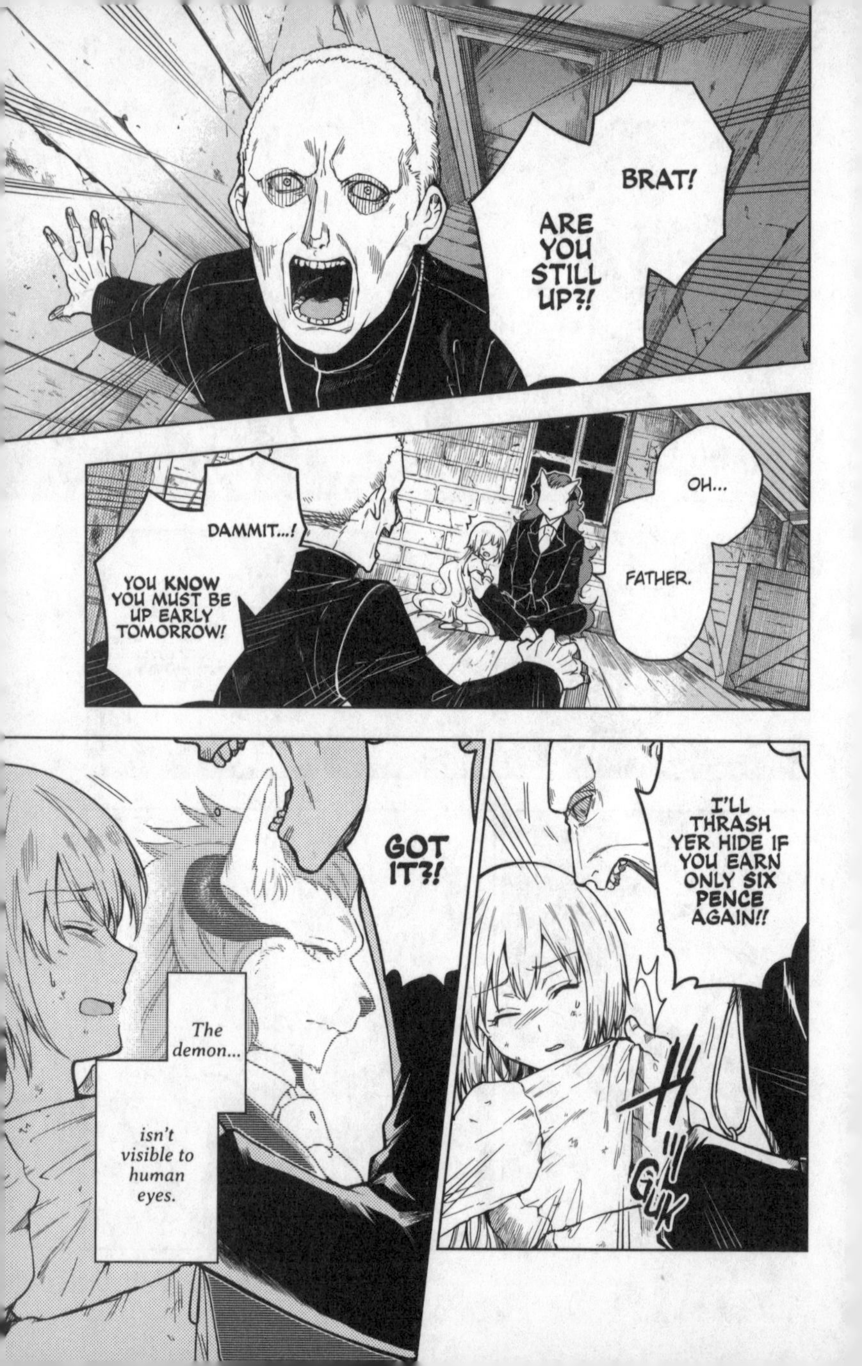
BRAT!
ARE YOU STILL UP?!
OH...
FATHER.
DAMMIT...!
YOU KNOW YOU MUST BE UP EARLY TOMORROW!
I'LL THRASH YER HIDE IF YOU EARN ONLY SIX PENCE AGAIN!!
GUK
GOT IT?!
The demon...
isn't visible to human eyes.

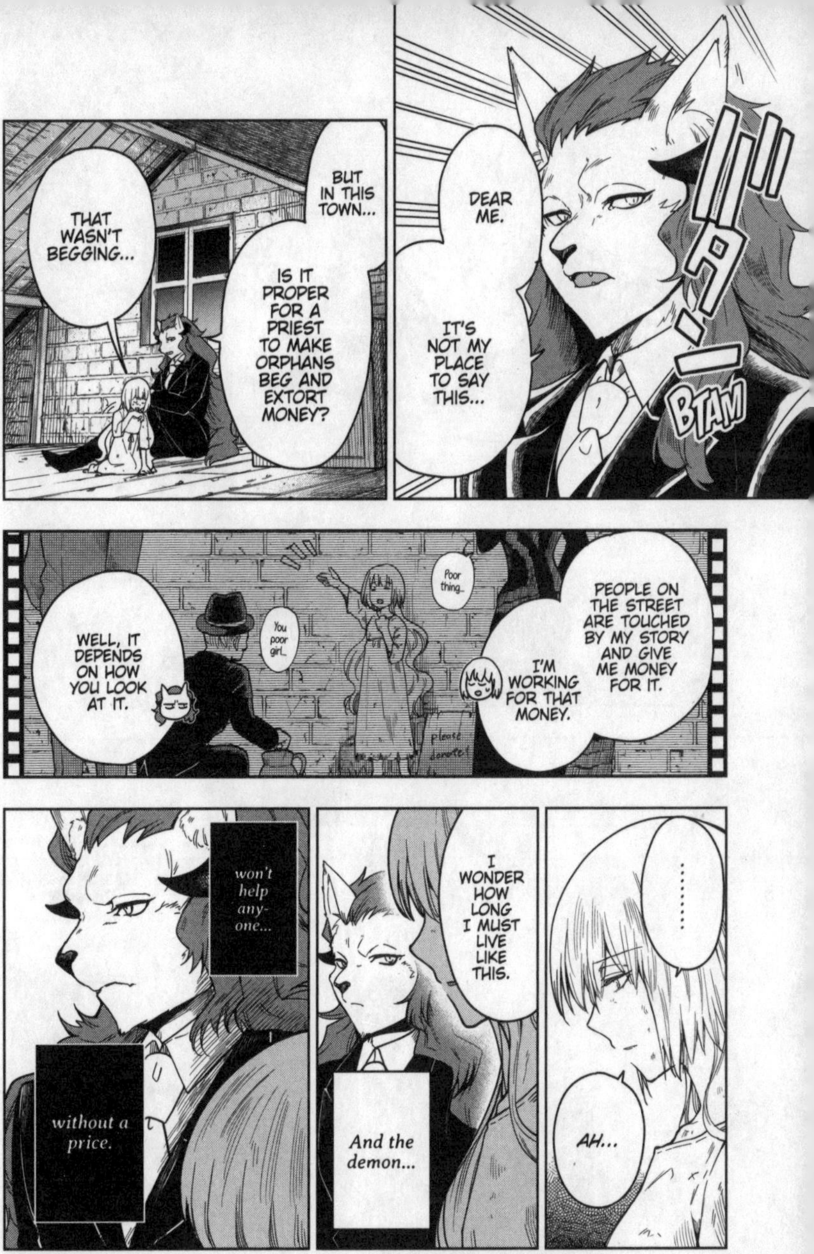
BTAM
DEAR ME.
IT'S NOT MY PLACE TO SAY THIS...
BUT IN THIS TOWN...
IS IT PROPER FOR A PRIEST TO MAKE ORPHANS BEG AND EXTORT MONEY?
THAT WASN'T BEGGING...
PEOPLE ON THE STREET ARE TOUCHED BY MY STORY AND GIVE ME MONEY FOR IT.
I'M WORKING FOR THAT MONEY.
Poor thing...
You poor girl...
please donate!
WELL, IT DEPENDS ON HOW YOU LOOK AT IT.
......
AH...
I WONDER HOW LONG I MUST LIVE LIKE THIS.
And the demon...
won't help any-one...
without a price.

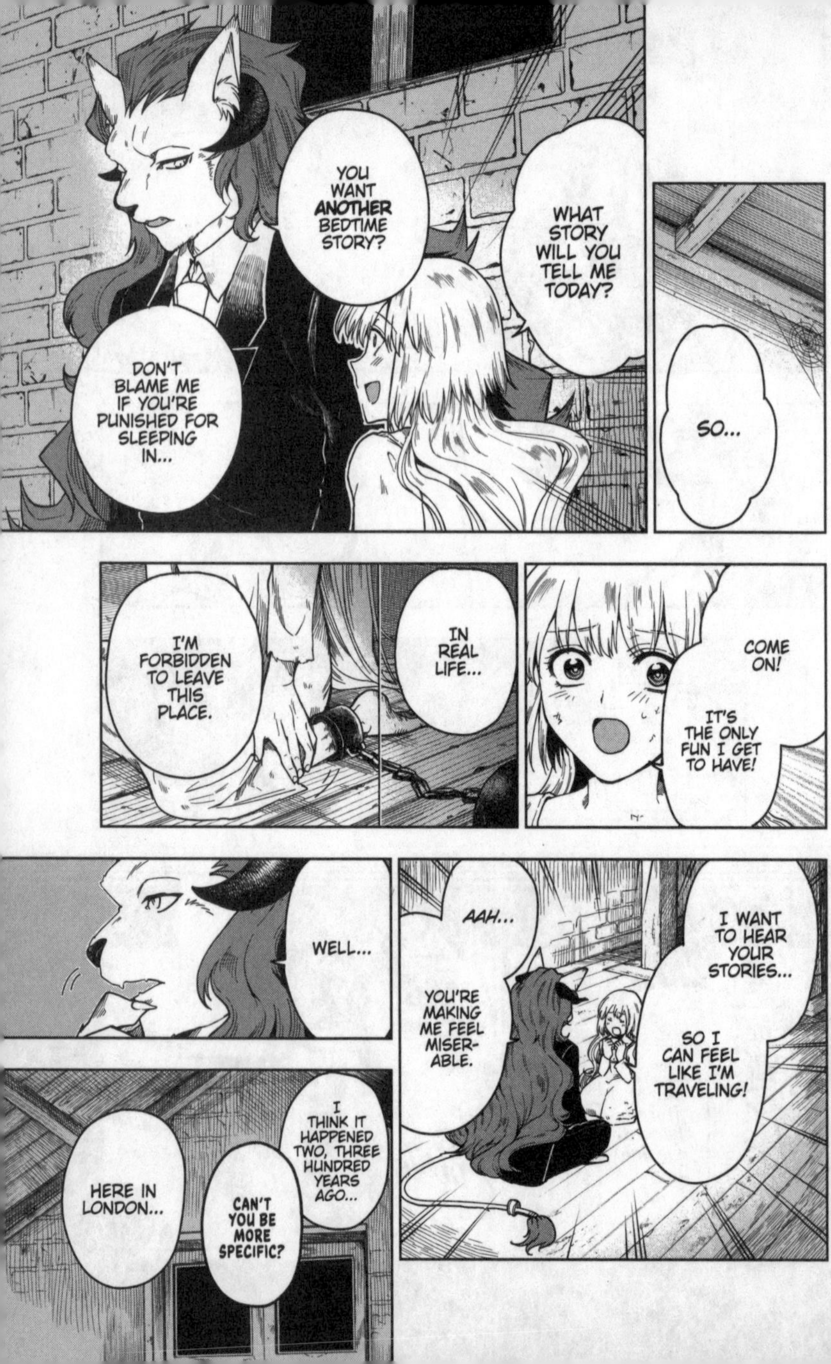
SO...
WHAT STORY WILL YOU TELL ME TODAY?
YOU WANT **ANOTHER** BEDTIME STORY?
DON'T BLAME ME IF YOU'RE PUNISHED FOR SLEEPING IN...
COME ON!
IT'S THE ONLY FUN I GET TO HAVE!
IN REAL LIFE...
I'M FORBIDDEN TO LEAVE THIS PLACE.
I WANT TO HEAR YOUR STORIES...
SO I CAN FEEL LIKE I'M TRAVELING!
AAH...
YOU'RE MAKING ME FEEL MISER-ABLE.
WELL...
I THINK IT HAPPENED TWO, THREE HUNDRED YEARS AGO...
HERE IN LONDON...
CAN'T YOU BE MORE SPECIFIC?

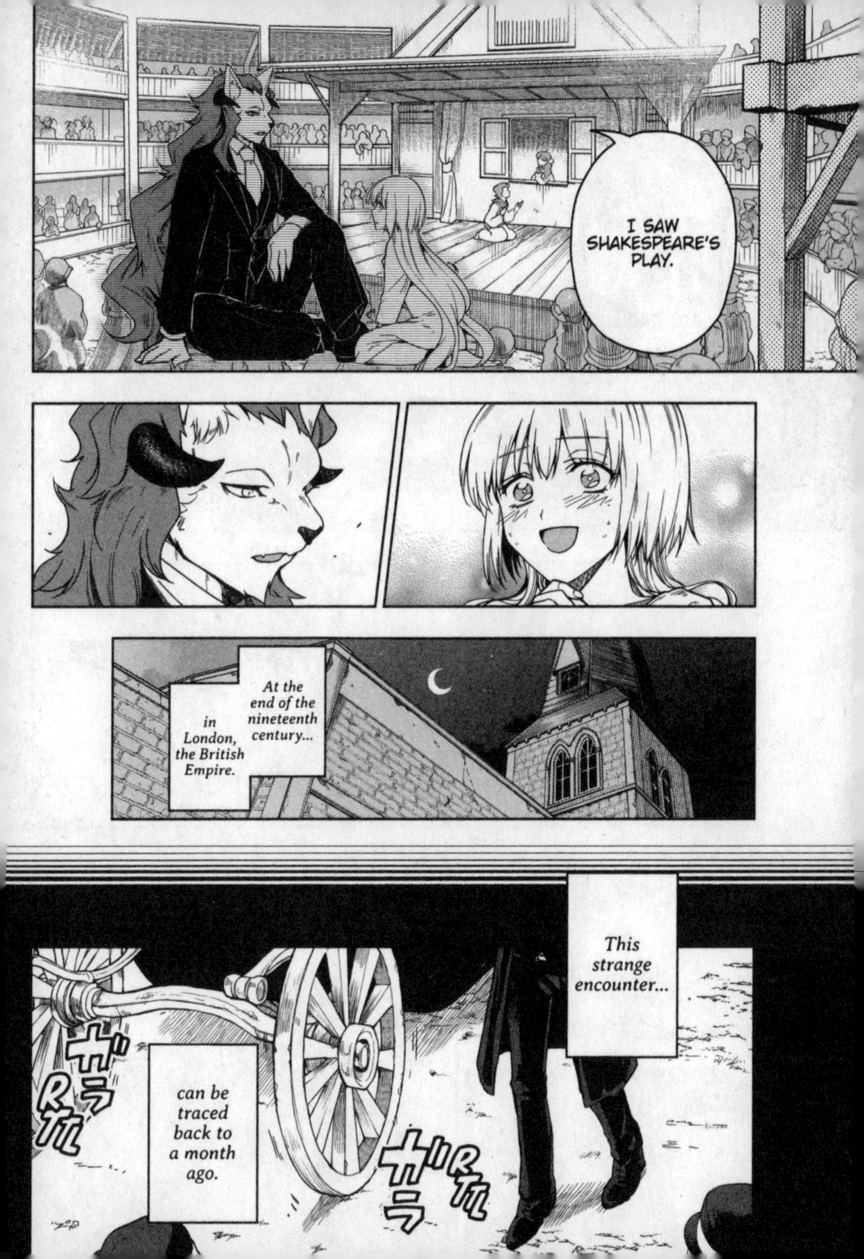
I SAW SHAKESPEARE'S PLAY.
At the end of the nineteenth century...
in London, the British Empire.
This strange encounter...
can be traced back to a month ago.
ガラ
ガラ

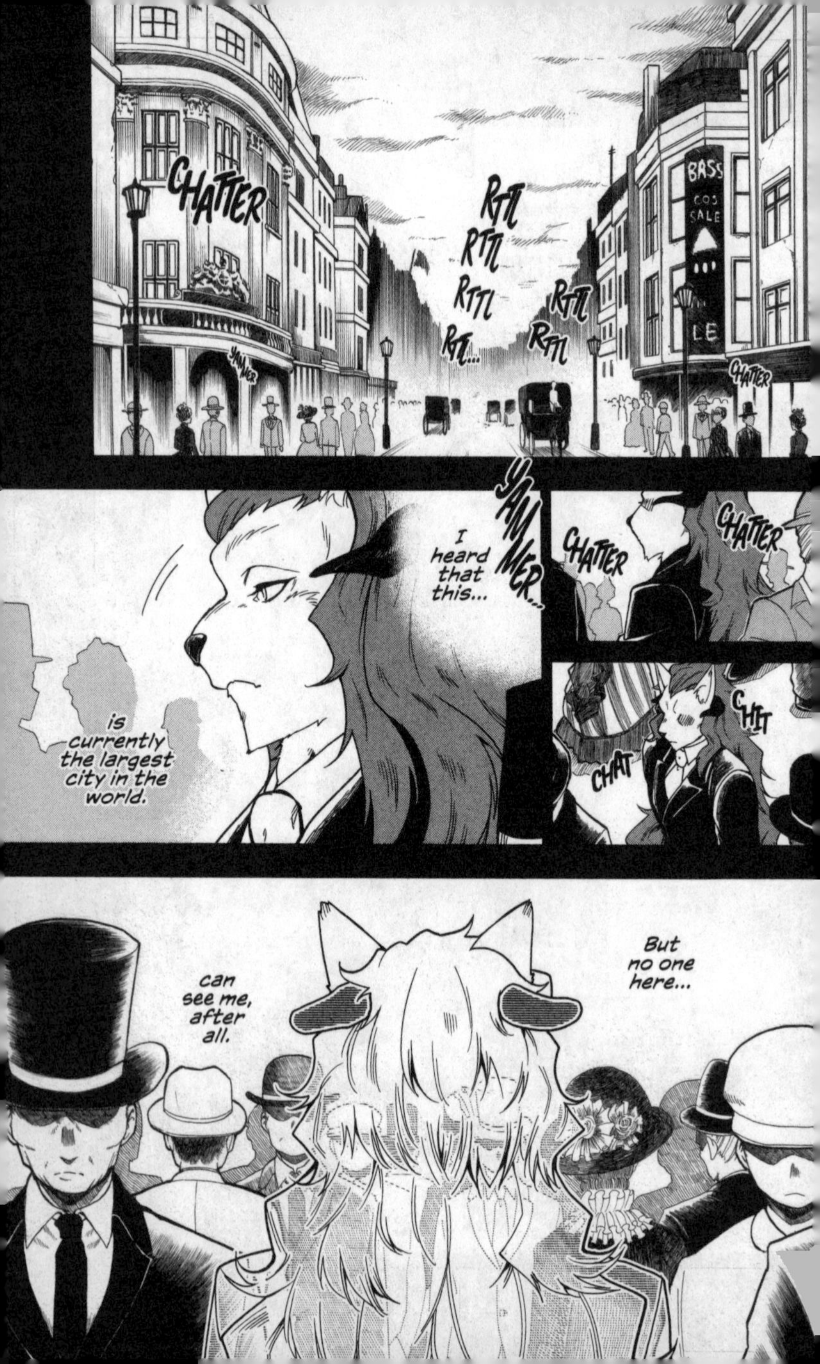
BASS
SALE
CHATTER
RTTL
RTTL
RTTL
RTTL
RTTL...
CHATTER
YAMMER
CHATTER
CHATTER
CHIT
CHAT
YAMMER...
I heard that this...
is currently the largest city in the world.
But no one here...
can see me, after all.

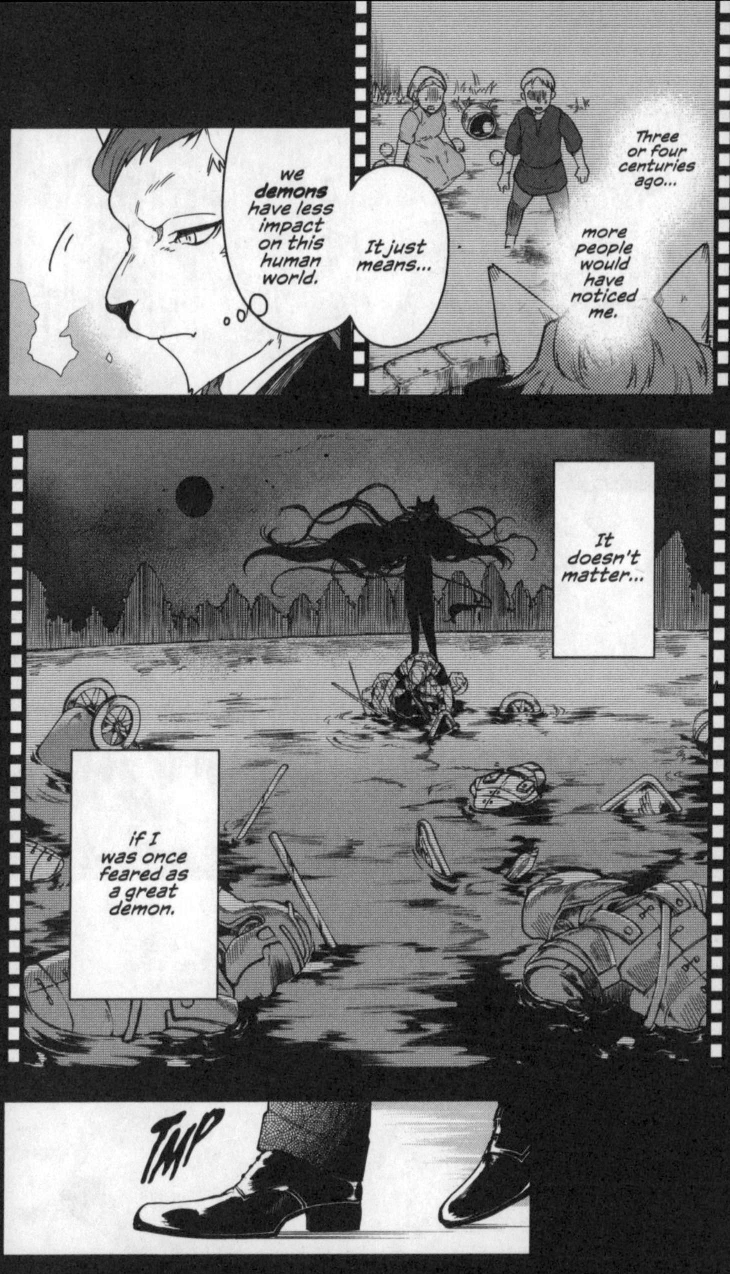
Three or four centuries ago...
more people would have noticed me.
It just means...
we demons have less impact on this human world.
It doesn't matter...
if I was once feared as a great demon.
TMP

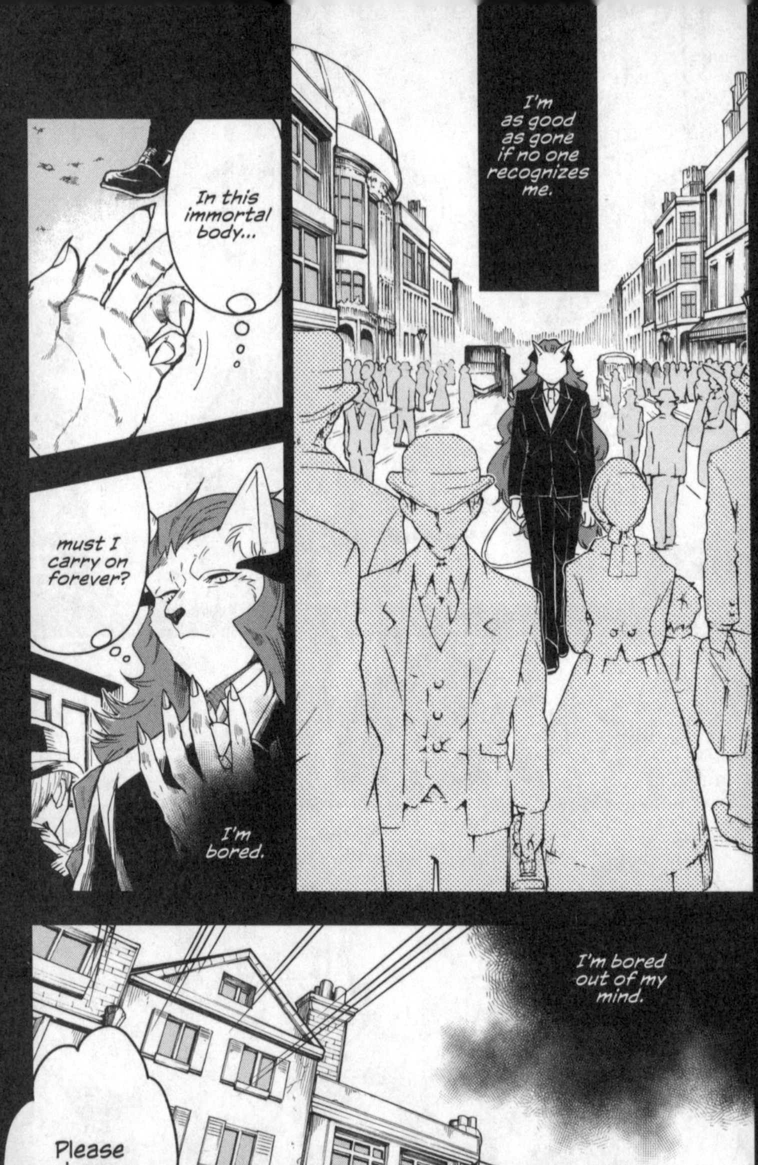
I'm as good as gone if no one recognizes me.
In this immortal body...
must I carry on forever?
I'm bored.
I'm bored out of my mind.
Please have mercy!

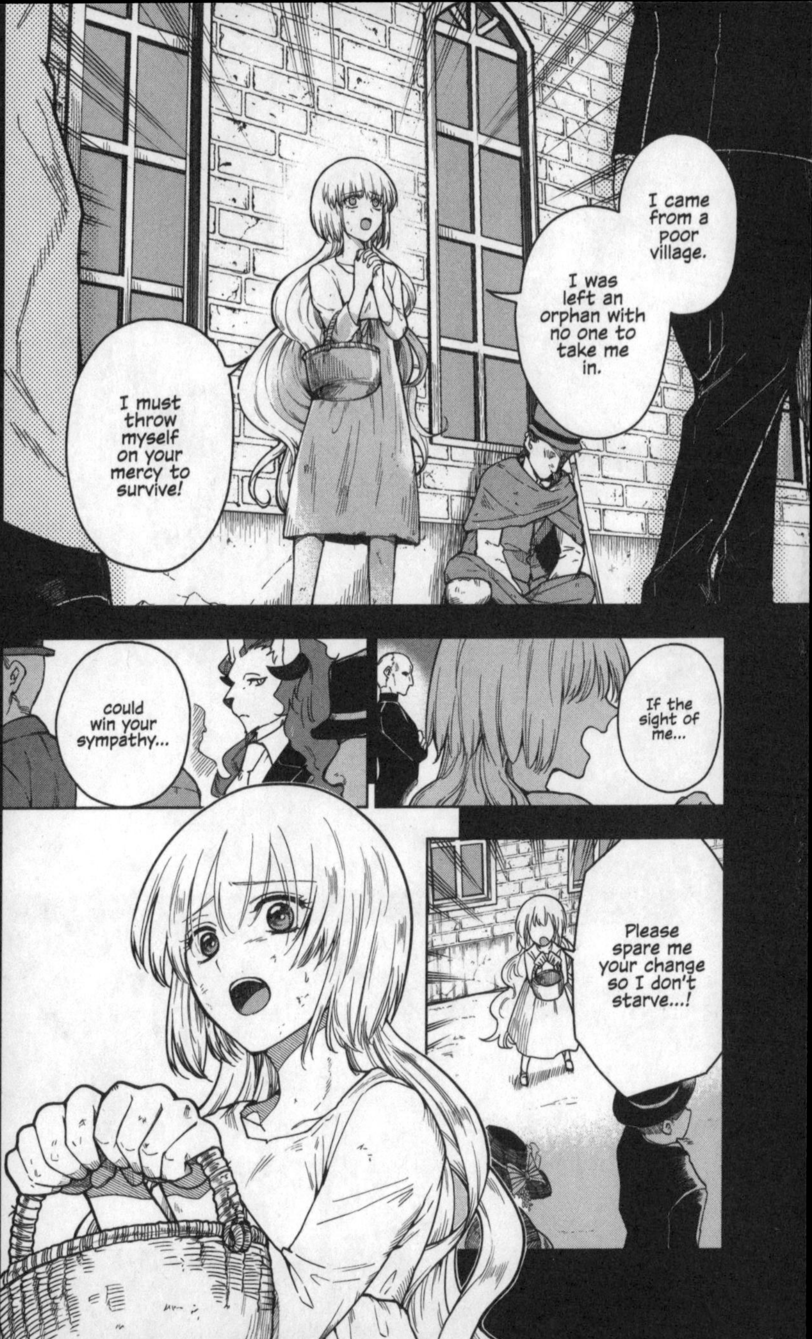
I came from a poor village.
I was left an orphan with no one to take me in.
I must throw myself on your mercy to survive!
If the sight of me...
could win your sympathy...
Please spare me your change so I don't starve...!

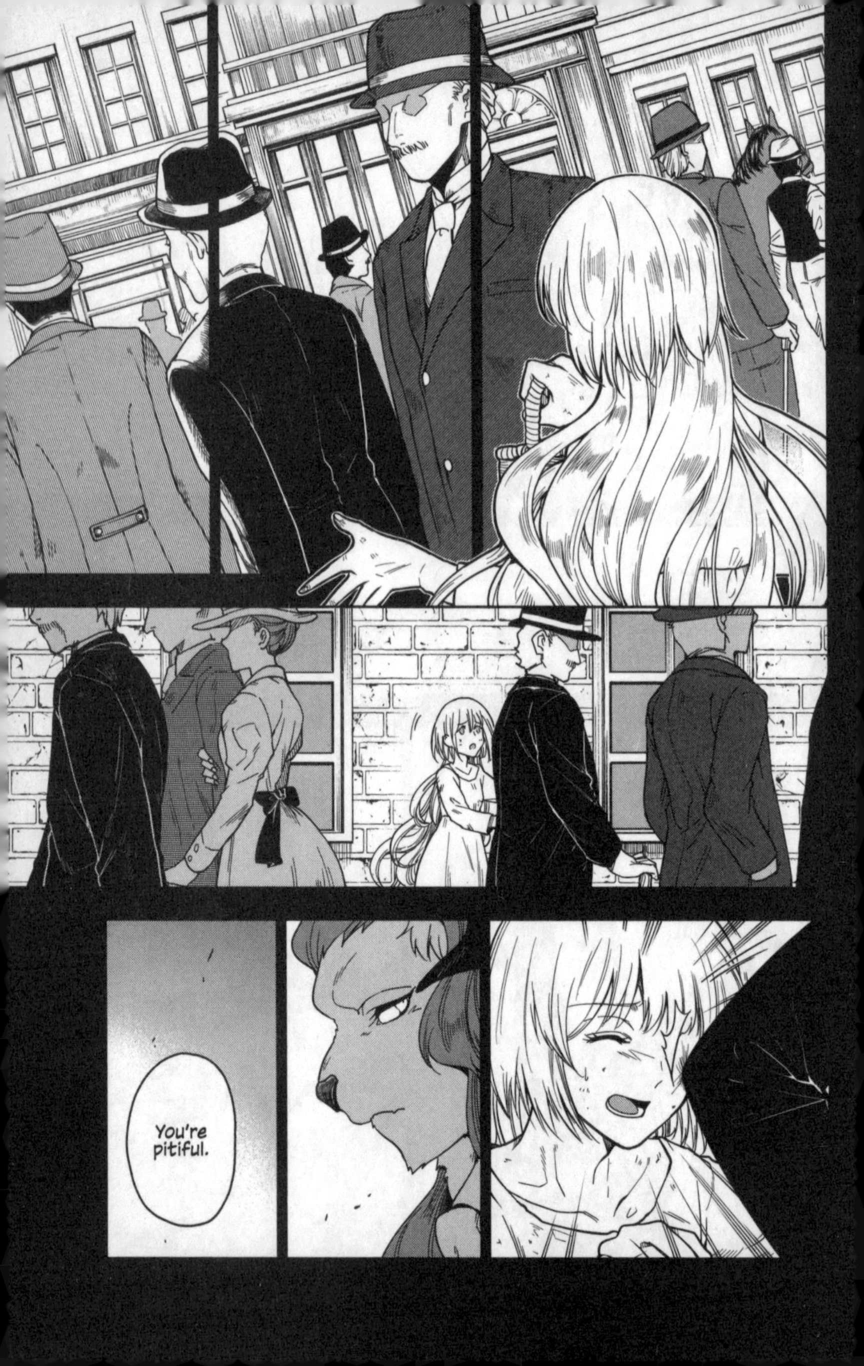
You're pitiful.

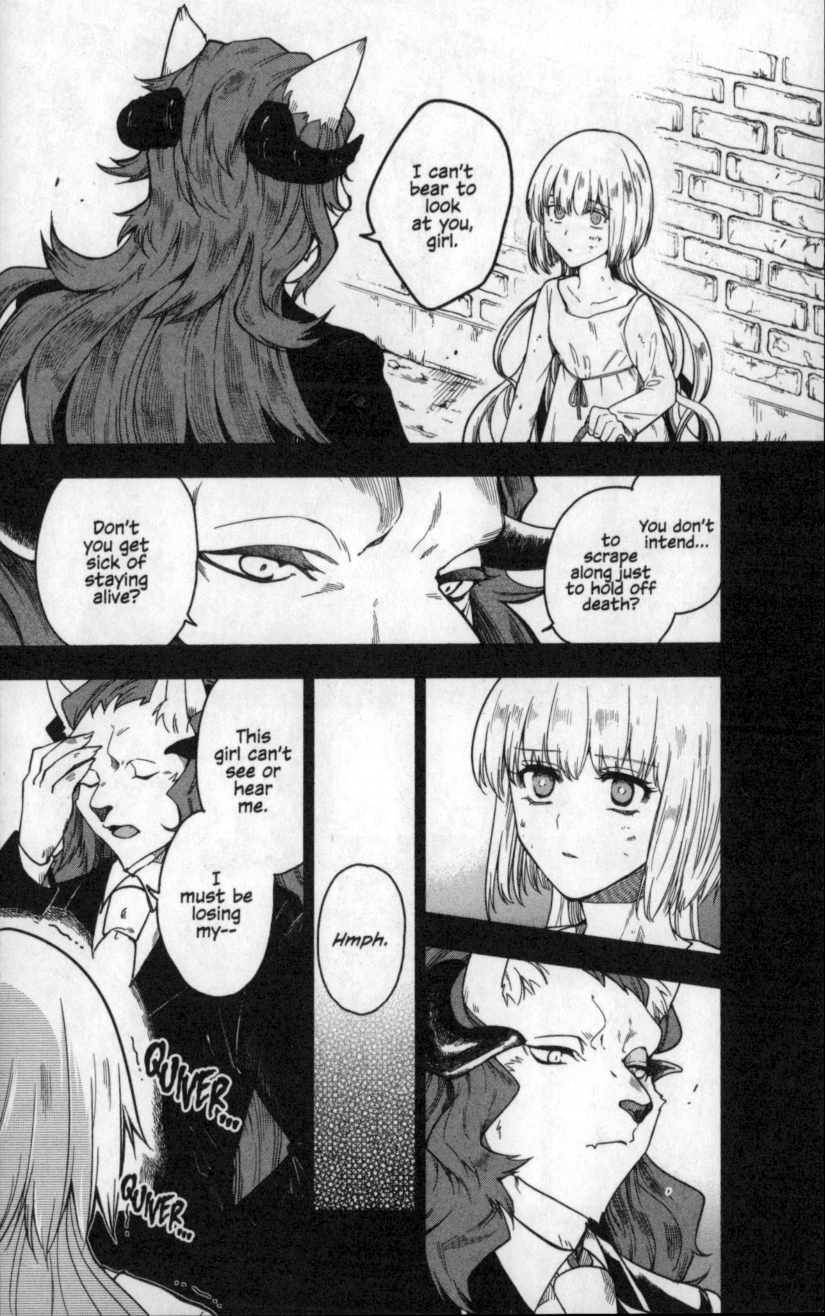
I can't bear to look at you, girl.
You don't intend... to scrape along just to hold off death?
Don't you get sick of staying alive?
Hmph.
This girl can't see or hear me.
I must be losing my--
QUIVER...
QUIVER...

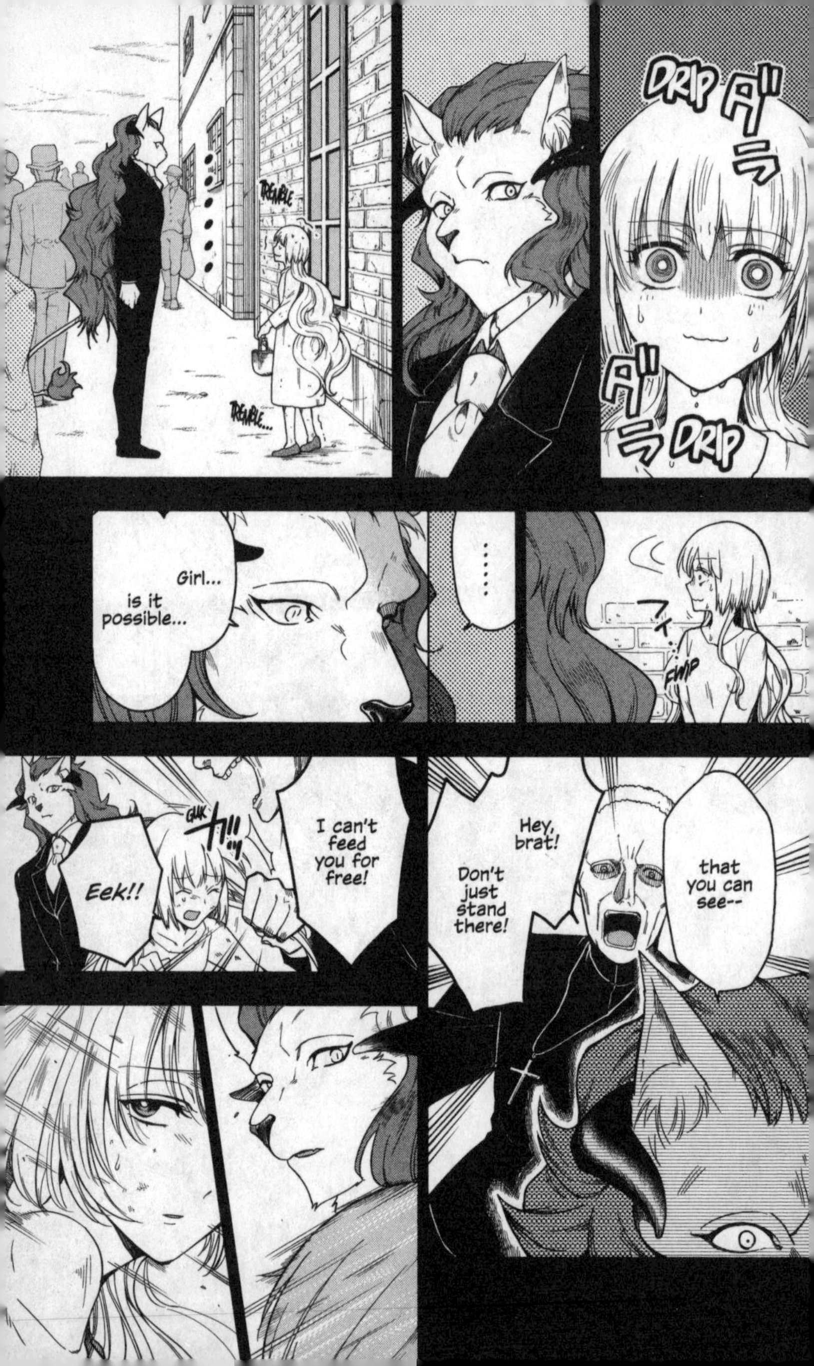
DRIP ダ ラ
ダ ラ DRIP
......
TREMBLE
TREMBLE...
フイ
FWIP
......
Girl... is it possible...
that you can see--
Hey, brat! Don't just stand there!
I can't feed you for free!
GUAK ガ!!
Eek!!

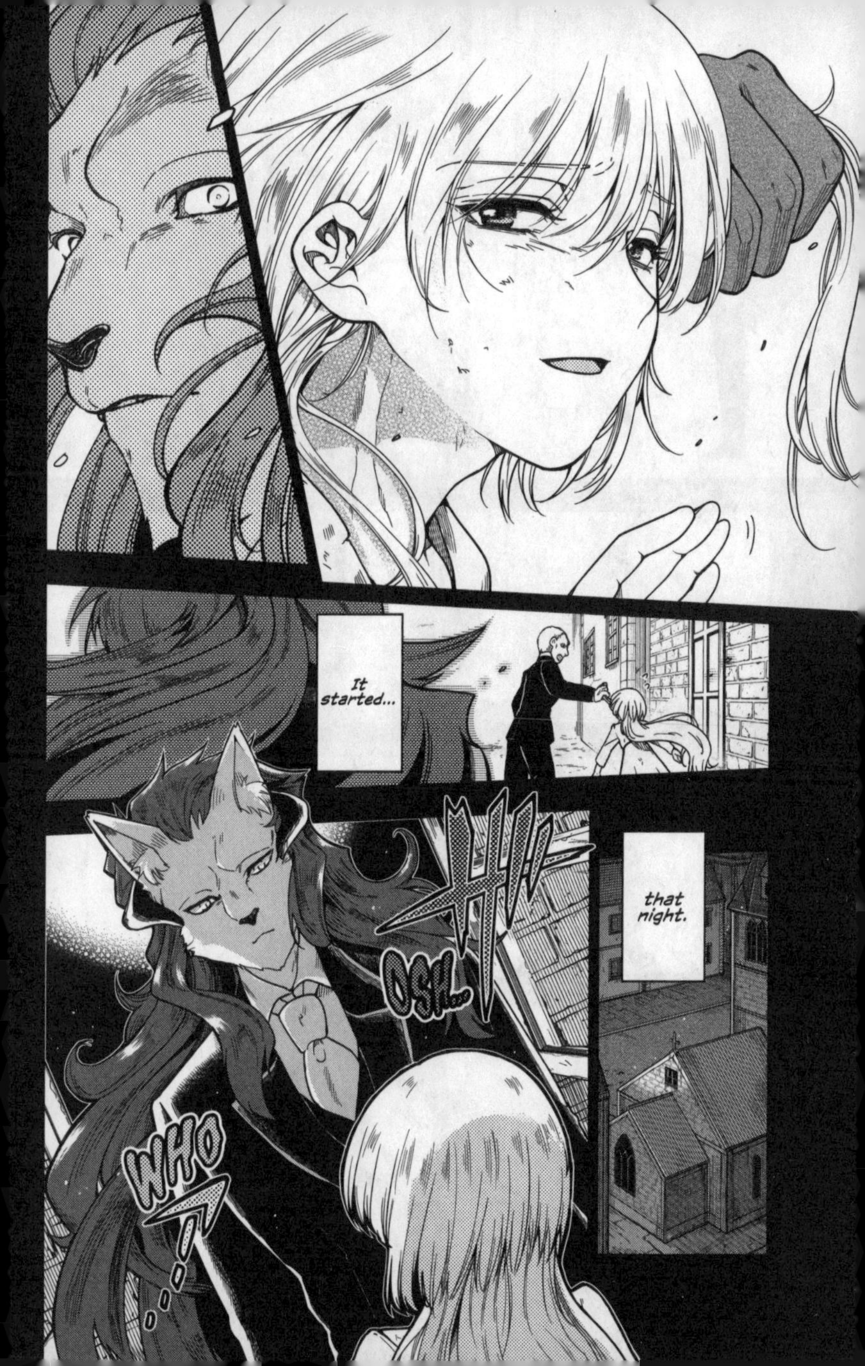
It started...
that night.
WHO
OSH...

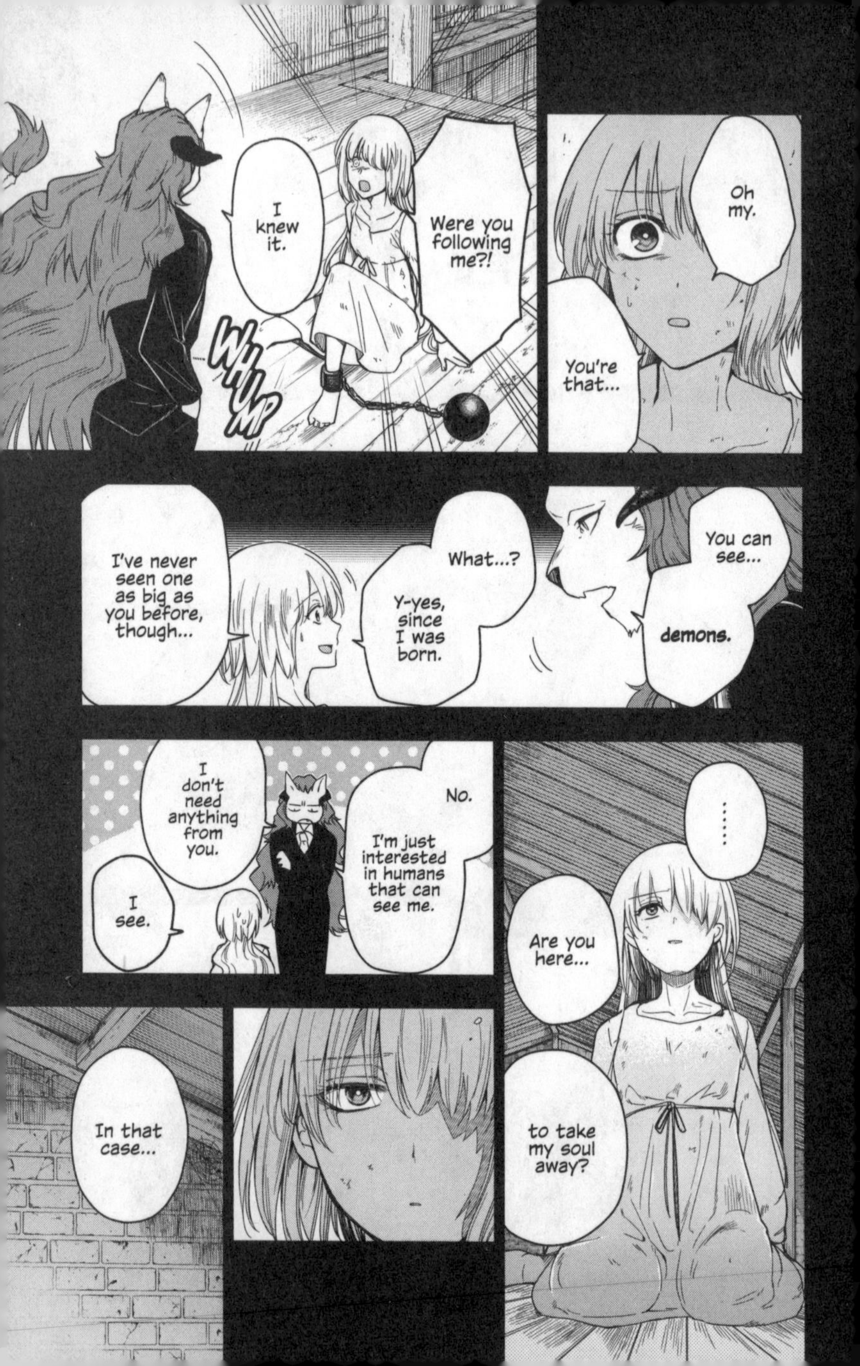
Oh my.
You're that...
Were you following me?!
I knew it.
WHUMP
You can see...
demons.
What...?
Y-yes, since I was born.
I've never seen one as big as you before, though...
......
Are you here...
to take my soul away?
No.
I'm just interested in humans that can see me.
I don't need anything from you.
I see.
In that case...

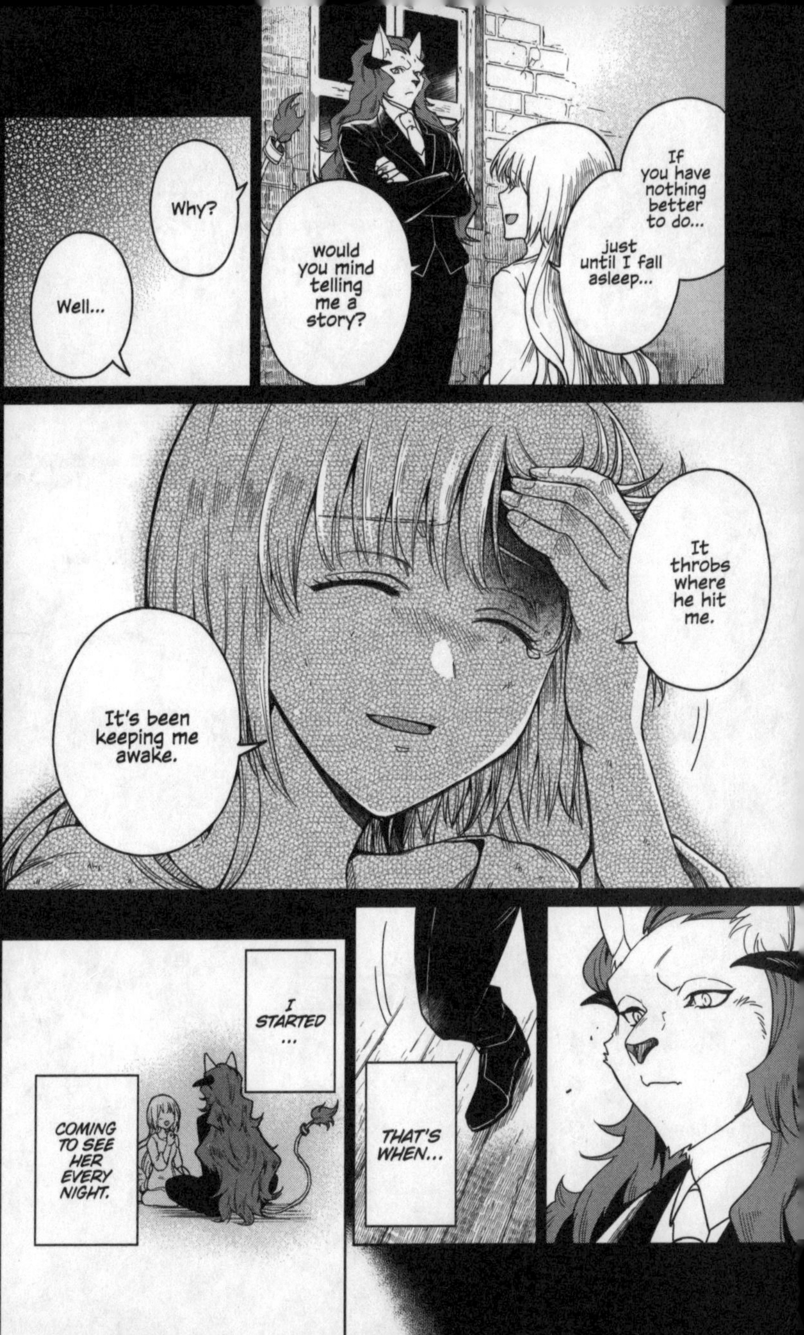
If you have nothing better to do...
just until I fall asleep...
would you mind telling me a story?
Why?
Well...
It throbs where he hit me.
It's been keeping me awake.
THAT'S WHEN...
I STARTED ...
COMING TO SEE HER EVERY NIGHT.

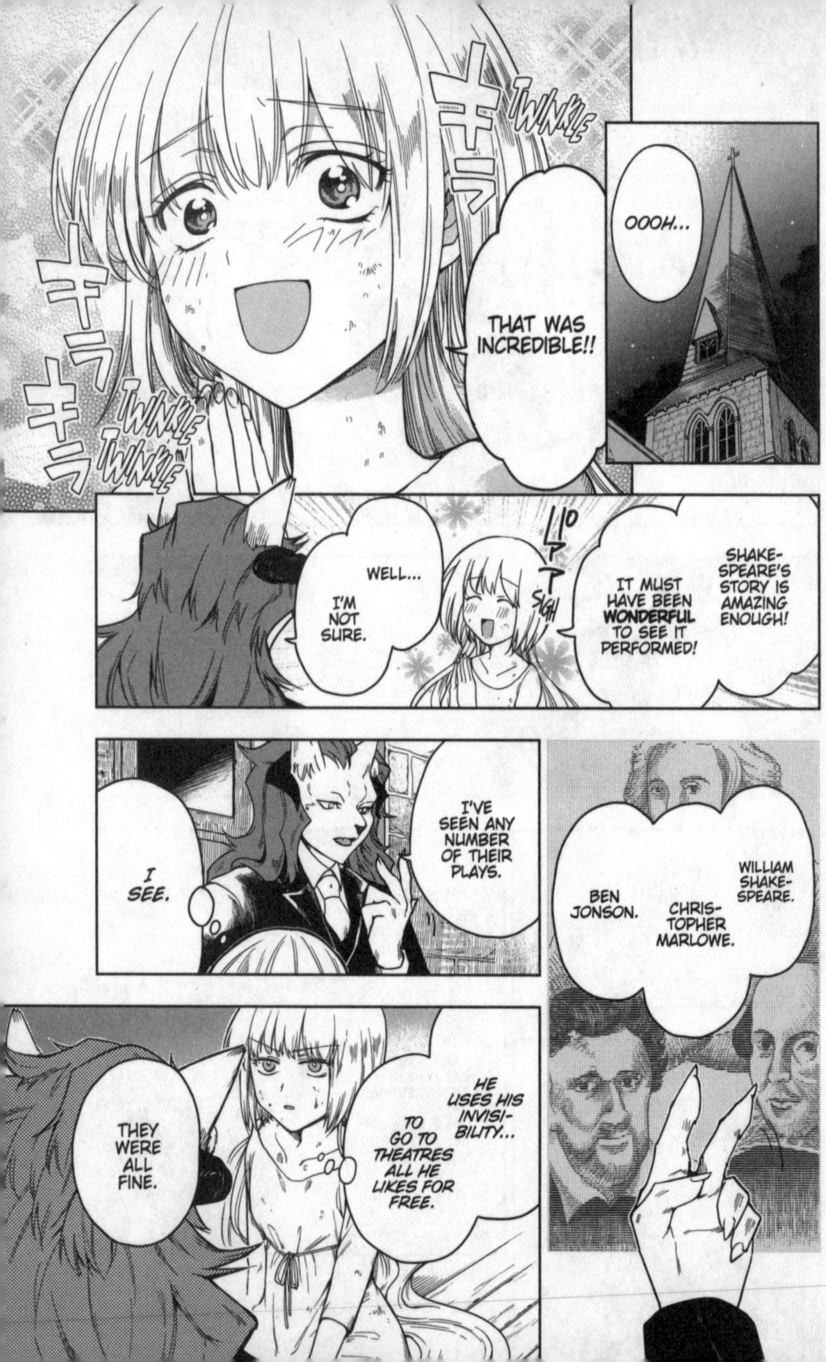
OOOH...
キラ
TWINKLE
キラキラ
TWINKLE TWINKLE
THAT WAS INCREDIBLE!!
SHAKESPEARE'S STORY IS AMAZING ENOUGH!
IT MUST HAVE BEEN **WONDERFUL** TO SEE IT PERFORMED!
SIGH
WELL...
I'M NOT SURE.
WILLIAM SHAKESPEARE.
CHRISTOPHER MARLOWE.
BEN JONSON.
I'VE SEEN ANY NUMBER OF THEIR PLAYS.
I SEE.
HE USES HIS INVISIBILITY...
TO GO TO THEATRES ALL HE LIKES FOR FREE.
THEY WERE ALL FINE.

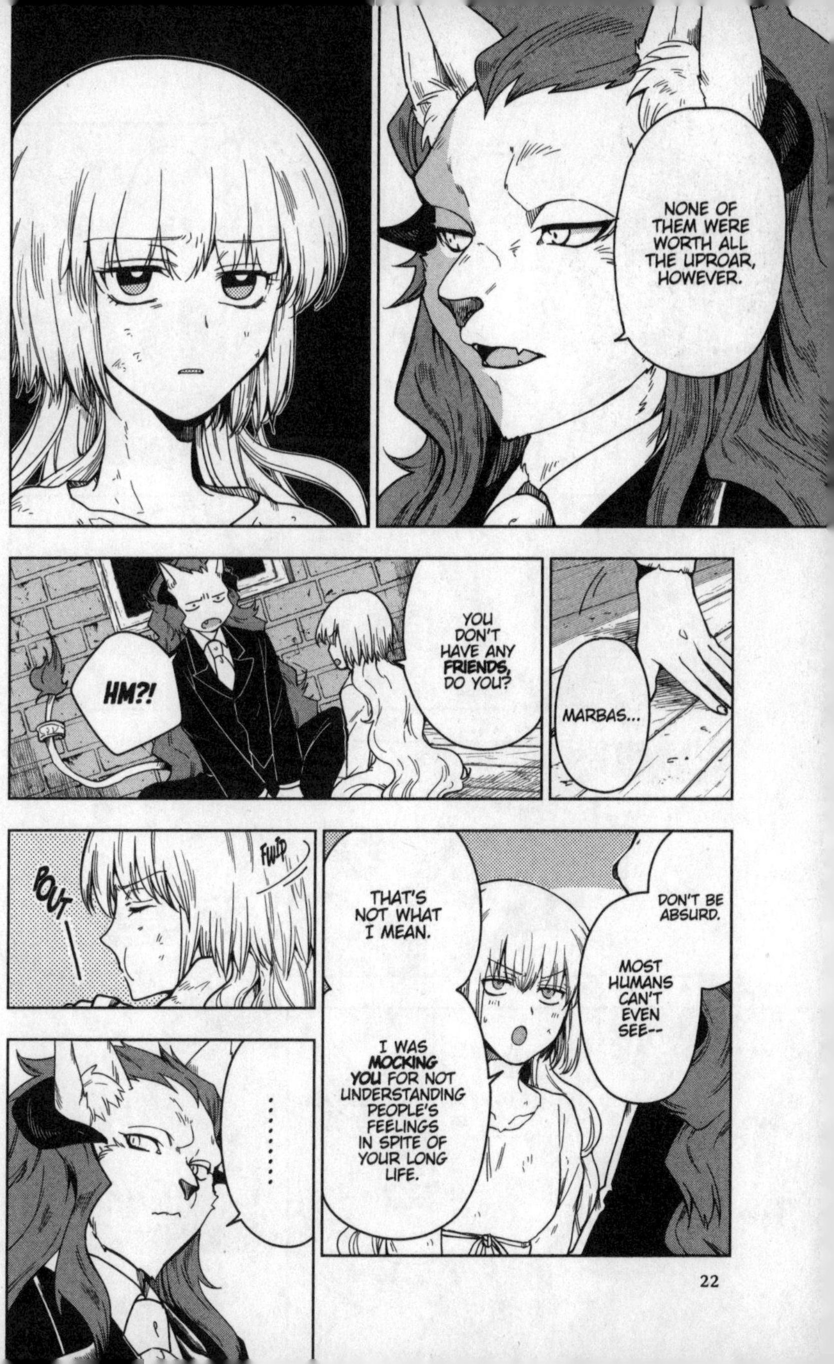
NONE OF THEM WERE WORTH ALL THE UPROAR, HOWEVER.
MARBAS...
YOU DON'T HAVE ANY FRIENDS, DO YOU?
HM?!
DON'T BE ABSURD.
MOST HUMANS CAN'T EVEN SEE--
THAT'S NOT WHAT I MEAN.
I WAS MOCKING YOU FOR NOT UNDERSTANDING PEOPLE'S FEELINGS IN SPITE OF YOUR LONG LIFE.
FWIP
POUT
......

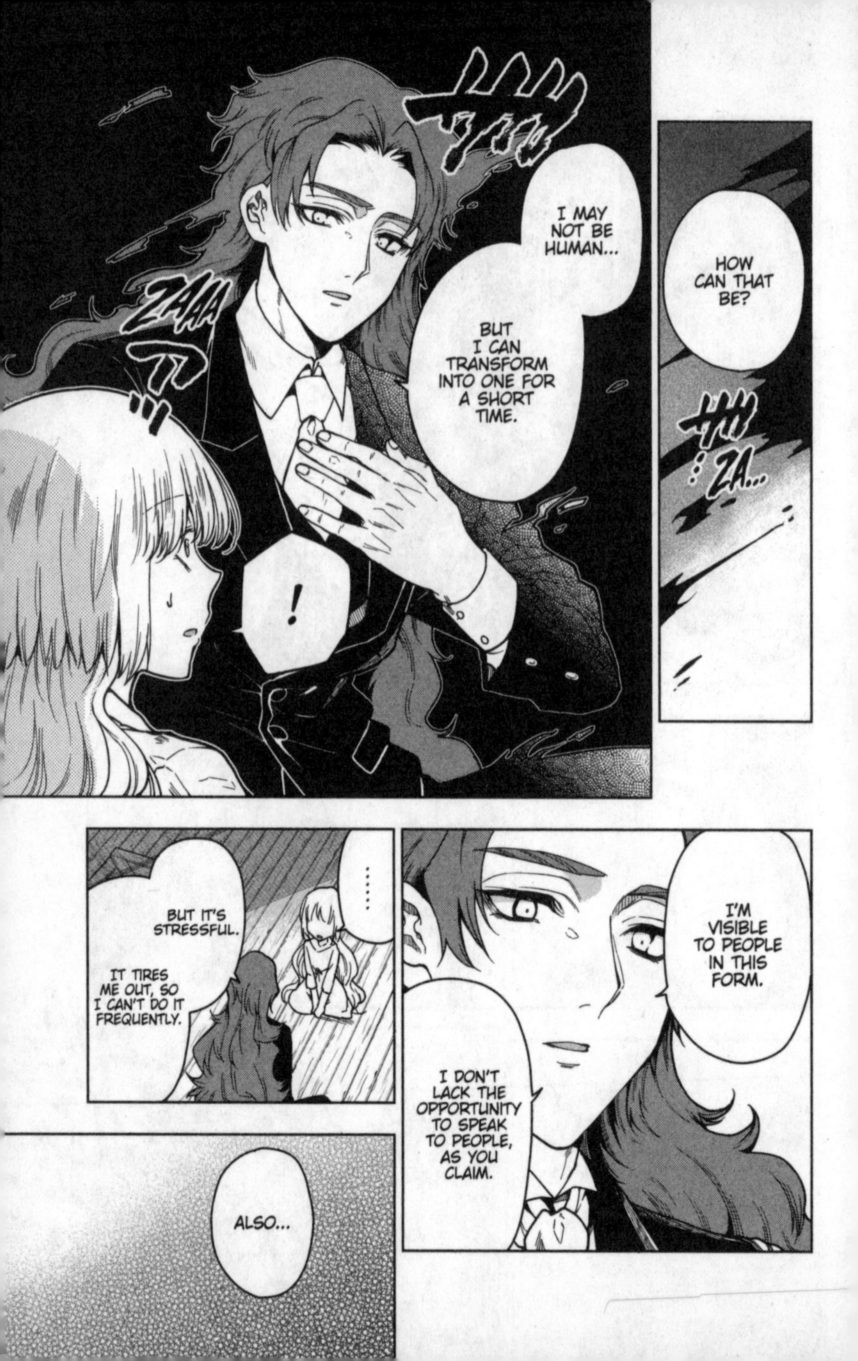
HOW CAN THAT BE?
ZA...
I MAY NOT BE HUMAN...
BUT I CAN TRANSFORM INTO ONE FOR A SHORT TIME.
ZAAA
!
I'M VISIBLE TO PEOPLE IN THIS FORM.
I DON'T LACK THE OPPORTUNITY TO SPEAK TO PEOPLE, AS YOU CLAIM.
......
BUT IT'S STRESSFUL.
IT TIRES ME OUT, SO I CAN'T DO IT FREQUENTLY.
ALSO...

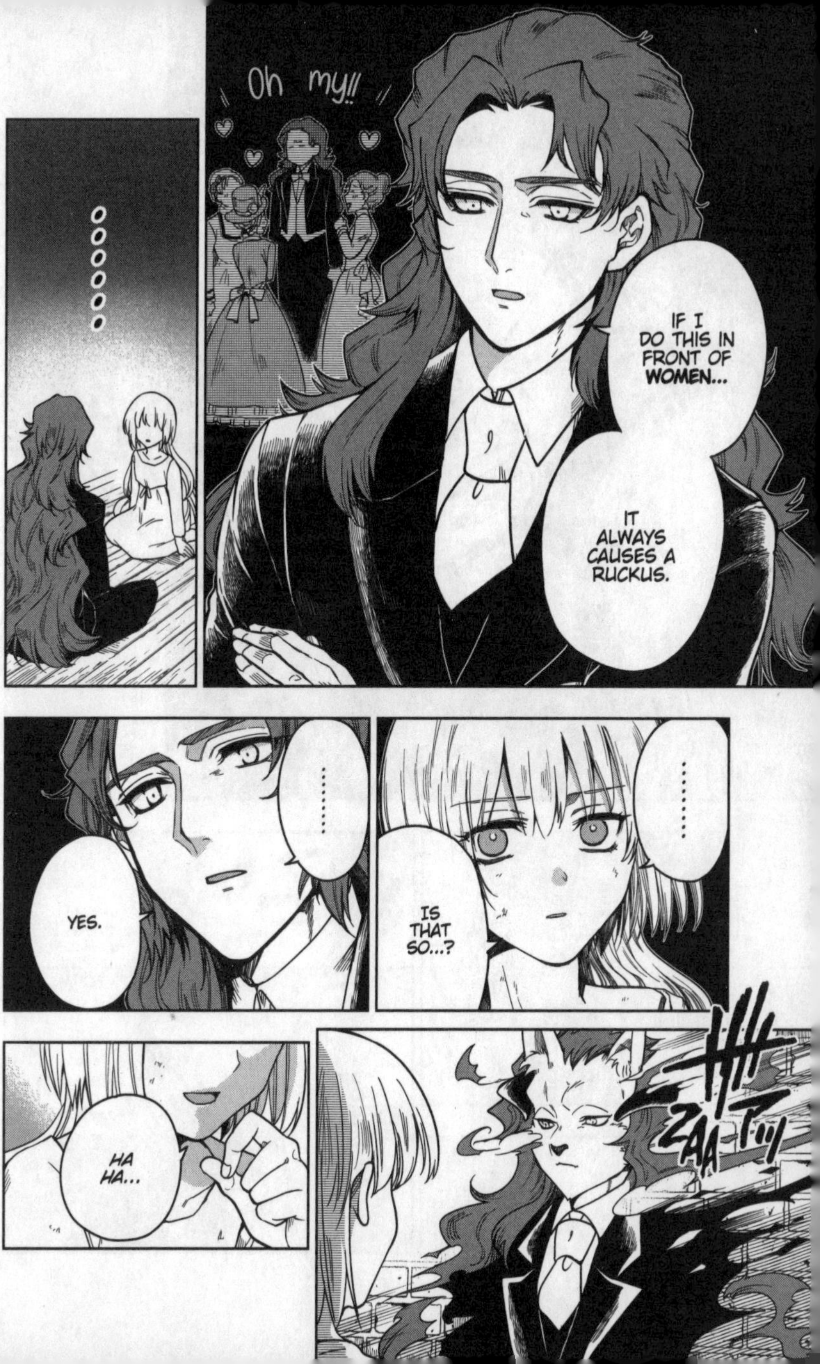
IF I DO THIS IN FRONT OF WOMEN...
IT ALWAYS CAUSES A RUCKUS.
Oh my!!
OOOOOOO
......
IS THAT SO...?
......
YES.
ZAA
HA HA...

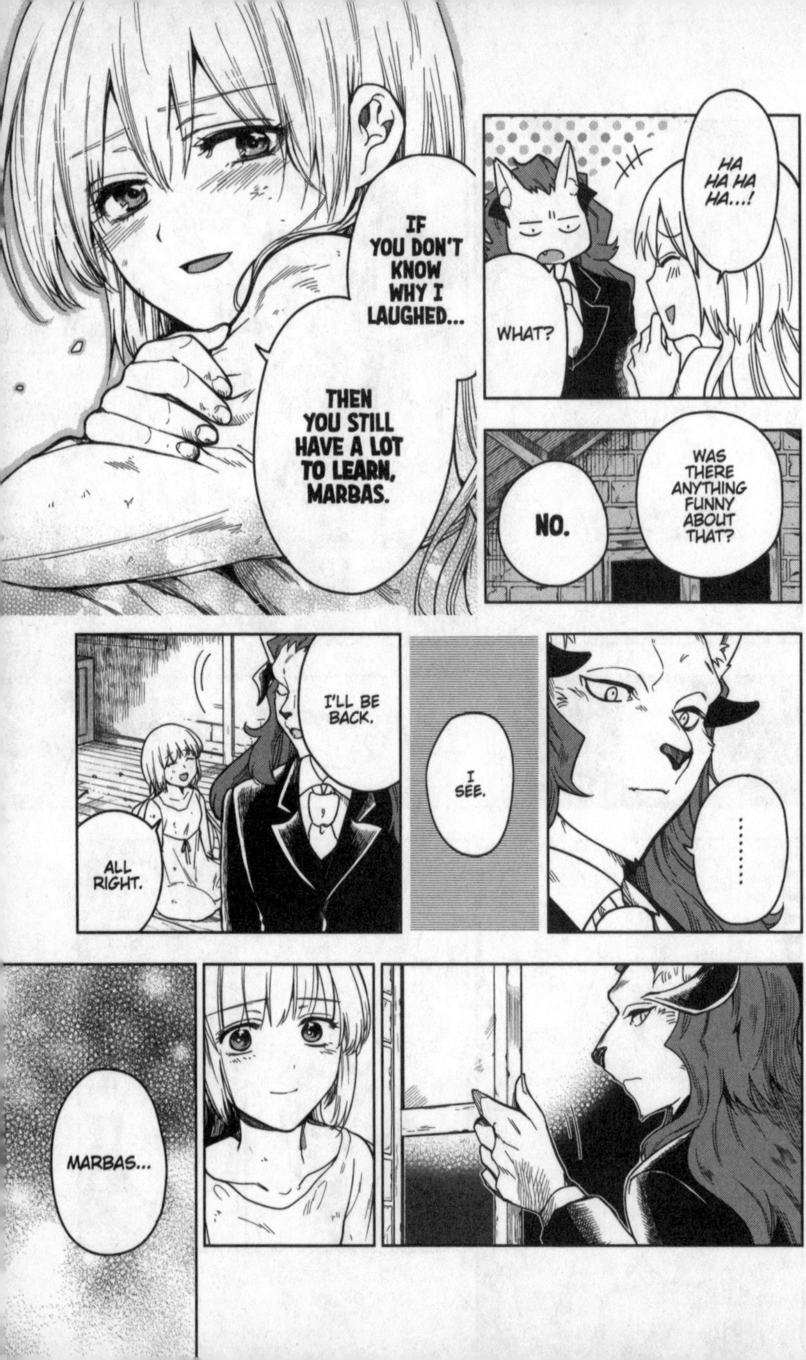
HA HA HA HA...!
WHAT?
WAS THERE ANYTHING FUNNY ABOUT THAT?
NO.
IF YOU DON'T KNOW WHY I LAUGHED...
THEN YOU STILL HAVE A LOT TO LEARN, MARBAS.
......
I SEE.
I'LL BE BACK.
ALL RIGHT.
MARBAS...

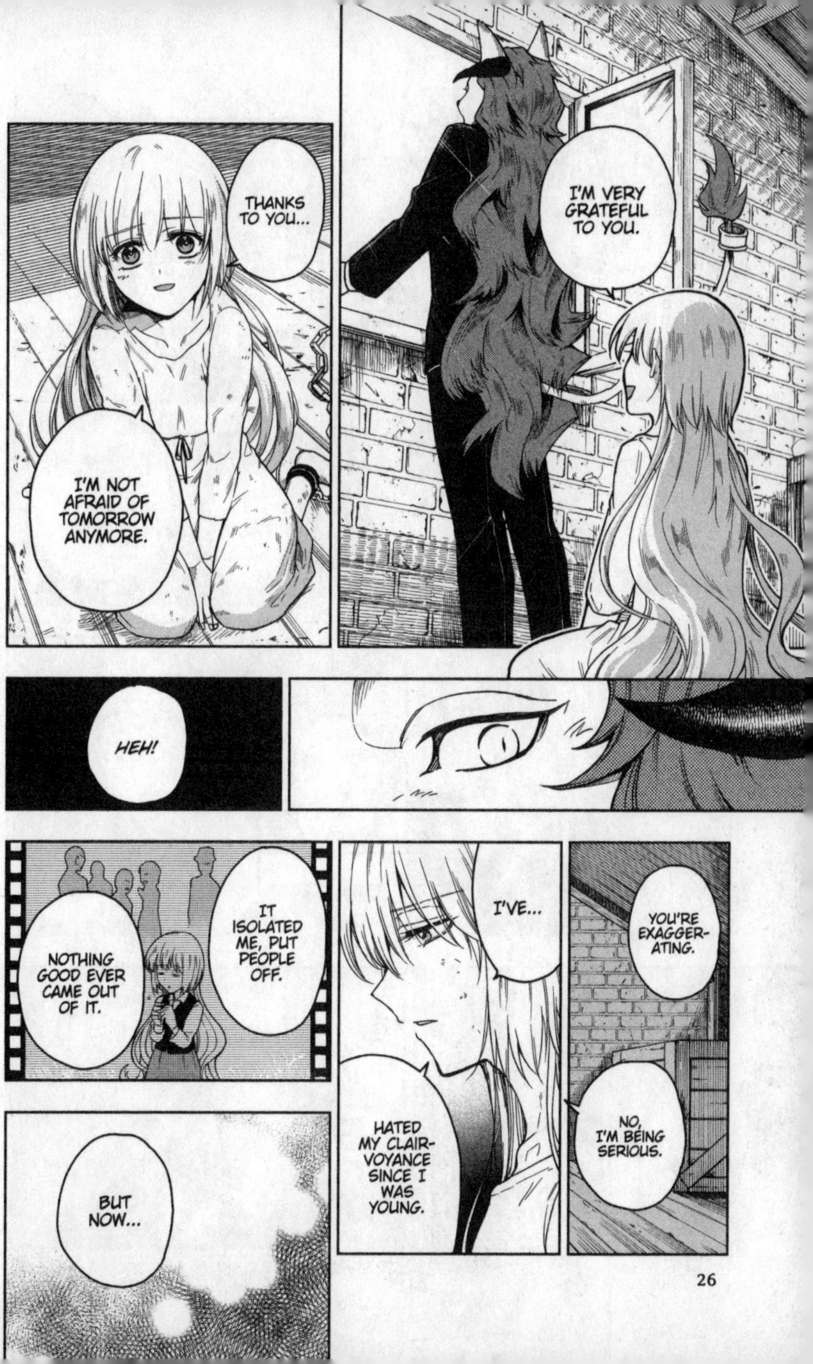
I'M VERY GRATEFUL TO YOU.
THANKS TO YOU...
I'M NOT AFRAID OF TOMORROW ANYMORE.
HEH!
YOU'RE EXAGGER-ATING.
NO, I'M BEING SERIOUS.
I'VE...
HATED MY CLAIR-VOYANCE SINCE I WAS YOUNG.
IT ISOLATED ME, PUT PEOPLE OFF.
NOTHING GOOD EVER CAME OUT OF IT.
BUT NOW...

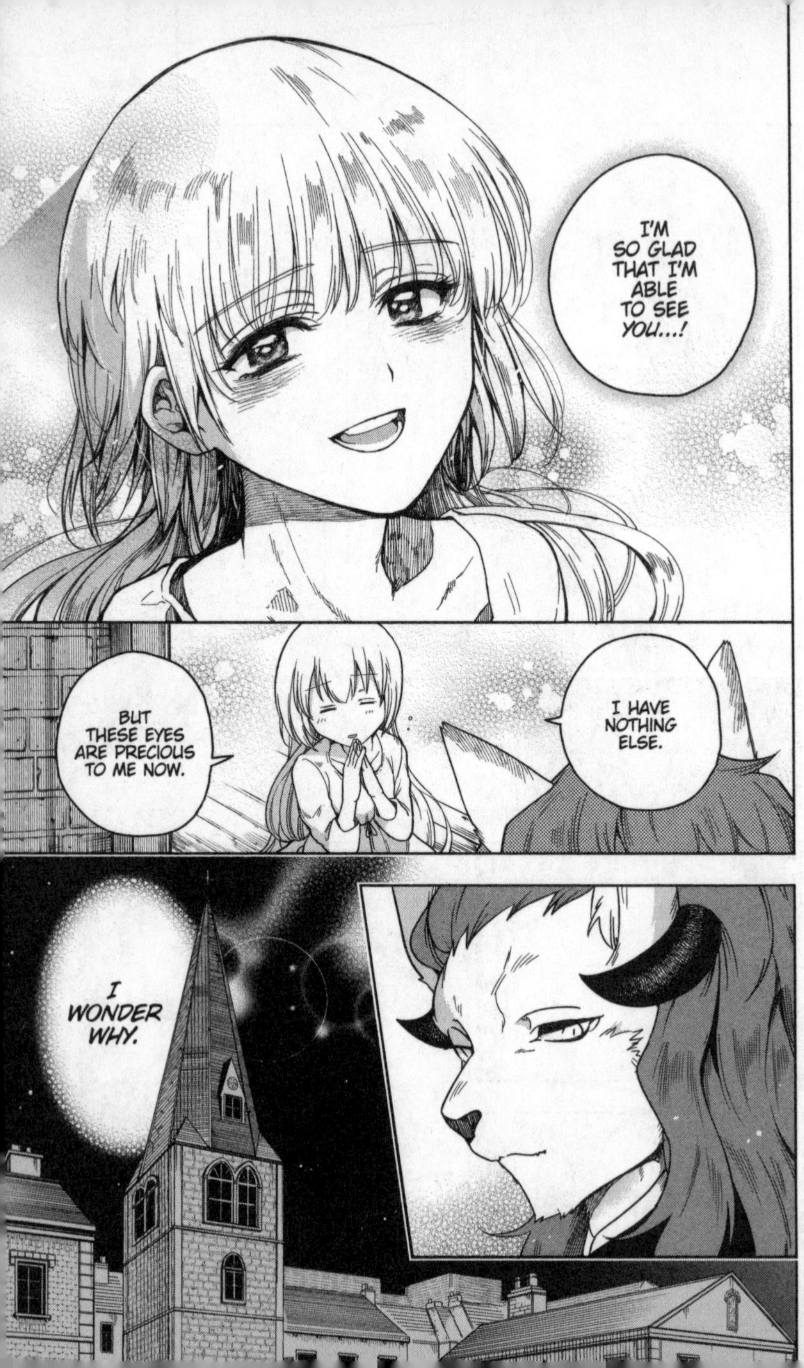
I'M SO GLAD THAT I'M ABLE TO SEE YOU...!
I HAVE NOTHING ELSE.
BUT THESE EYES ARE PRECIOUS TO ME NOW.
I WONDER WHY.

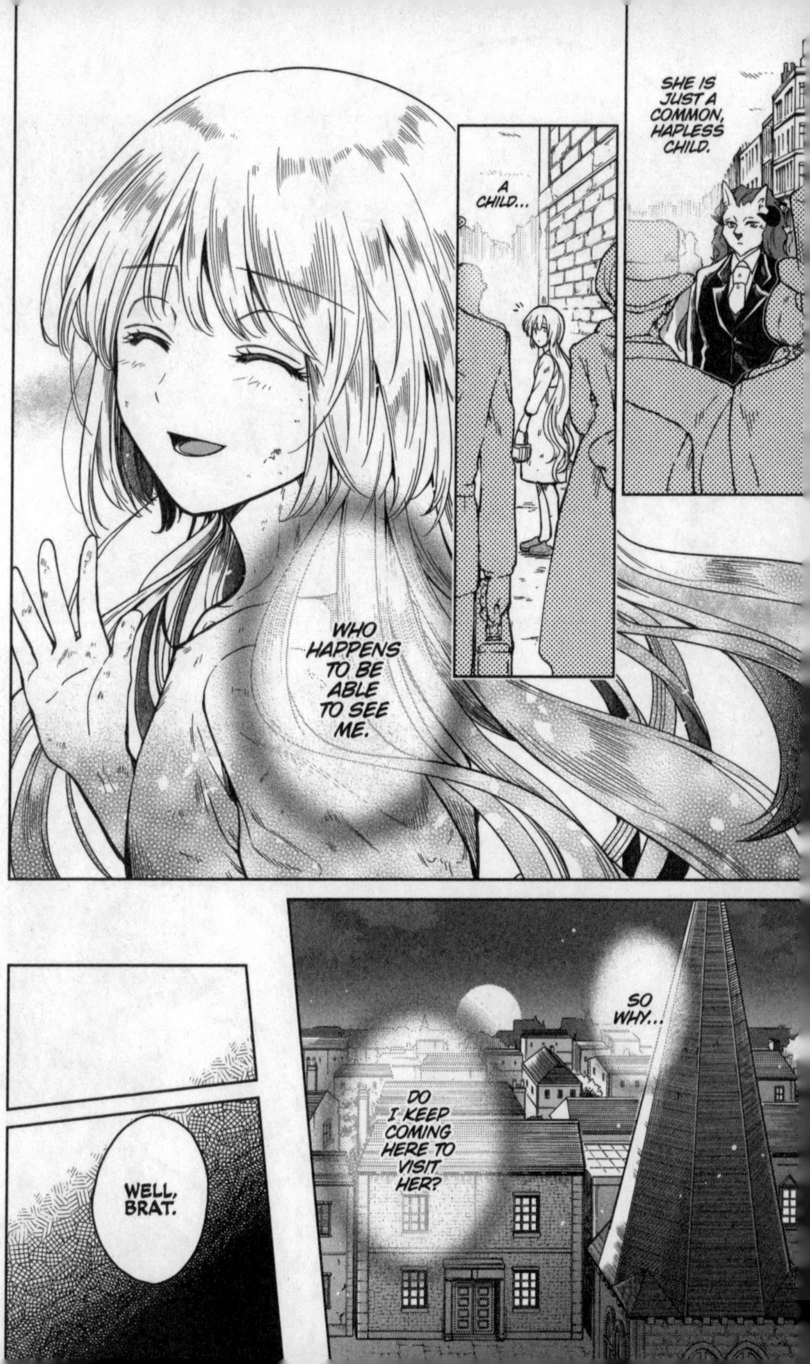
SHE IS JUST A COMMON, HAPLESS CHILD.
A CHILD...
WHO HAPPENS TO BE ABLE TO SEE ME.
SO WHY...
DO I KEEP COMING HERE TO VISIT HER?
WELL, BRAT.

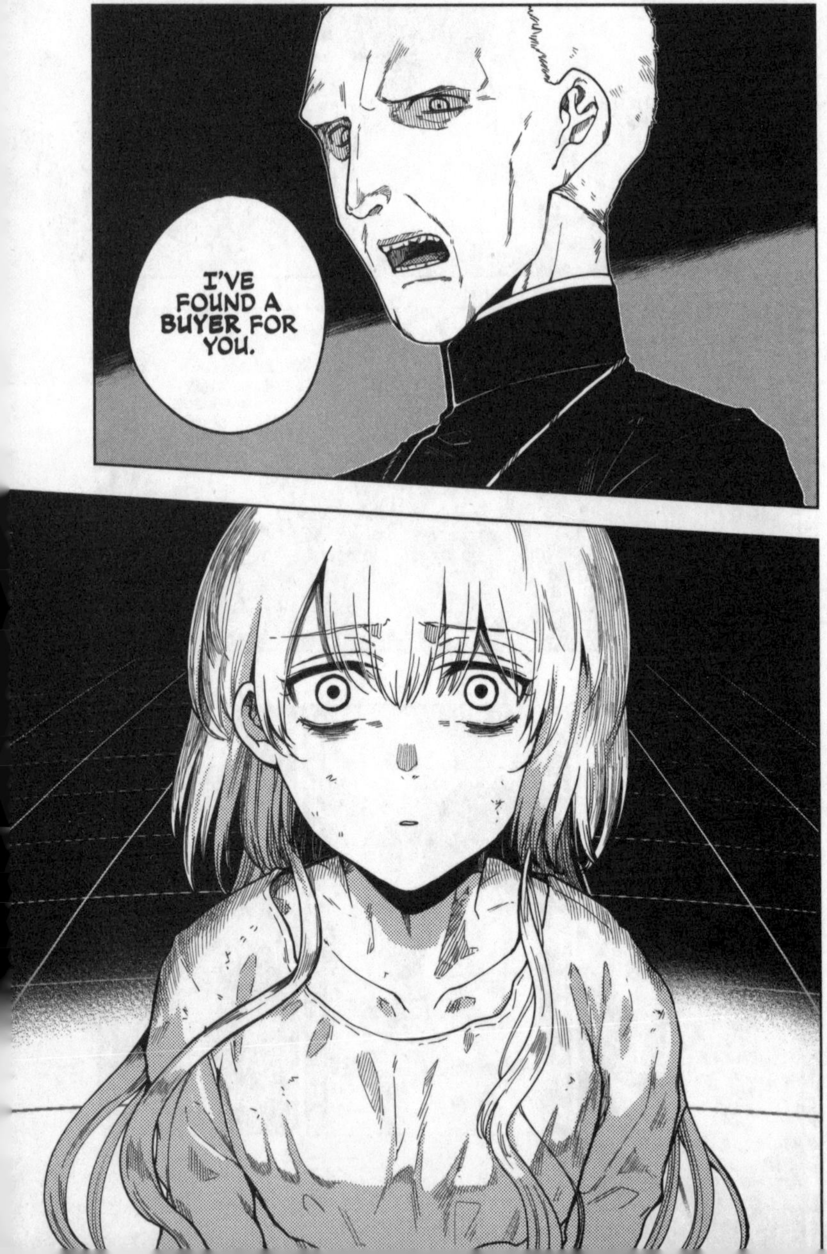
I'VE FOUND A BUYER FOR YOU.

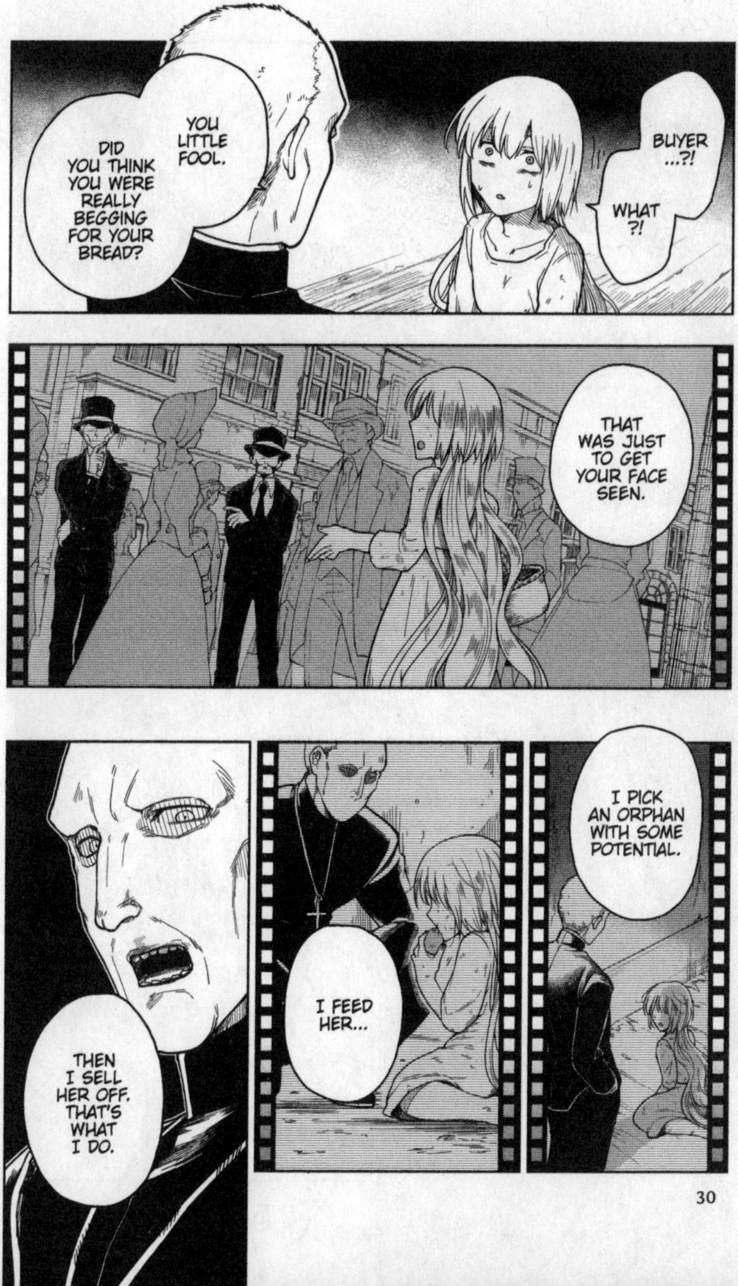
BUYER ...?! WHAT ?!
YOU LITTLE FOOL.
DID YOU THINK YOU WERE REALLY BEGGING FOR YOUR BREAD?
THAT WAS JUST TO GET YOUR FACE SEEN.
I PICK AN ORPHAN WITH SOME POTENTIAL.
I FEED HER...
THEN I SELL HER OFF. THAT'S WHAT I DO.

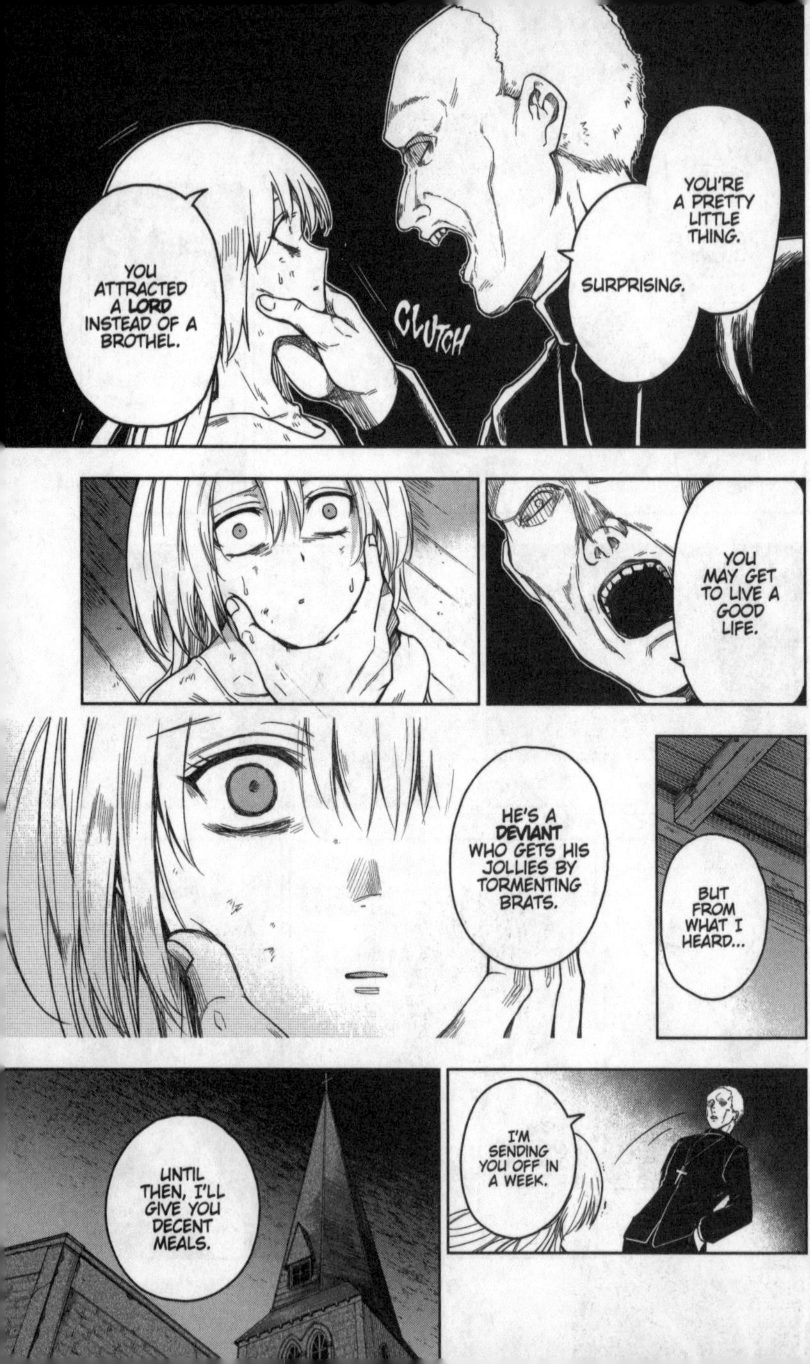
YOU'RE A PRETTY LITTLE THING.
SURPRISING.
CLUTCH
YOU ATTRACTED A LORD INSTEAD OF A BROTHEL.
YOU MAY GET TO LIVE A GOOD LIFE.
BUT FROM WHAT I HEARD...
HE'S A DEVIANT WHO GETS HIS JOLLIES BY TORMENTING BRATS.
I'M SENDING YOU OFF IN A WEEK.
UNTIL THEN, I'LL GIVE YOU DECENT MEALS.

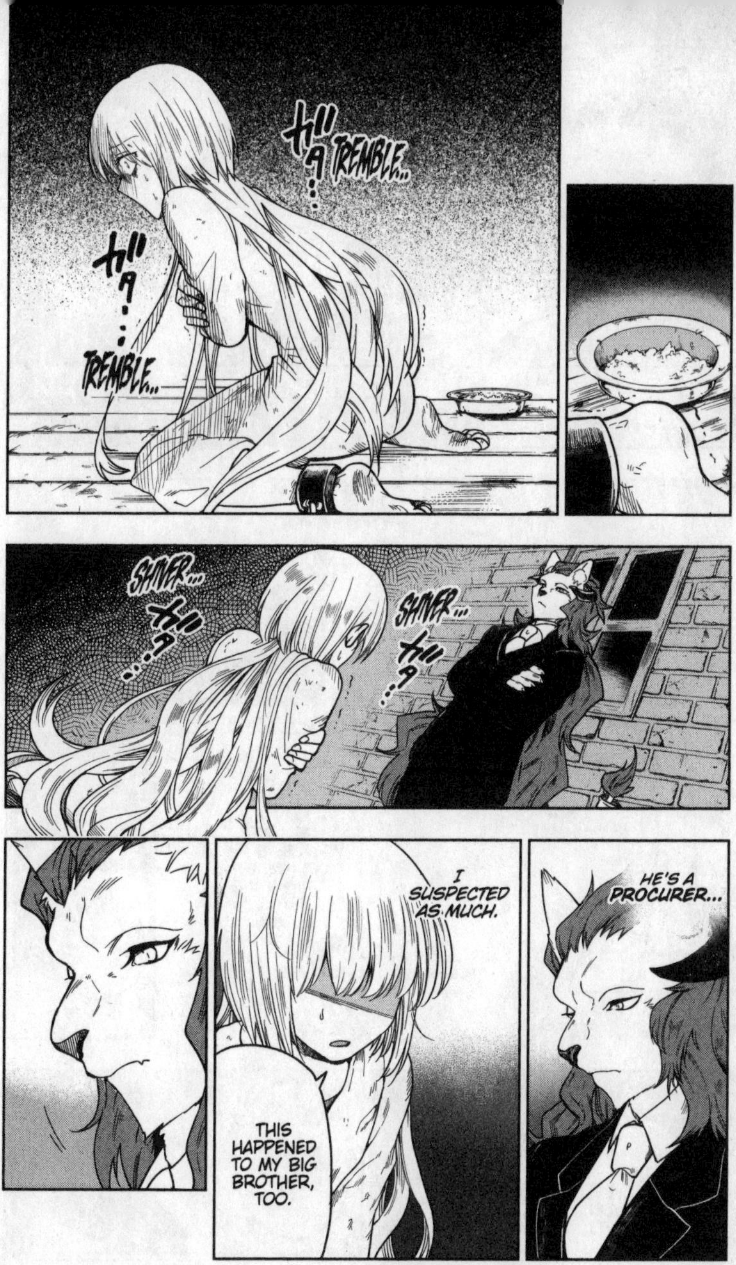
ガタ...
TREMBLE...
ガタ...
TREMBLE...
SHIVER...
ガタ...
SHIVER...
ガタ...
HE'S A PROCURER...
I SUSPECTED AS MUCH.
THIS HAPPENED TO MY BIG BROTHER, TOO.

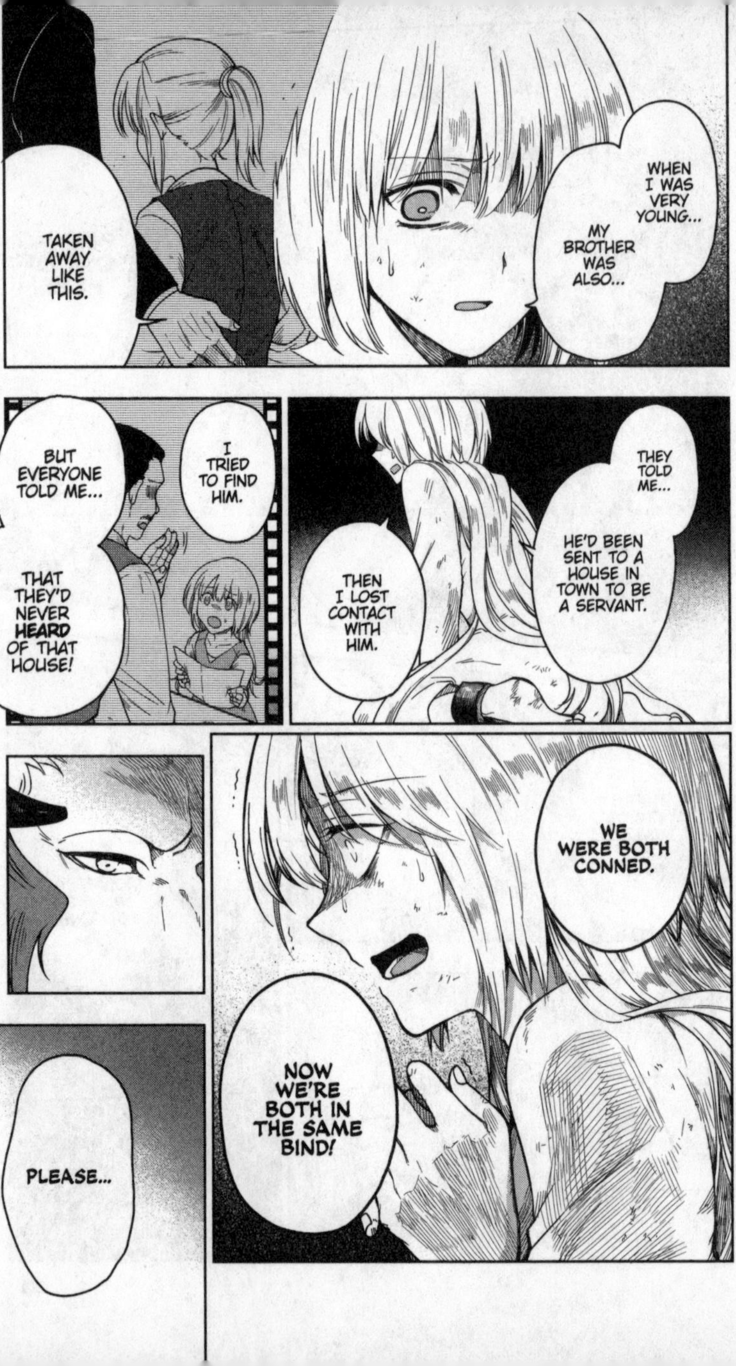
WHEN I WAS VERY YOUNG...
MY BROTHER WAS ALSO...
TAKEN AWAY LIKE THIS.
THEY TOLD ME...
HE'D BEEN SENT TO A HOUSE IN TOWN TO BE A SERVANT.
THEN I LOST CONTACT WITH HIM.
I TRIED TO FIND HIM.
BUT EVERYONE TOLD ME...
THAT THEY'D NEVER **HEARD** OF THAT HOUSE!
WE WERE BOTH CONNED.
NOW WE'RE BOTH IN THE SAME BIND!
PLEASE...

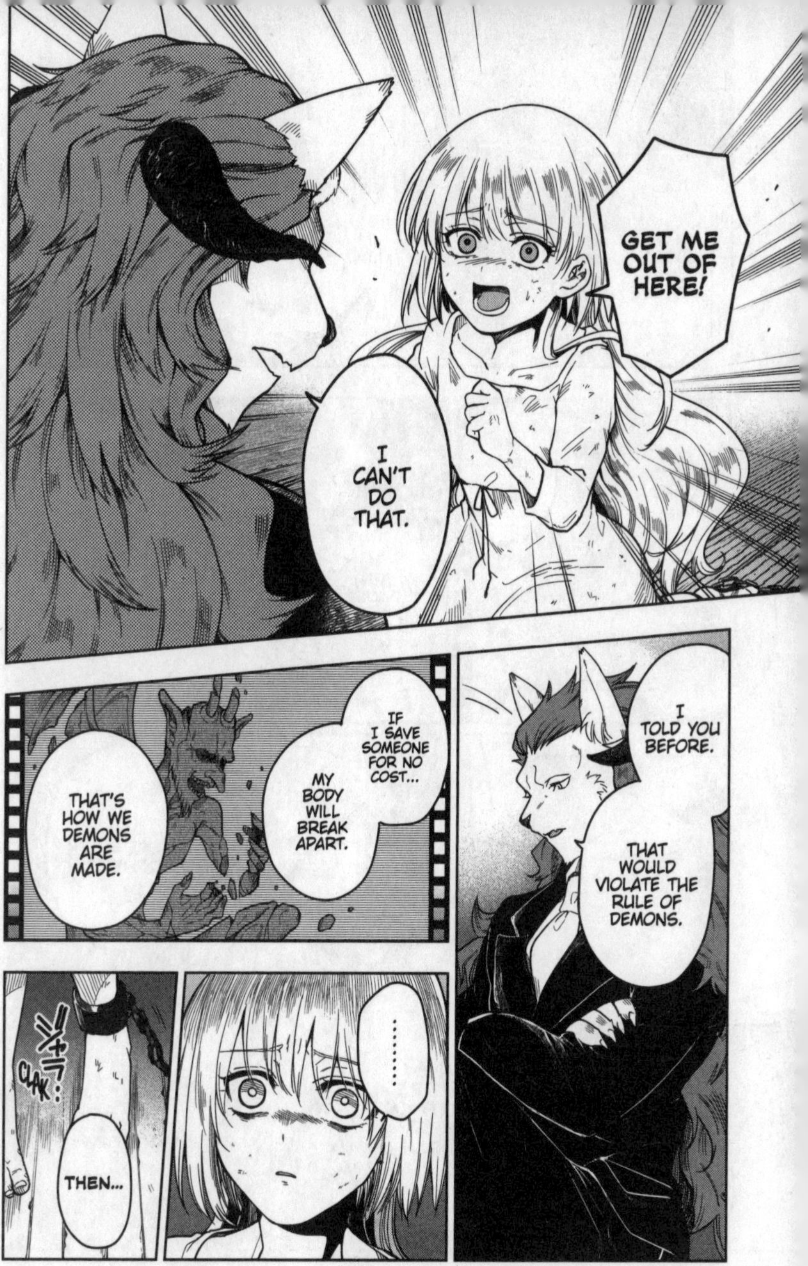
GET ME OUT OF HERE!
I CAN'T DO THAT.
I TOLD YOU BEFORE.
THAT WOULD VIOLATE THE RULE OF DEMONS.
IF I SAVE SOMEONE FOR NO COST...
MY BODY WILL BREAK APART.
THAT'S HOW WE DEMONS ARE MADE.
......
CLAK
THEN...

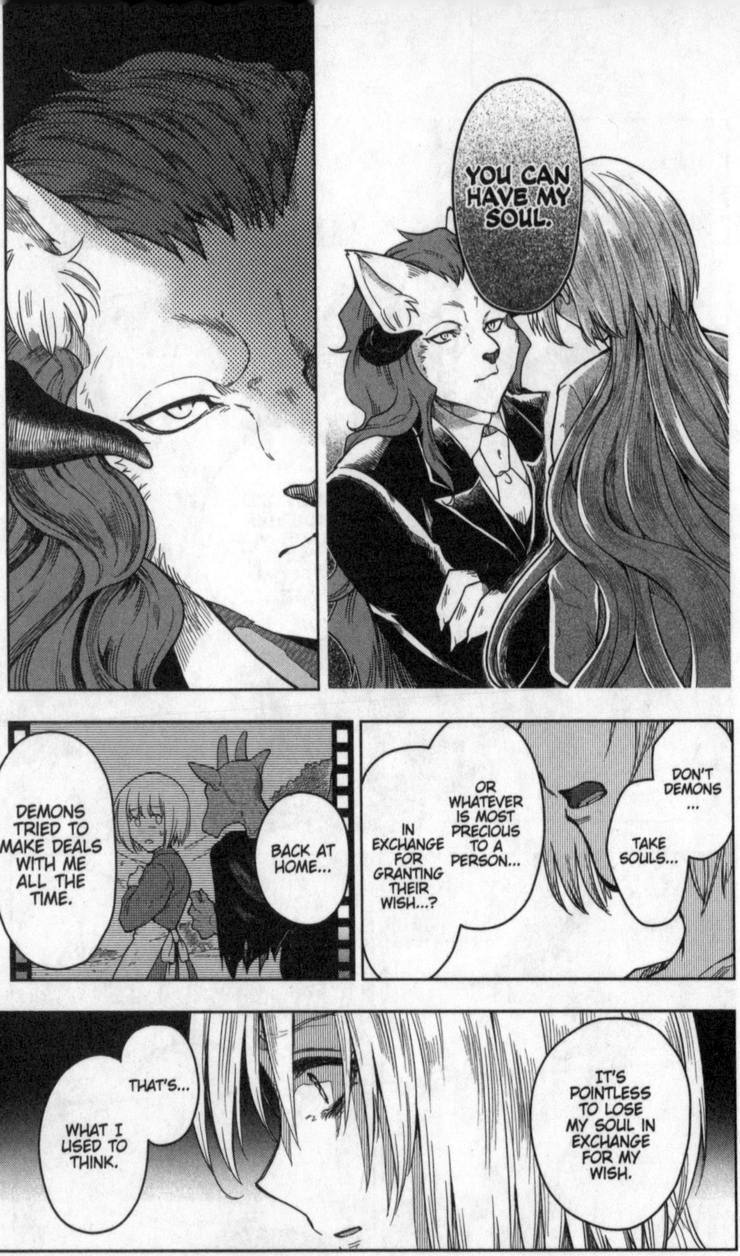
YOU CAN HAVE MY SOUL.
DON'T DEMONS ...
TAKE SOULS...
OR WHATEVER IS MOST PRECIOUS TO A PERSON...
IN EXCHANGE FOR GRANTING THEIR WISH...?
BACK AT HOME...
DEMONS TRIED TO MAKE DEALS WITH ME ALL THE TIME.
IT'S POINTLESS TO LOSE MY SOUL IN EXCHANGE FOR MY WISH.
THAT'S...
WHAT I USED TO THINK.

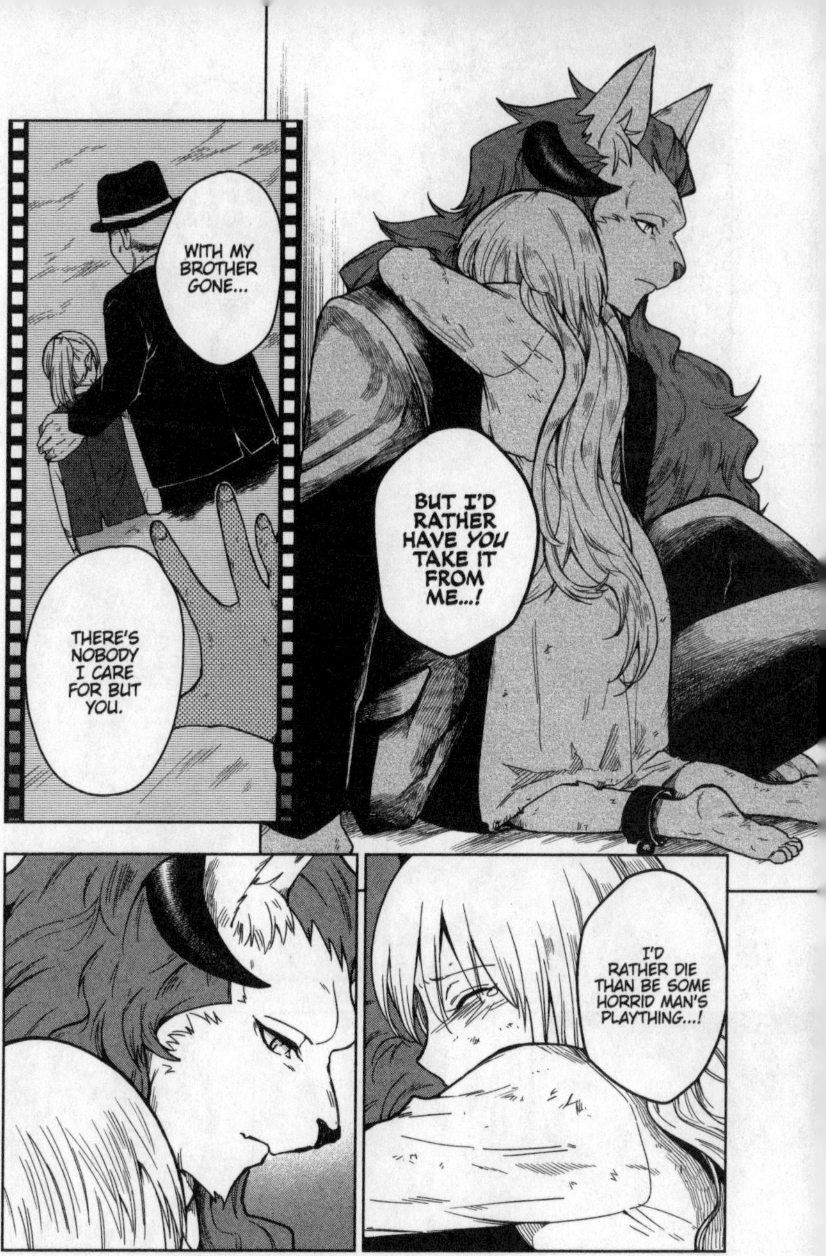
BUT I'D RATHER HAVE *YOU* TAKE IT FROM ME...!
WITH MY BROTHER GONE...
THERE'S NOBODY I CARE FOR BUT YOU.
I'D RATHER DIE THAN BE SOME HORRID MAN'S PLAYTHING...!

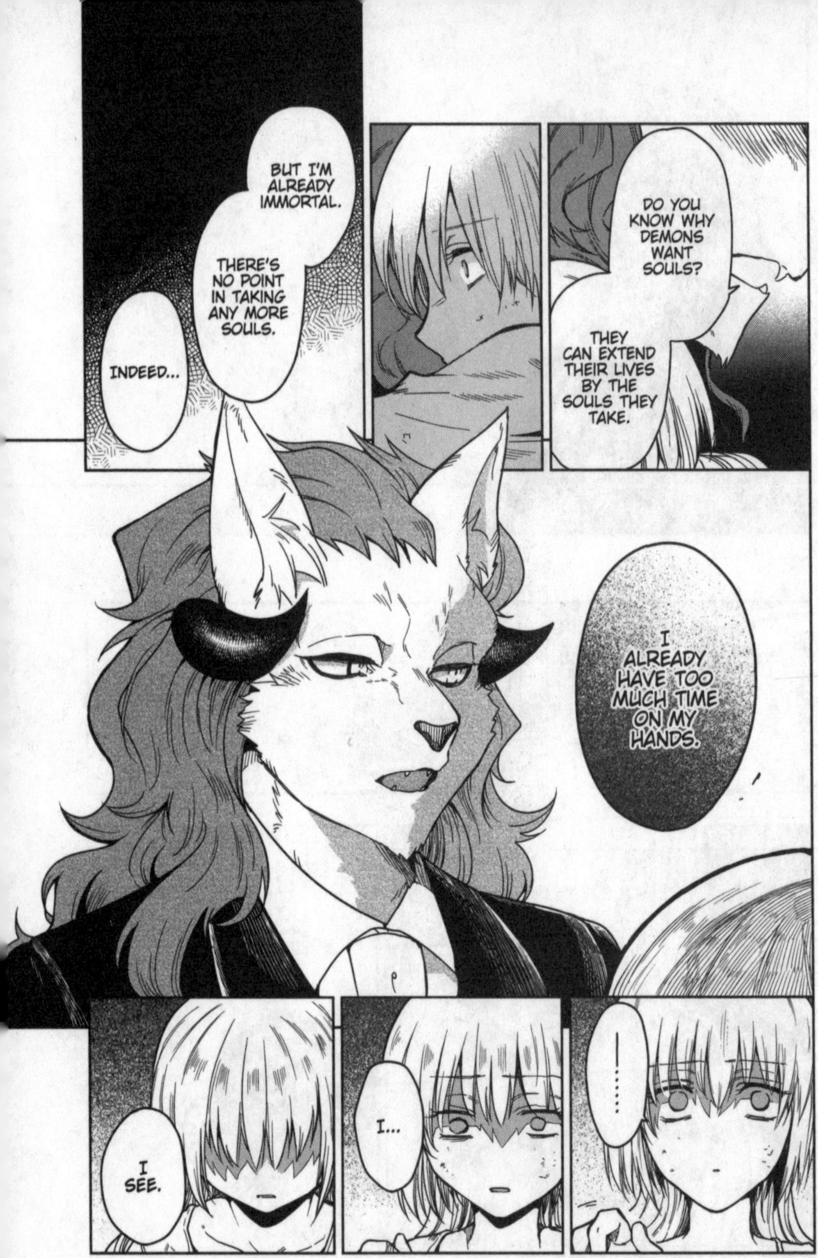
DO YOU KNOW WHY DEMONS WANT SOULS?
THEY CAN EXTEND THEIR LIVES BY THE SOULS THEY TAKE.
BUT I'M ALREADY IMMORTAL.
THERE'S NO POINT IN TAKING ANY MORE SOULS.
INDEED...
I ALREADY HAVE TOO MUCH TIME ON MY HANDS.
......
I...
I SEE.

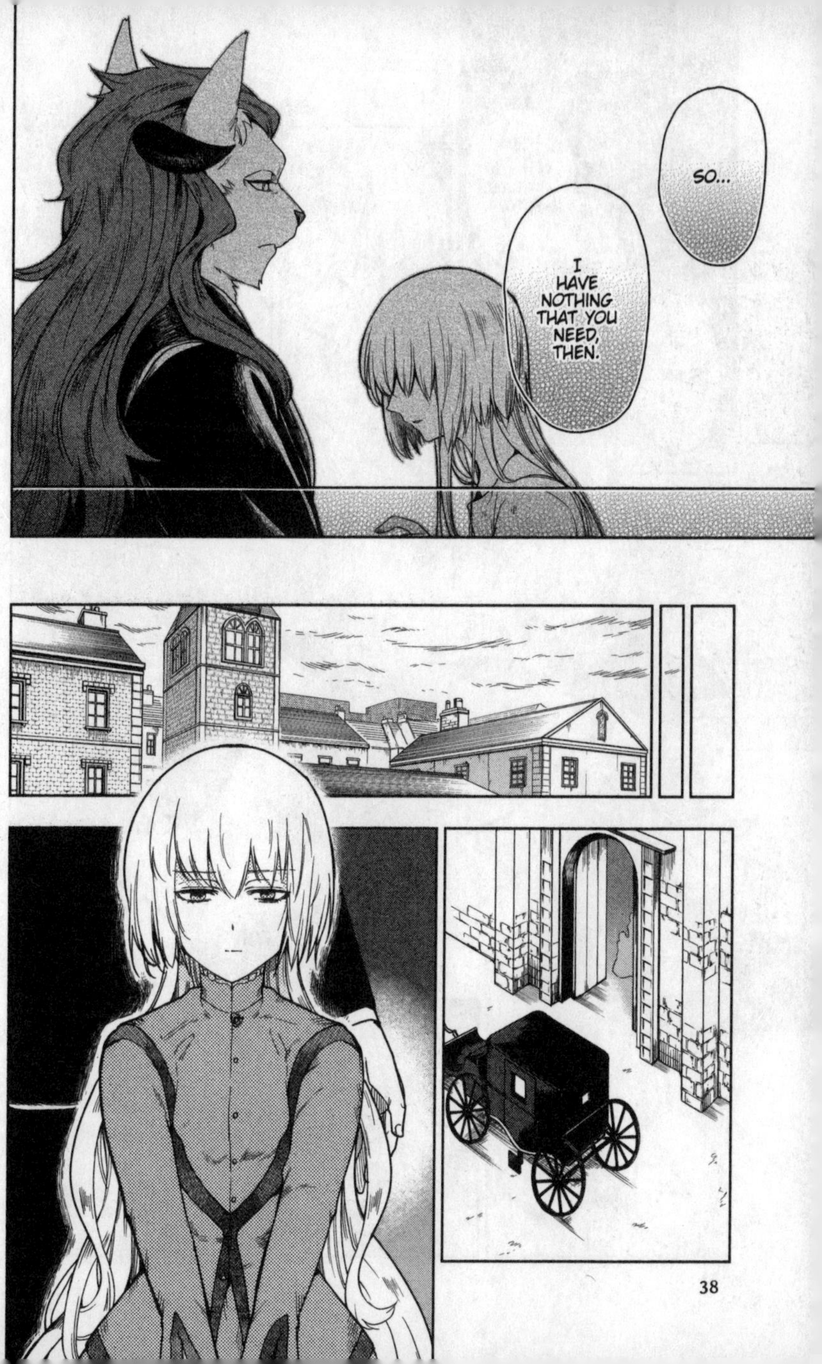

SO...
I HAVE NOTHING THAT YOU NEED, THEN.

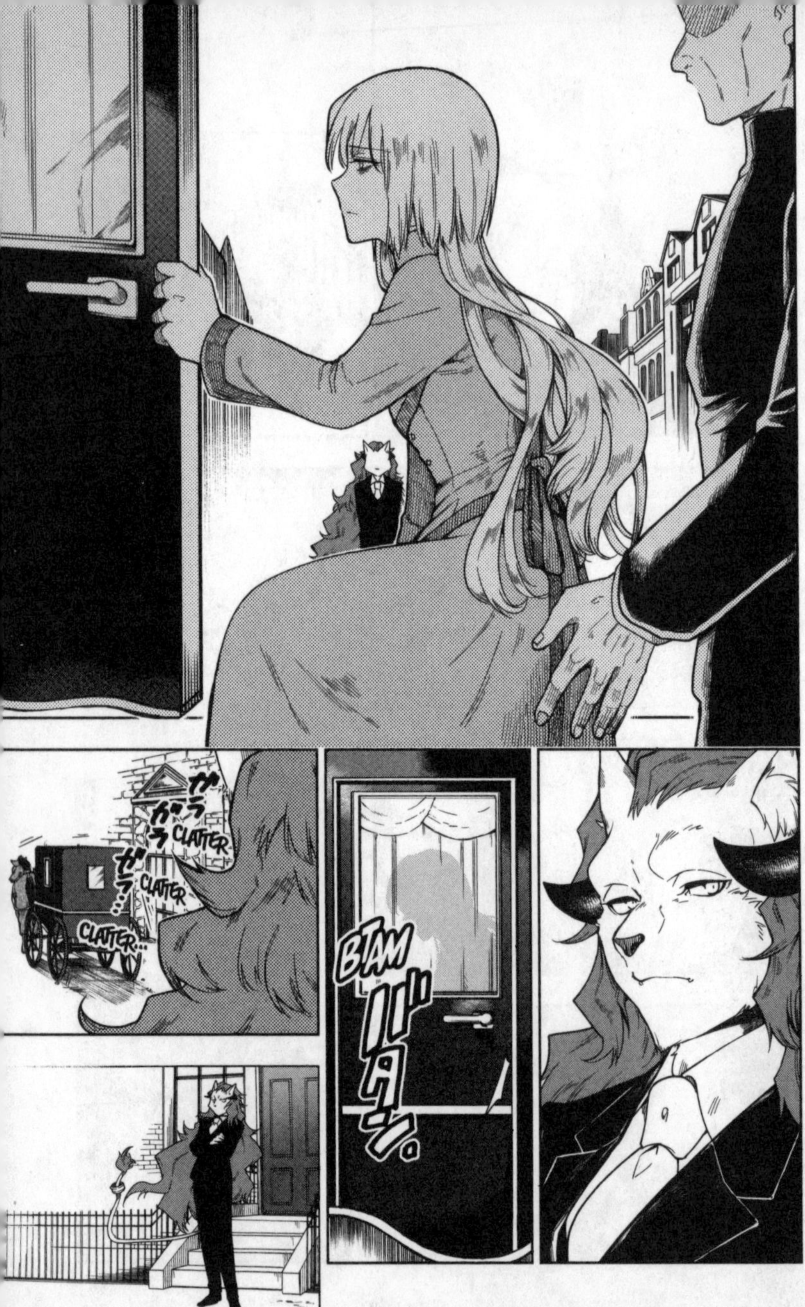
BTAM
バタン。
ガラガラ
CLATTER
ガラ…
CLATTER
CLATTER...

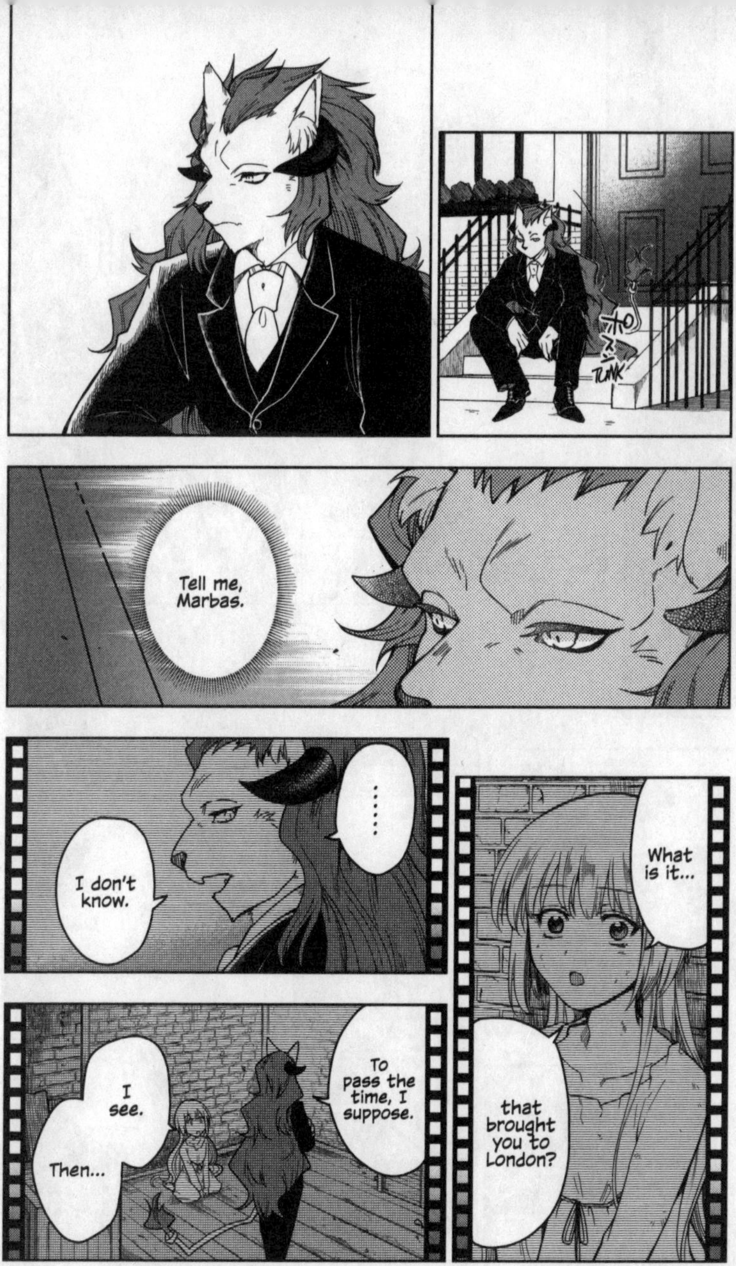
TUNK
Tell me, Marbas.
What is it...
that brought you to London?
......
I don't know.
To pass the time, I suppose.
I see.
Then...

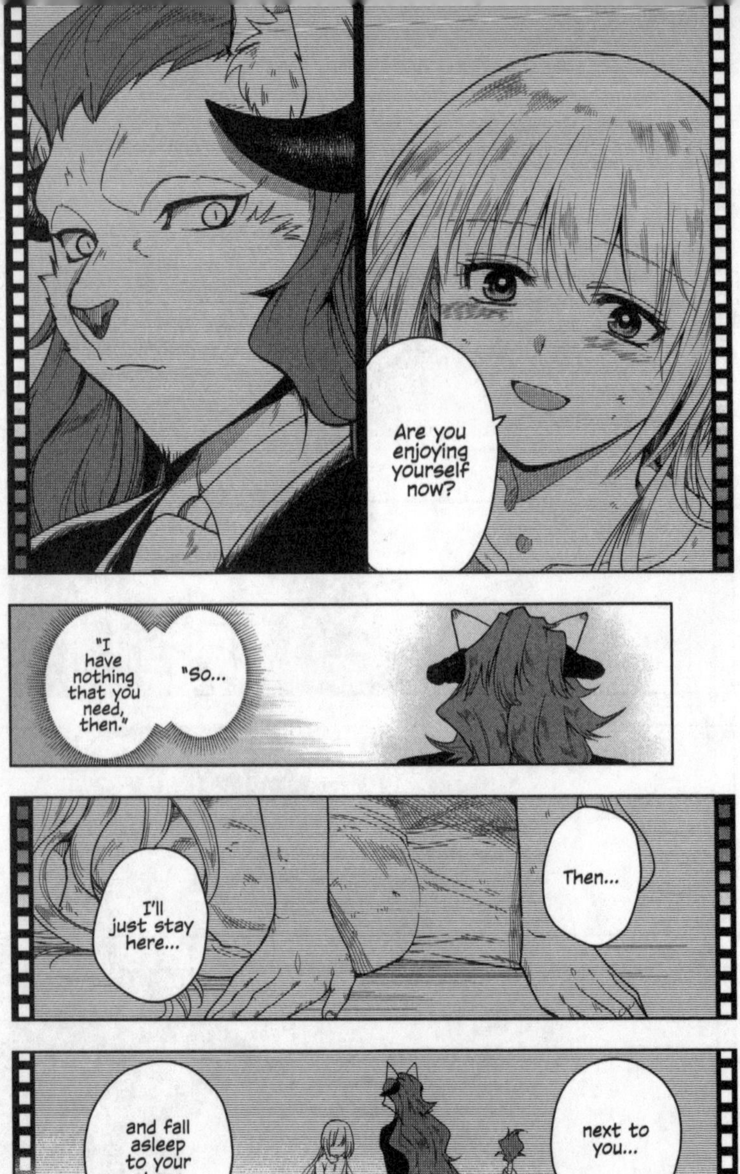
Are you enjoying yourself now?
"So...
"I have nothing that you need, then."
Then...
I'll just stay here...
next to you...
and fall asleep to your story.

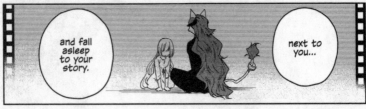

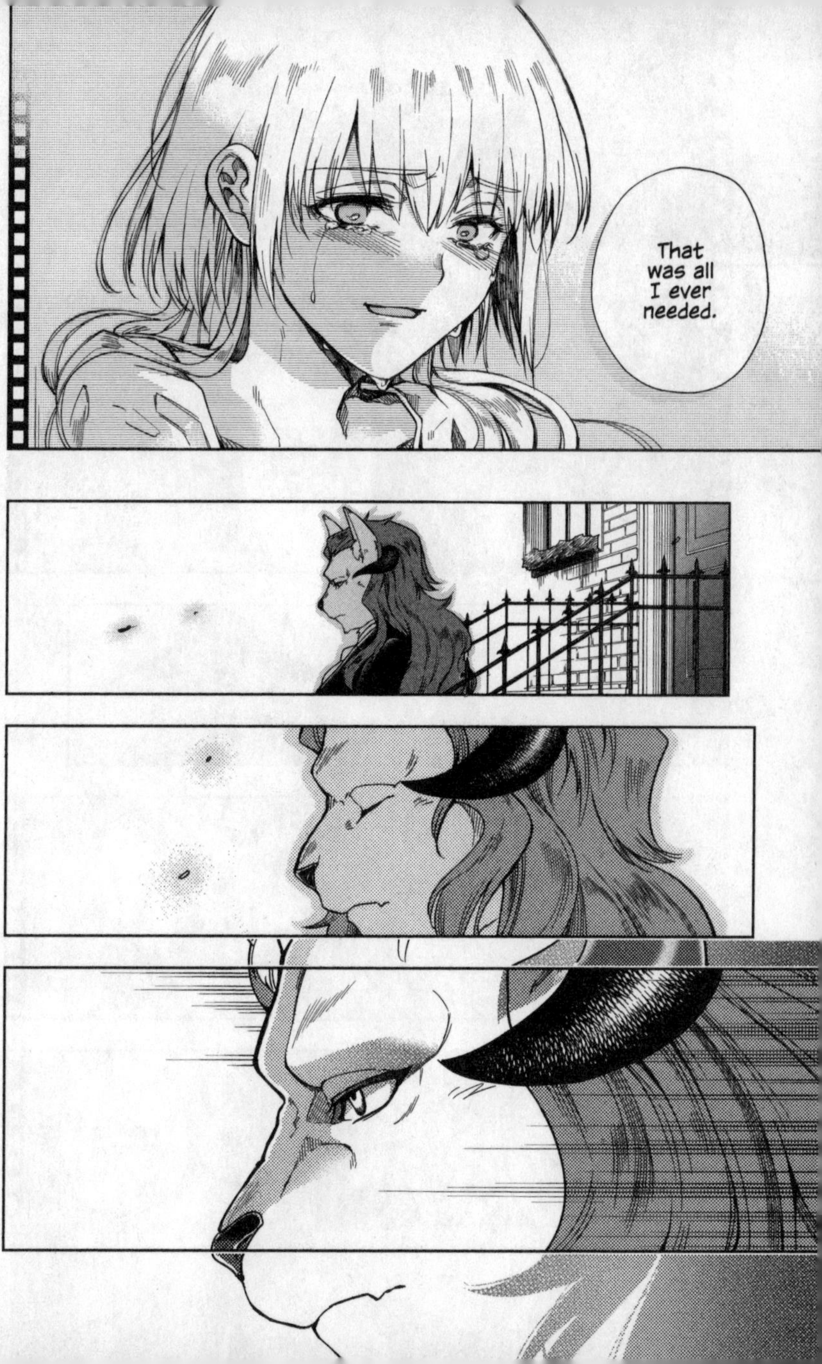
That was all I ever needed.

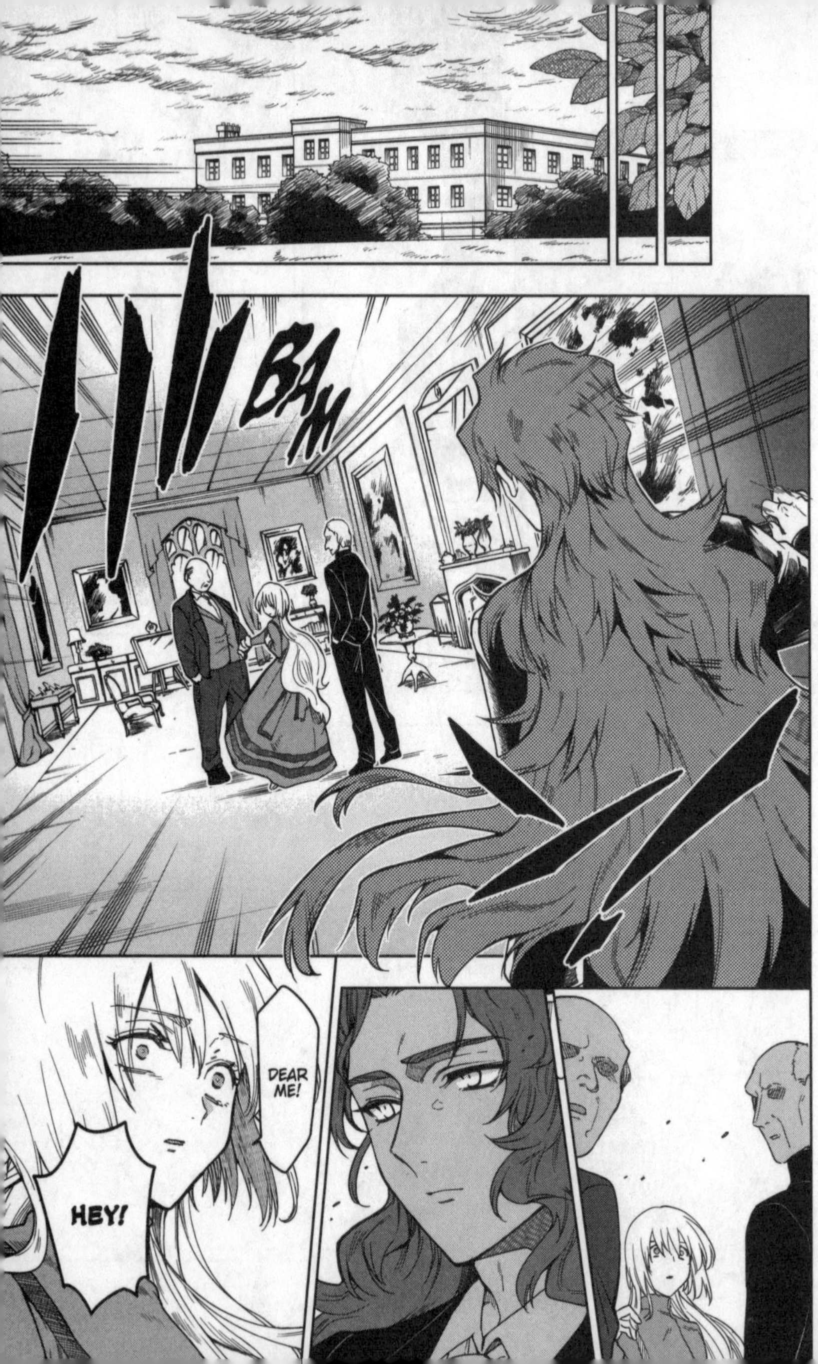
BAM
DEAR ME!
HEY!

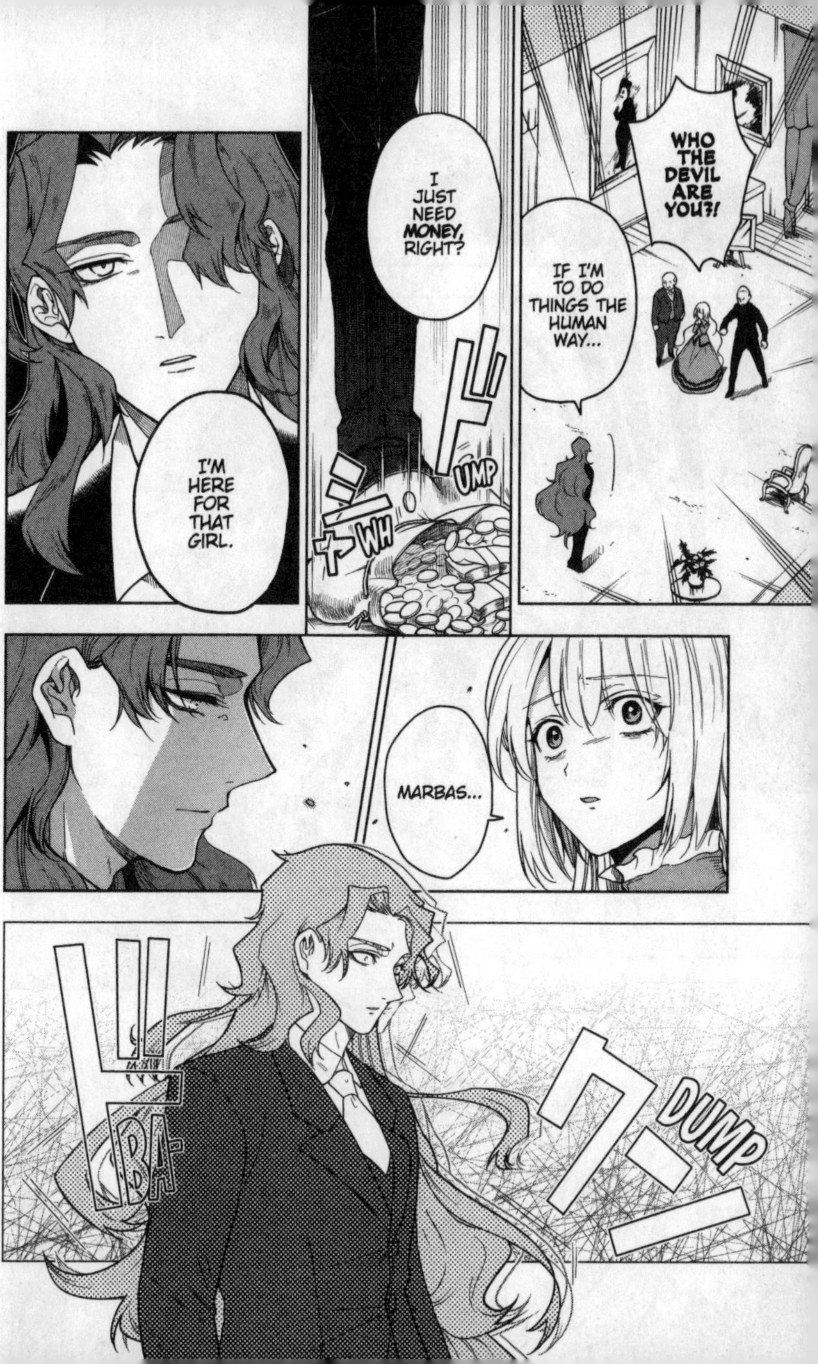
WHO THE DEVIL ARE YOU?!
IF I'M TO DO THINGS THE HUMAN WAY...
I JUST NEED MONEY, RIGHT?
WH
UMP
I'M HERE FOR THAT GIRL.
MARBAS...
BA-
DUMP

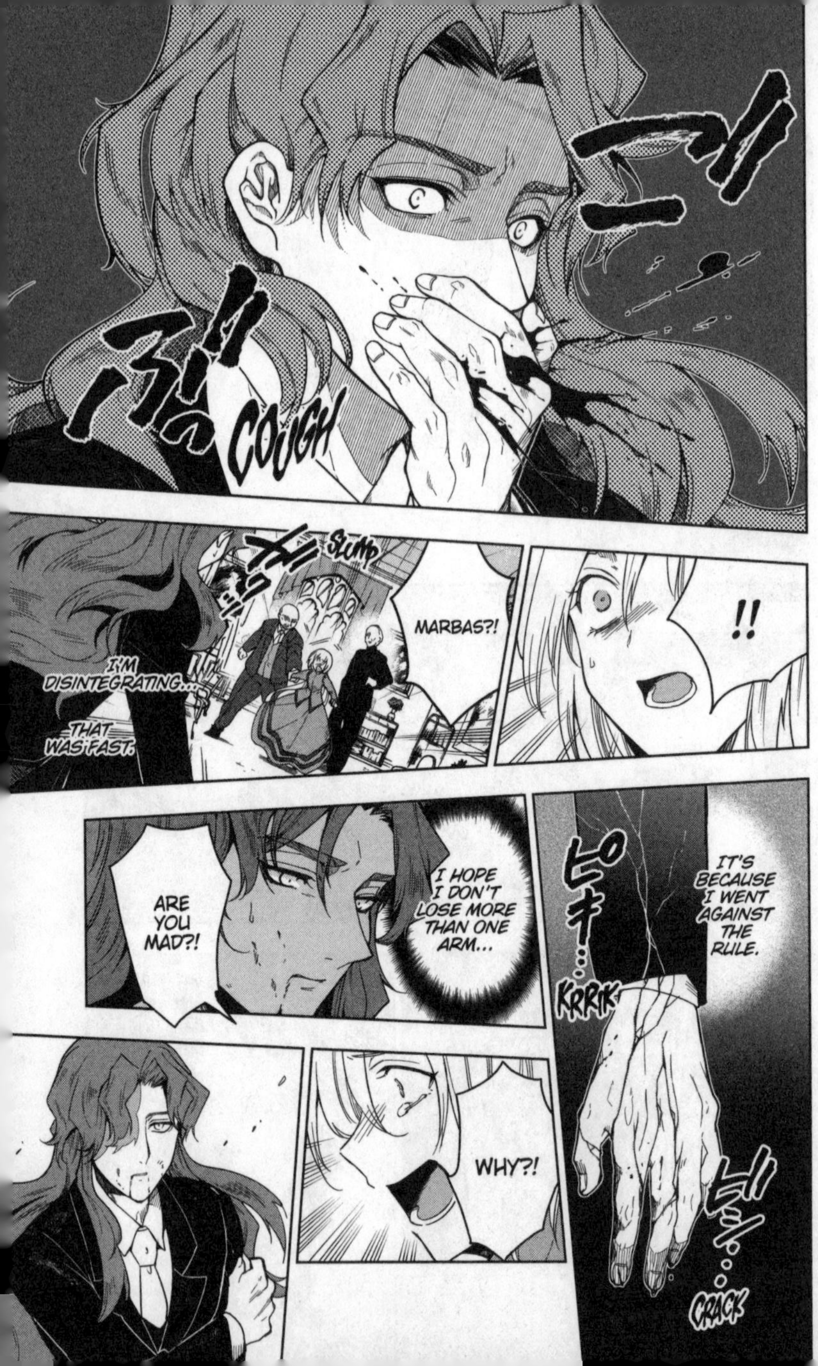
COUGH
!!
MARBAS?!
SLUMP
I'M DISINTEGRATING...
THAT WAS FAST.
IT'S BECAUSE I WENT AGAINST THE RULE.
KRRIK
CRACK
I HOPE I DON'T LOSE MORE THAN ONE ARM...
ARE YOU MAD?!
WHY?!

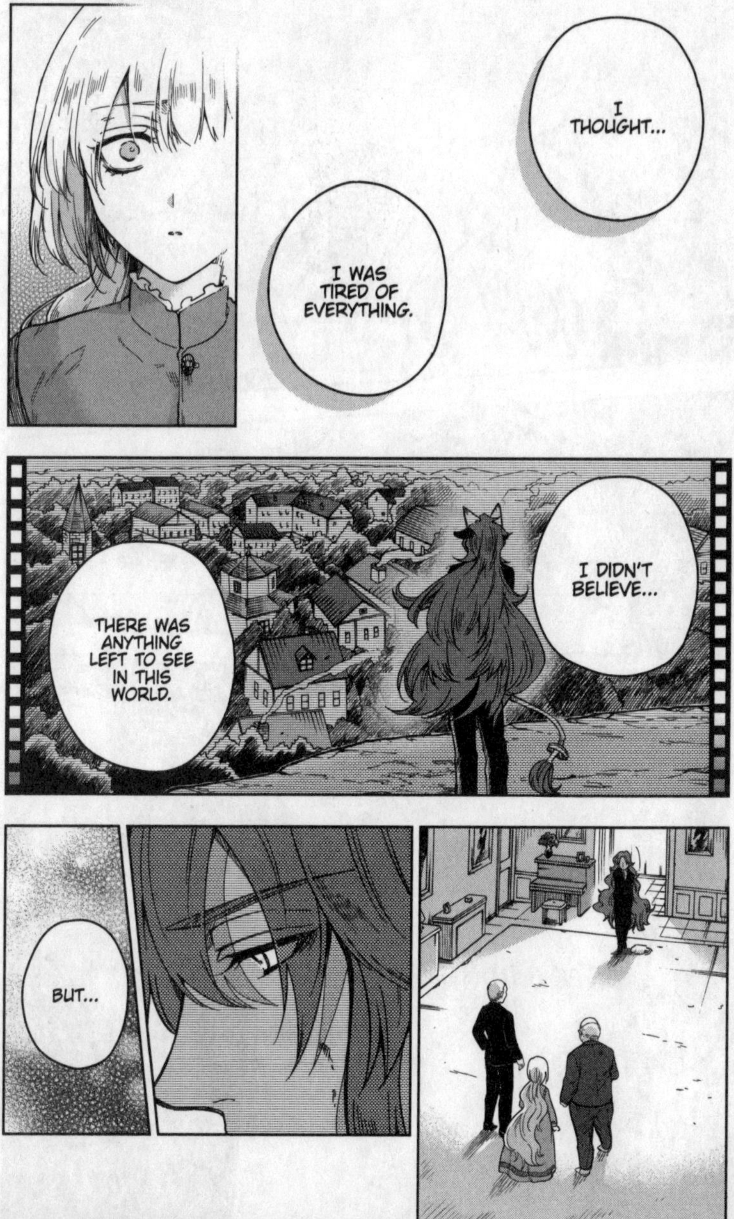
I THOUGHT...
I WAS TIRED OF EVERYTHING.
I DIDN'T BELIEVE...
THERE WAS ANYTHING LEFT TO SEE IN THIS WORLD.
BUT...

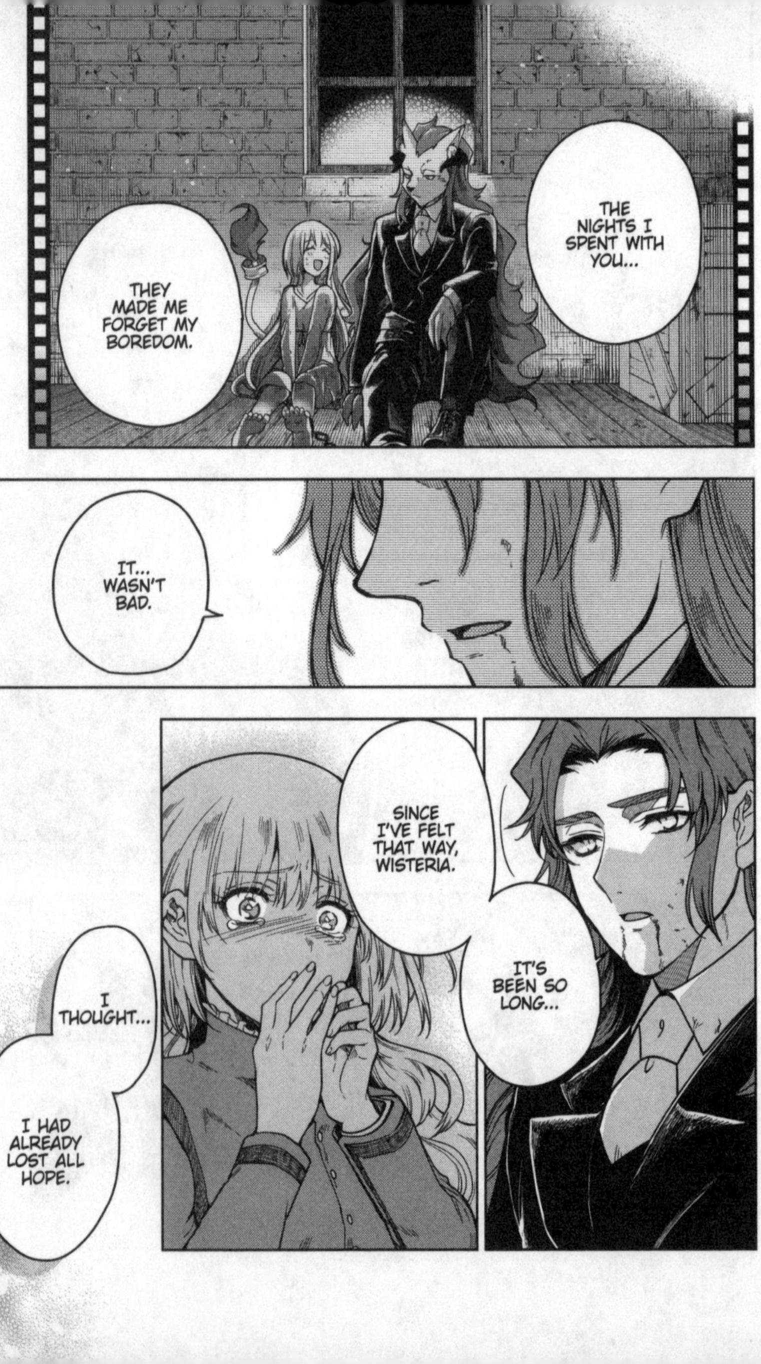
THE NIGHTS I SPENT WITH YOU...
THEY MADE ME FORGET MY BOREDOM.
IT... WASN'T BAD.
IT'S BEEN SO LONG...
SINCE I'VE FELT THAT WAY, WISTERIA.
I THOUGHT...
I HAD ALREADY LOST ALL HOPE.

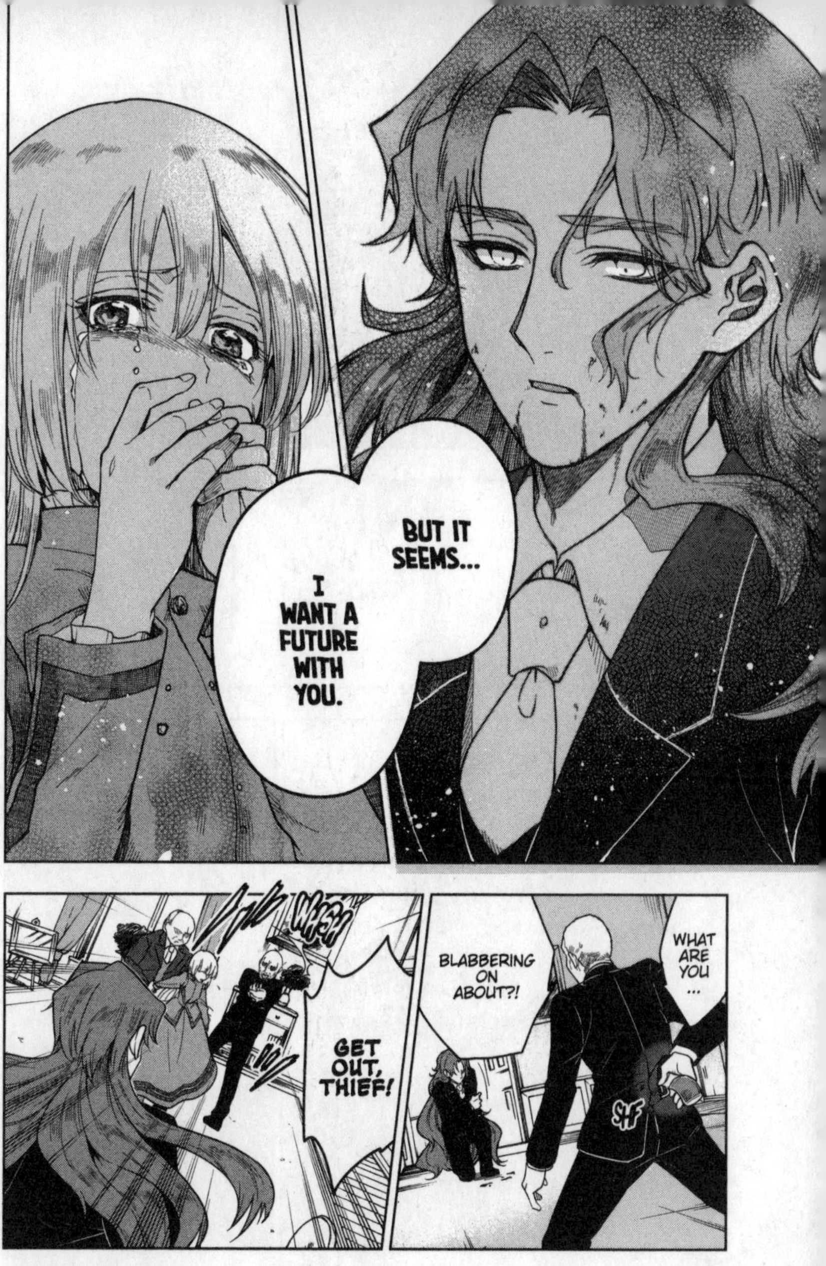
BUT IT SEEMS...
I WANT A FUTURE WITH YOU.
WHAT ARE YOU ...
BLABBERING ON ABOUT?!
SHF
WHSH
GET OUT, THIEF!

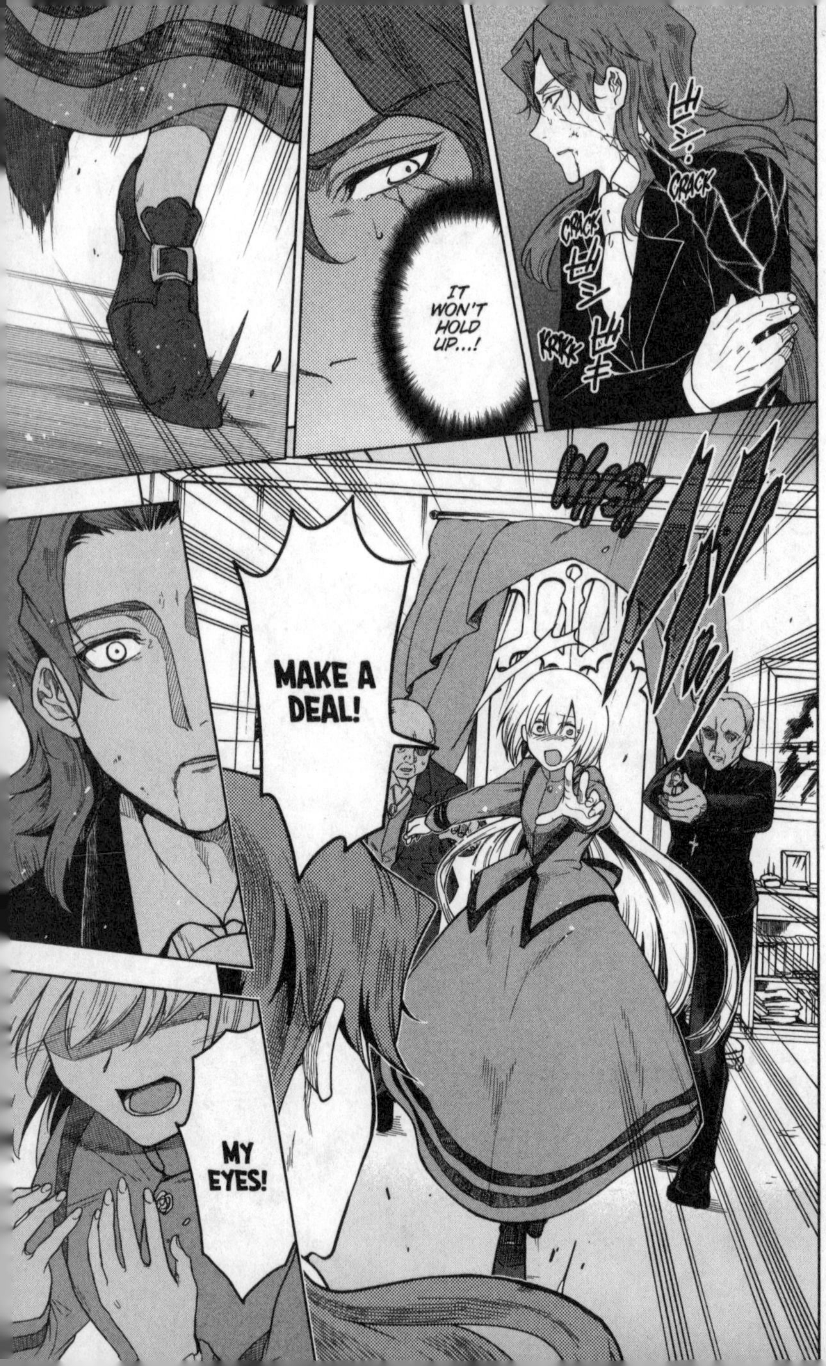
CRACK
CRACK
KRAKK
IT WON'T HOLD UP...!
WHSSH
MAKE A DEAL!
MY EYES!

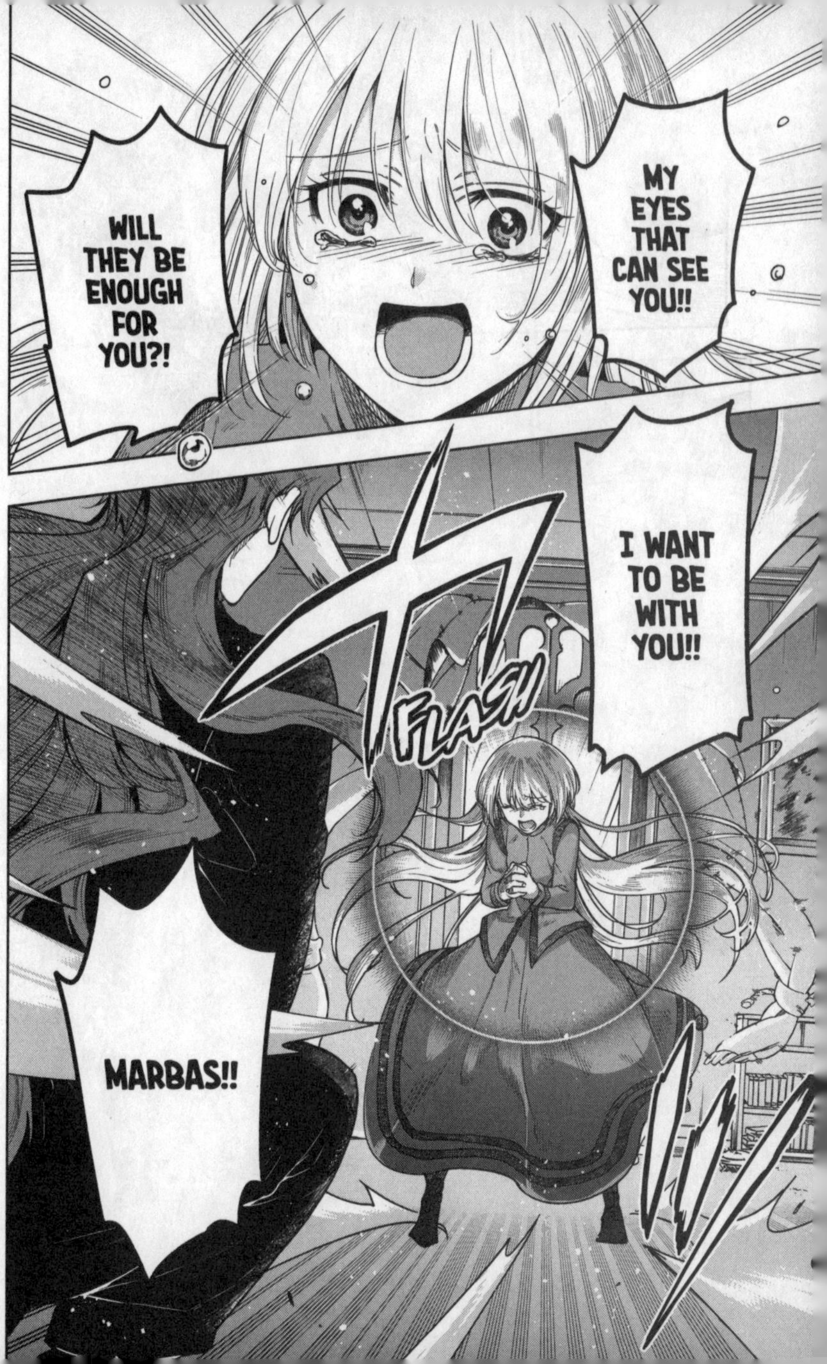
MY EYES THAT CAN SEE YOU!!
WILL THEY BE ENOUGH FOR YOU?!
I WANT TO BE WITH YOU!!
FLASH
MARBAS!!

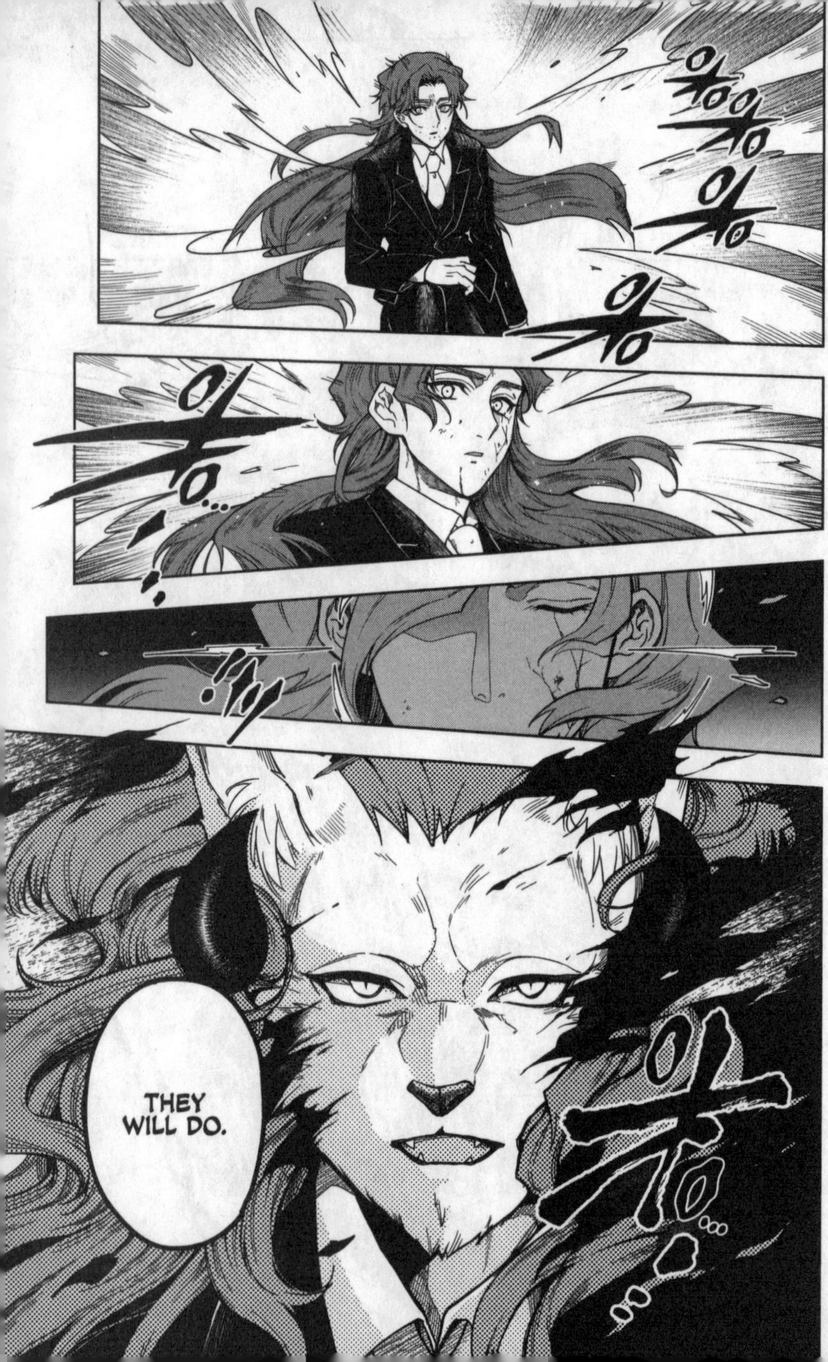
THEY WILL DO.

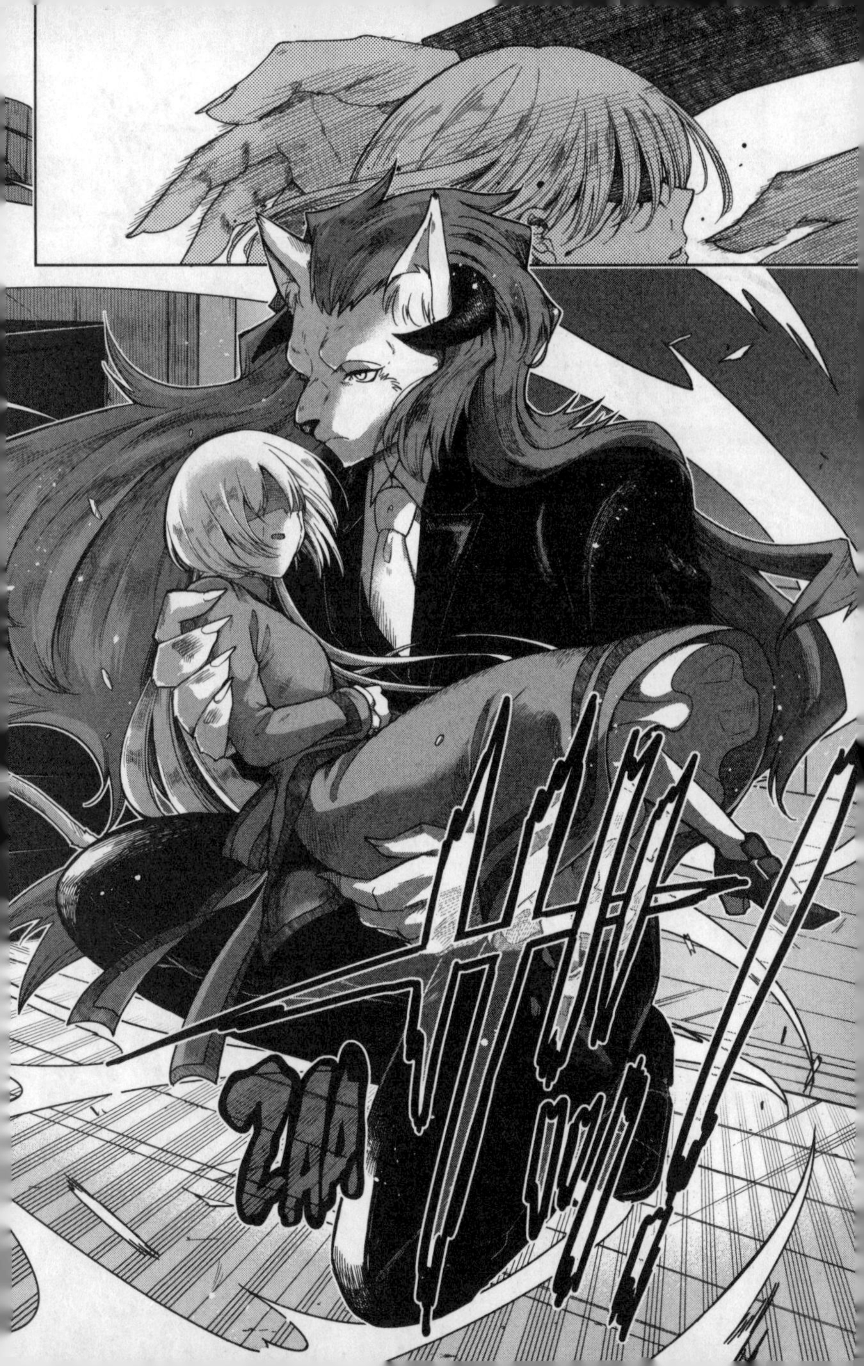
ZAP

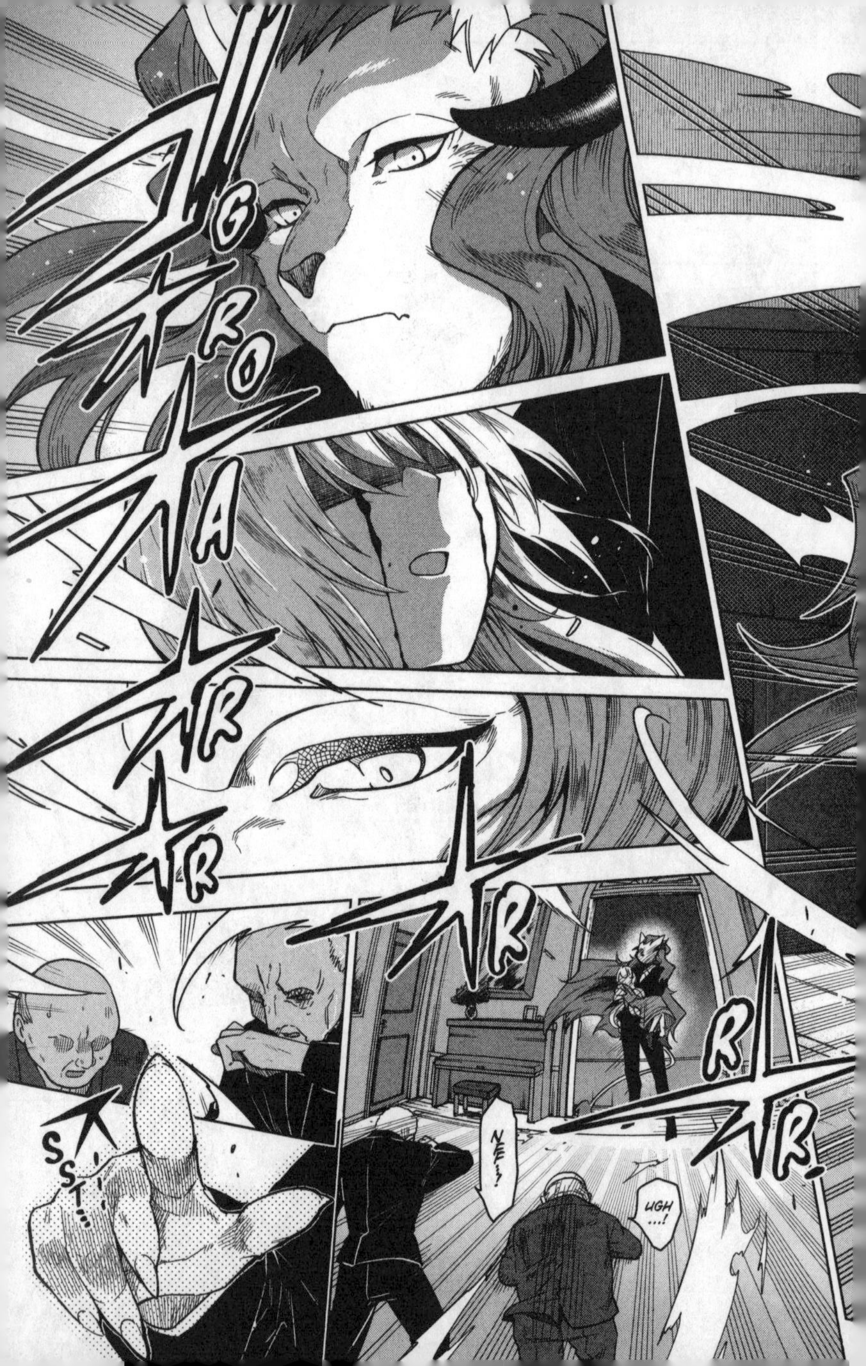
GROARRRRRR!
UGH...!
NFF...!
SSST...

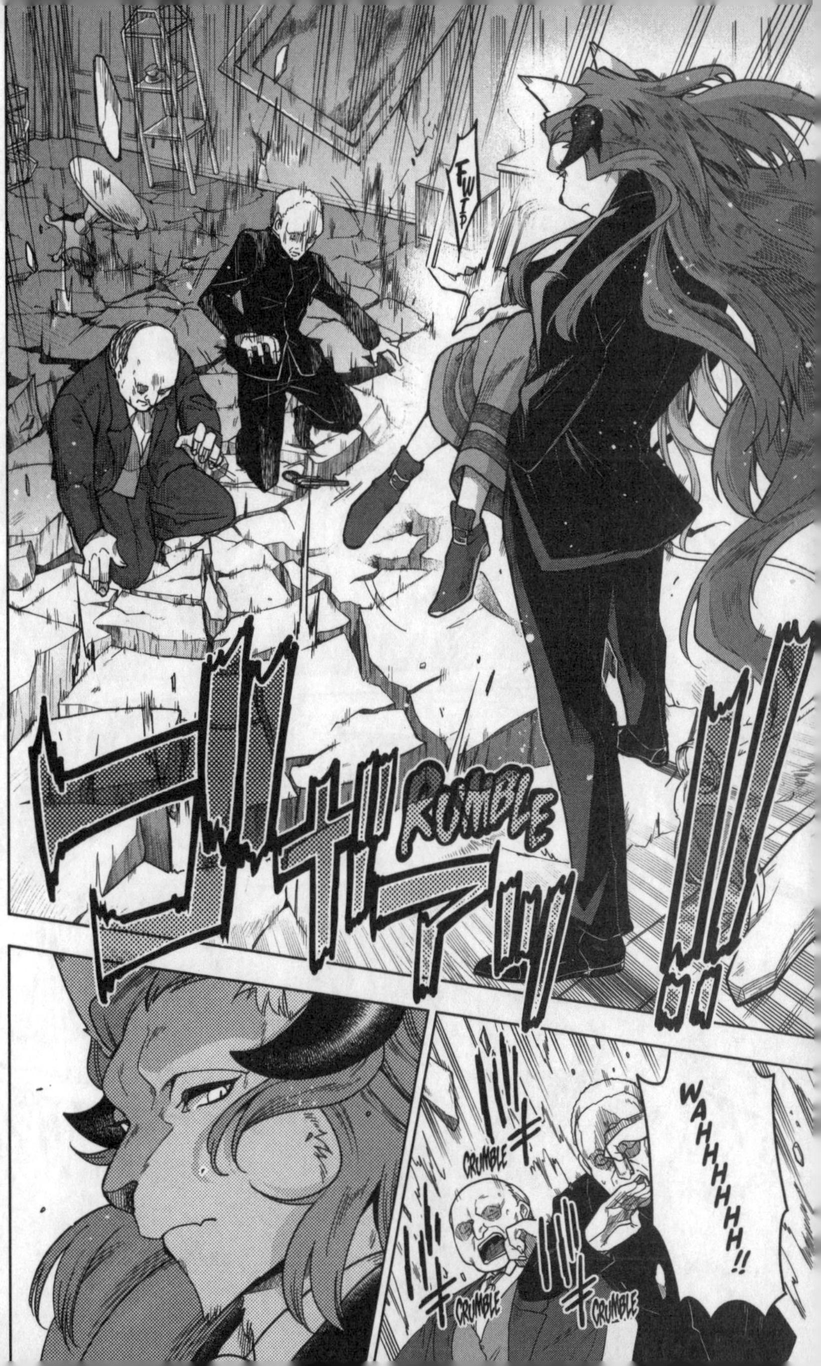
FWIP
RUMBLE
WAHHHHHHH!!
CRUMBLE
CRUMBLE
CRUMBLE

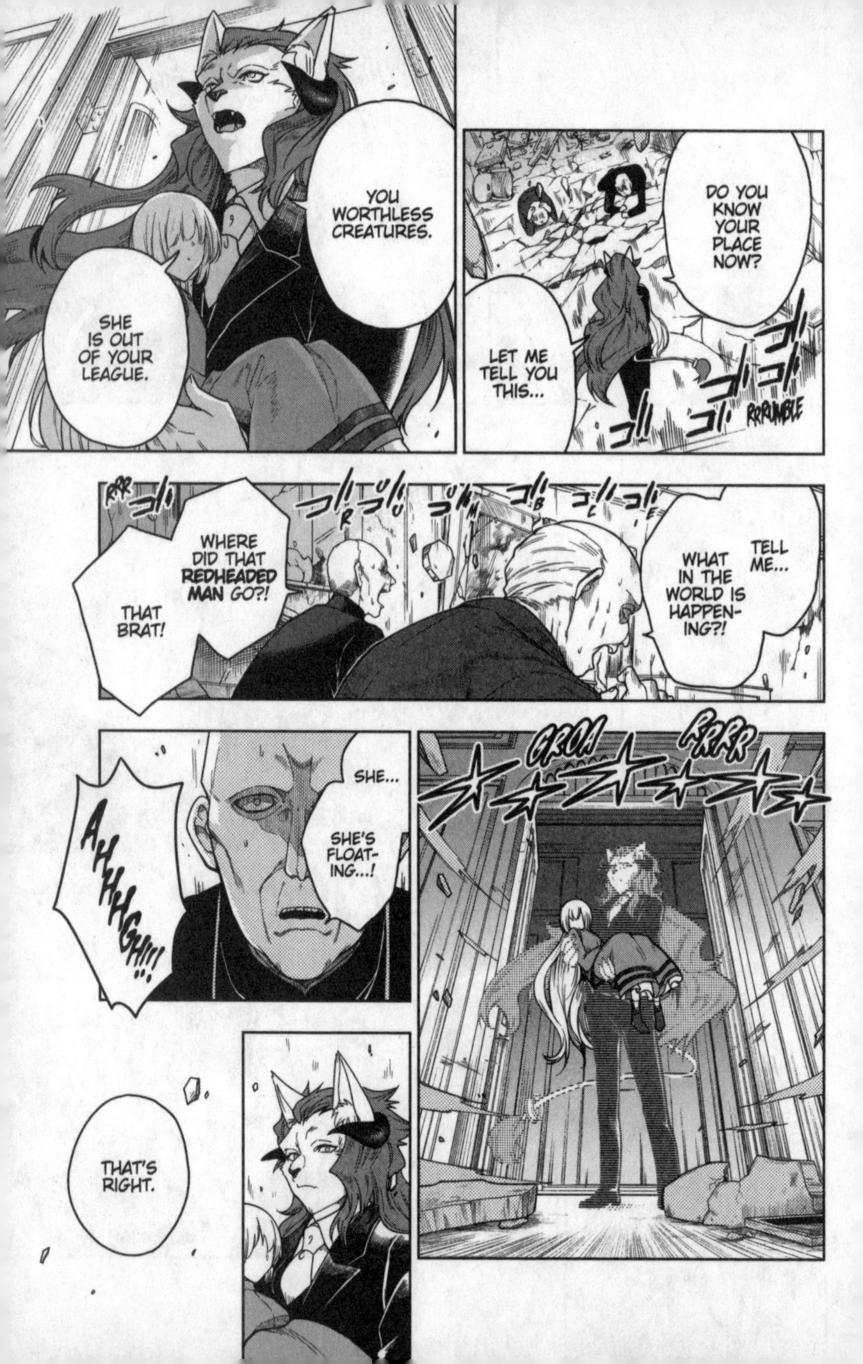
DO YOU KNOW YOUR PLACE NOW?
LET ME TELL YOU THIS...
RRRUMBLE
YOU WORTHLESS CREATURES.
SHE IS OUT OF YOUR LEAGUE.
RRR
RUMBLE
TELL ME...
WHAT IN THE WORLD IS HAPPENING?!
WHERE DID THAT **REDHEADED MAN** GO?!
THAT BRAT!
GROA
RRRR
SHE...
SHE'S FLOATING...!
AHHHGH!!!
THAT'S RIGHT.

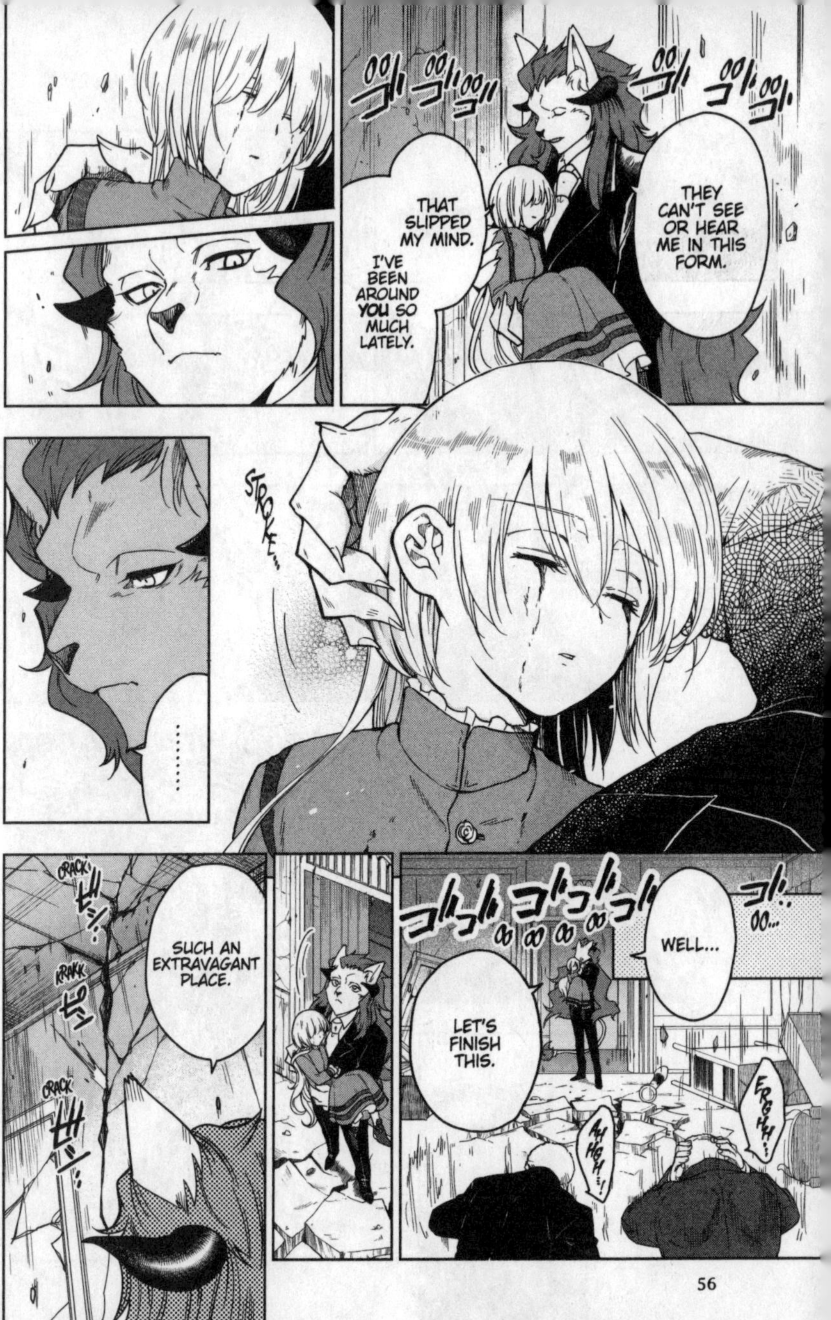
THEY CAN'T SEE OR HEAR ME IN THIS FORM.
THAT SLIPPED MY MIND.
I'VE BEEN AROUND YOU SO MUCH LATELY.
STROKE...
......
WELL...
LET'S FINISH THIS.
ERGHH...
AHHGH...!
SUCH AN EXTRAVAGANT PLACE.
CRACK
KRAKK
CRACK

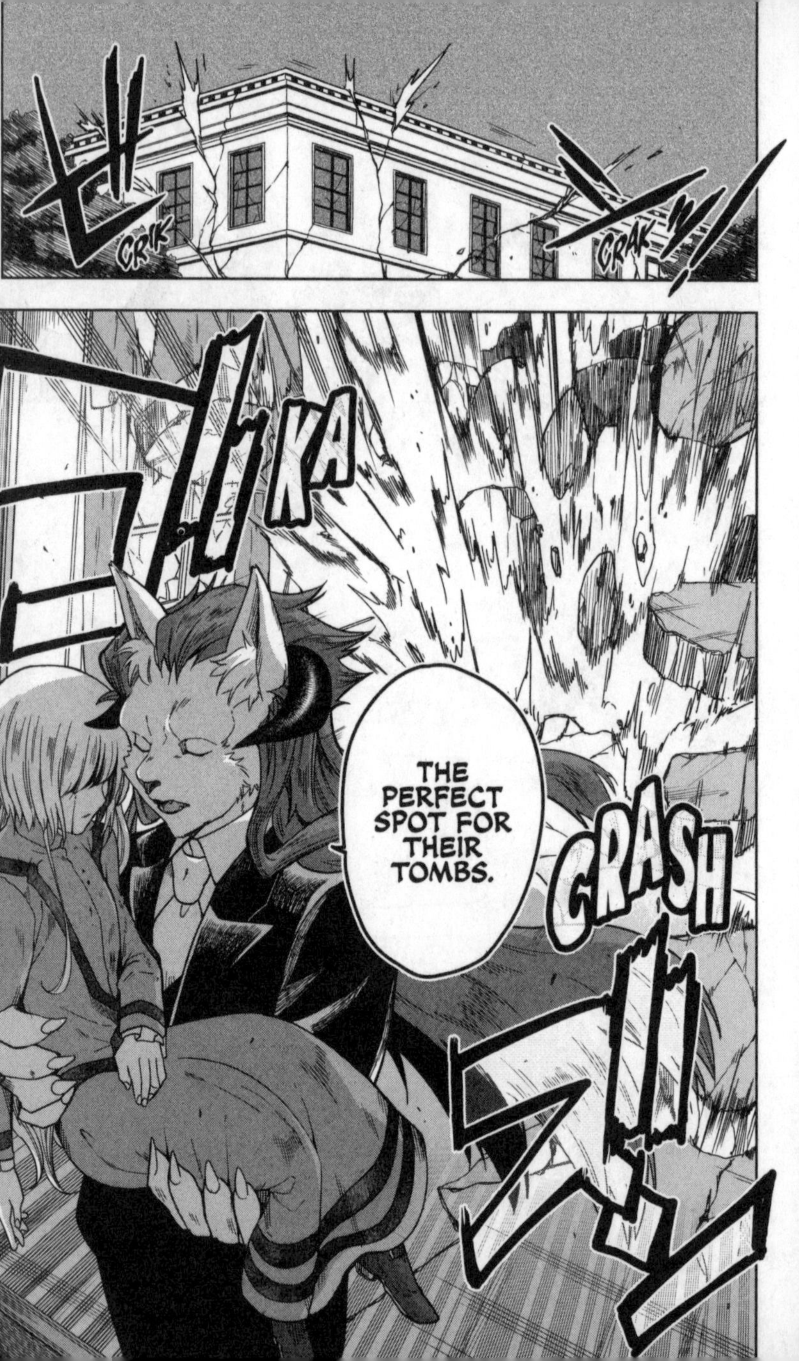
CRAK
CRIK
KA
THE PERFECT SPOT FOR THEIR TOMBS.
CRASH

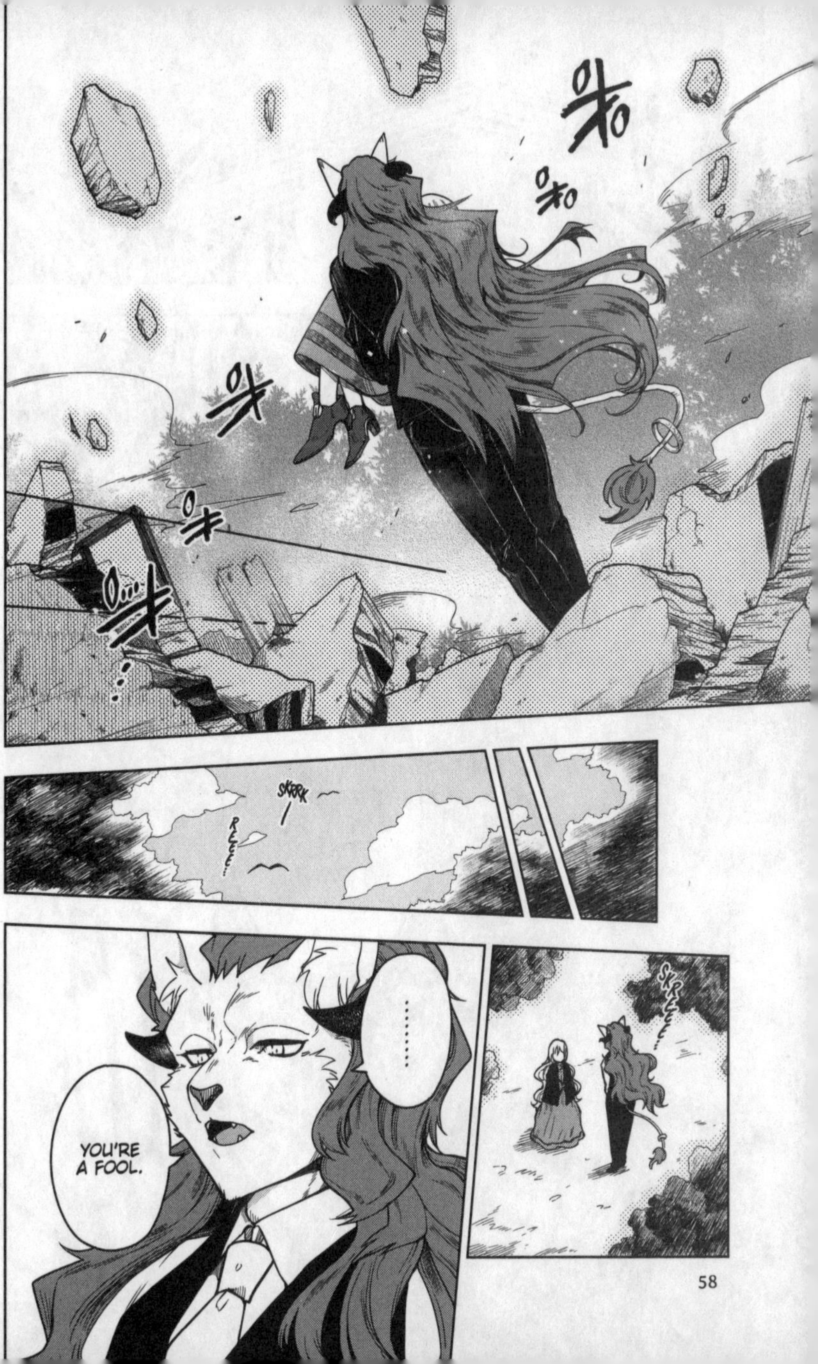
SKRRK-
REEE...
SKREEE...
......
YOU'RE A FOOL.

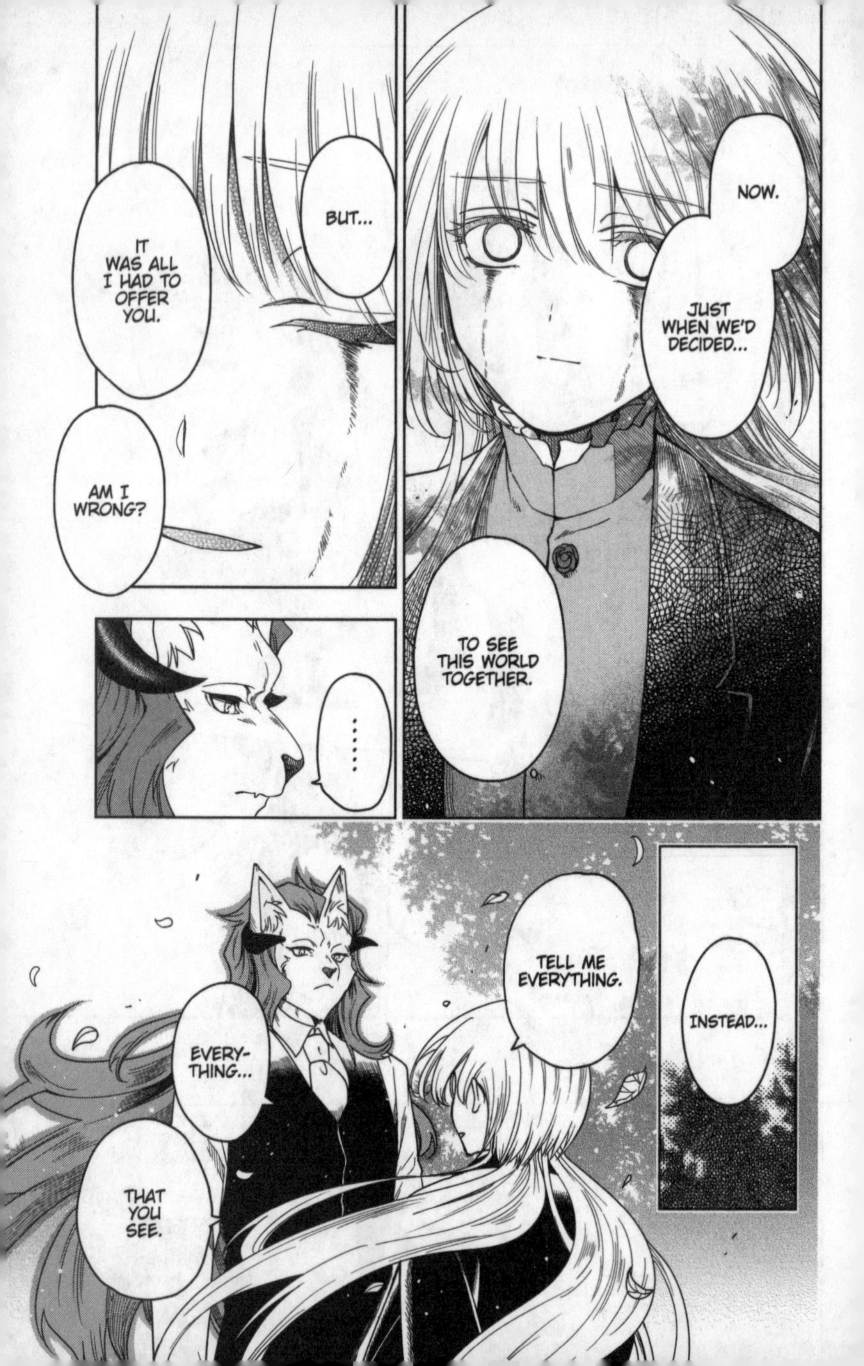
NOW.
JUST WHEN WE'D DECIDED...
TO SEE THIS WORLD TOGETHER.
BUT...
IT WAS ALL I HAD TO OFFER YOU.
AM I WRONG?
......
INSTEAD...
TELL ME EVERYTHING.
EVERY-THING...
THAT YOU SEE.

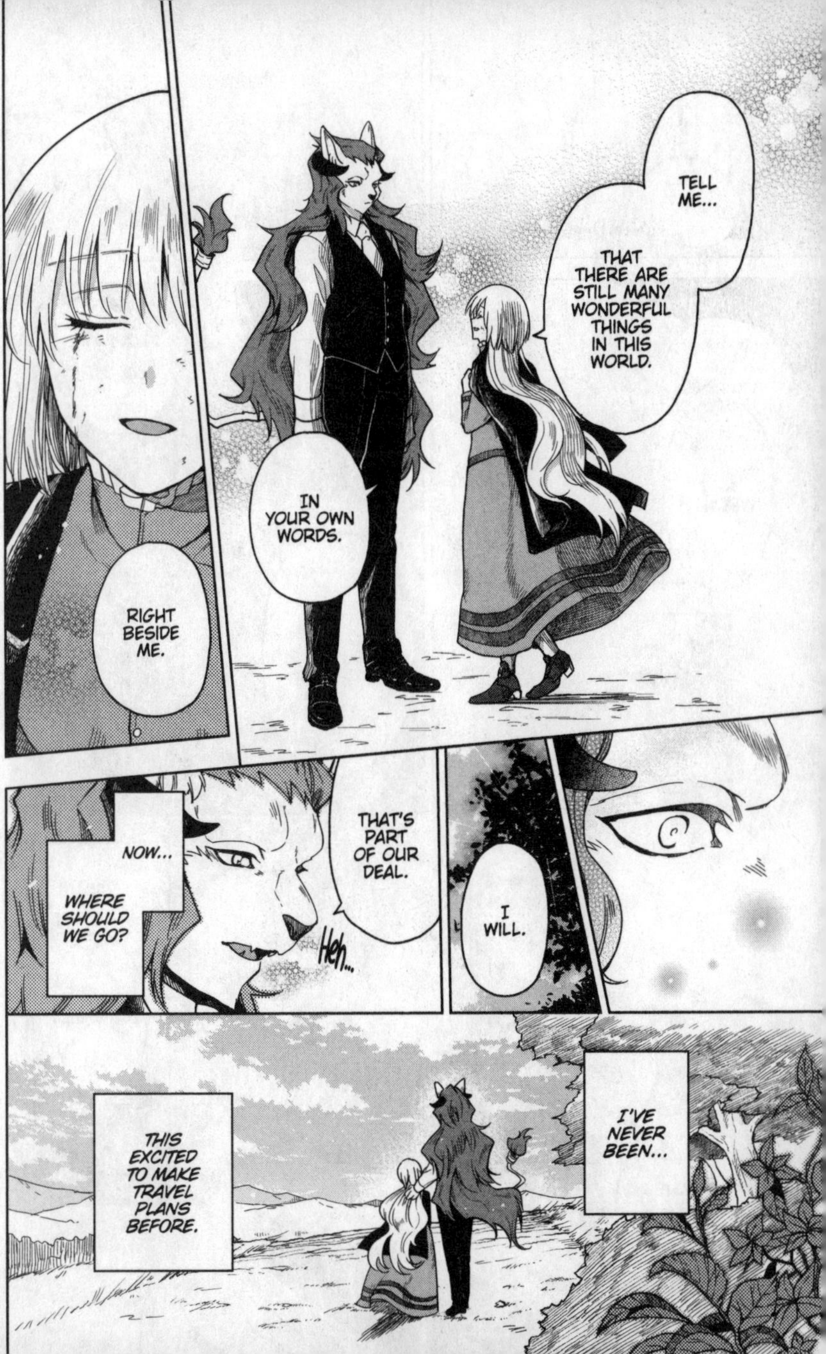
TELL ME...
THAT THERE ARE STILL MANY WONDERFUL THINGS IN THIS WORLD.
IN YOUR OWN WORDS.
RIGHT BESIDE ME.
I WILL.
THAT'S PART OF OUR DEAL.
Heh...
NOW...
WHERE SHOULD WE GO?
I'VE NEVER BEEN...
THIS EXCITED TO MAKE TRAVEL PLANS BEFORE.

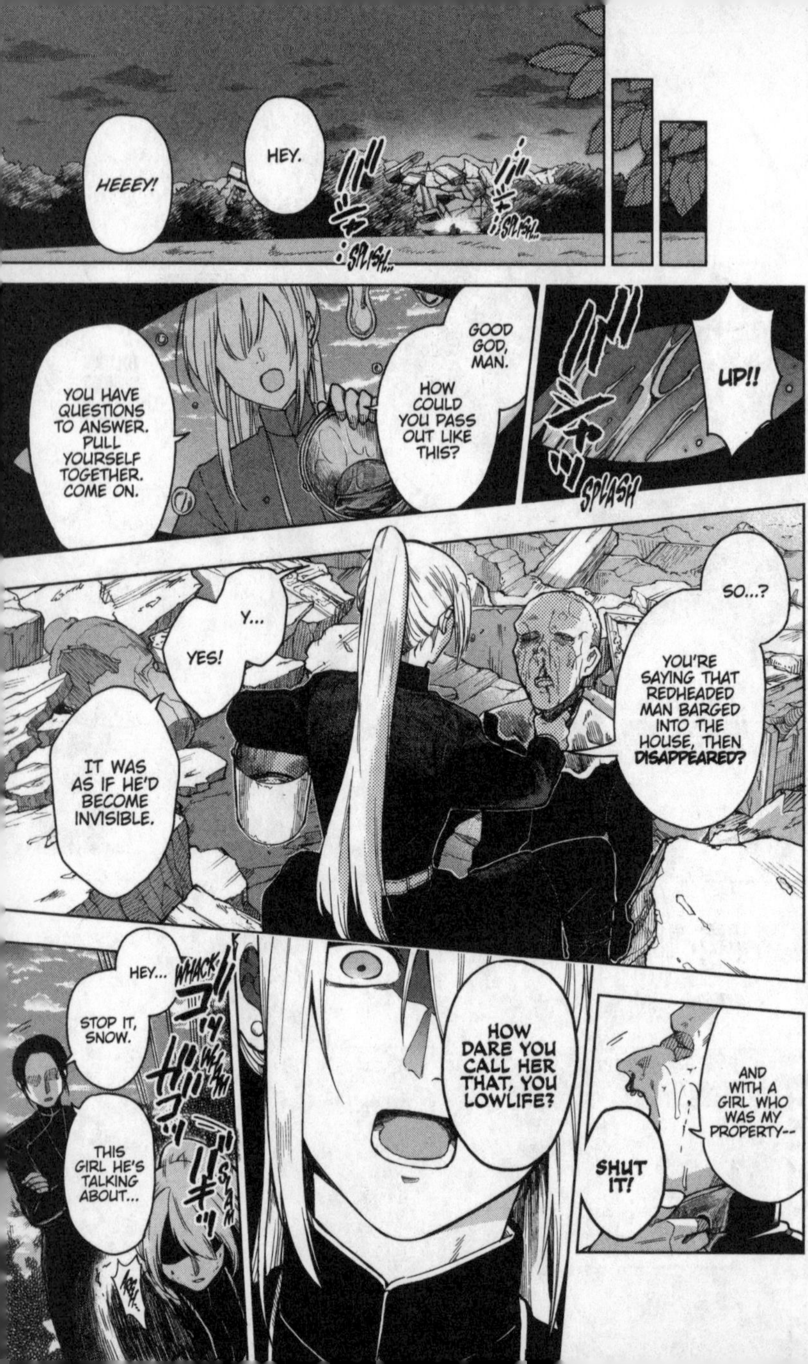
SPLISH...
HEY.
SPLISH...
HEEEY!
UP!!
SPLASH
GOOD GOD, MAN.
HOW COULD YOU PASS OUT LIKE THIS?
YOU HAVE QUESTIONS TO ANSWER. PULL YOURSELF TOGETHER. COME ON.
SO...?
YOU'RE SAYING THAT REDHEADED MAN BARGED INTO THE HOUSE, THEN **DISAPPEARED?**
Y...
YES!
IT WAS AS IF HE'D BECOME INVISIBLE.
AND WITH A GIRL WHO WAS MY PROPERTY--
SHUT IT!
HOW DARE YOU CALL HER THAT, YOU LOWLIFE?
WHACK
WHAM
SLAM
HEY...
STOP IT, SNOW.
THIS GIRL HE'S TALKING ABOUT...

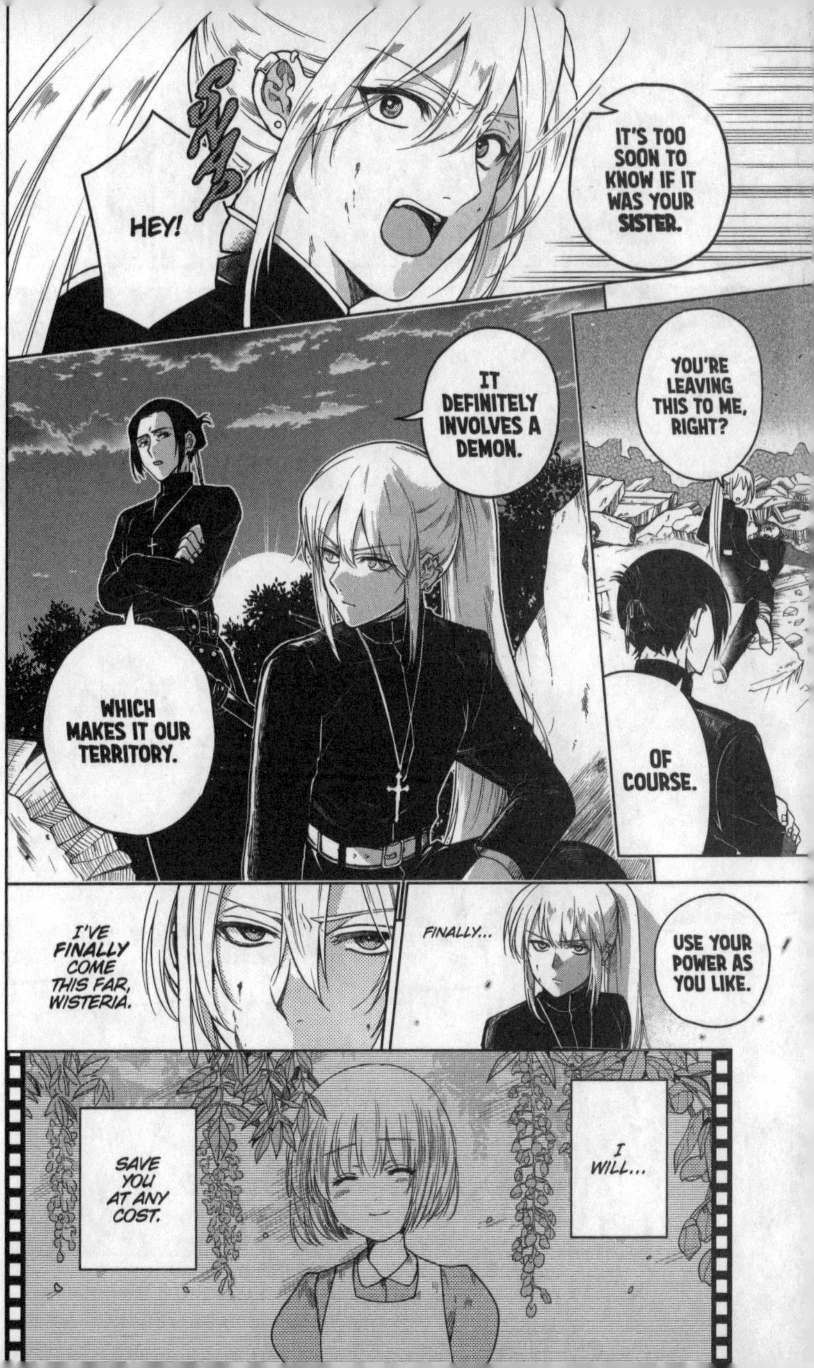
IT'S TOO SOON TO KNOW IF IT WAS YOUR SISTER.
SNAP
HEY!
YOU'RE LEAVING THIS TO ME, RIGHT?
OF COURSE.
IT DEFINITELY INVOLVES A DEMON.
WHICH MAKES IT OUR TERRITORY.
USE YOUR POWER AS YOU LIKE.
FINALLY...
I'VE FINALLY COME THIS FAR, WISTERIA.
I WILL...
SAVE YOU AT ANY COST.

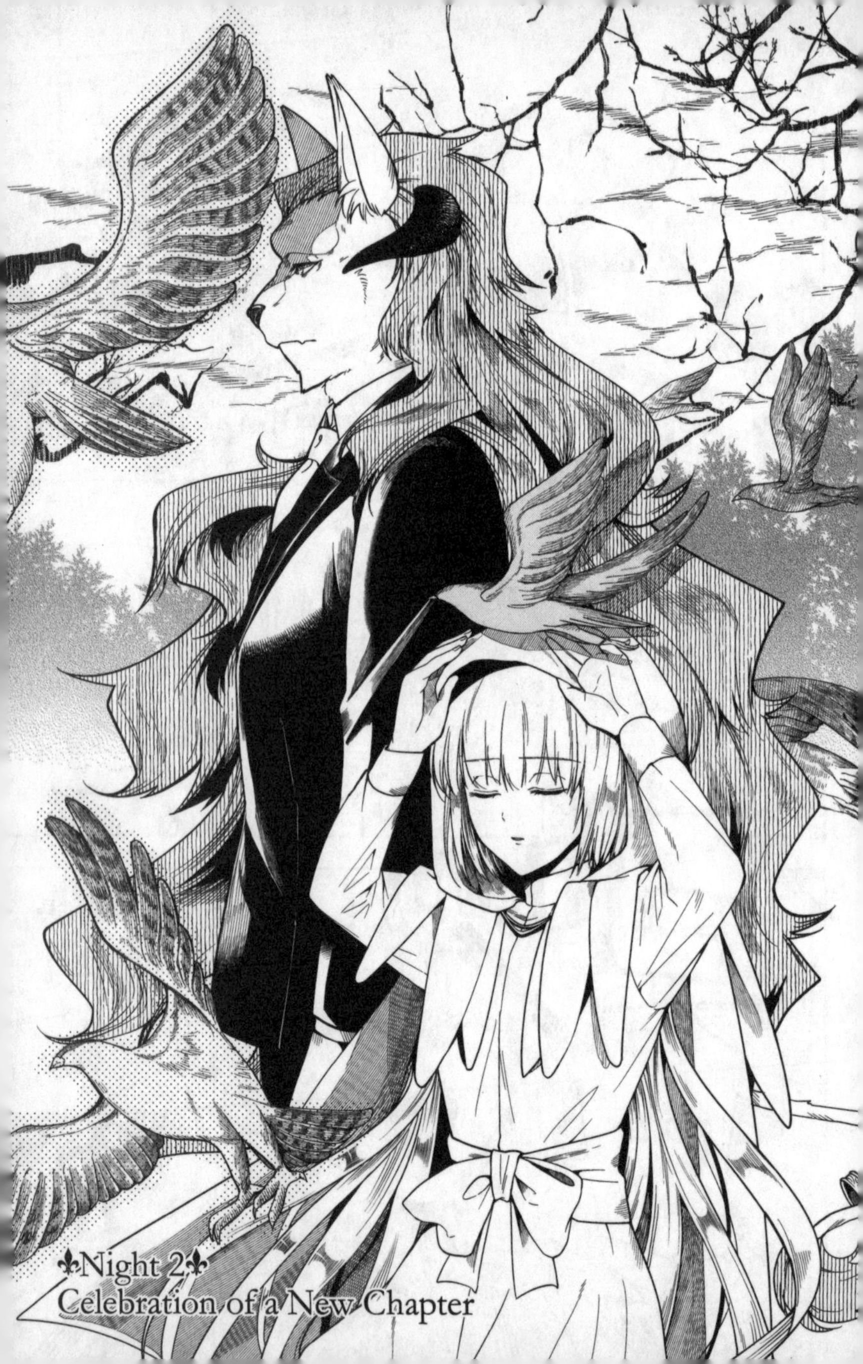

⚜Night 2⚜ Celebration of a New Chapter

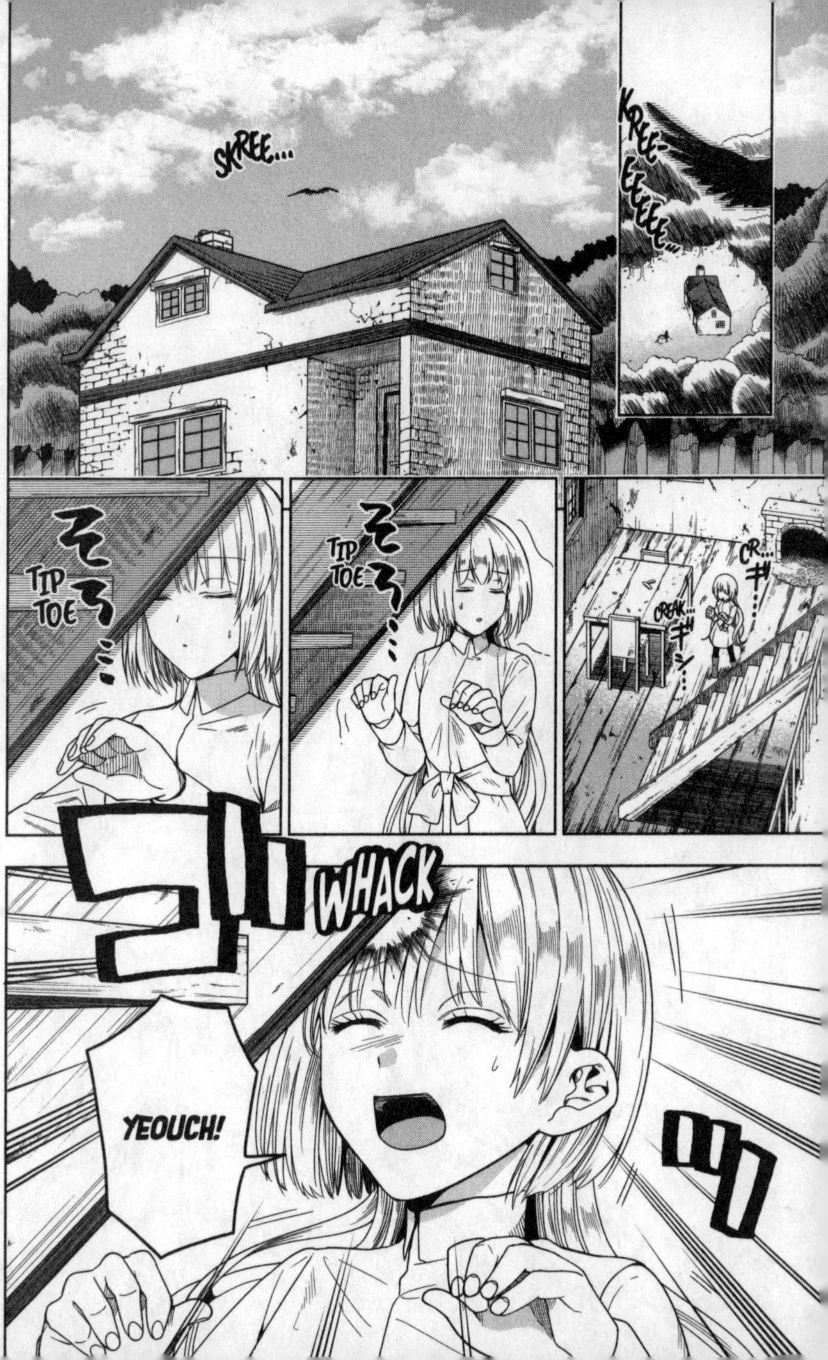
KREE-EEEEE...
SKREE...
CR...
ギ...
CREAK...
ギシ...
TIP TOE
そろ...
TIP TOE
そろ...
ゴン
WHACK
ッ
YEOUCH!

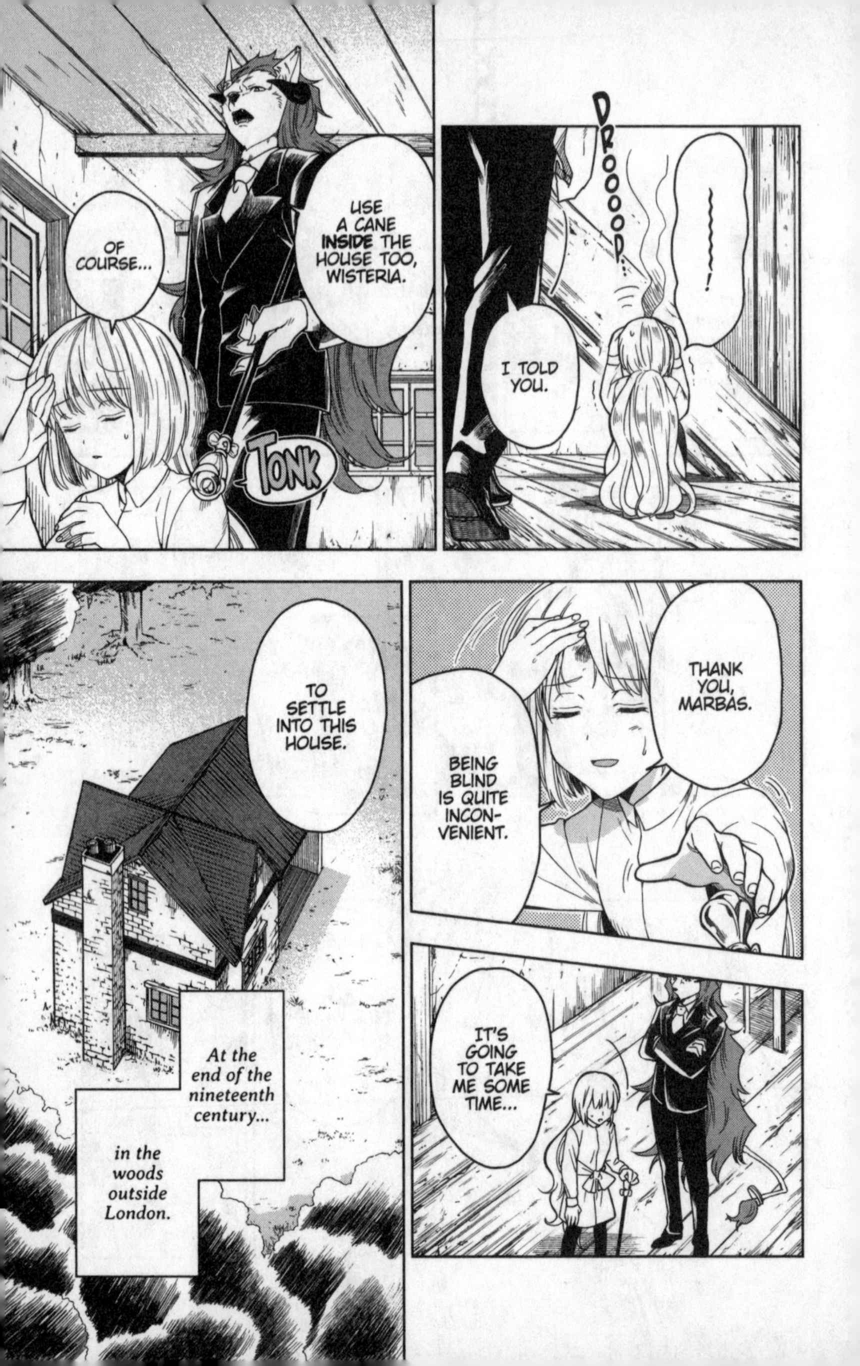

DROOOOD...
——!
I TOLD YOU.
USE A CANE INSIDE THE HOUSE TOO, WISTERIA.
OF COURSE...
TONK
THANK YOU, MARBAS.
BEING BLIND IS QUITE INCON-VENIENT.
IT'S GOING TO TAKE ME SOME TIME...
TO SETTLE INTO THIS HOUSE.
At the end of the nineteenth century...
in the woods outside London.

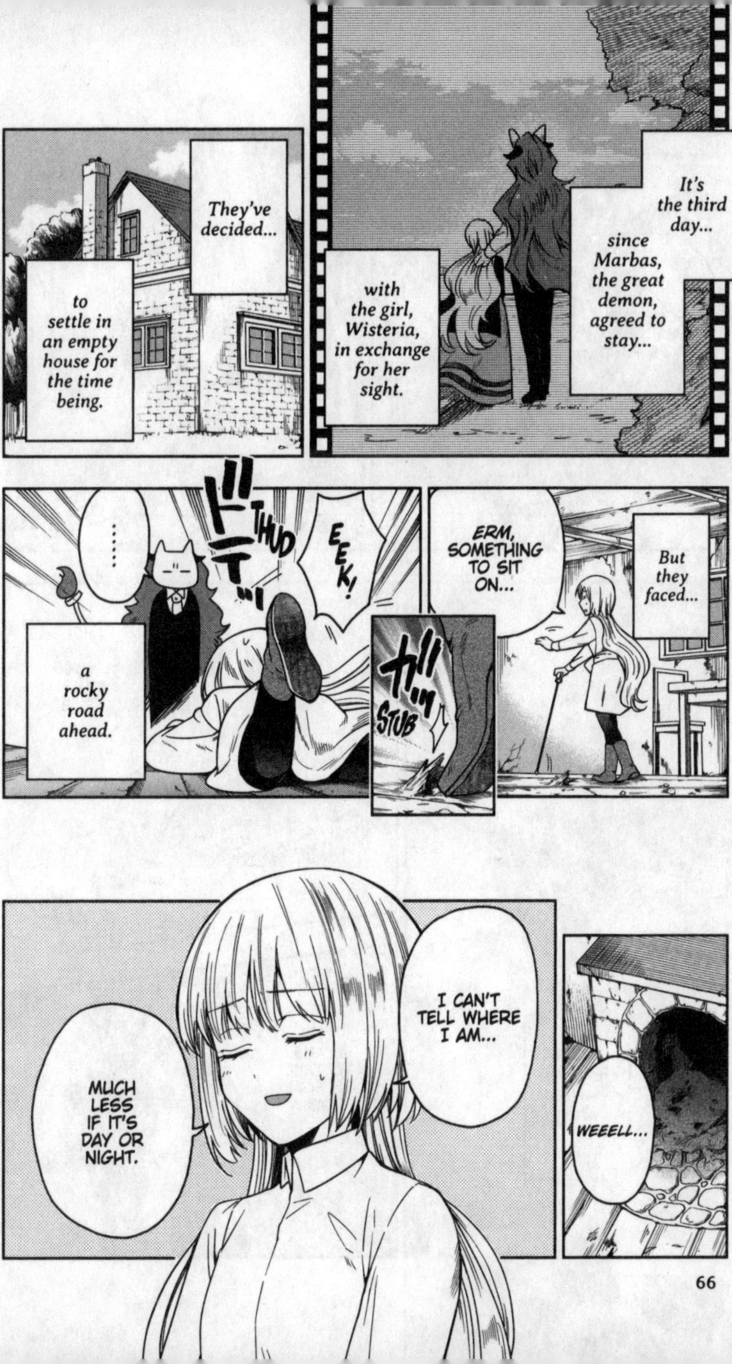
It's the third day...
since Marbas, the great demon, agreed to stay...
with the girl, Wisteria, in exchange for her sight.
They've decided...
to settle in an empty house for the time being.
But they faced...
ERM, SOMETHING TO SIT ON...
STUB
EEK!
THUD
......
a rocky road ahead.
WEEELL...
I CAN'T TELL WHERE I AM...
MUCH LESS IF IT'S DAY OR NIGHT.

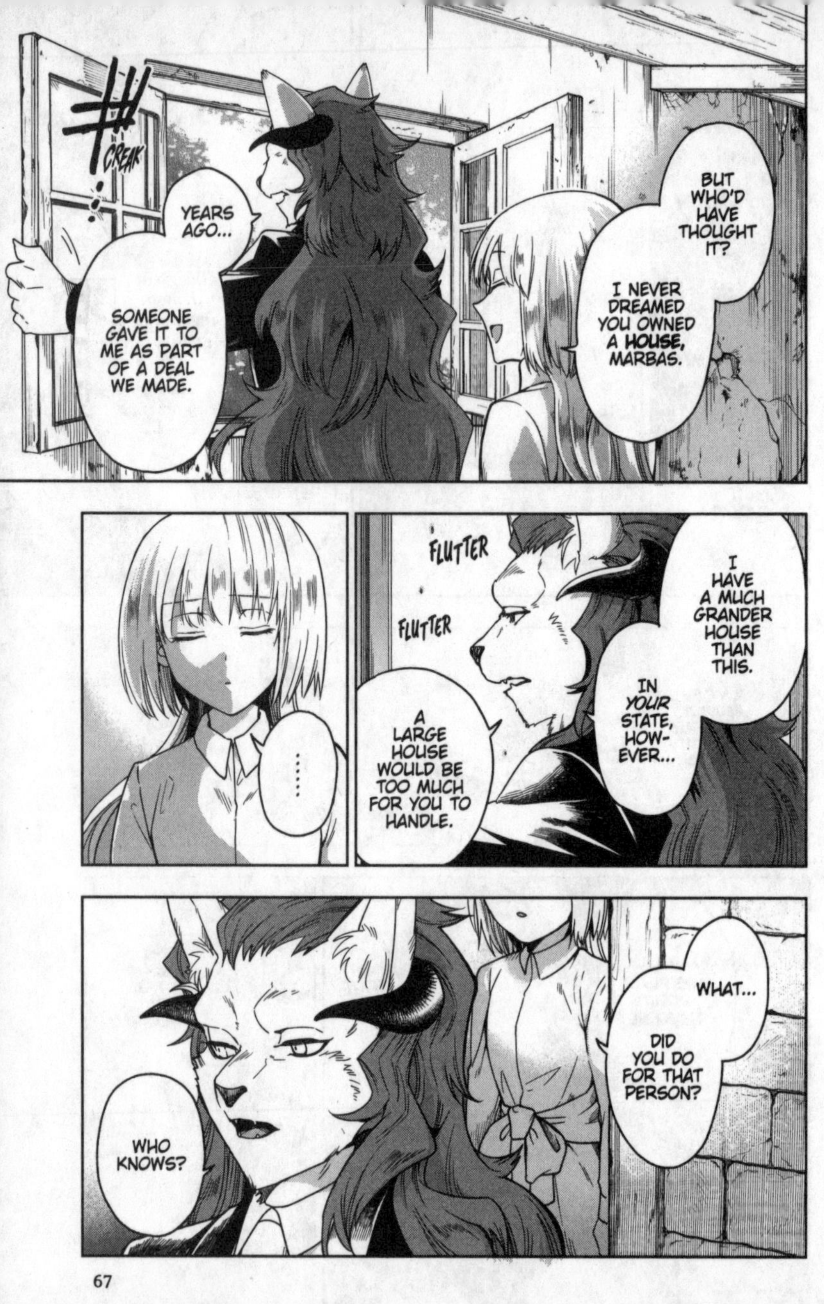
BUT WHO'D HAVE THOUGHT IT?
I NEVER DREAMED YOU OWNED A HOUSE, MARBAS.
YEARS AGO...
SOMEONE GAVE IT TO ME AS PART OF A DEAL WE MADE.
CREAK
FLUTTER
FLUTTER
I HAVE A MUCH GRANDER HOUSE THAN THIS.
IN YOUR STATE, HOW-EVER...
A LARGE HOUSE WOULD BE TOO MUCH FOR YOU TO HANDLE.
......
WHAT...
DID YOU DO FOR THAT PERSON?
WHO KNOWS?

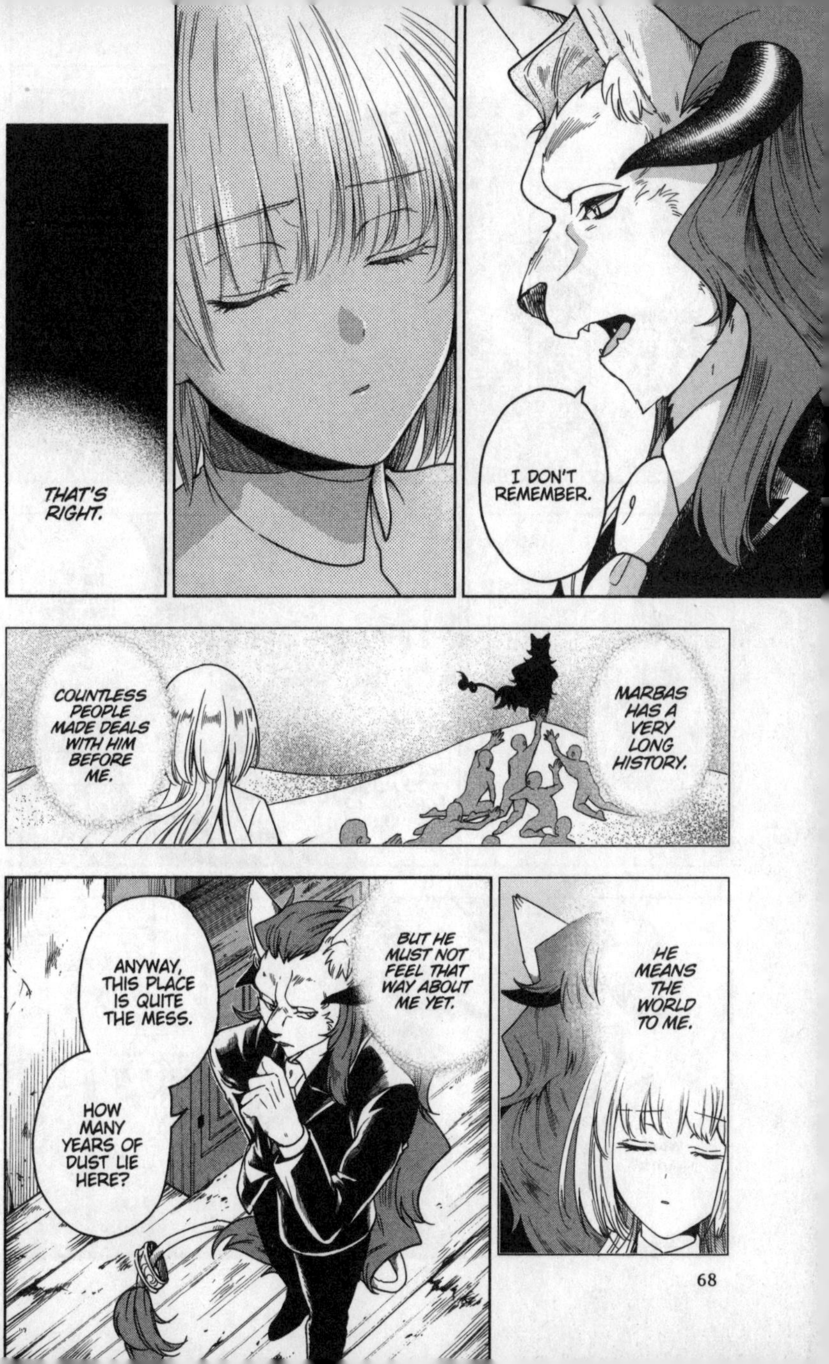
I DON'T REMEMBER.
THAT'S RIGHT.
MARBAS HAS A VERY LONG HISTORY.
COUNTLESS PEOPLE MADE DEALS WITH HIM BEFORE ME.
HE MEANS THE WORLD TO ME.
BUT HE MUST NOT FEEL THAT WAY ABOUT ME YET.
ANYWAY, THIS PLACE IS QUITE THE MESS.
HOW MANY YEARS OF DUST LIE HERE?

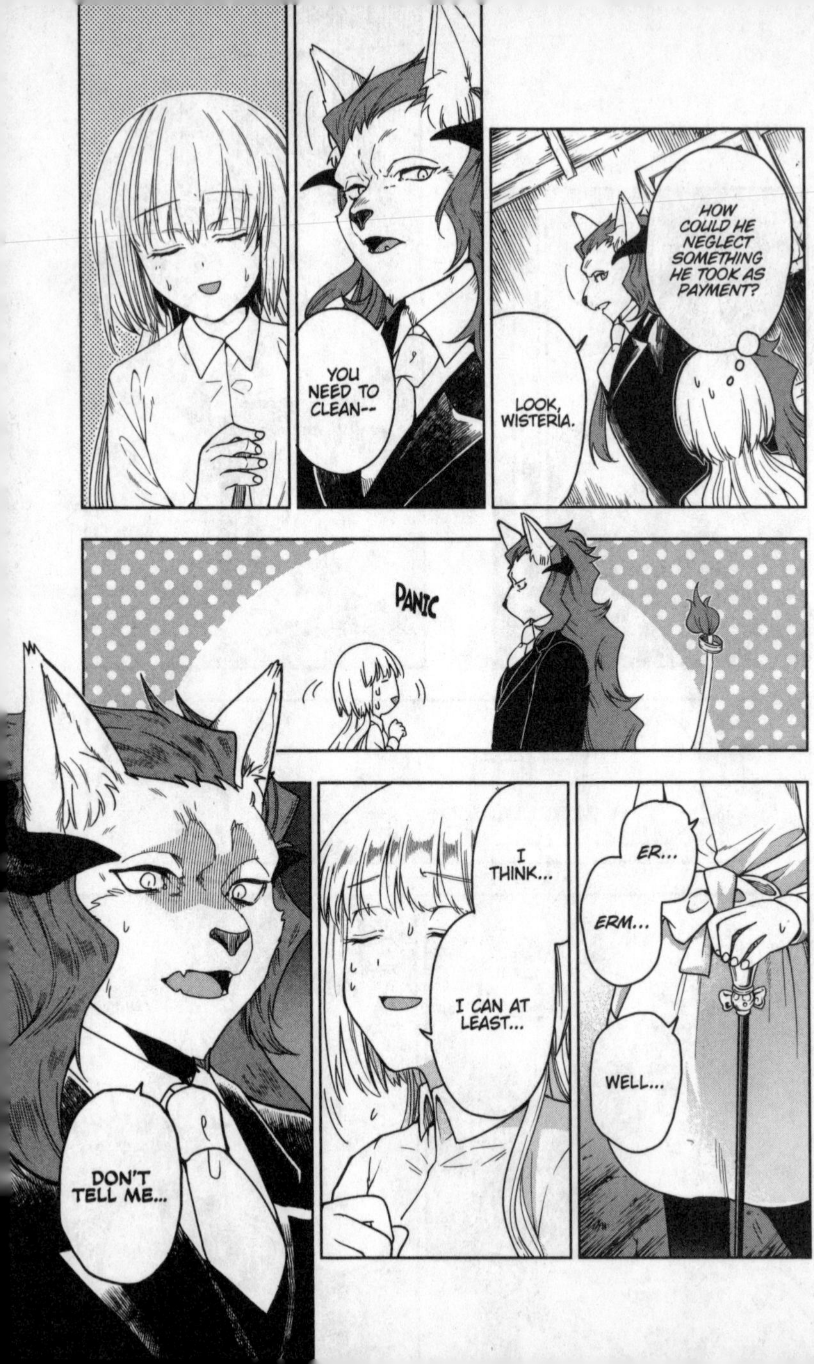
HOW COULD HE NEGLECT SOMETHING HE TOOK AS PAYMENT?
LOOK, WISTERIA.
YOU NEED TO CLEAN--
PANIC
ER...
ERM...
WELL...
I THINK...
I CAN AT LEAST...
DON'T TELL ME...

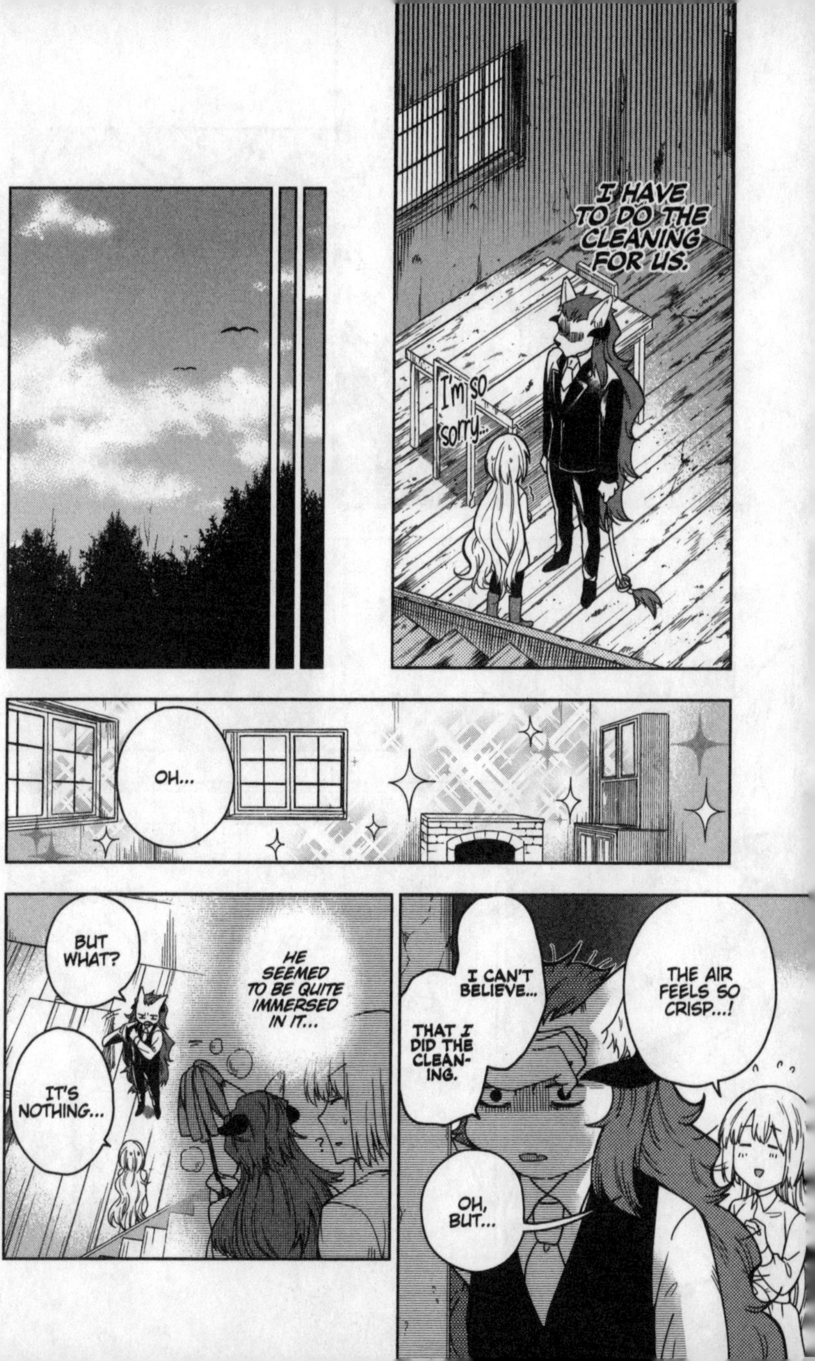
I HAVE TO DO THE CLEANING FOR US.
I'm so sorry...
OH...
THE AIR FEELS SO CRISP...!
I CAN'T BELIEVE...
THAT I DID THE CLEAN-ING.
OH, BUT...
BUT WHAT?
IT'S NOTHING...
HE SEEMED TO BE QUITE IMMERSED IN IT...

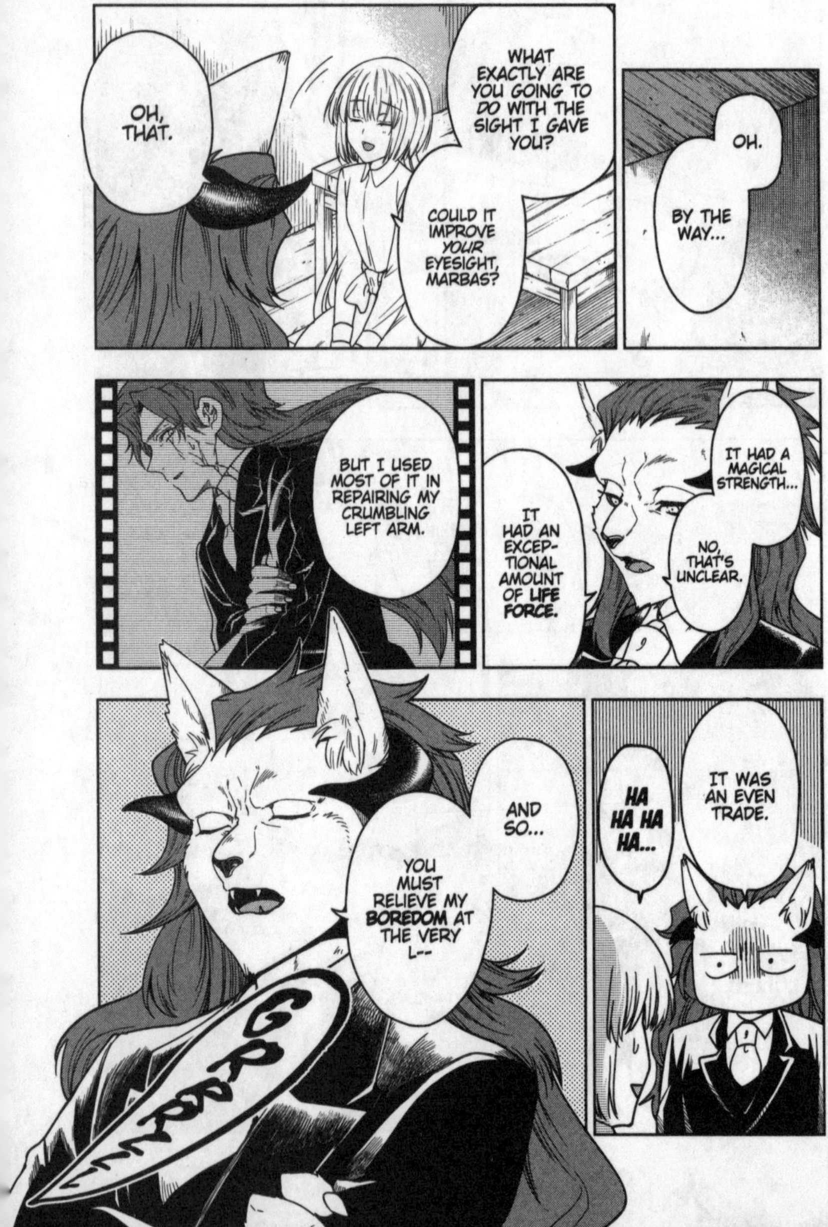
OH.
BY THE WAY...
WHAT EXACTLY ARE YOU GOING TO *DO* WITH THE SIGHT I GAVE YOU?
COULD IT IMPROVE *YOUR* EYESIGHT, MARBAS?
OH, THAT.
IT HAD A MAGICAL STRENGTH...
NO, THAT'S UNCLEAR.
IT HAD AN EXCEP-TIONAL AMOUNT OF **LIFE FORCE**.
BUT I USED MOST OF IT IN REPAIRING MY CRUMBLING LEFT ARM.
IT WAS AN EVEN TRADE.
HA HA HA HA...
AND SO...
YOU MUST RELIEVE MY **BOREDOM** AT THE VERY L--
GRRRULL

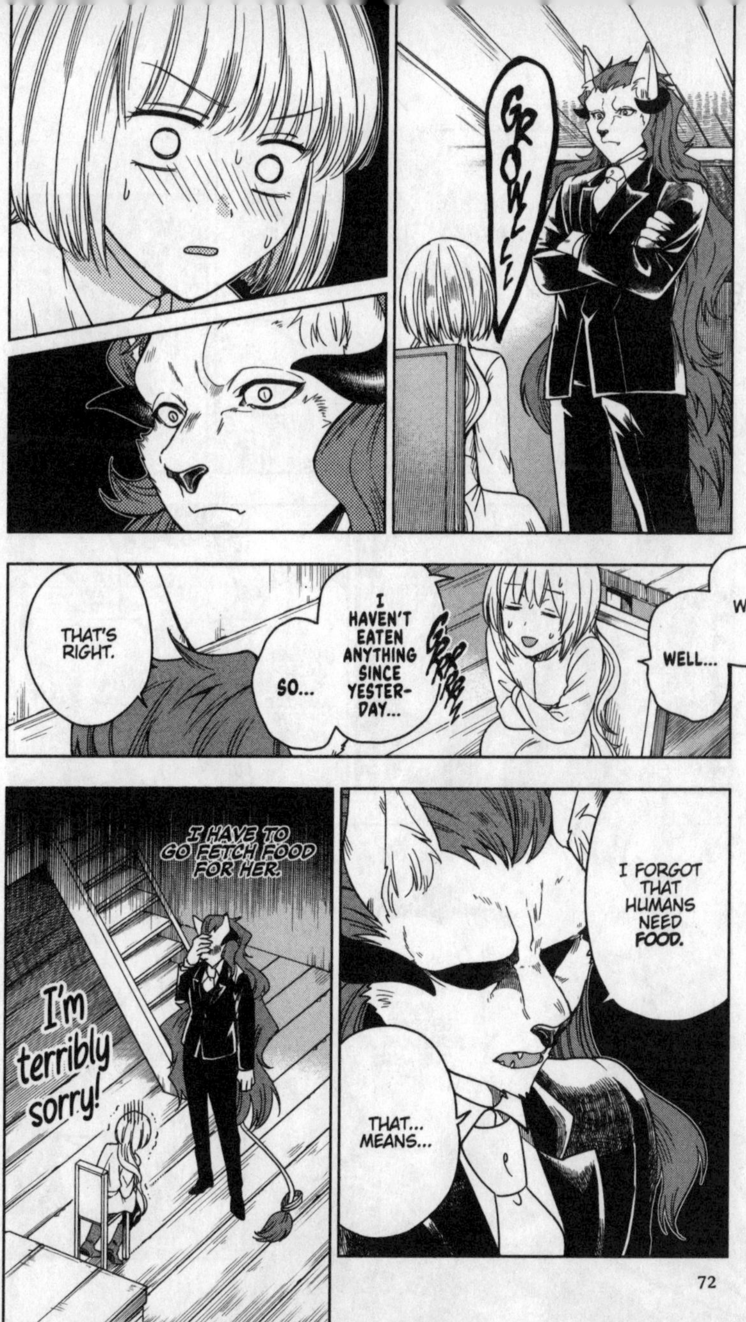
GROWLLL
W...
WELL...
I HAVEN'T EATEN ANYTHING SINCE YESTER-DAY...
SO...
THAT'S RIGHT.
I FORGOT THAT HUMANS NEED FOOD.
THAT... MEANS...
I HAVE TO GO FETCH FOOD FOR HER.
I'm terribly sorry!

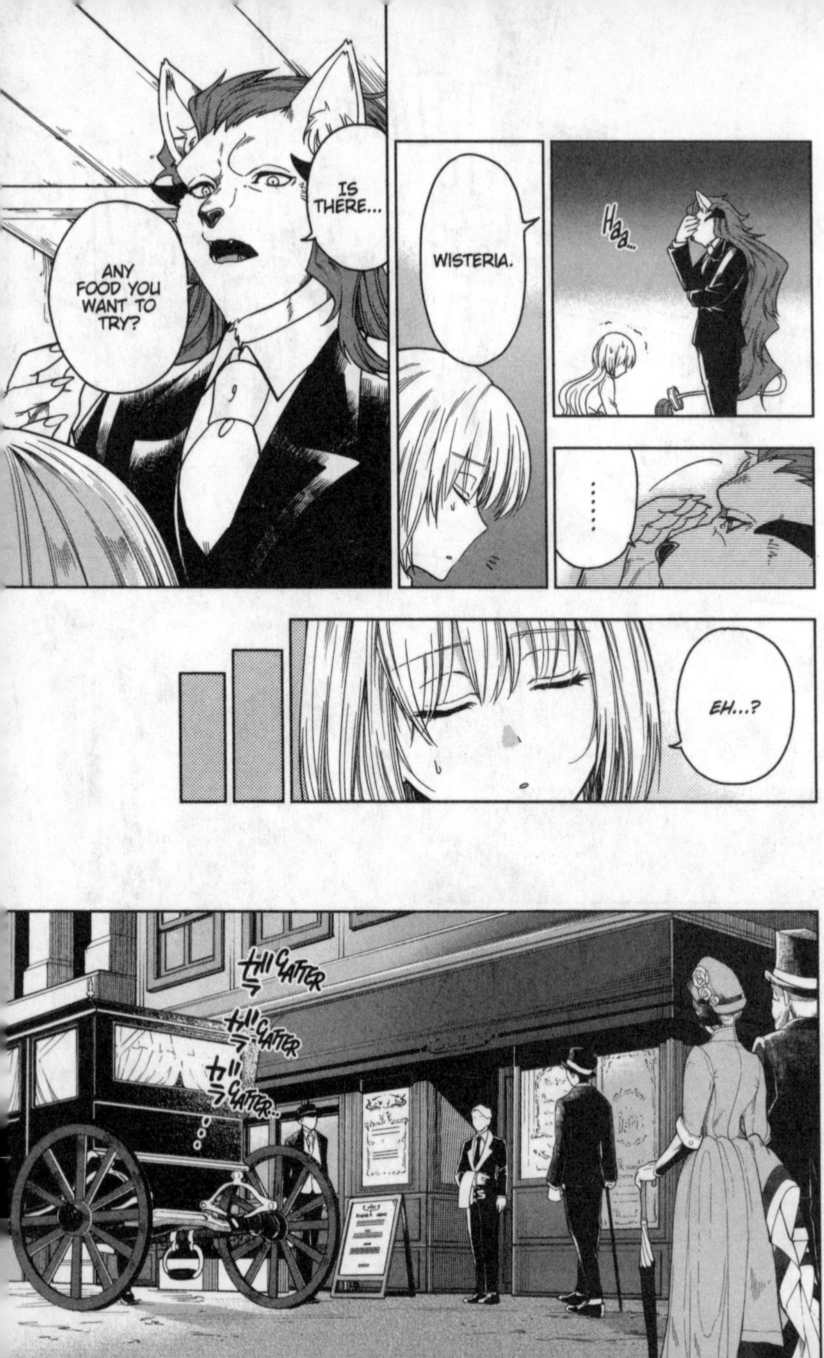
Haa...
......
WISTERIA.
IS THERE...
ANY FOOD YOU WANT TO TRY?
EH...?
CLATTER
CLATTER
CLATTER...

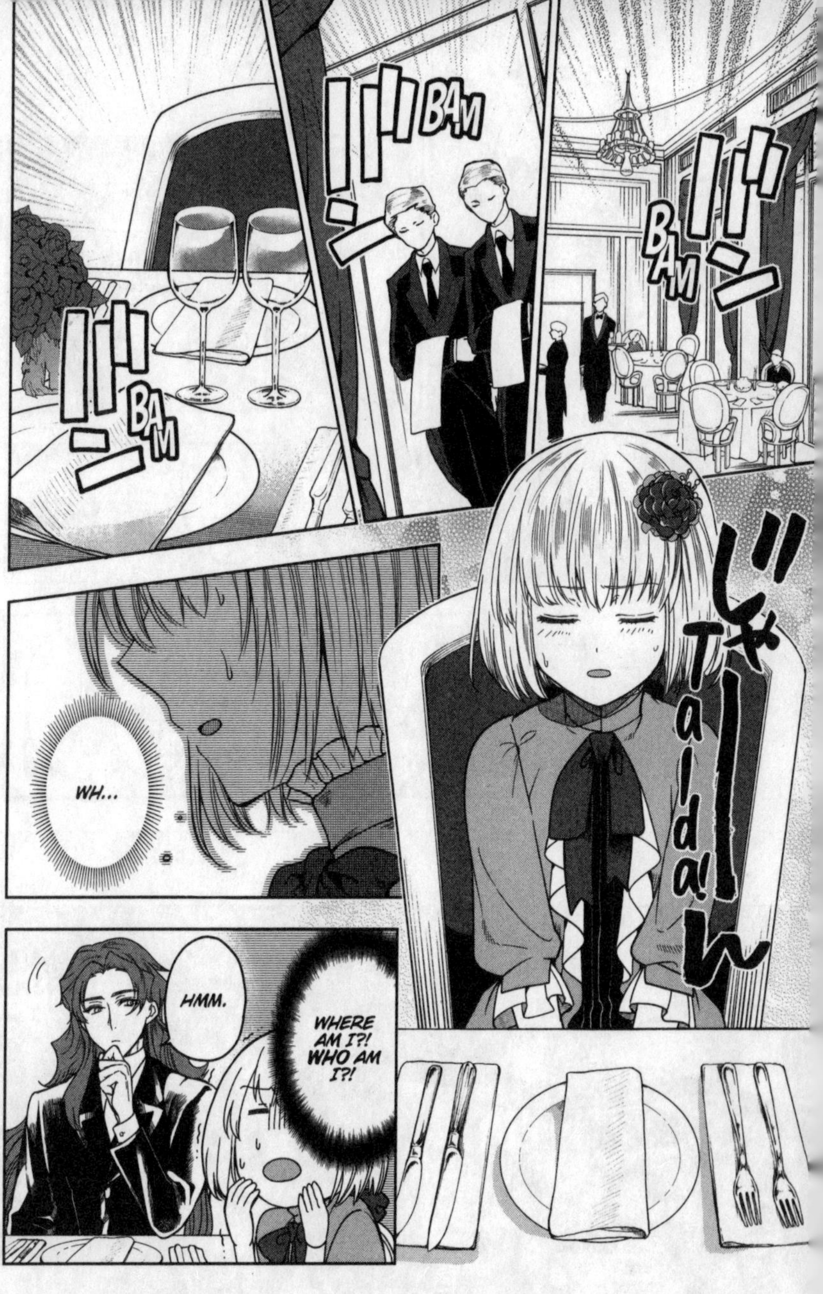
BAM
BAM
BAM
Ta-da!
WH...
HMM.
WHERE AM I?! WHO AM I?!

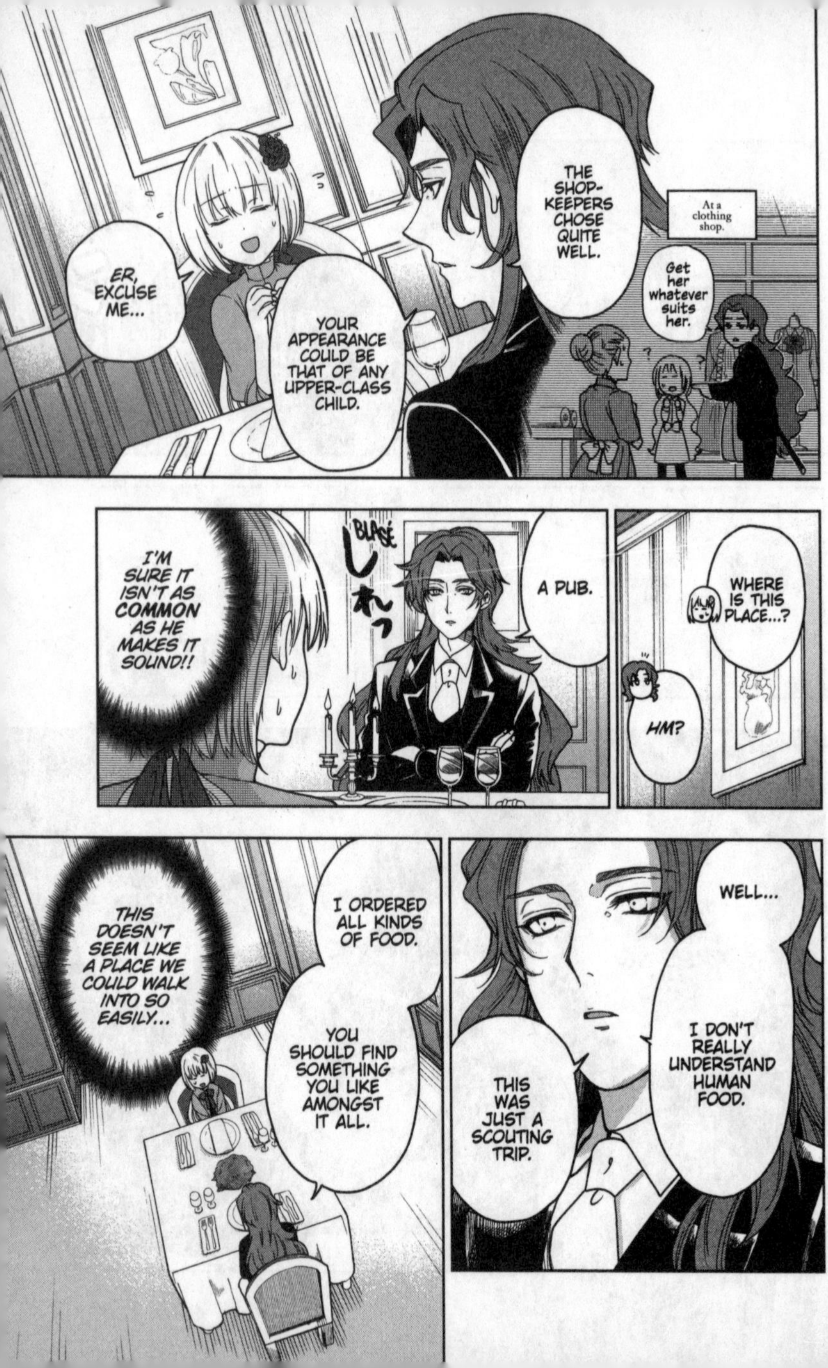
THE SHOP-KEEPERS CHOSE QUITE WELL.
At a clothing shop.
Get her whatever suits her.
YOUR APPEARANCE COULD BE THAT OF ANY UPPER-CLASS CHILD.
ER, EXCUSE ME...
WHERE IS THIS PLACE...?
HM?
A PUB.
BLASÉ
しれっ
I'M SURE IT ISN'T AS COMMON AS HE MAKES IT SOUND!!
WELL...
I DON'T REALLY UNDERSTAND HUMAN FOOD.
THIS WAS JUST A SCOUTING TRIP.
I ORDERED ALL KINDS OF FOOD.
YOU SHOULD FIND SOMETHING YOU LIKE AMONGST IT ALL.
THIS DOESN'T SEEM LIKE A PLACE WE COULD WALK INTO SO EASILY...

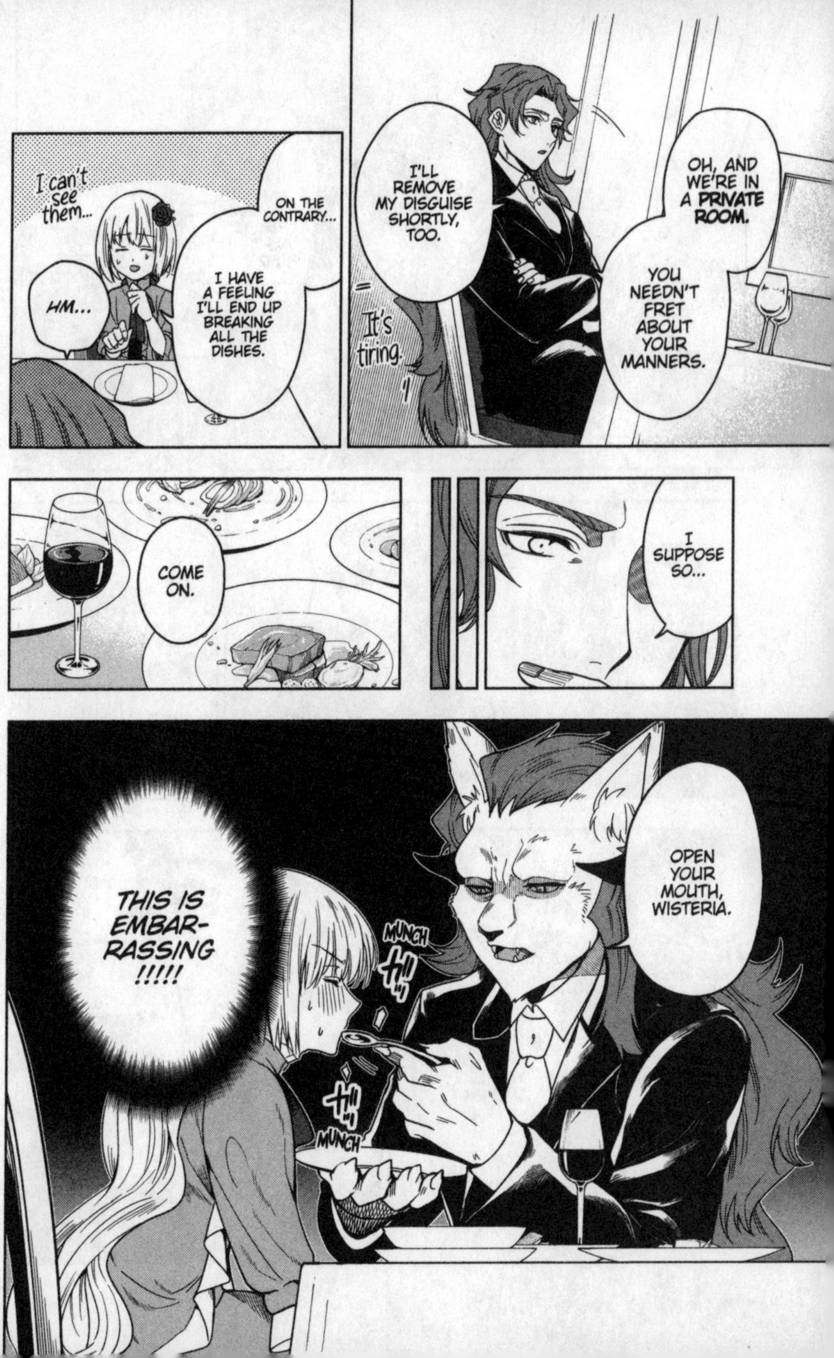
OH, AND WE'RE IN A **PRIVATE ROOM.**
YOU NEEDN'T FRET ABOUT YOUR MANNERS.
I'LL REMOVE MY DISGUISE SHORTLY, TOO.
It's tiring.
ON THE CONTRARY...
I HAVE A FEELING I'LL END UP BREAKING ALL THE DISHES.
I can't see them...
HM...
I SUPPOSE SO...
COME ON.
OPEN YOUR MOUTH, WISTERIA.
MUNCH
THIS IS EMBAR-RASSING!!!!!
MUNCH

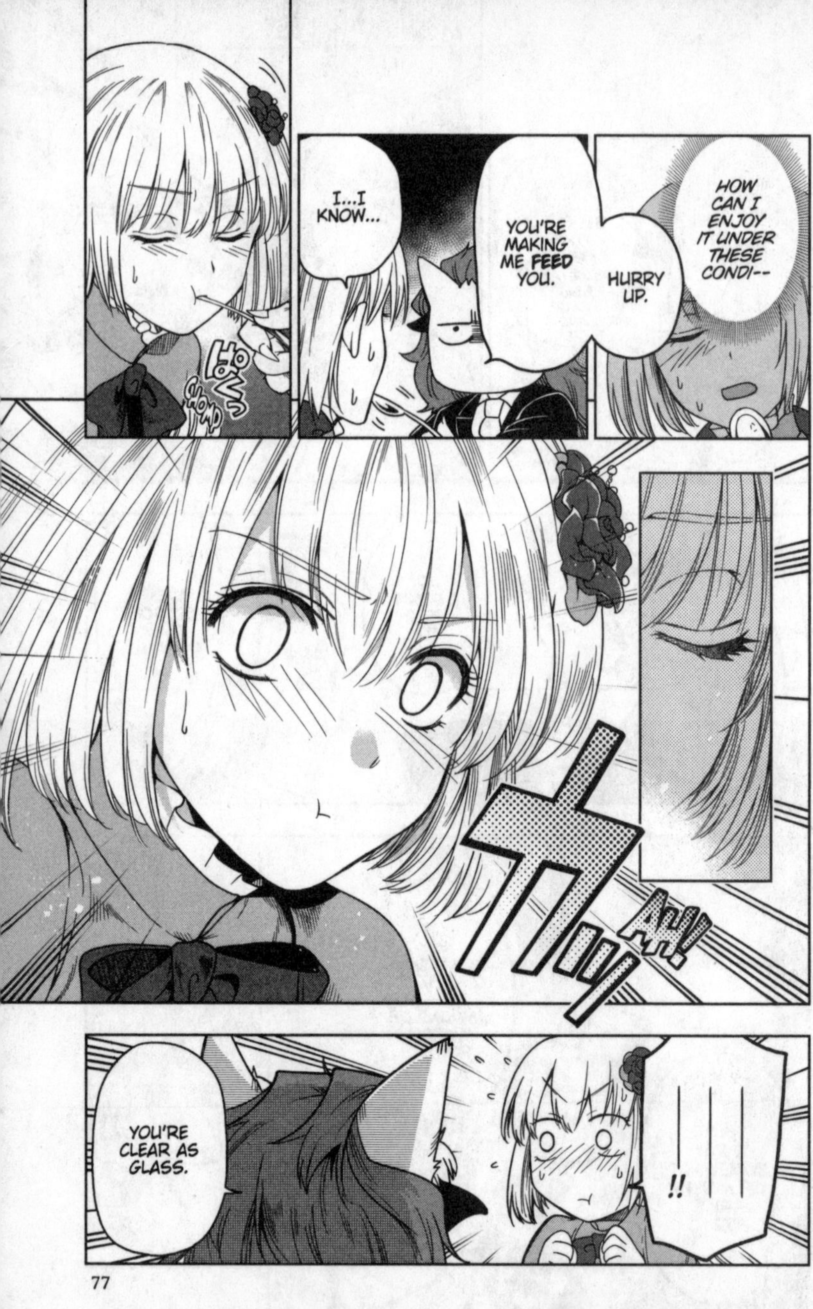
HOW CAN I ENJOY IT UNDER THESE CONDI--
YOU'RE MAKING ME FEED YOU.
HURRY UP.
I...I KNOW...
chomp
AH!
!!
YOU'RE CLEAR AS GLASS.

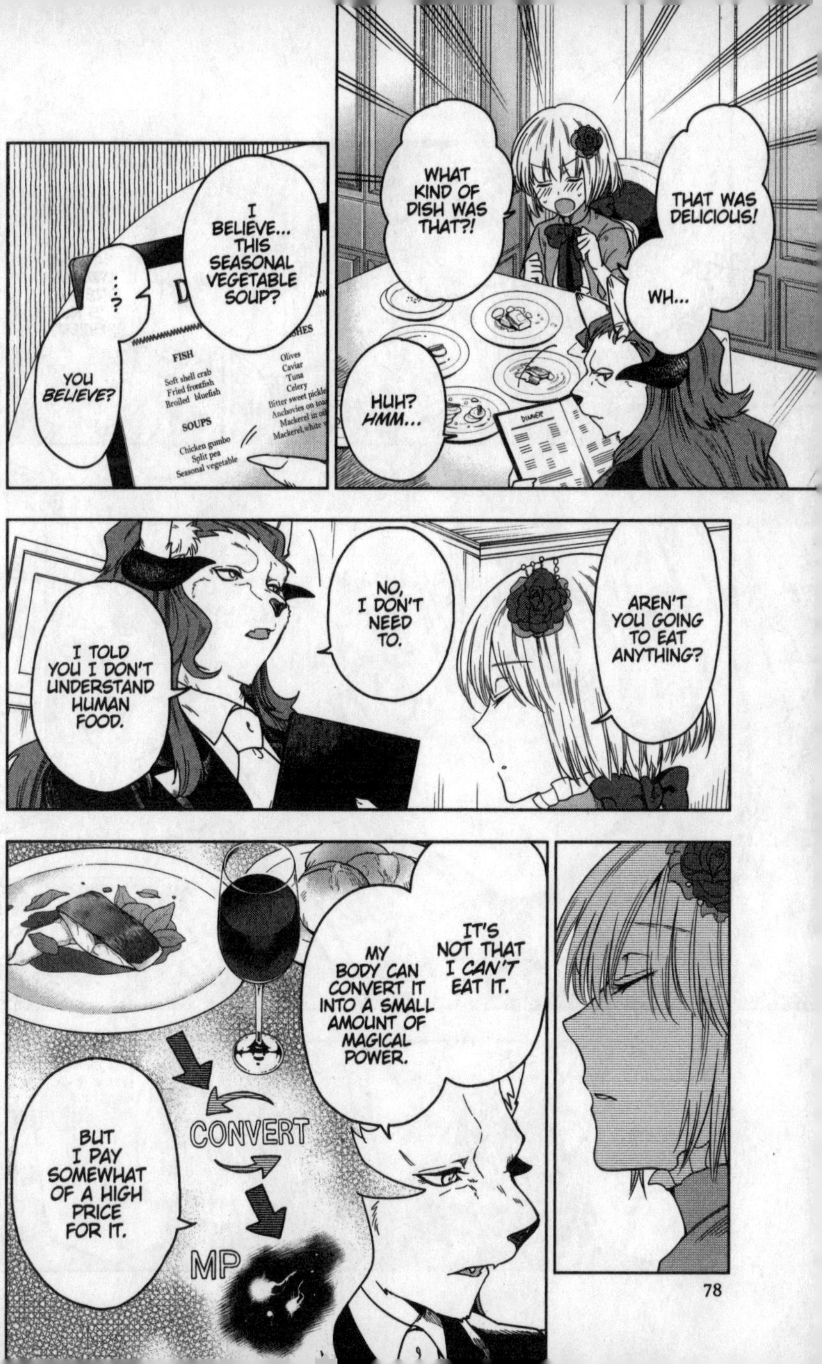
THAT WAS DELICIOUS!
WH...
WHAT KIND OF DISH WAS THAT?!
HUH? *HMM...*
I BELIEVE... THIS SEASONAL VEGETABLE SOUP?
...?
YOU *BELIEVE?*
FISH
Soft shell crab
Fried frostfish
Broiled bluefish
SOUPS
Chicken gumbo
Split pea
Seasonal vegetable
Olives
Caviar
Tuna
Celery
AREN'T YOU GOING TO EAT ANYTHING?
NO, I DON'T NEED TO.
I TOLD YOU I DON'T UNDERSTAND HUMAN FOOD.
IT'S NOT THAT I *CAN'T* EAT IT.
MY BODY CAN CONVERT IT INTO A SMALL AMOUNT OF MAGICAL POWER.
CONVERT
MP
BUT I PAY SOMEWHAT OF A HIGH PRICE FOR IT.

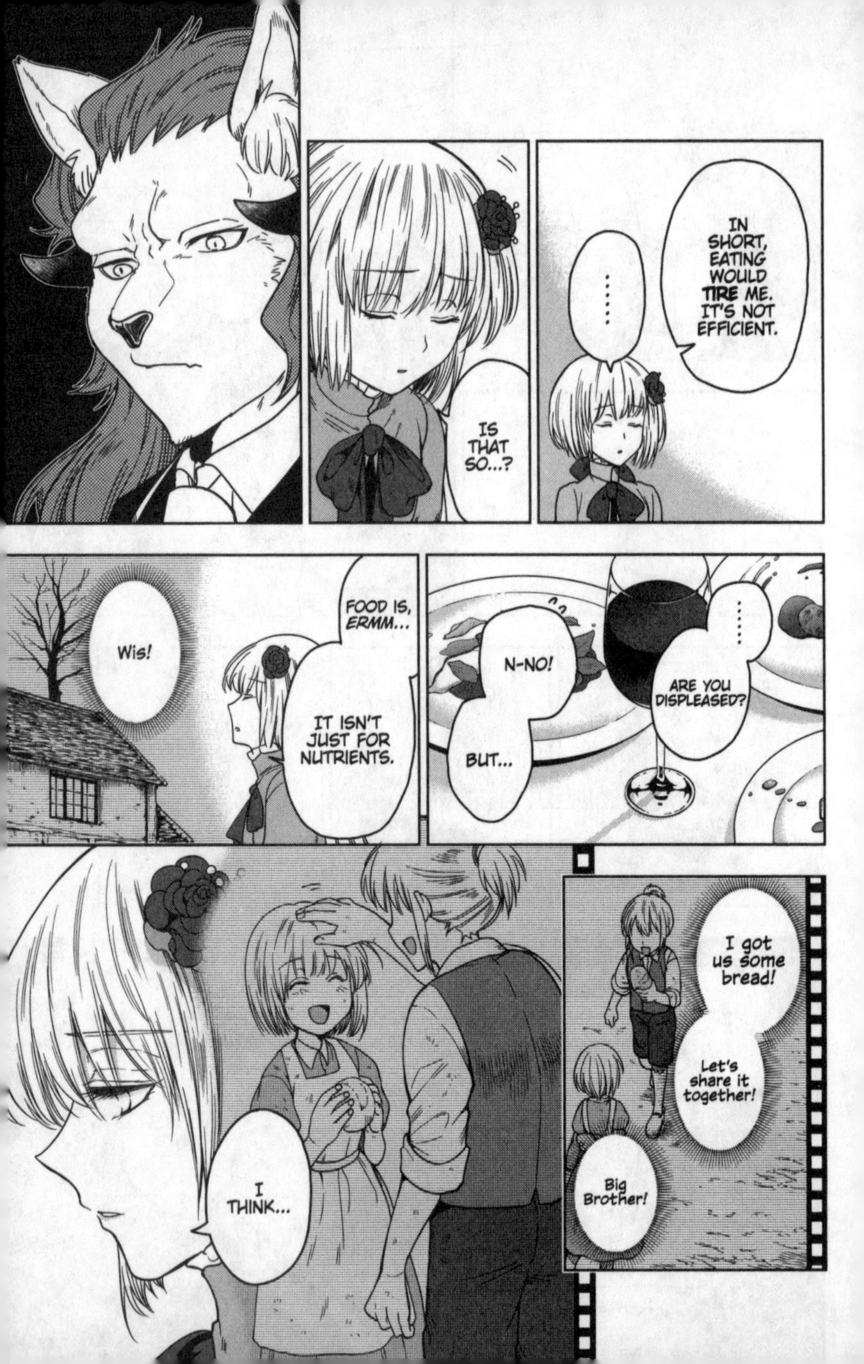
IN SHORT, EATING WOULD TIRE ME. IT'S NOT EFFICIENT.
......
IS THAT SO...?
......
ARE YOU DISPLEASED?
N-NO!
BUT...
FOOD IS, ERMM...
IT ISN'T JUST FOR NUTRIENTS.
Wis!
I got us some bread!
Let's share it together!
Big Brother!
I THINK...

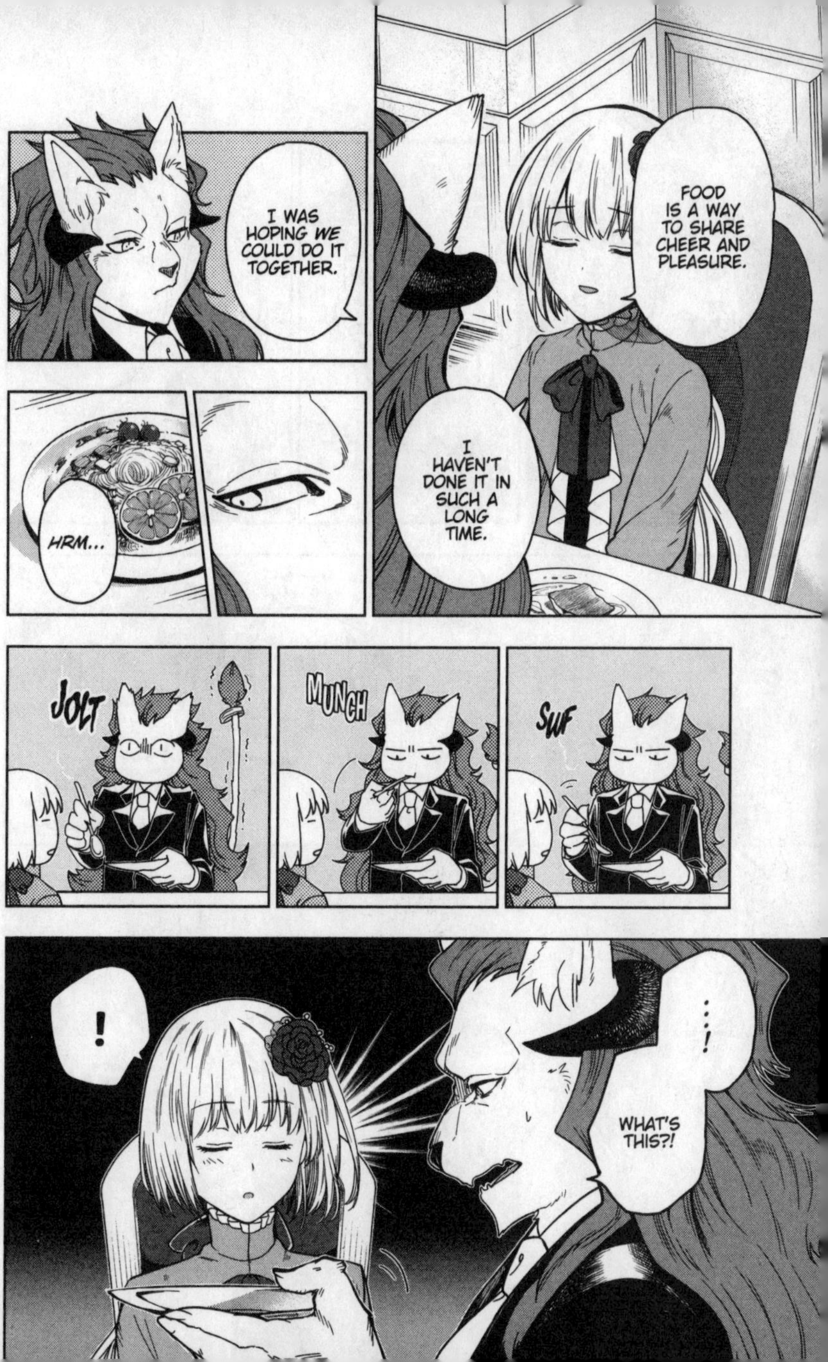
FOOD IS A WAY TO SHARE CHEER AND PLEASURE.
I HAVEN'T DONE IT IN SUCH A LONG TIME.
I WAS HOPING *WE* COULD DO IT TOGETHER.
HRM...
SUF
MUNCH
JOLT
...!
WHAT'S THIS?!
!

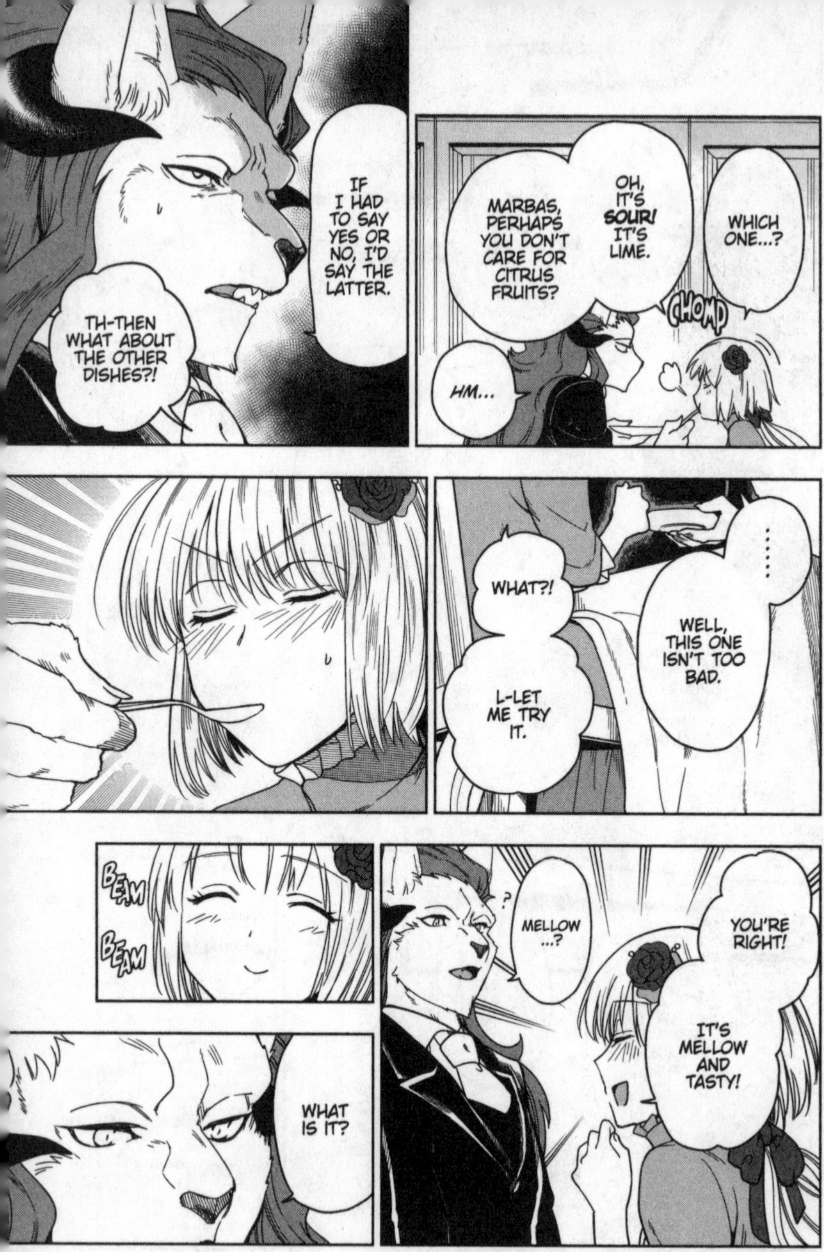
WHICH ONE...?
CHOMP
OH, IT'S SOUR! IT'S LIME.
MARBAS, PERHAPS YOU DON'T CARE FOR CITRUS FRUITS?
HM...
IF I HAD TO SAY YES OR NO, I'D SAY THE LATTER.
TH-THEN WHAT ABOUT THE OTHER DISHES?!
......
WELL, THIS ONE ISN'T TOO BAD.
WHAT?!
L-LET ME TRY IT.
YOU'RE RIGHT!
IT'S MELLOW AND TASTY!
MELLOW ...?
BEAM
BEAM
WHAT IS IT?

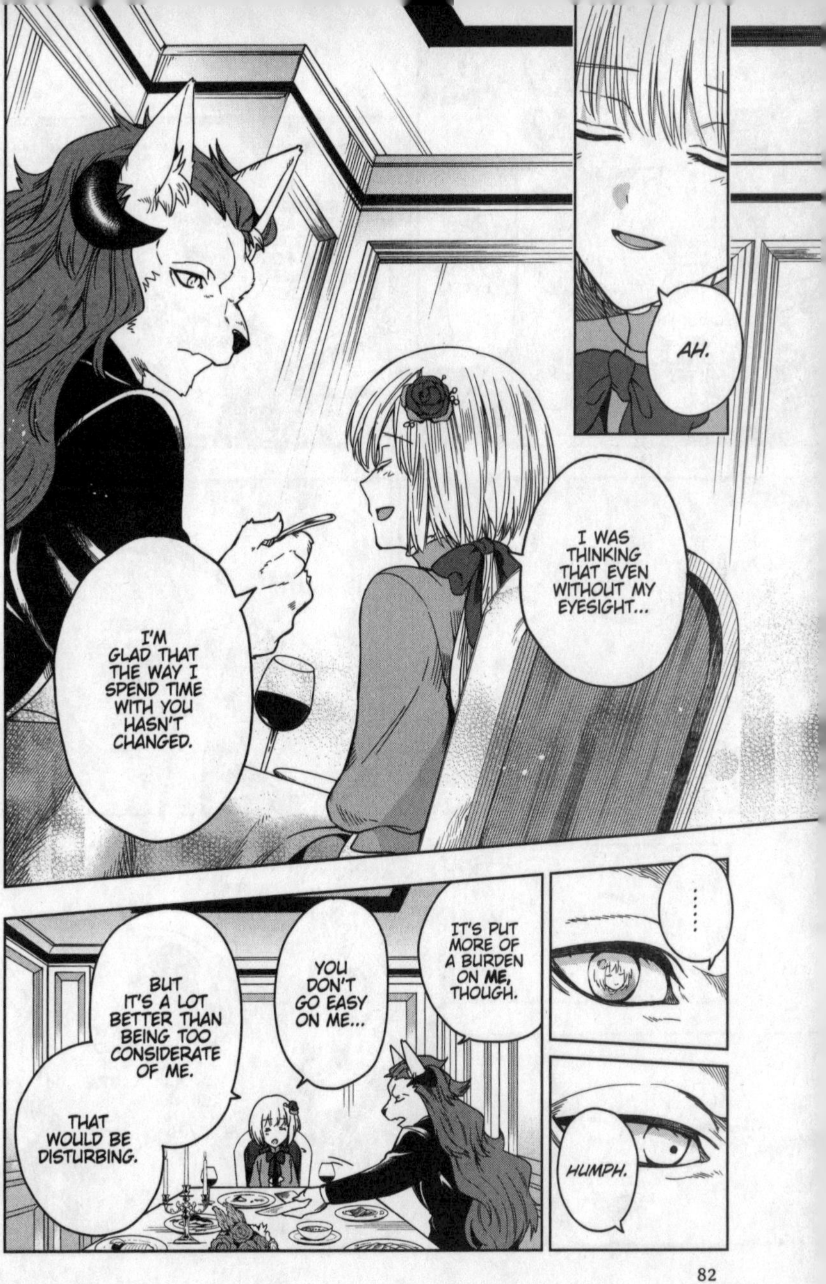
AH.
I WAS THINKING THAT EVEN WITHOUT MY EYESIGHT...
I'M GLAD THAT THE WAY I SPEND TIME WITH YOU HASN'T CHANGED.
......
HUMPH.
IT'S PUT MORE OF A BURDEN ON ME, THOUGH.
YOU DON'T GO EASY ON ME...
BUT IT'S A LOT BETTER THAN BEING TOO CONSIDERATE OF ME.
THAT WOULD BE DISTURBING.

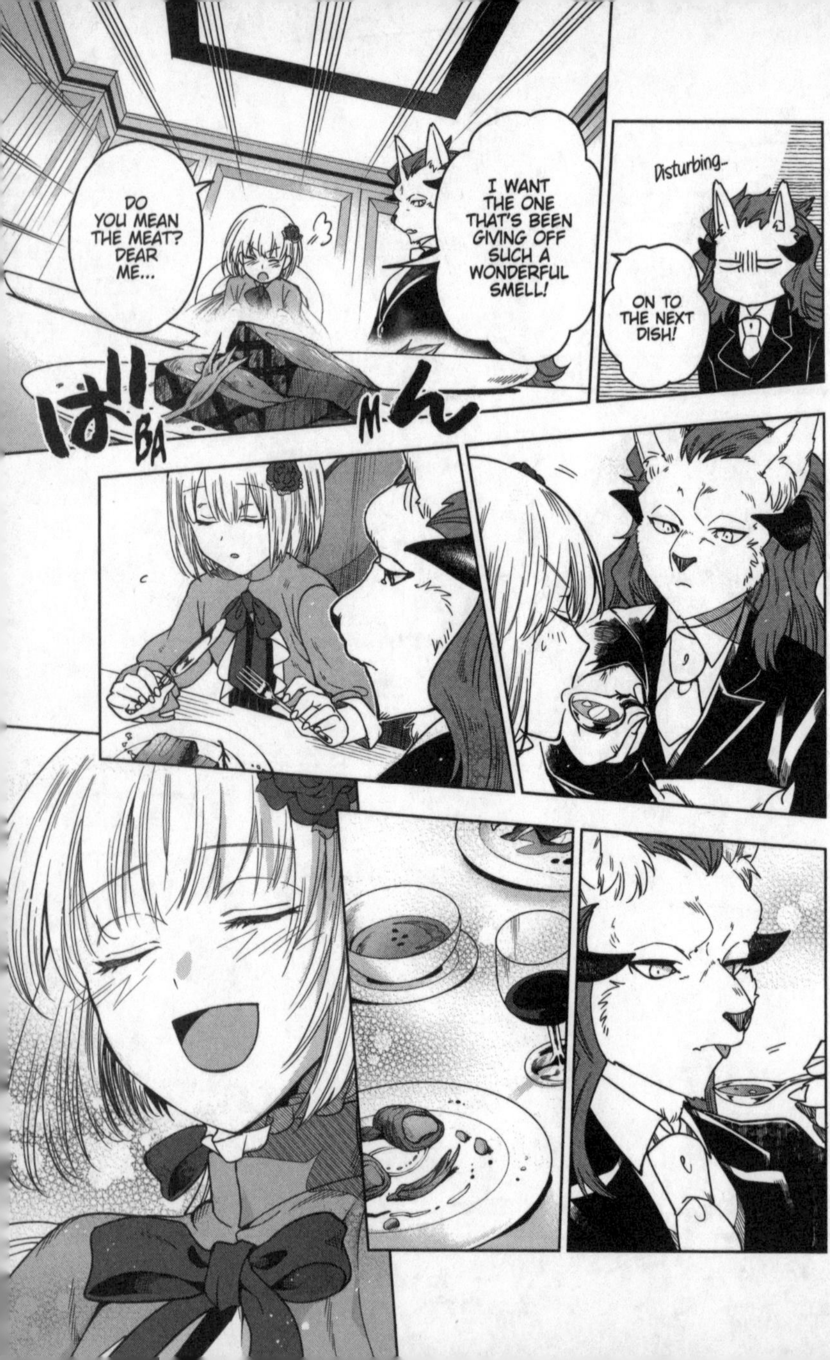
Disturbing...
ON TO THE NEXT DISH!
I WANT THE ONE THAT'S BEEN GIVING OFF SUCH A WONDERFUL SMELL!
DO YOU MEAN THE MEAT? DEAR ME...
ば!ん
BAM

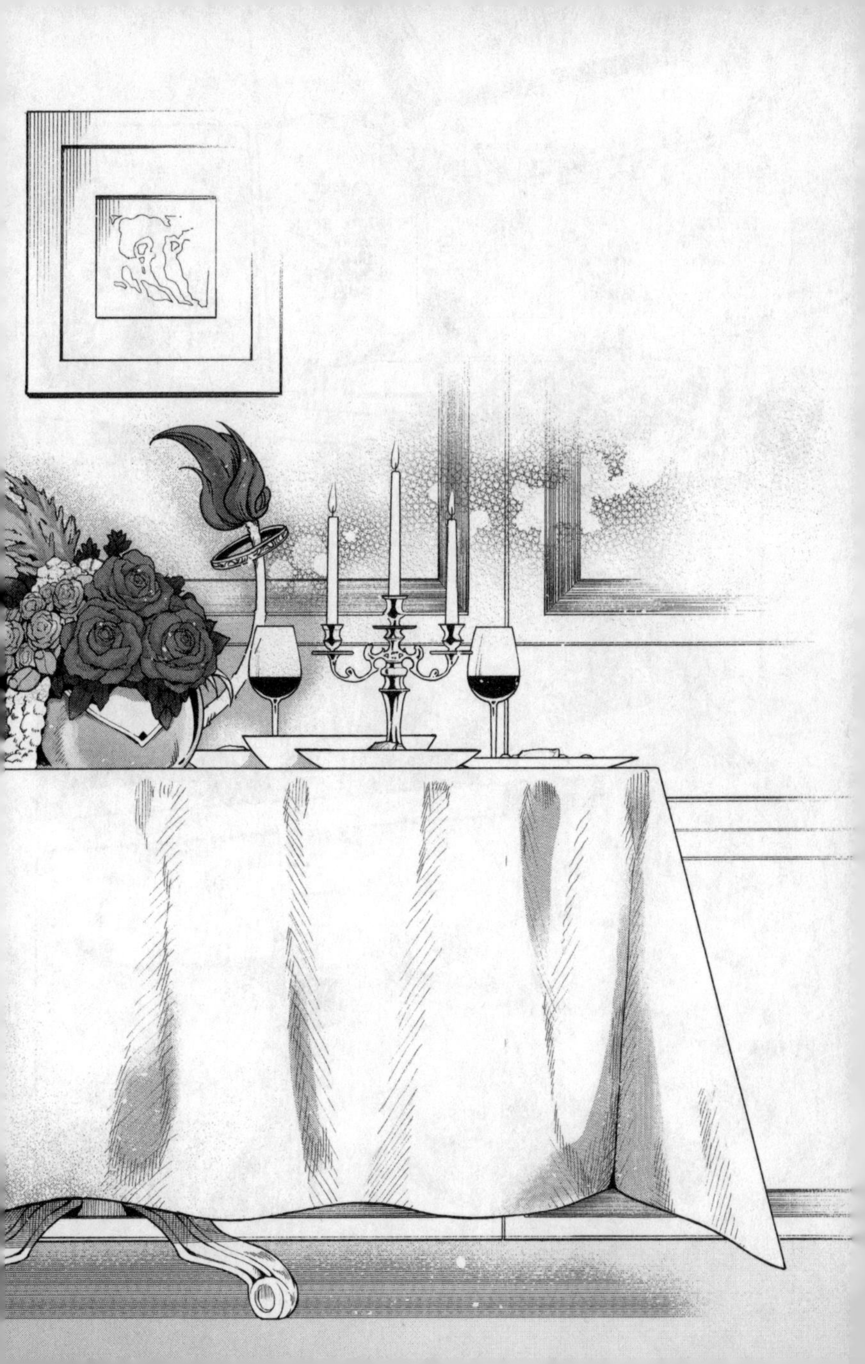

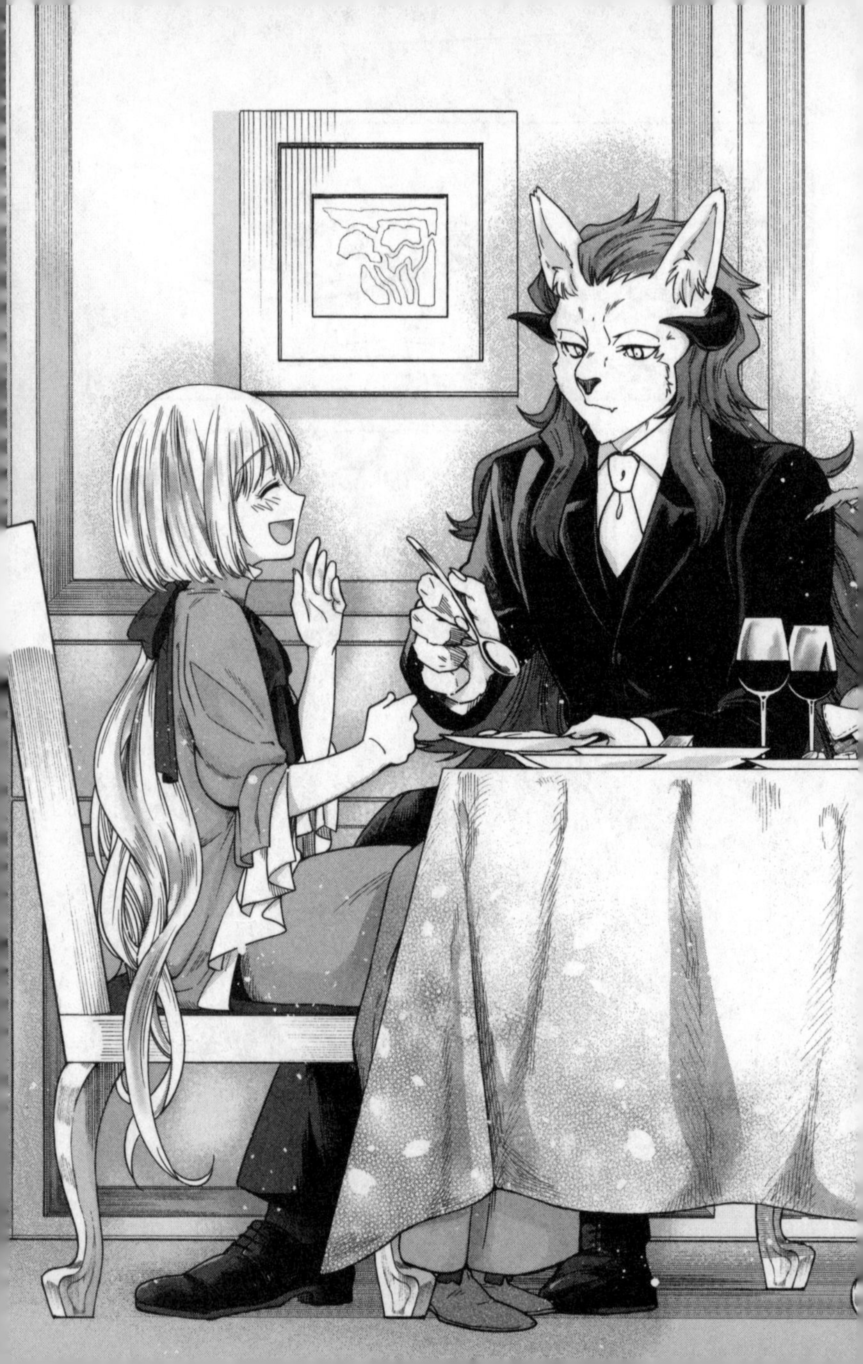

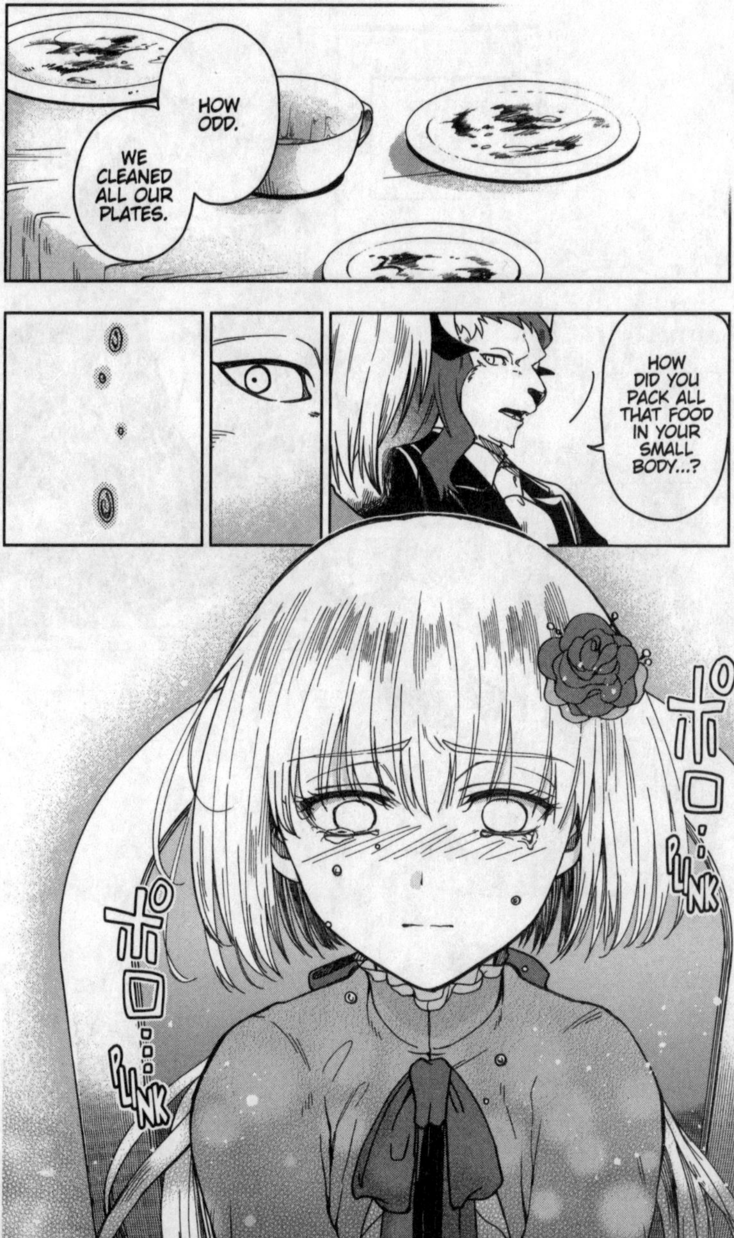
HOW ODD.
WE CLEANED ALL OUR PLATES.
HOW DID YOU PACK ALL THAT FOOD IN YOUR SMALL BODY...?
ポロ...
PLINK
ポロ...
PLINK

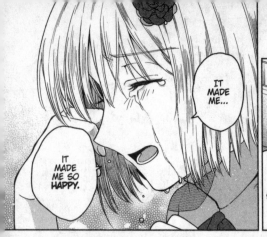

IT MADE ME...

IT MADE ME SO HAPPY.

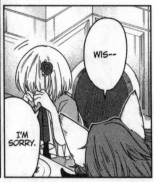

WIS--

I'M SORRY.

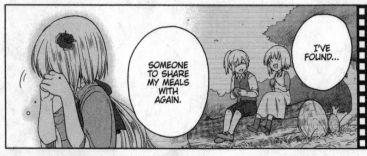

SOMEONE TO SHARE MY MEALS WITH AGAIN.

I'VE FOUND...

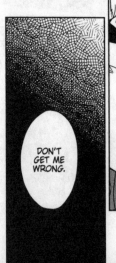

DON'T GET ME WRONG.

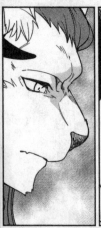

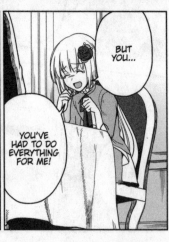

BUT YOU...

YOU'VE HAD TO DO EVERYTHING FOR ME!

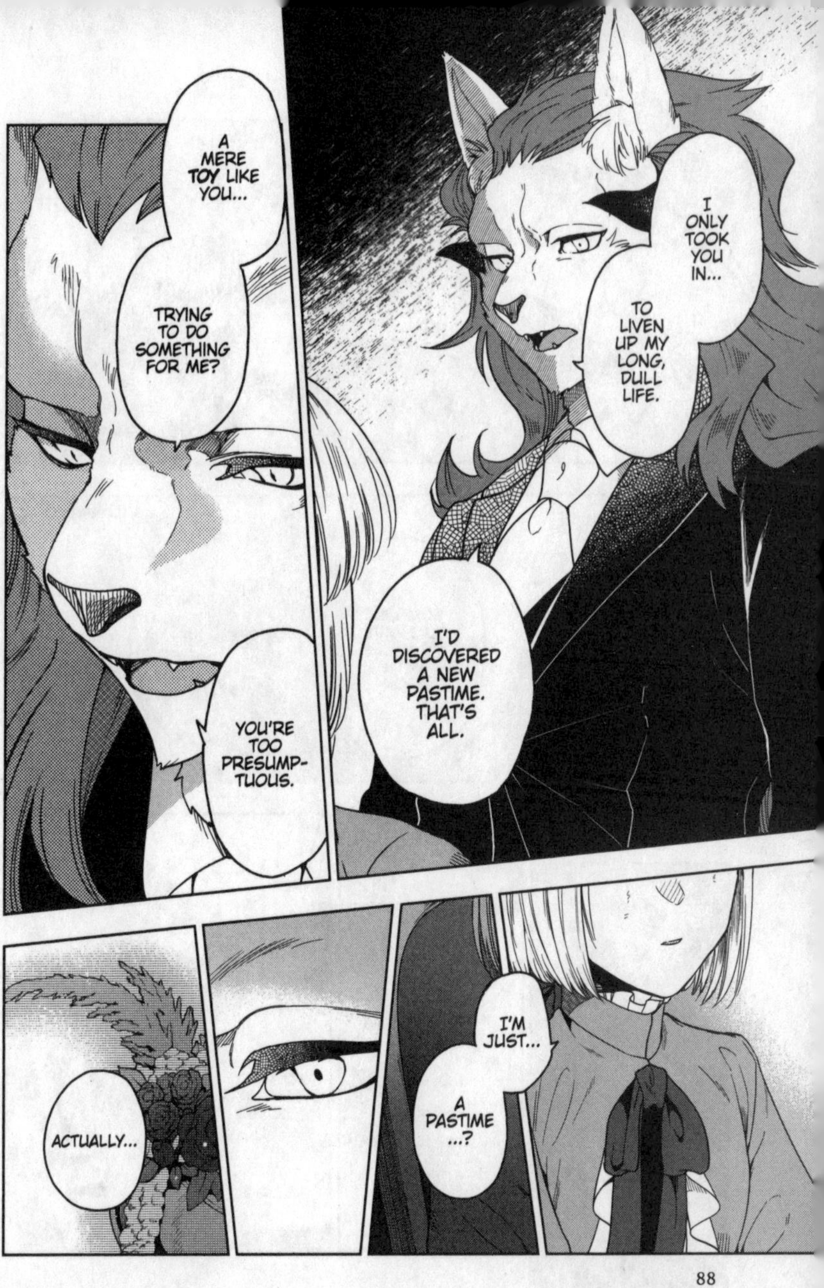
I ONLY TOOK YOU IN...
TO LIVEN UP MY LONG, DULL LIFE.
I'D DISCOVERED A NEW PASTIME. THAT'S ALL.
A MERE TOY LIKE YOU...
TRYING TO DO SOMETHING FOR ME?
YOU'RE TOO PRESUMP-TUOUS.
I'M JUST...
A PASTIME ...?
ACTUALLY...

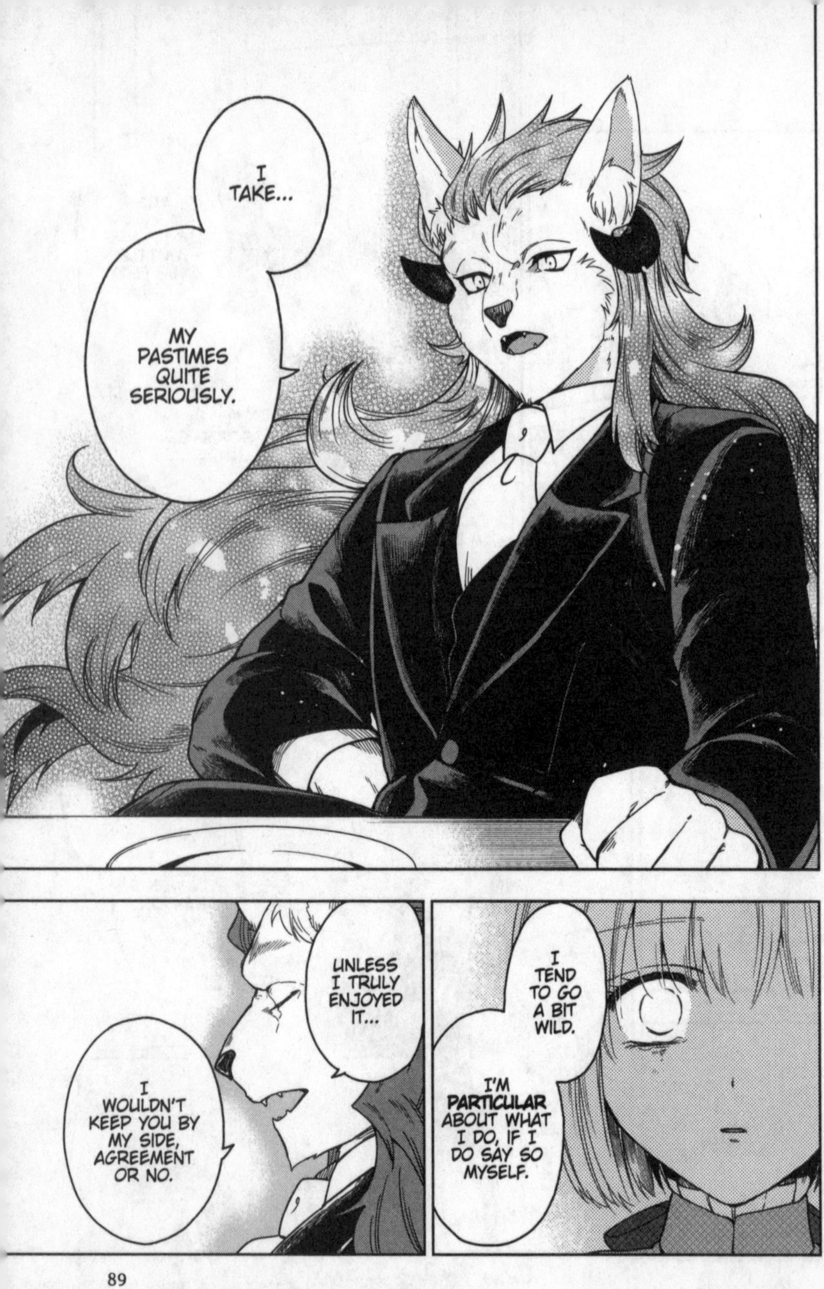
I TAKE...
MY PASTIMES QUITE SERIOUSLY.
I TEND TO GO A BIT WILD.
I'M **PARTICULAR** ABOUT WHAT I DO, IF I DO SAY SO MYSELF.
UNLESS I TRULY ENJOYED IT...
I WOULDN'T KEEP YOU BY MY SIDE, AGREEMENT OR NO.

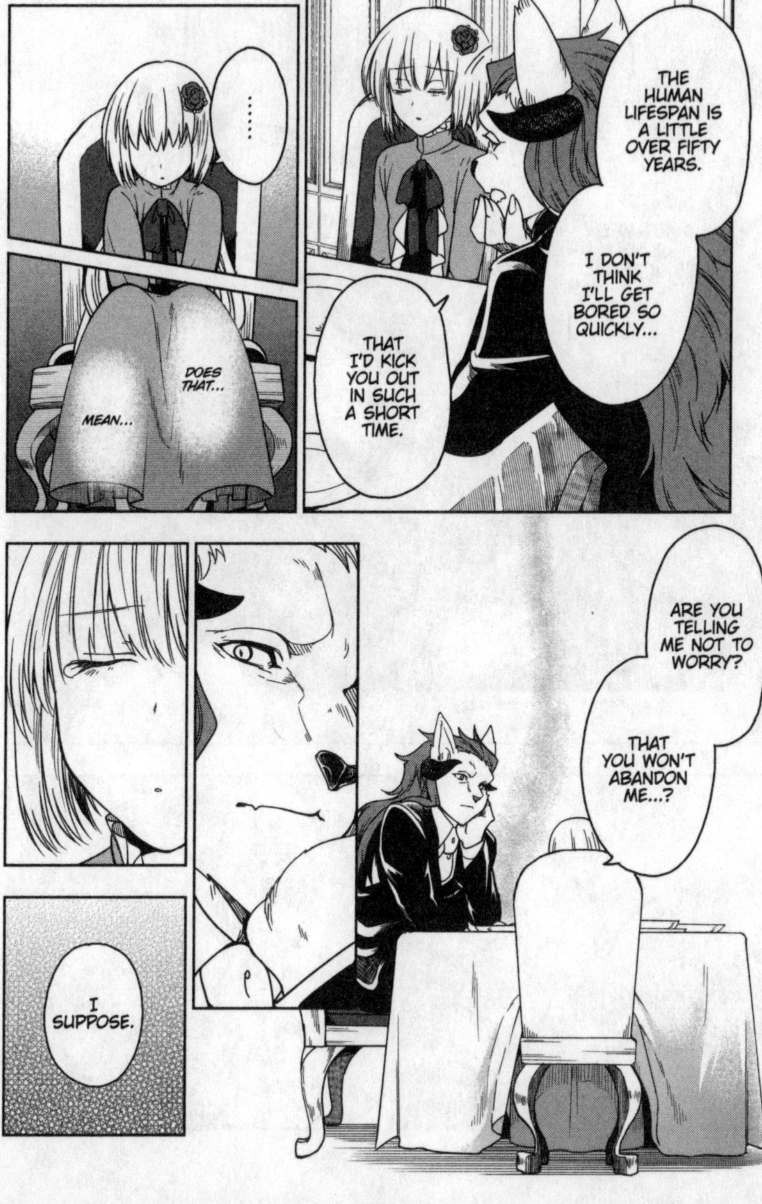
THE HUMAN LIFESPAN IS A LITTLE OVER FIFTY YEARS.
I DON'T THINK I'LL GET BORED SO QUICKLY...
THAT I'D KICK YOU OUT IN SUCH A SHORT TIME.
......
DOES THAT...
MEAN...
ARE YOU TELLING ME NOT TO WORRY?
THAT YOU WON'T ABANDON ME...?
I SUPPOSE.

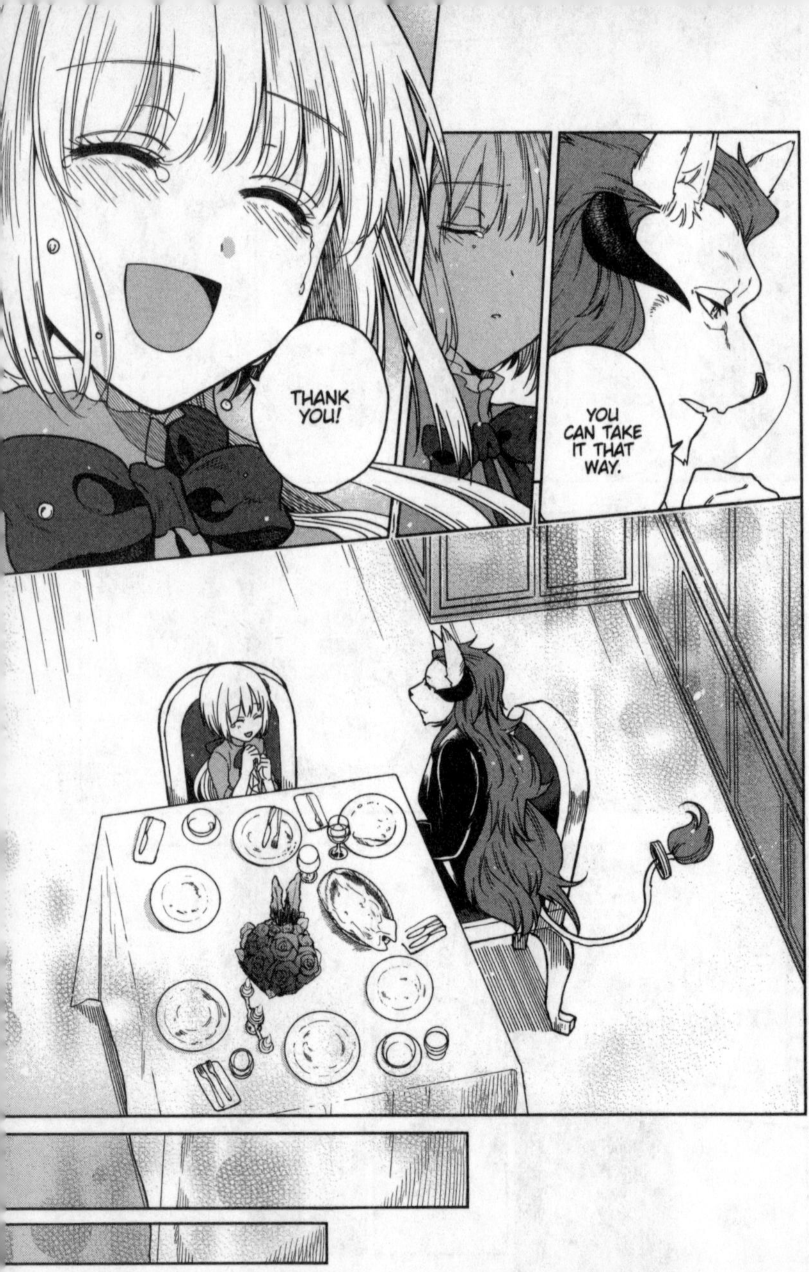
YOU CAN TAKE IT THAT WAY.
THANK YOU!

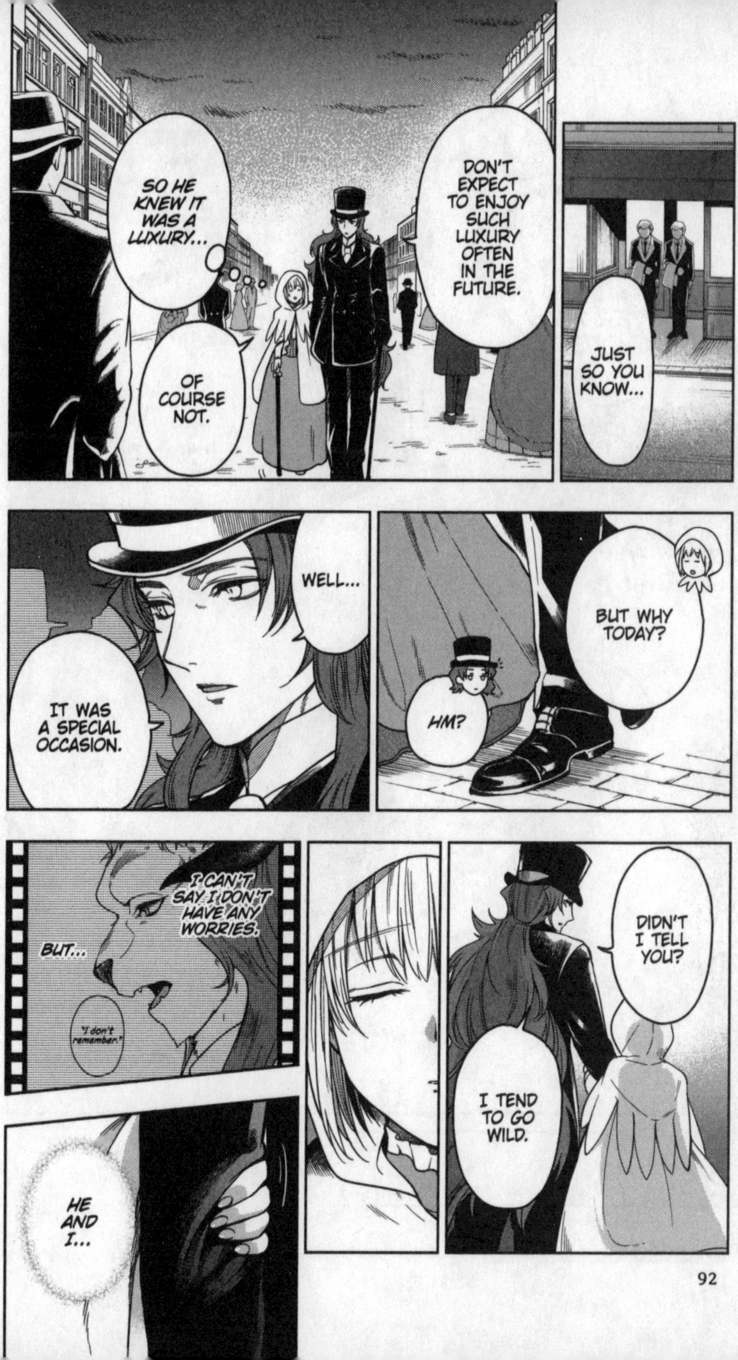
JUST SO YOU KNOW...
DON'T EXPECT TO ENJOY SUCH LUXURY OFTEN IN THE FUTURE.
SO HE KNEW IT WAS A LUXURY...
OF COURSE NOT.
BUT WHY TODAY?
HM?
WELL...
IT WAS A SPECIAL OCCASION.
DIDN'T I TELL YOU?
I TEND TO GO WILD.
I CAN'T SAY I DON'T HAVE ANY WORRIES.
BUT...
"I don't remember."
HE AND I...

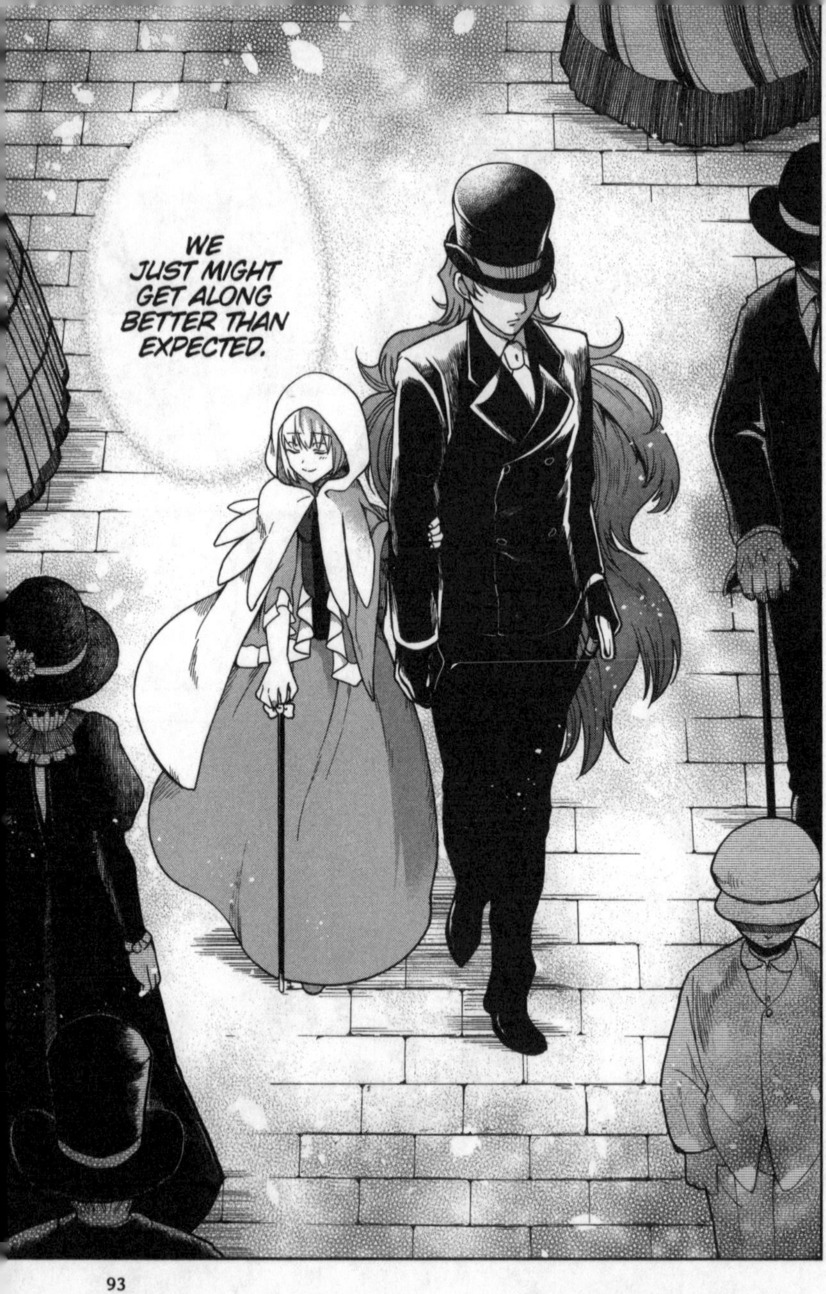
WE JUST MIGHT GET ALONG BETTER THAN EXPECTED.

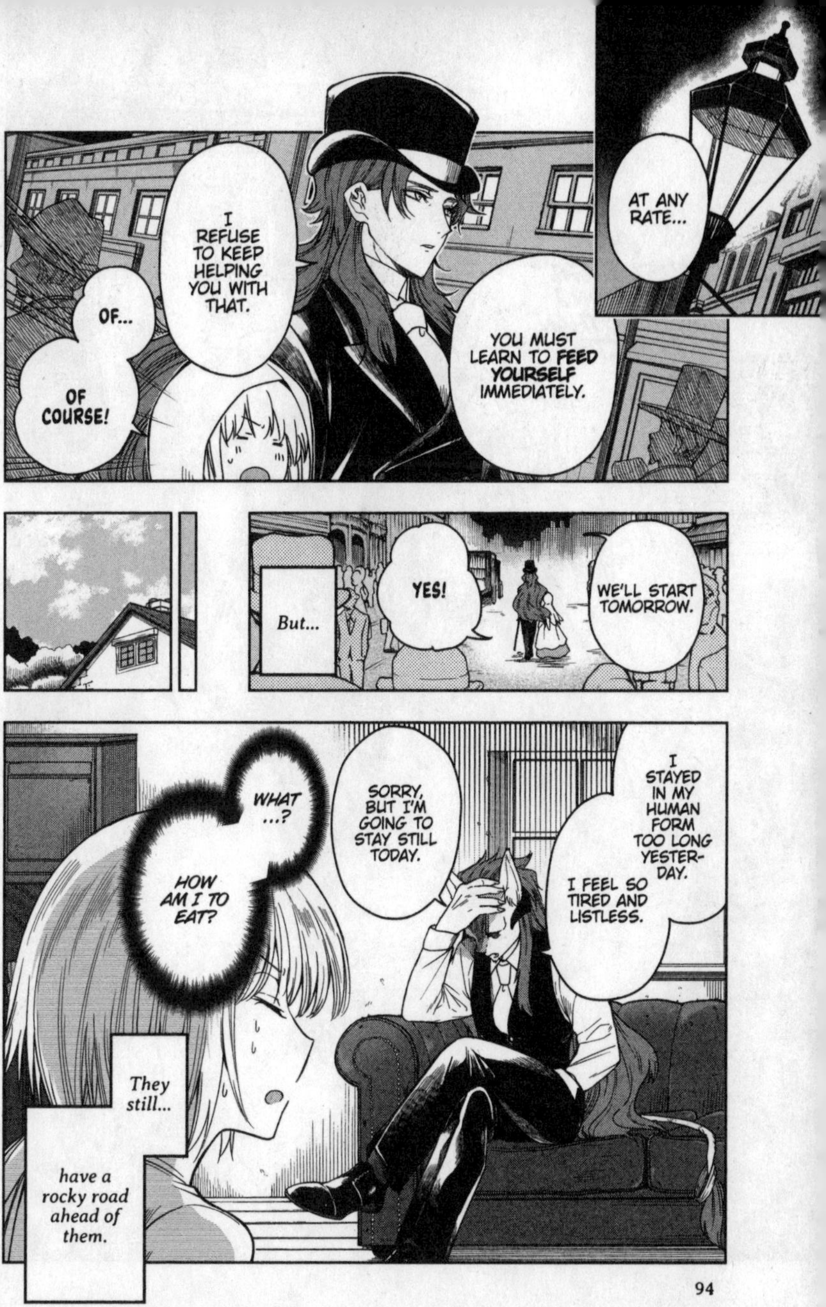
AT ANY RATE...
YOU MUST LEARN TO FEED YOURSELF IMMEDIATELY.
I REFUSE TO KEEP HELPING YOU WITH THAT.
OF...
OF COURSE!
WE'LL START TOMORROW.
YES!
But...
I STAYED IN MY HUMAN FORM TOO LONG YESTERDAY.
I FEEL SO TIRED AND LISTLESS.
SORRY, BUT I'M GOING TO STAY STILL TODAY.
WHAT ...?
HOW AM I TO EAT?
They still...
have a rocky road ahead of them.

Night 3 Late Night Visitor

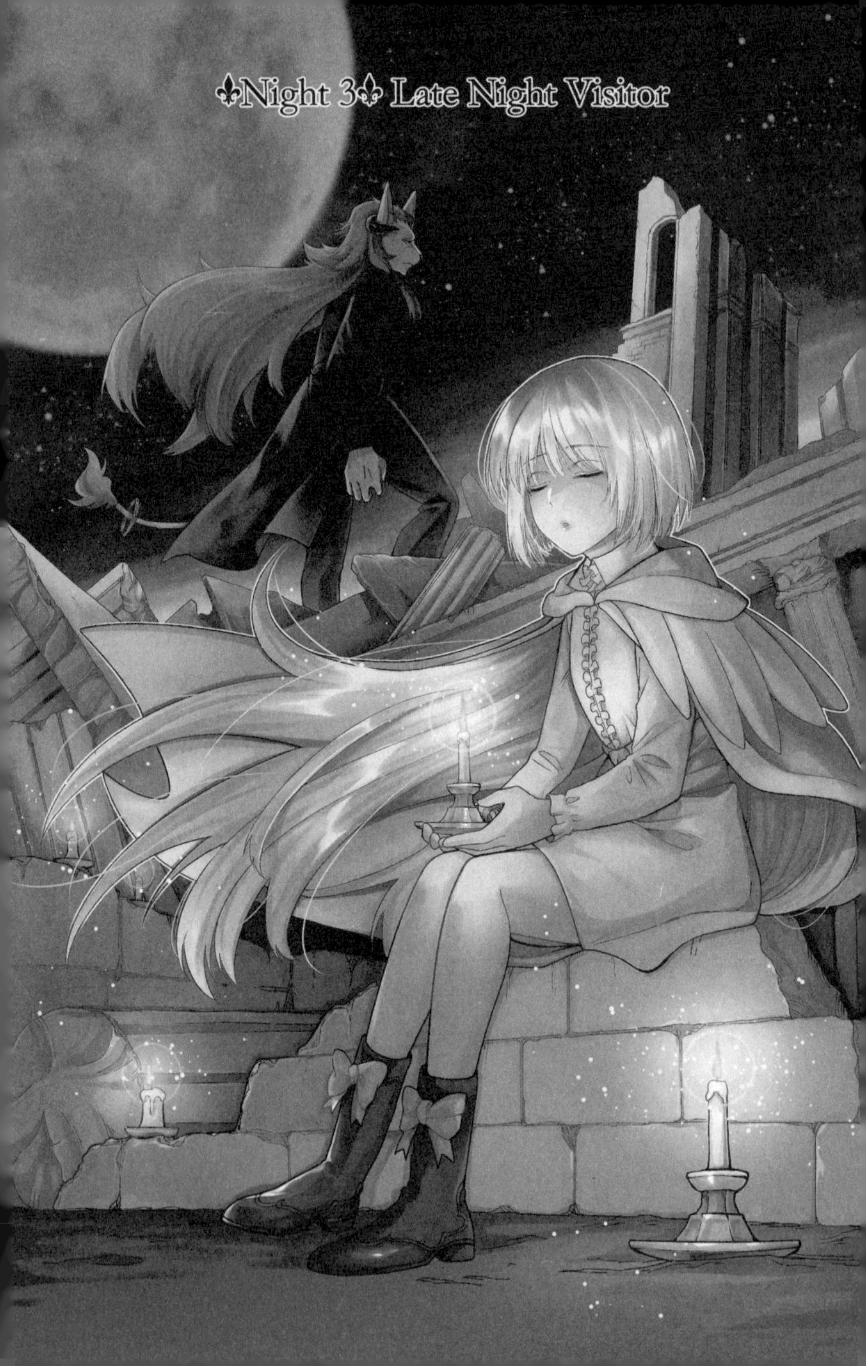

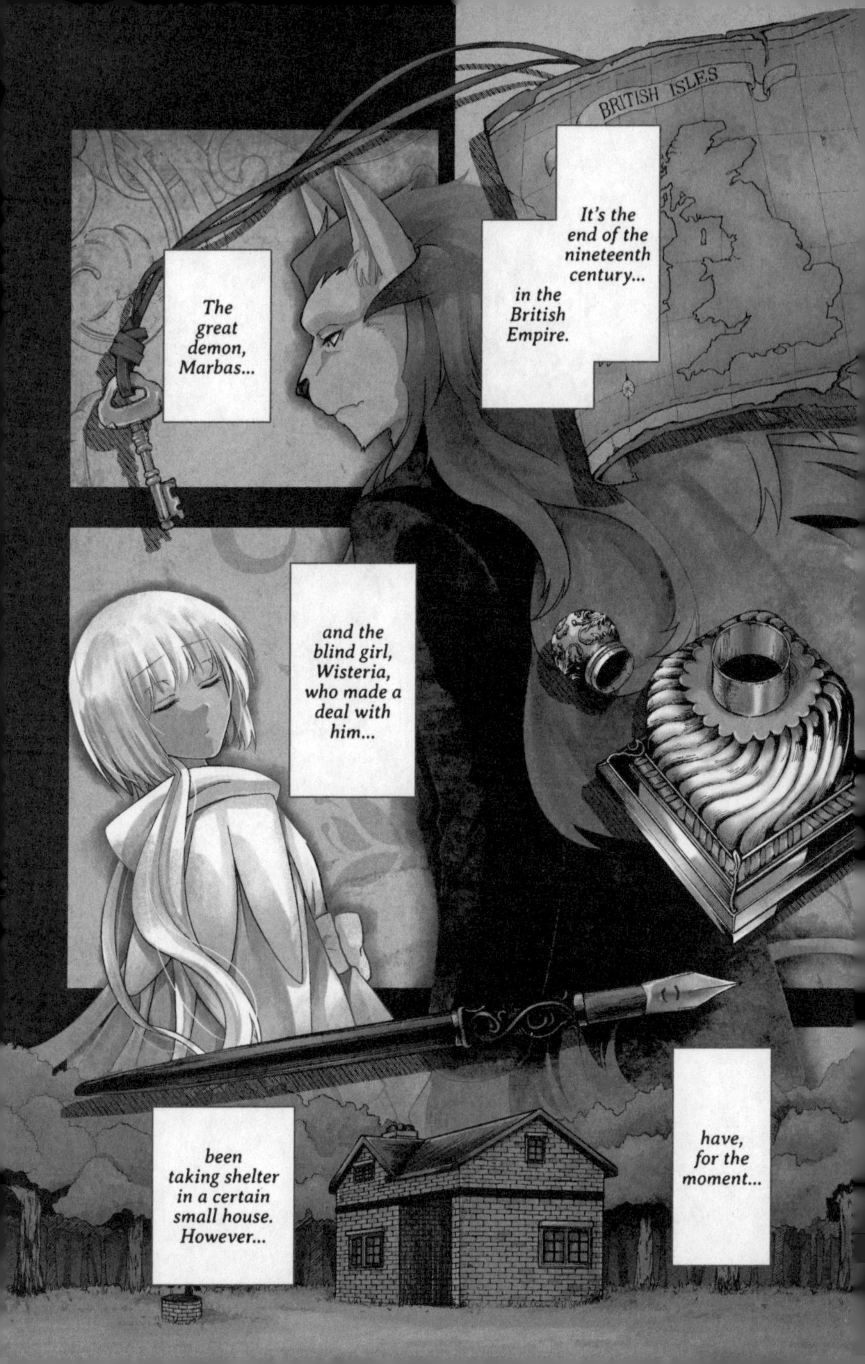
BRITISH ISLES
It's the end of the nineteenth century...
in the British Empire.
The great demon, Marbas...
and the blind girl, Wisteria, who made a deal with him...
have, for the moment...
been taking shelter in a certain small house. However...

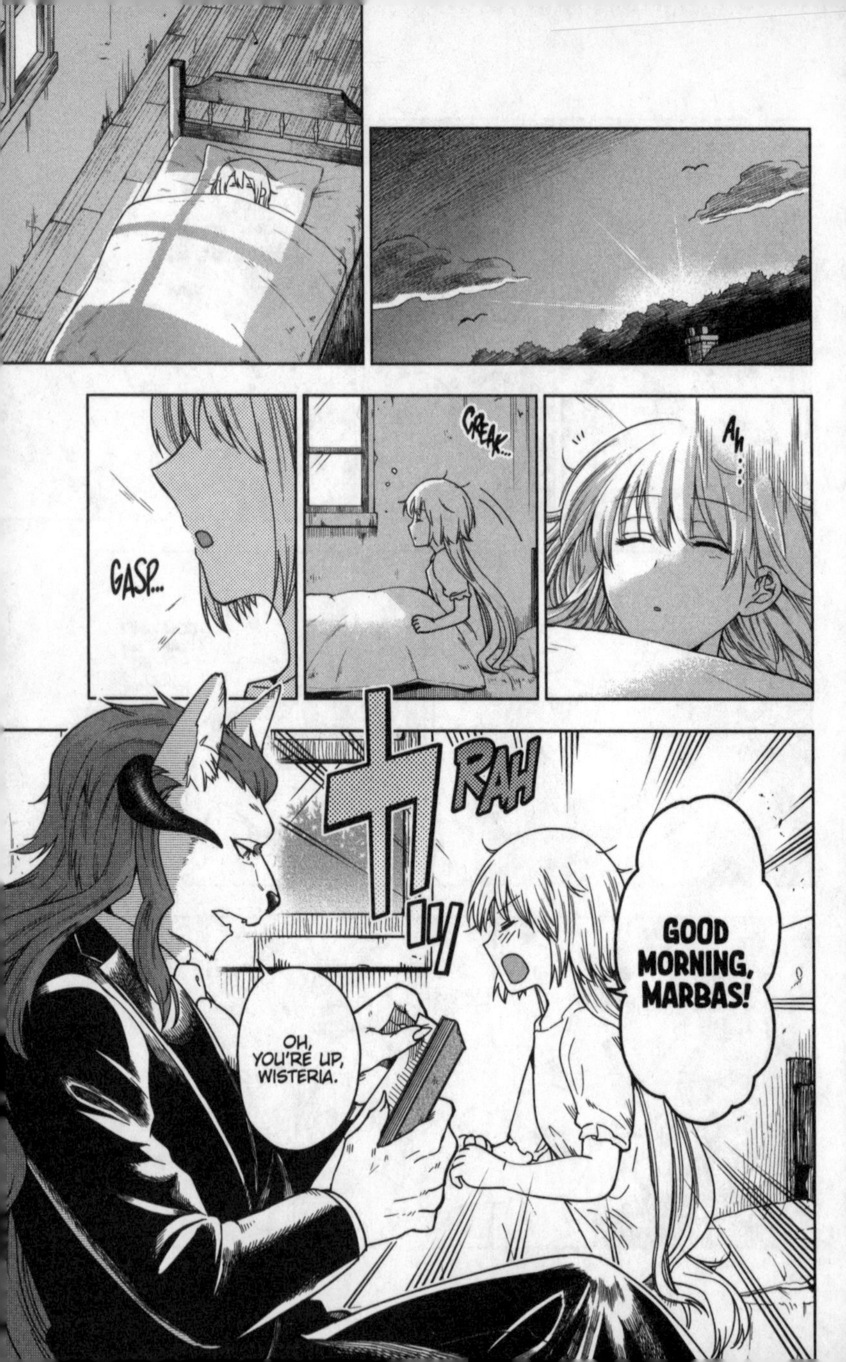
AH...
CREAK...
GASP...
RAH
GOOD MORNING, MARBAS!
OH, YOU'RE UP, WISTERIA.

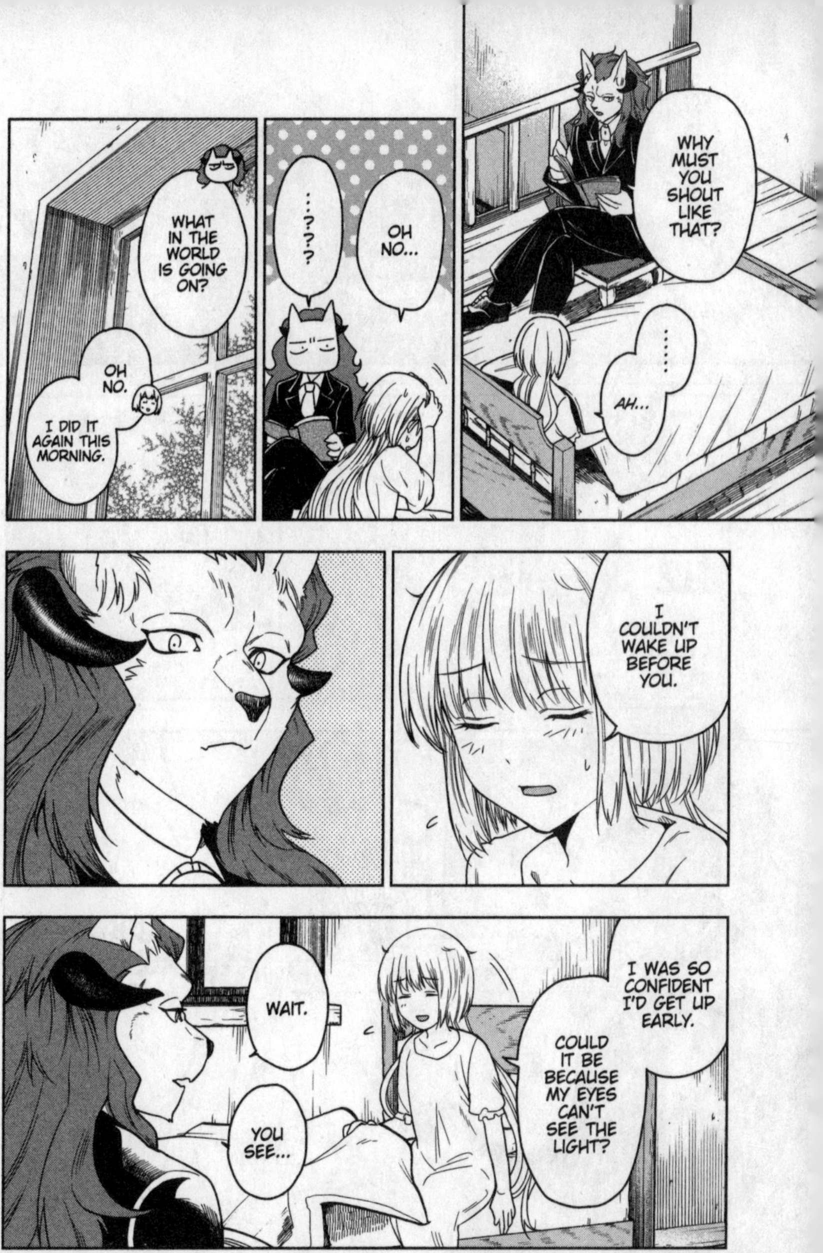

WHY MUST YOU SHOUT LIKE THAT?
......
AH...
OH NO...
...???
WHAT IN THE WORLD IS GOING ON?
OH NO.
I DID IT AGAIN THIS MORNING.
I COULDN'T WAKE UP BEFORE YOU.
I WAS SO CONFIDENT I'D GET UP EARLY.
COULD IT BE BECAUSE MY EYES CAN'T SEE THE LIGHT?
WAIT.
YOU SEE...

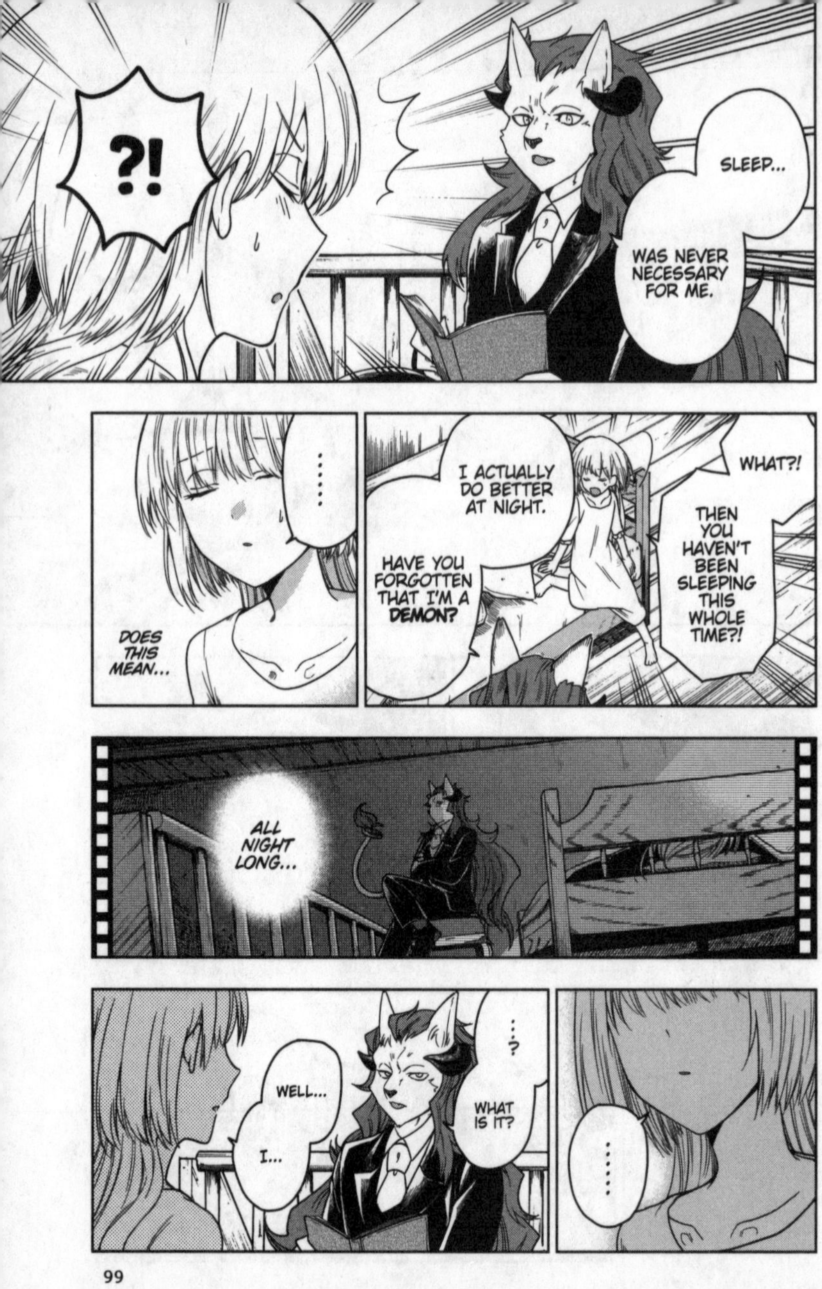
SLEEP...
WAS NEVER NECESSARY FOR ME.
?!
WHAT?!
THEN YOU HAVEN'T BEEN SLEEPING THIS WHOLE TIME?!
I ACTUALLY DO BETTER AT NIGHT.
HAVE YOU FORGOTTEN THAT I'M A DEMON?
......
DOES THIS MEAN...
ALL NIGHT LONG...
......
...?
WHAT IS IT?
WELL...
I...

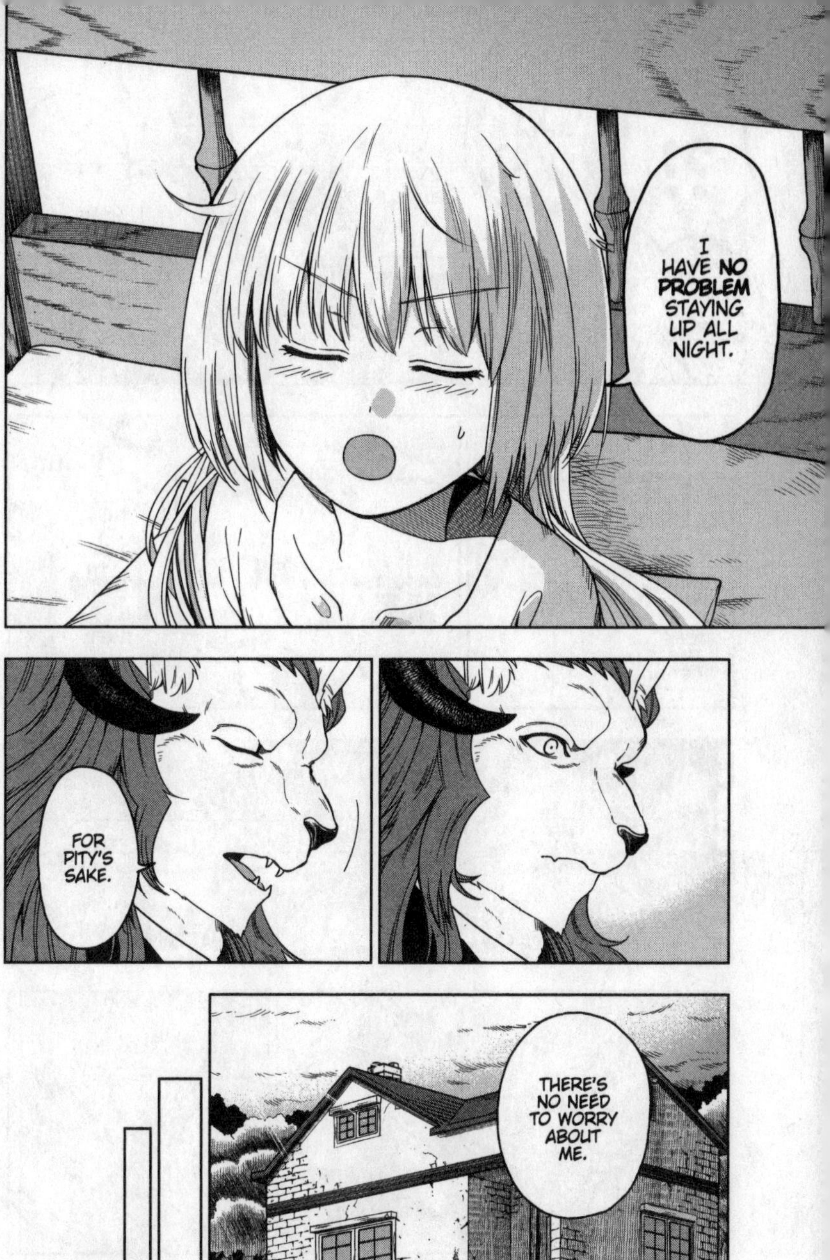
I HAVE NO PROBLEM STAYING UP ALL NIGHT.
FOR PITY'S SAKE.
THERE'S NO NEED TO WORRY ABOUT ME.

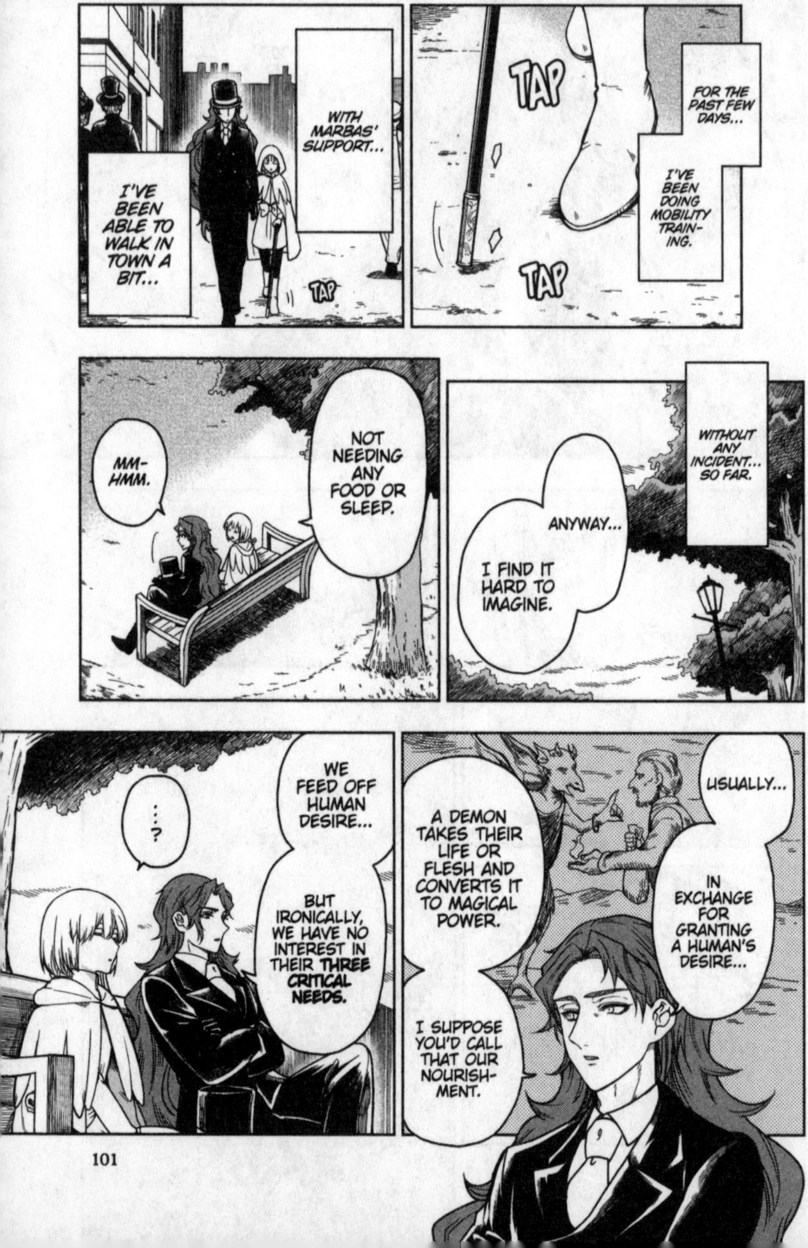
TAP
FOR THE PAST FEW DAYS...
I'VE BEEN DOING MOBILITY TRAIN-ING.
TAP
WITH MARBAS' SUPPORT...
I'VE BEEN ABLE TO WALK IN TOWN A BIT...
TAP
WITHOUT ANY INCIDENT... SO FAR.
ANYWAY...
I FIND IT HARD TO IMAGINE.
NOT NEEDING ANY FOOD OR SLEEP.
MM-HMM.
USUALLY...
IN EXCHANGE FOR GRANTING A HUMAN'S DESIRE...
A DEMON TAKES THEIR LIFE OR FLESH AND CONVERTS IT TO MAGICAL POWER.
I SUPPOSE YOU'D CALL THAT OUR NOURISH-MENT.
WE FEED OFF HUMAN DESIRE...
BUT IRONICALLY, WE HAVE NO INTEREST IN THEIR **THREE CRITICAL NEEDS.**
...?

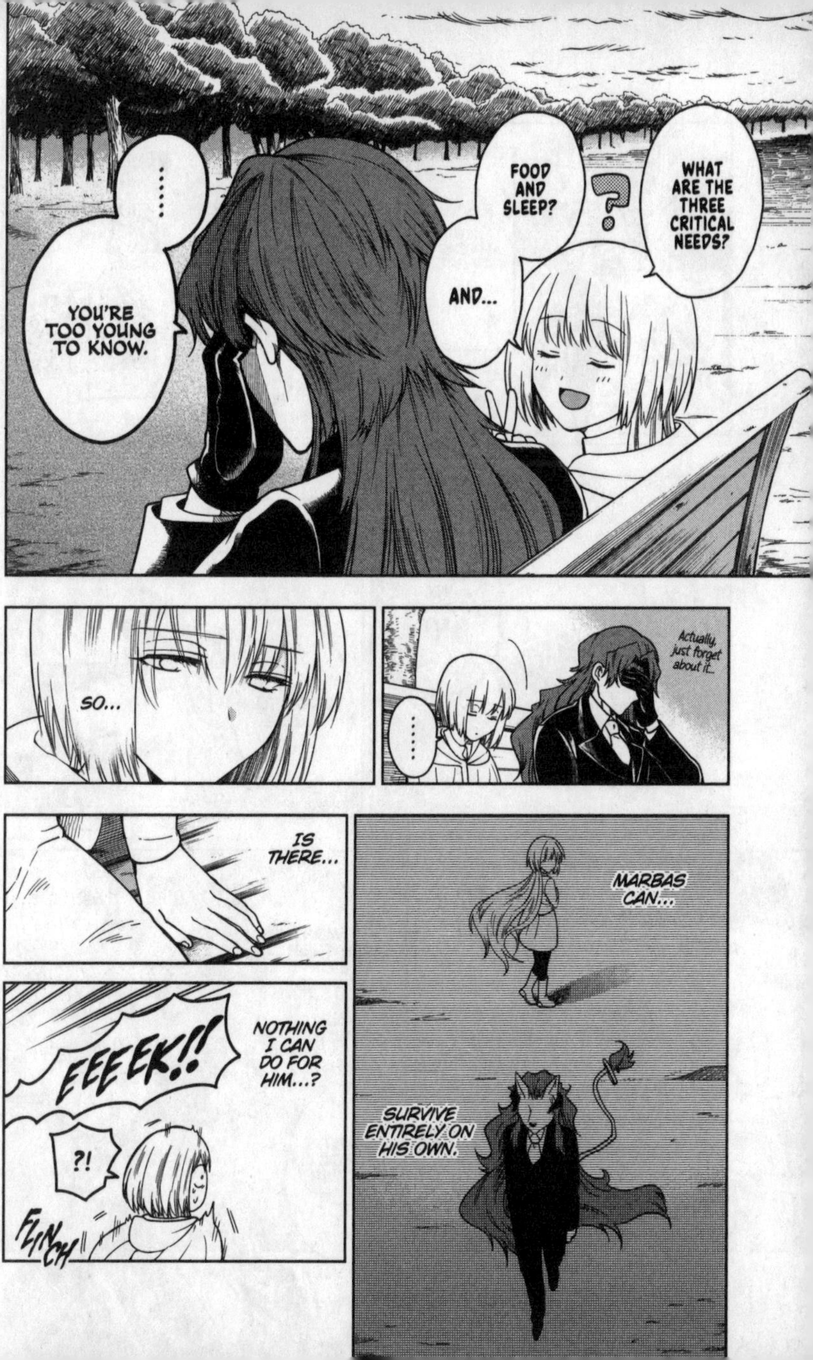
WHAT ARE THE THREE CRITICAL NEEDS?
?
FOOD AND SLEEP?
AND...
......
YOU'RE TOO YOUNG TO KNOW.
Actually, just forget about it...
......
SO...
MARBAS CAN...
SURVIVE ENTIRELY ON HIS OWN.
IS THERE...
NOTHING I CAN DO FOR HIM...?
EEEEK!!
?!
FLINCH

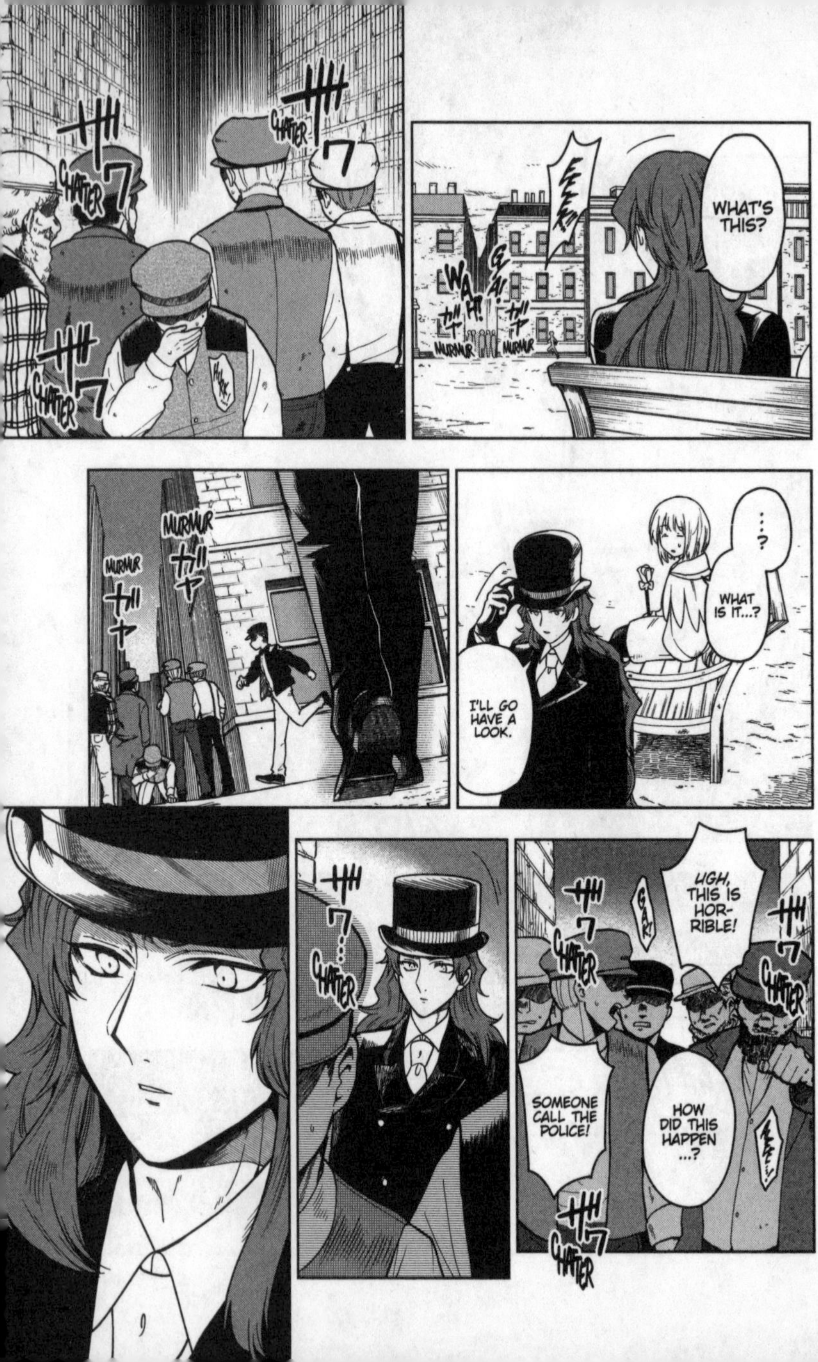
WHAT'S THIS?
EEEK!
GYAA!
WAAH!
MURMUR
MURMUR
CHATTER
CHATTER
CHATTER
HURK...!
...?
WHAT IS IT...?
I'LL GO HAVE A LOOK.
MURMUR
MURMUR
UGH, THIS IS HOR-RIBLE!
GAK!
CHATTER
CHATTER
HOW DID THIS HAPPEN...?
SOMEONE CALL THE POLICE!
CHATTER
CHATTER

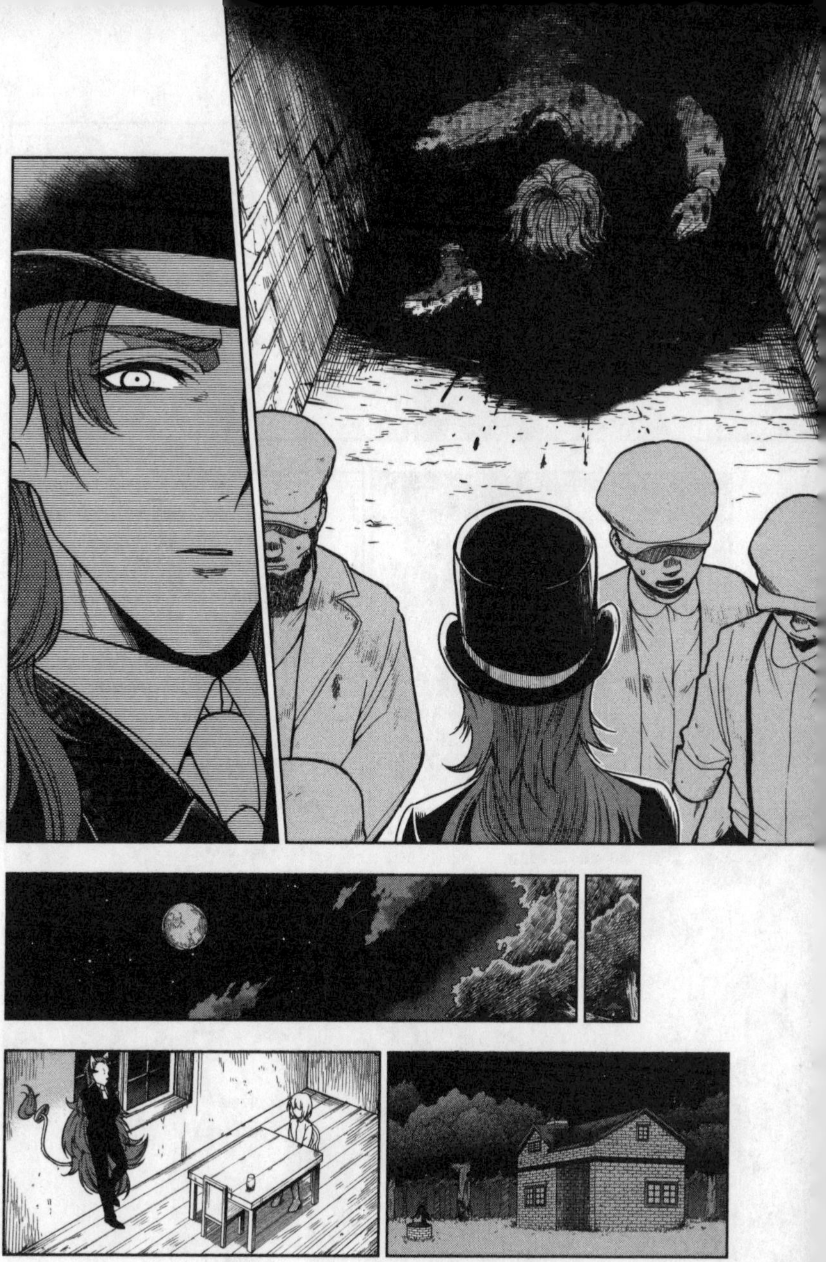

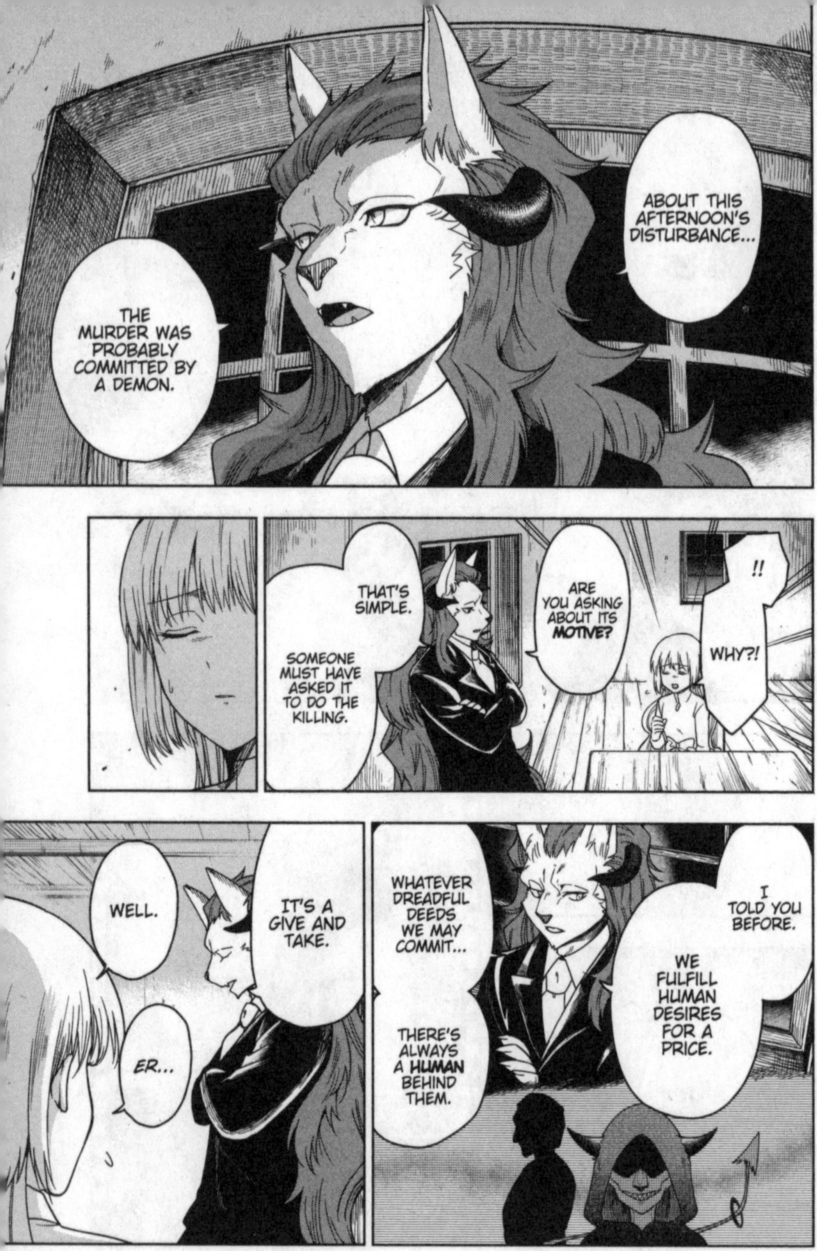
ABOUT THIS AFTERNOON'S DISTURBANCE...
THE MURDER WAS PROBABLY COMMITTED BY A DEMON.
!!
WHY?!
ARE YOU ASKING ABOUT ITS **MOTIVE?**
THAT'S SIMPLE.
SOMEONE MUST HAVE ASKED IT TO DO THE KILLING.
I TOLD YOU BEFORE.
WE FULFILL HUMAN DESIRES FOR A PRICE.
WHATEVER DREADFUL DEEDS WE MAY COMMIT...
THERE'S ALWAYS A **HUMAN** BEHIND THEM.
IT'S A GIVE AND TAKE.
WELL.
ER...

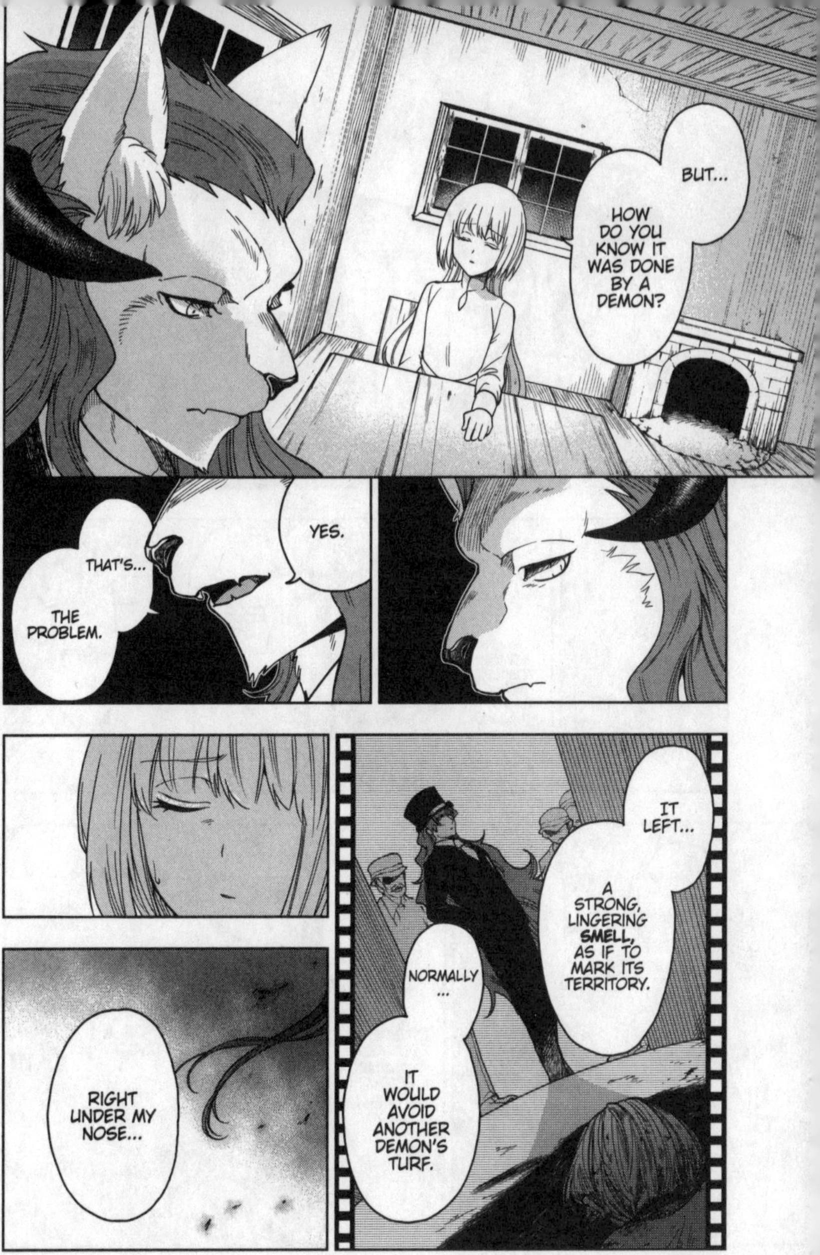
BUT...
HOW DO YOU KNOW IT WAS DONE BY A DEMON?
YES.
THAT'S...
THE PROBLEM.
IT LEFT...
A STRONG, LINGERING **SMELL**, AS IF TO MARK ITS TERRITORY.
NORMALLY...
IT WOULD AVOID ANOTHER DEMON'S TURF.
RIGHT UNDER MY NOSE...

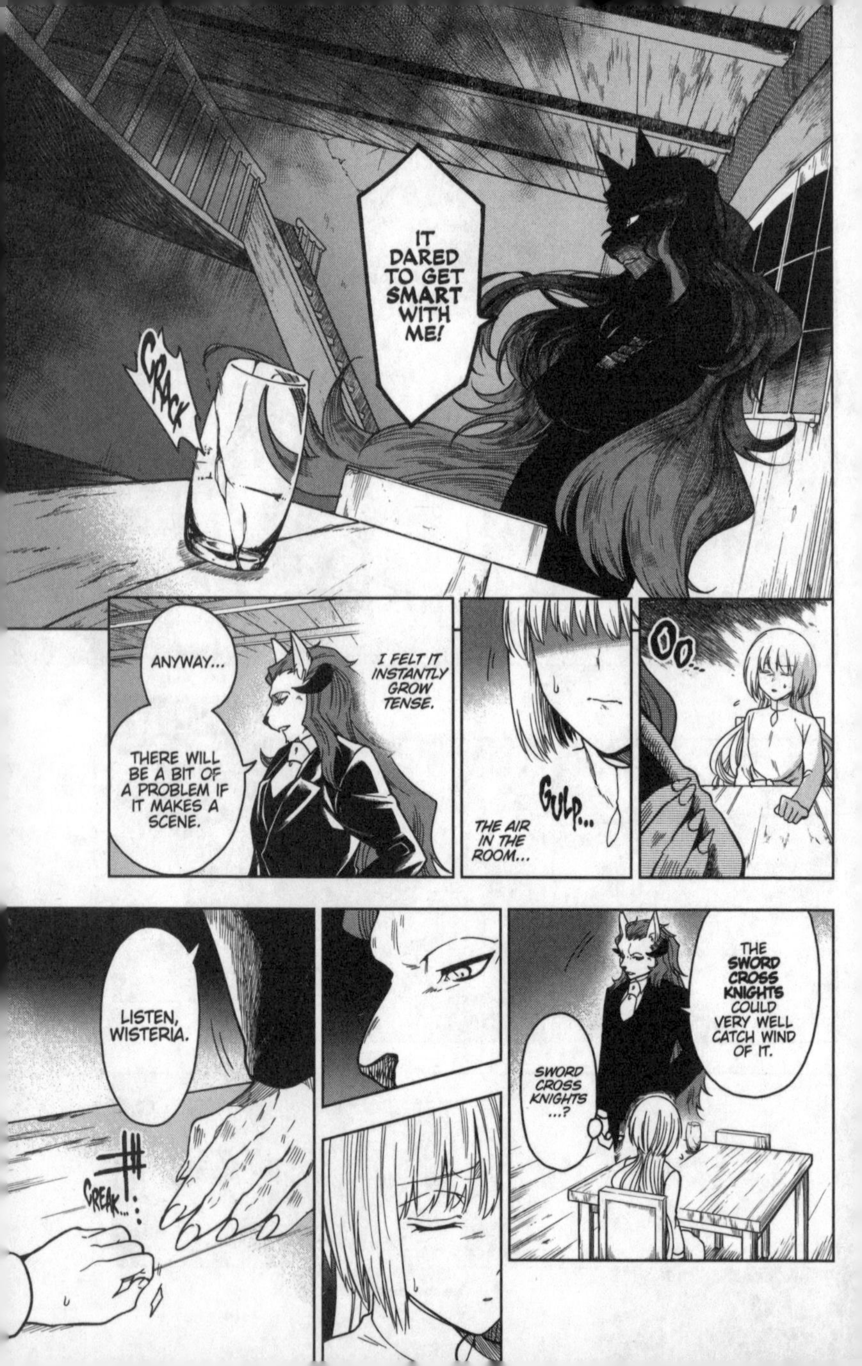
IT DARED TO GET SMART WITH ME!
CRACK
OO...
GULP...
THE AIR IN THE ROOM...
I FELT IT INSTANTLY GROW TENSE.
ANYWAY...
THERE WILL BE A BIT OF A PROBLEM IF IT MAKES A SCENE.
THE SWORD CROSS KNIGHTS COULD VERY WELL CATCH WIND OF IT.
SWORD CROSS KNIGHTS ...?
LISTEN, WISTERIA.
CREAK...

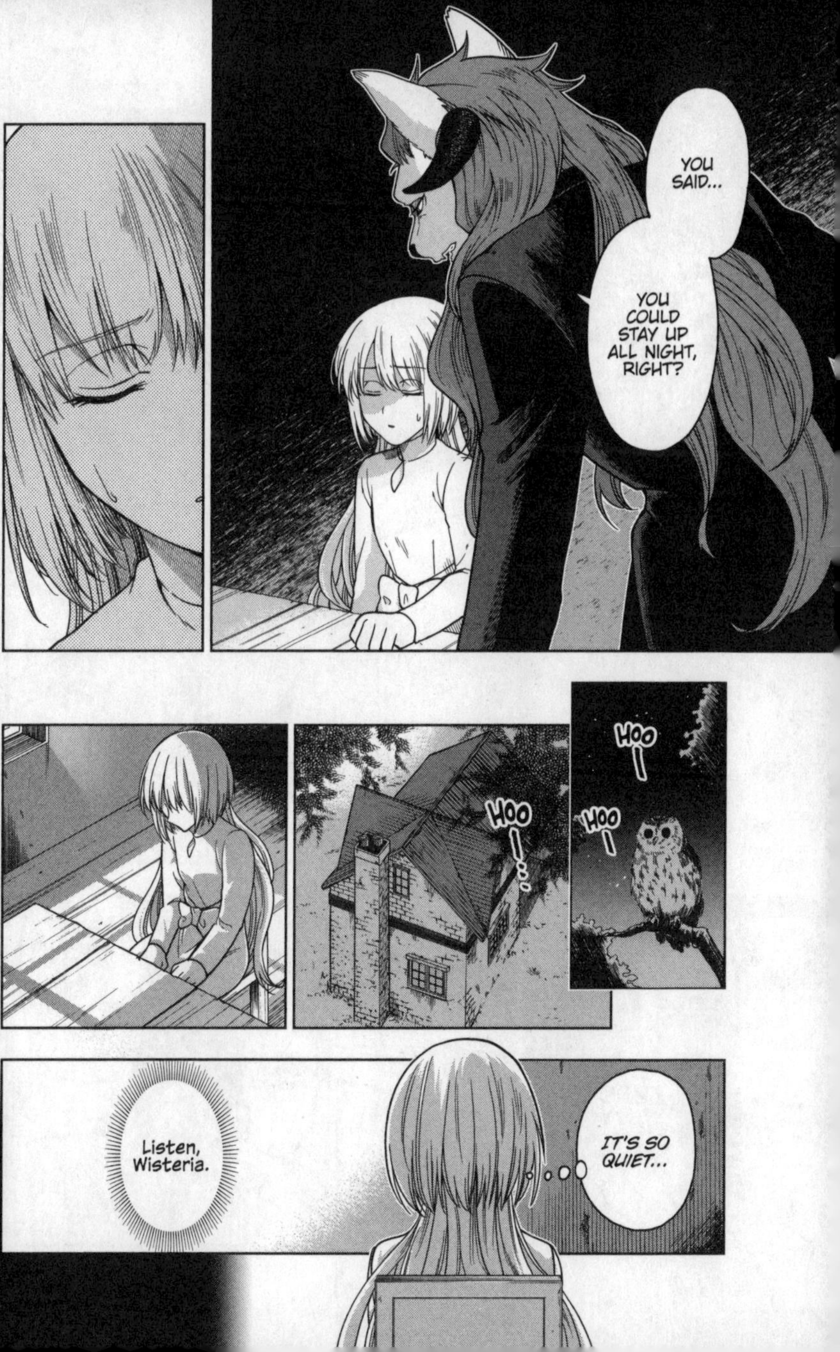
YOU SAID...
YOU COULD STAY UP ALL NIGHT, RIGHT?
HOO
HOO
HOO
IT'S SO QUIET...
Listen, Wisteria.

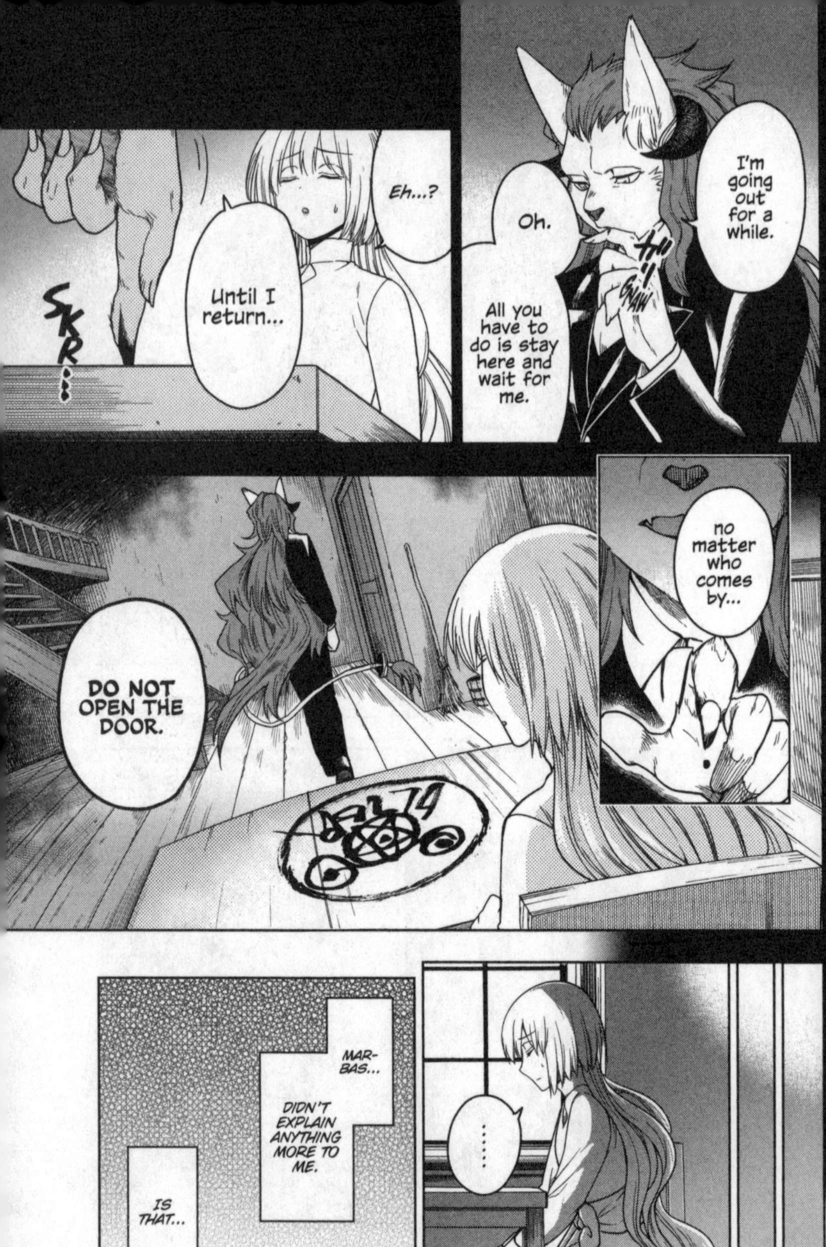
I'm going out for a while.
GNAW
Oh.
All you have to do is stay here and wait for me.
Eh...?
Until I return...
SKR..
no matter who comes by...
DO NOT OPEN THE DOOR.
......
MAR-BAS...
DIDN'T EXPLAIN ANYTHING MORE TO ME.
IS THAT...

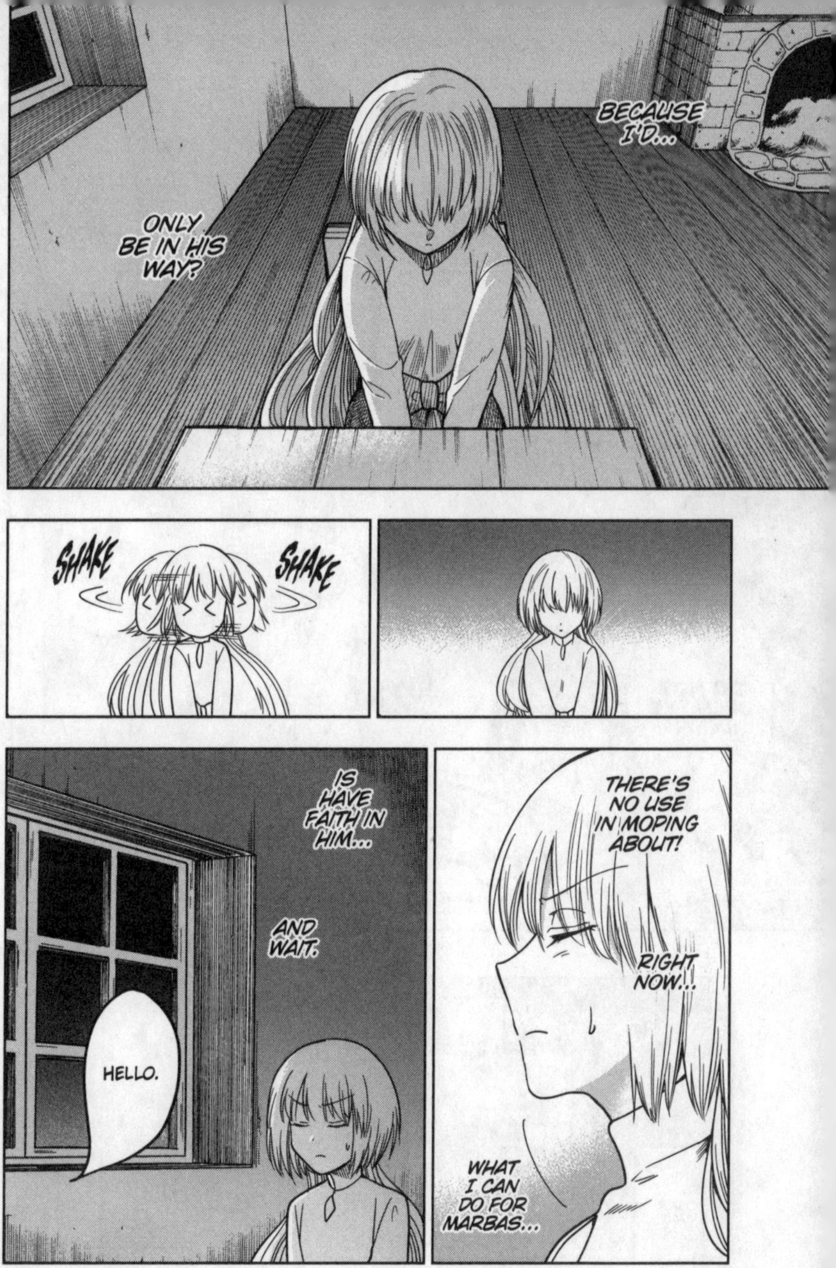
BECAUSE I'D...
ONLY BE IN HIS WAY?
SHAKE
SHAKE
THERE'S NO USE IN MOPING ABOUT!
RIGHT NOW...
WHAT I CAN DO FOR MARBAS...
IS HAVE FAITH IN HIM...
AND WAIT.
HELLO.

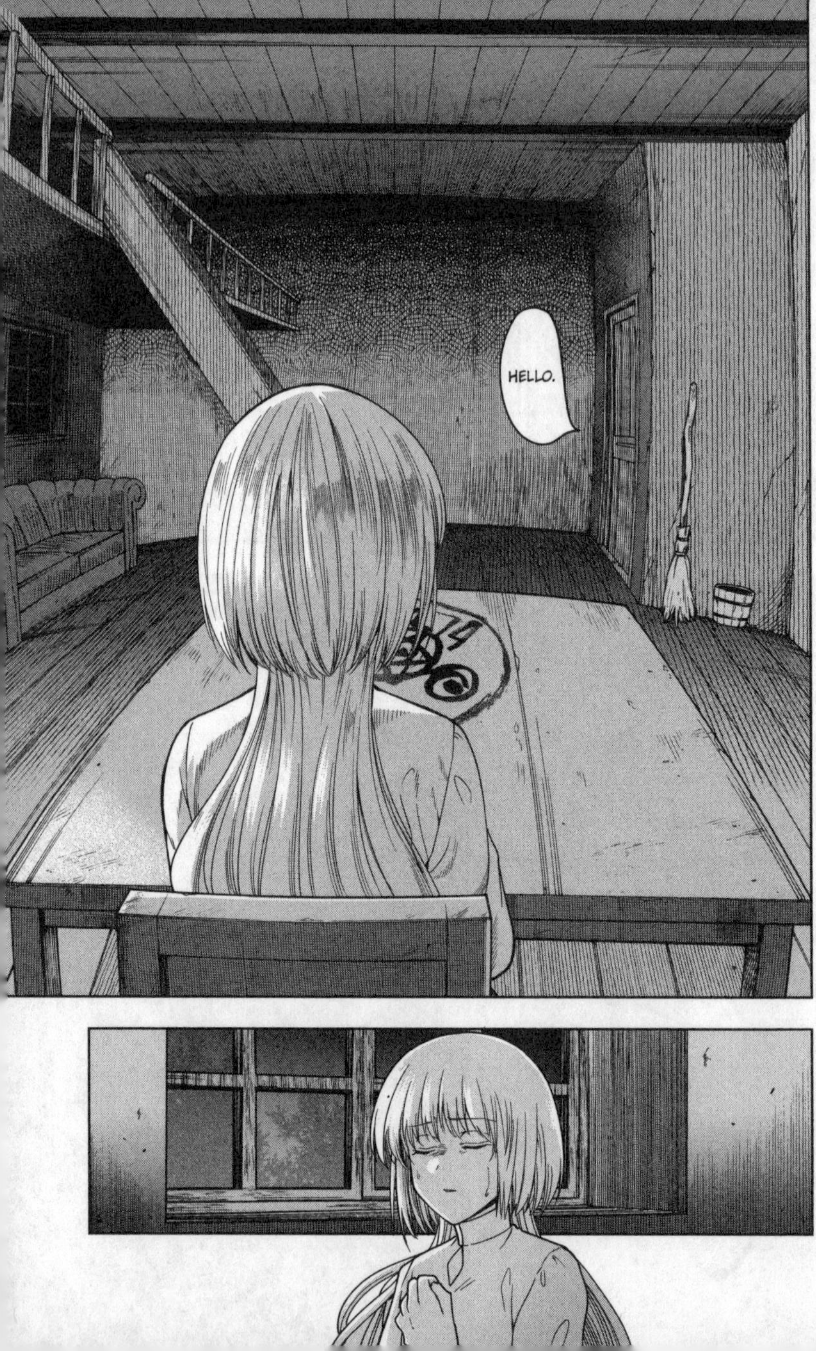
HELLO.

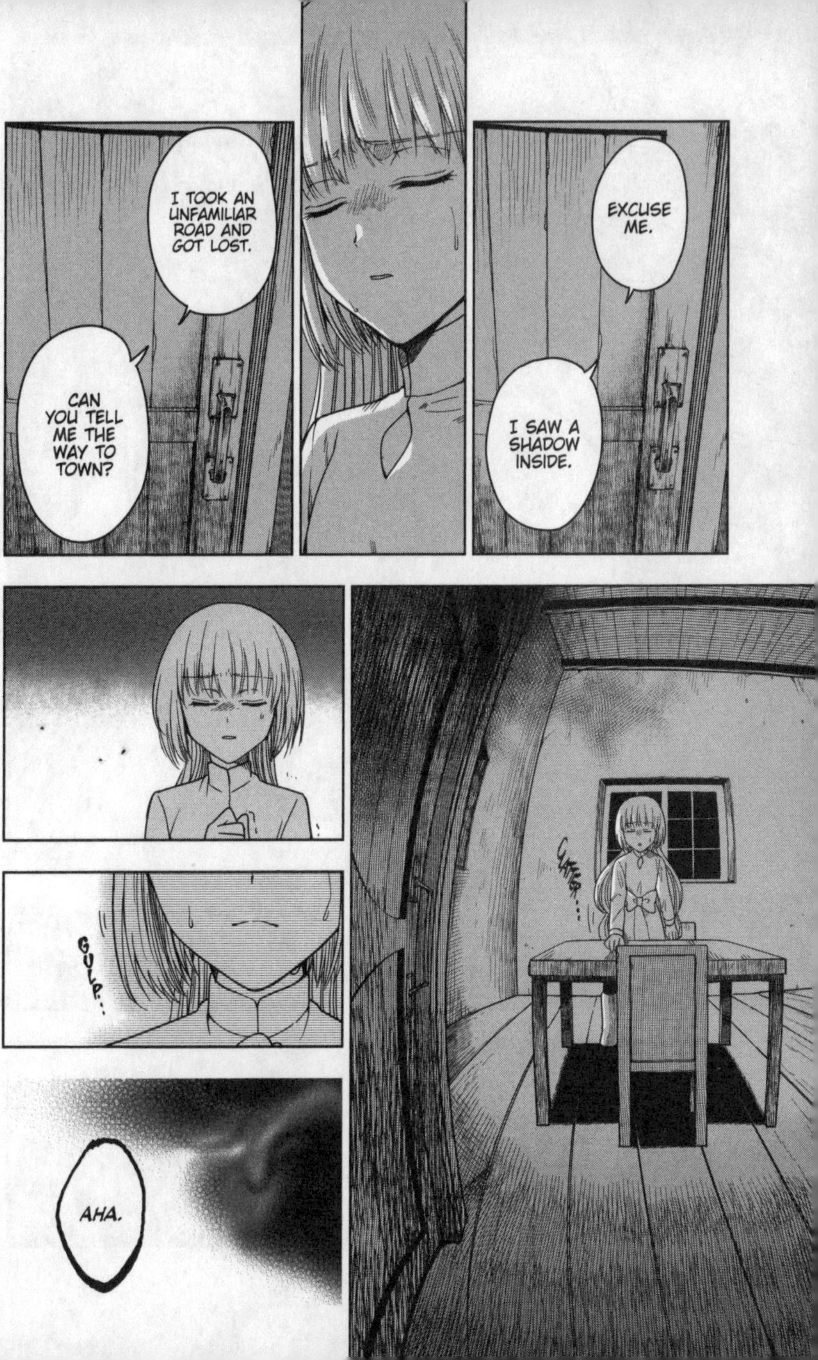
EXCUSE ME.
I SAW A SHADOW INSIDE.
I TOOK AN UNFAMILIAR ROAD AND GOT LOST.
CAN YOU TELL ME THE WAY TO TOWN?
...
GULP...
AHA.

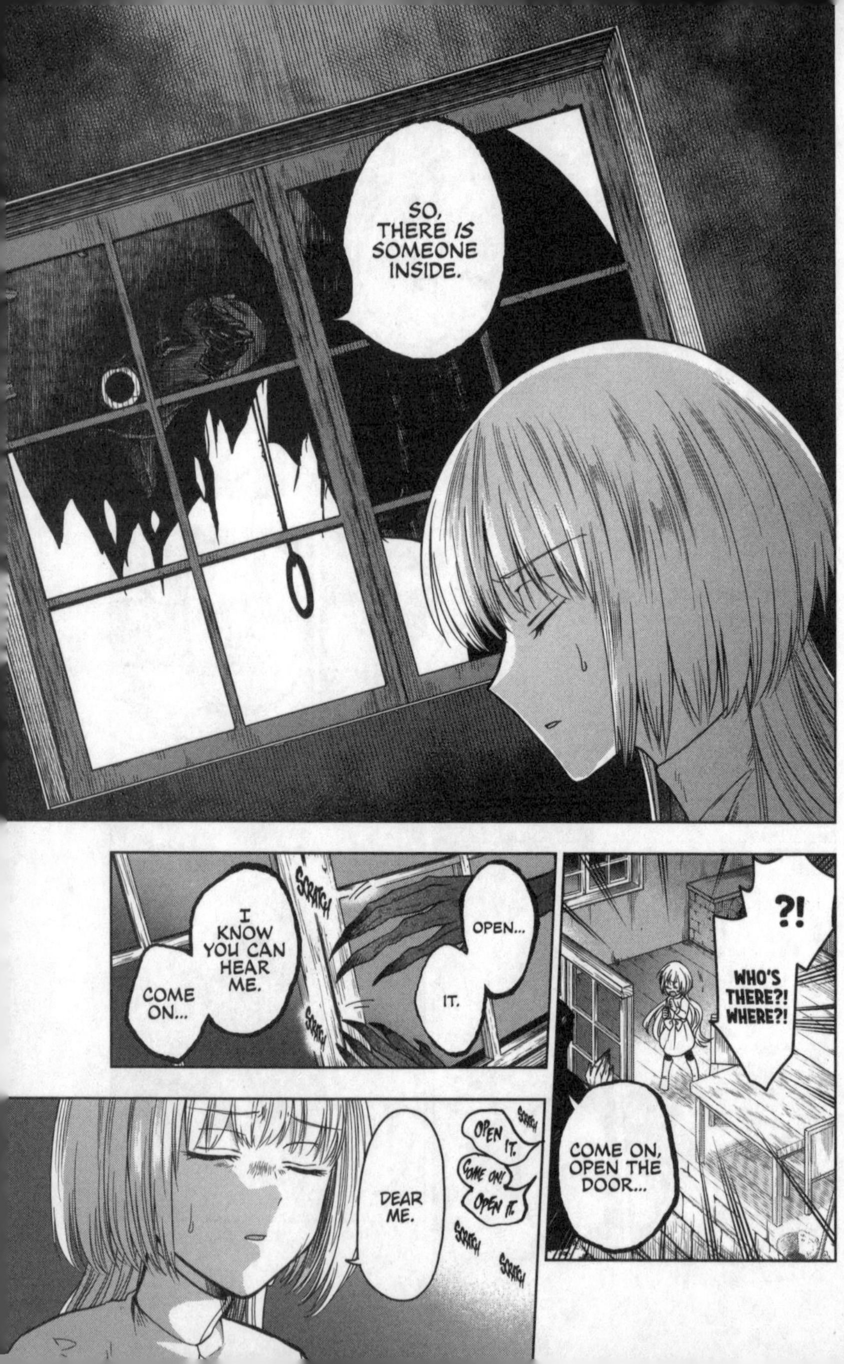
SO, THERE IS SOMEONE INSIDE.
?!
WHO'S THERE?! WHERE?!
COME ON, OPEN THE DOOR...
SCRATCH
OPEN...
IT.
I KNOW YOU CAN HEAR ME.
COME ON...
SCRATCH
SCRATCH
OPEN IT.
COME ON!
OPEN IT.
SCRATCH
SCRATCH
DEAR ME.

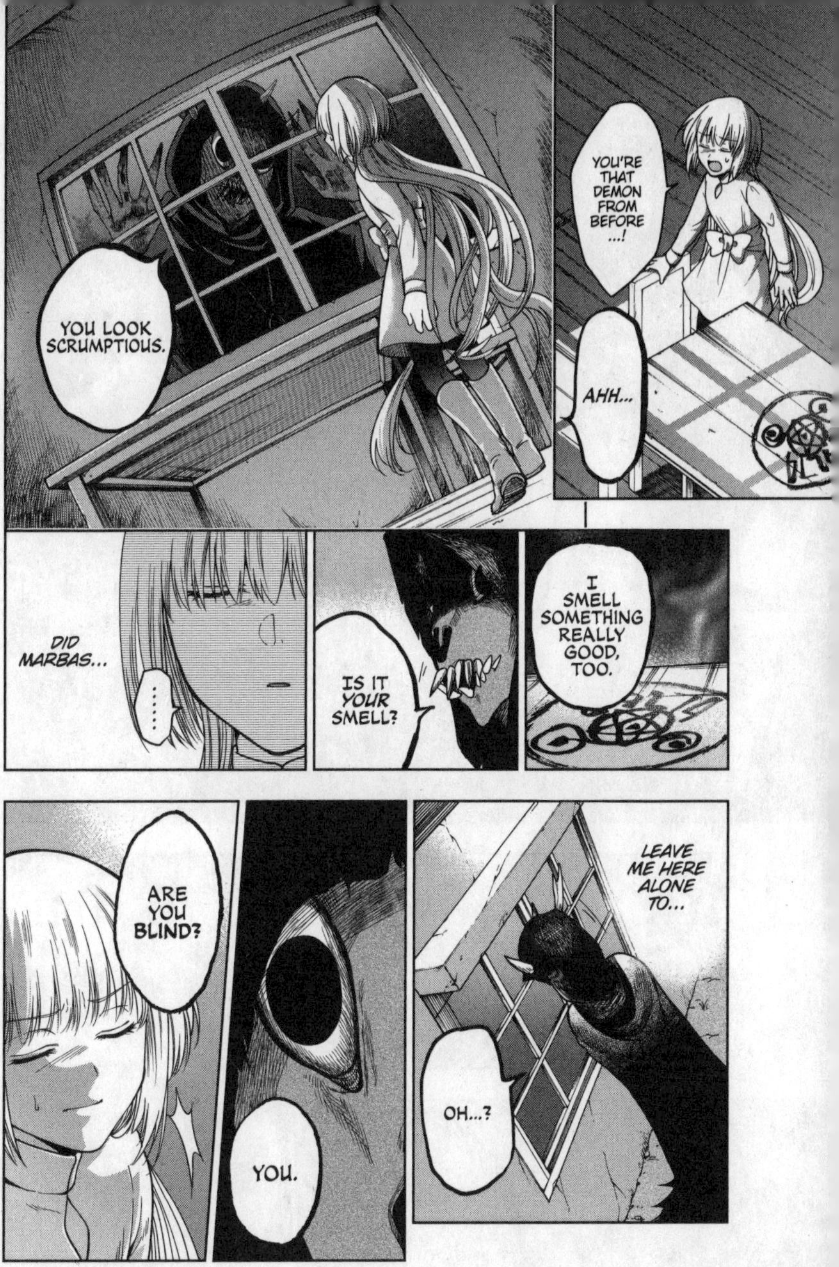
YOU'RE THAT DEMON FROM BEFORE ...!
AHH...
YOU LOOK SCRUMPTIOUS.
I SMELL SOMETHING REALLY GOOD, TOO.
IS IT *YOUR* SMELL?
......
DID MARBAS...
LEAVE ME HERE ALONE TO...
OH...?
YOU.
ARE YOU BLIND?

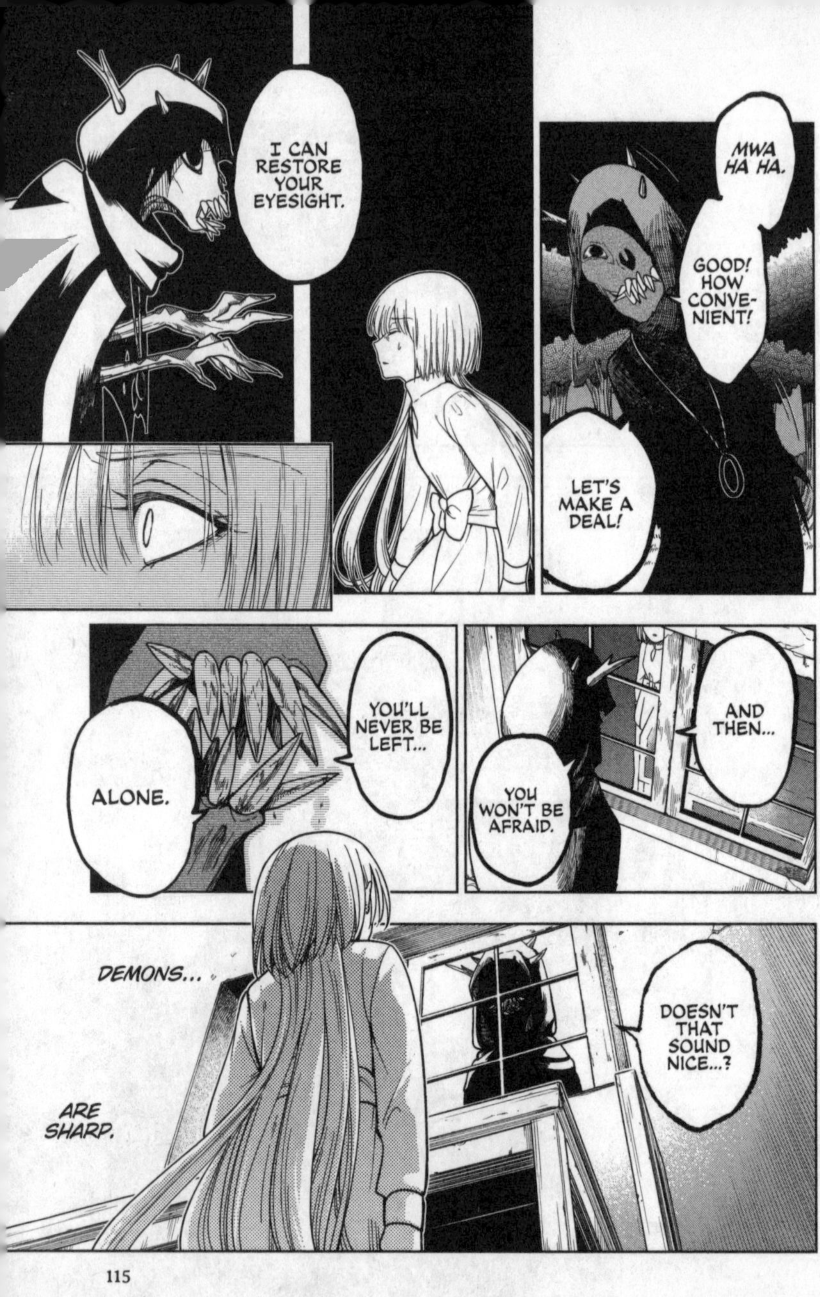
MWA HA HA.
GOOD! HOW CONVENIENT!
LET'S MAKE A DEAL!
I CAN RESTORE YOUR EYESIGHT.
AND THEN...
YOU WON'T BE AFRAID.
YOU'LL NEVER BE LEFT...
ALONE.
DOESN'T THAT SOUND NICE...?
DEMONS...
ARE SHARP.

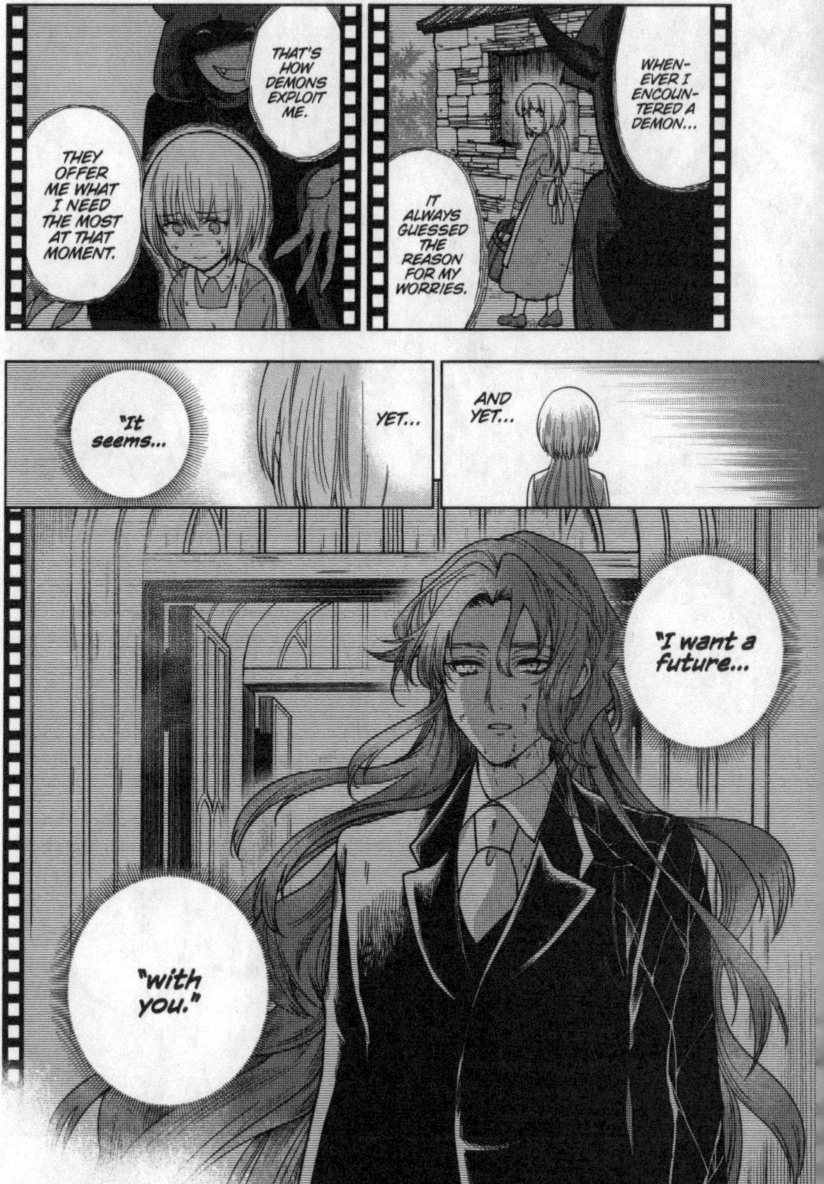
WHEN-EVER I ENCOUN-TERED A DEMON...
IT ALWAYS GUESSED THE REASON FOR MY WORRIES.
THAT'S HOW DEMONS EXPLOIT ME.
THEY OFFER ME WHAT I NEED THE MOST AT THAT MOMENT.
AND YET...
YET...
"It seems...
"I want a future...
"with you."

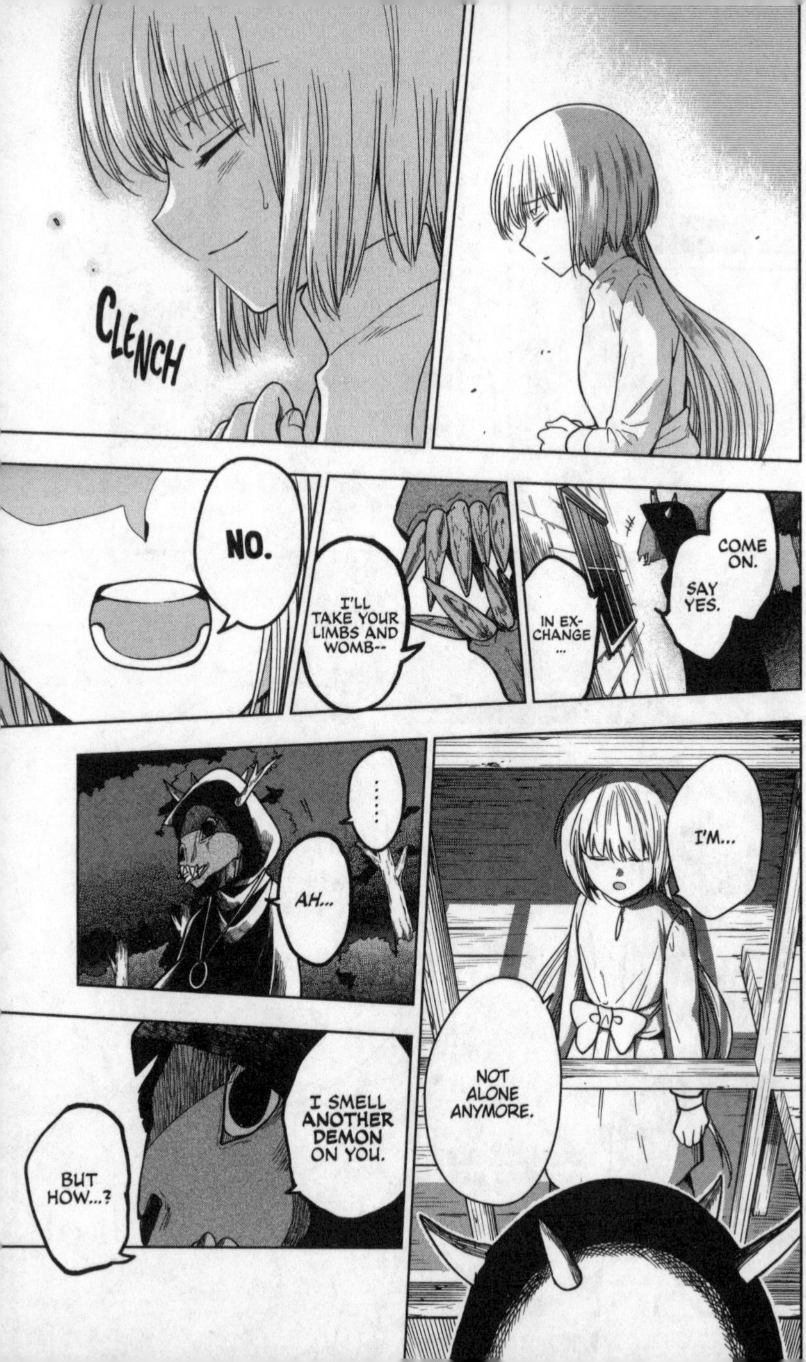
CLENCH
COME ON.
SAY YES.
IN EX-CHANGE...
I'LL TAKE YOUR LIMBS AND WOMB--
NO.
I'M...
NOT ALONE ANYMORE.
......
AH...
I SMELL ANOTHER DEMON ON YOU.
BUT HOW...?

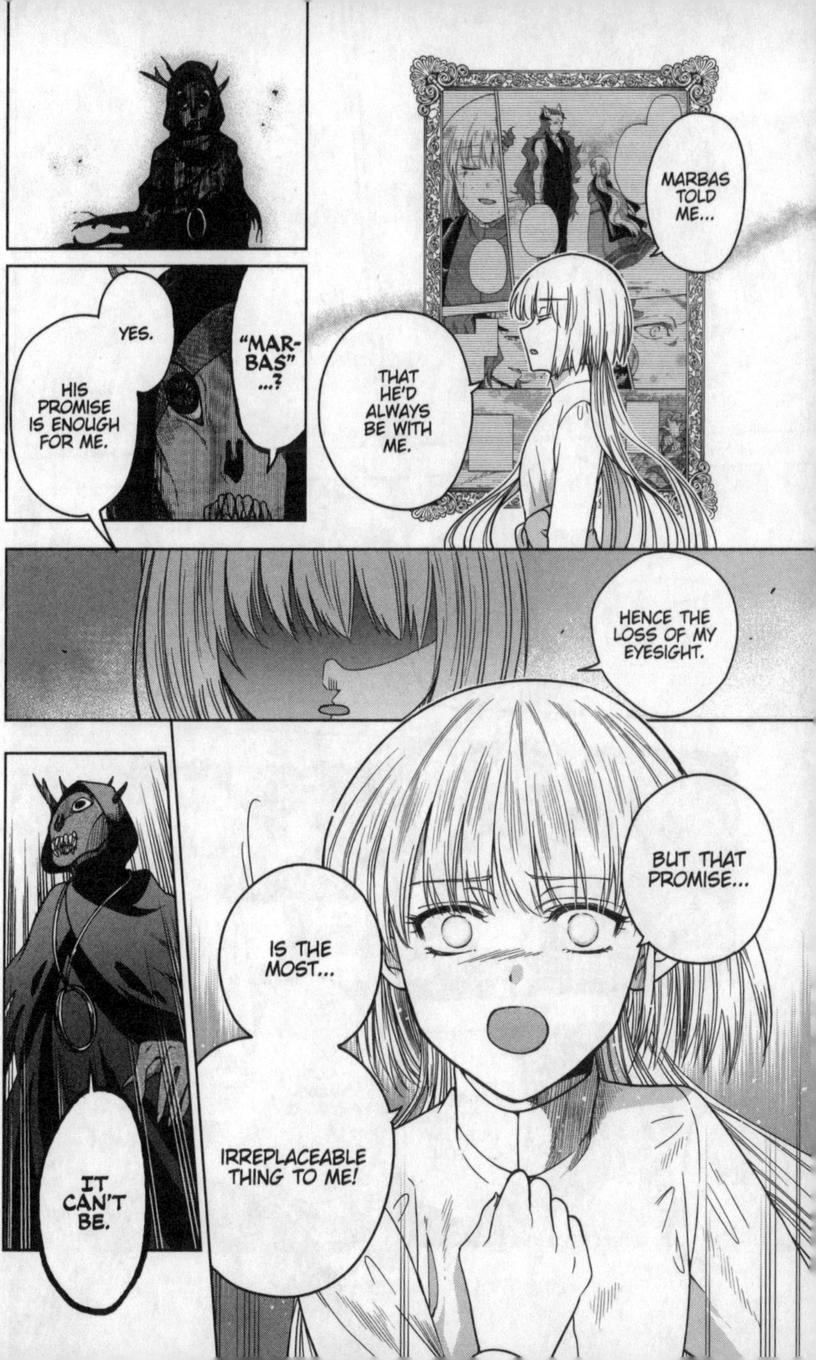
MARBAS TOLD ME...
THAT HE'D ALWAYS BE WITH ME.
“MAR-BAS” ...?
YES. HIS PROMISE IS ENOUGH FOR ME.
HENCE THE LOSS OF MY EYESIGHT.
BUT THAT PROMISE...
IS THE MOST...
IRREPLACEABLE THING TO ME!
IT CAN'T BE.

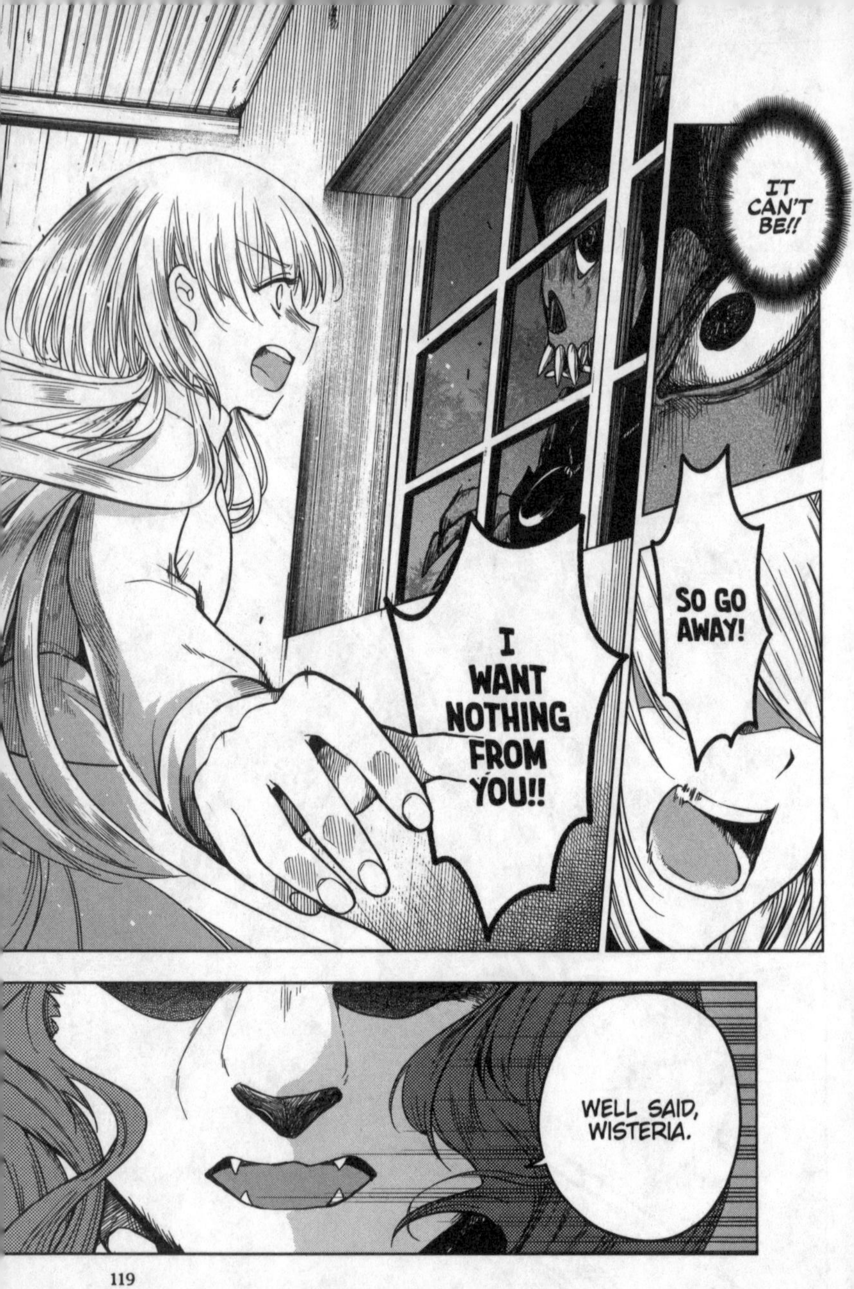
IT CAN'T BE!!
SO GO AWAY!
I WANT NOTHING FROM YOU!!
WELL SAID, WISTERIA.

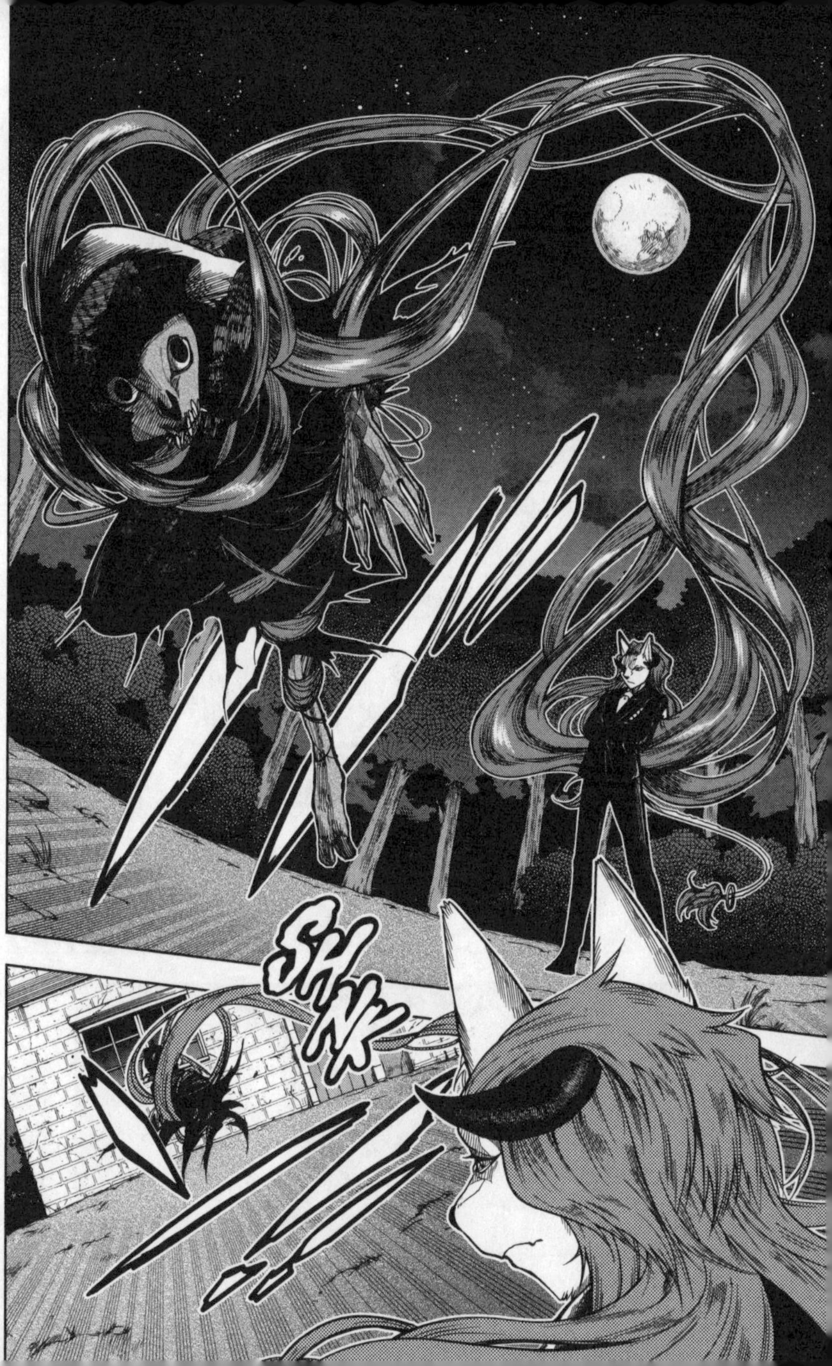
SHNK

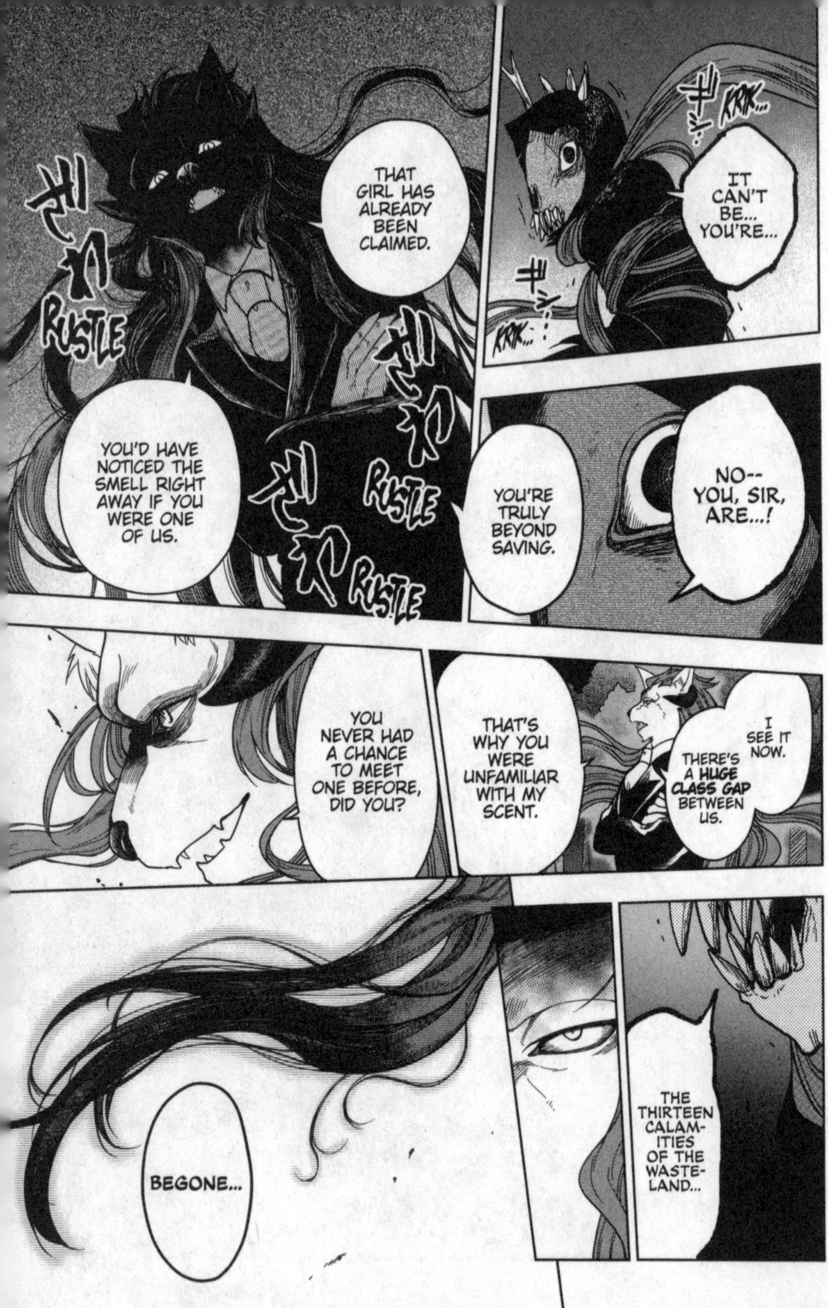
KRIK...
IT CAN'T BE... YOU'RE...
KRIK...
NO-- YOU, SIR, ARE...!
YOU'RE TRULY BEYOND SAVING.
THAT GIRL HAS ALREADY BEEN CLAIMED.
RUSTLE
RUSTLE
YOU'D HAVE NOTICED THE SMELL RIGHT AWAY IF YOU WERE ONE OF US.
RUSTLE
I SEE IT NOW.
THERE'S A **HUGE CLASS GAP** BETWEEN US.
THAT'S WHY YOU WERE UNFAMILIAR WITH MY SCENT.
YOU NEVER HAD A CHANCE TO MEET ONE BEFORE, DID YOU?
THE THIRTEEN CALAMITIES OF THE WASTELAND...
BEGONE...

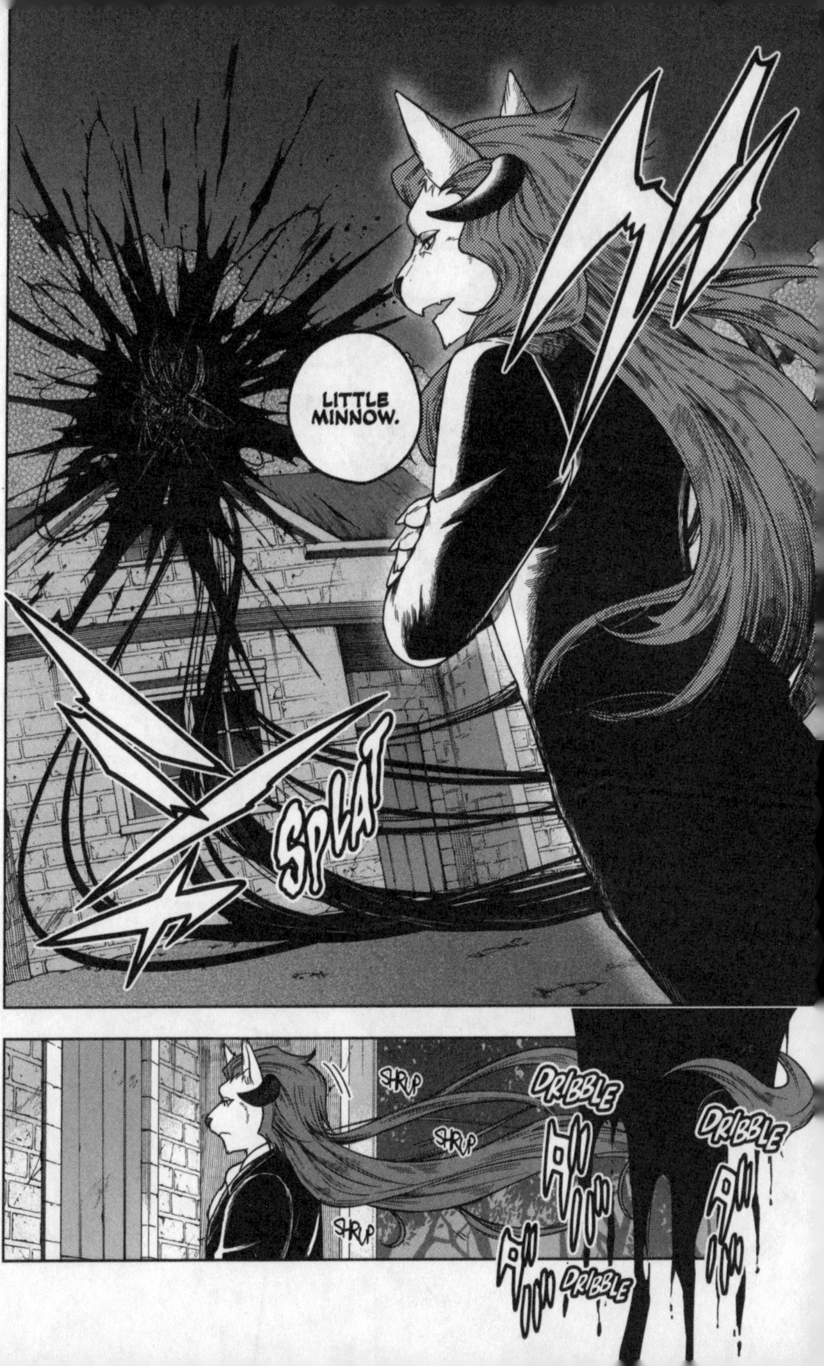
LITTLE MINNOW.
SPLAT
DRIBBLE
DRIBBLE
SHRUP
SHRUP
DRIBBLE
SHRUP

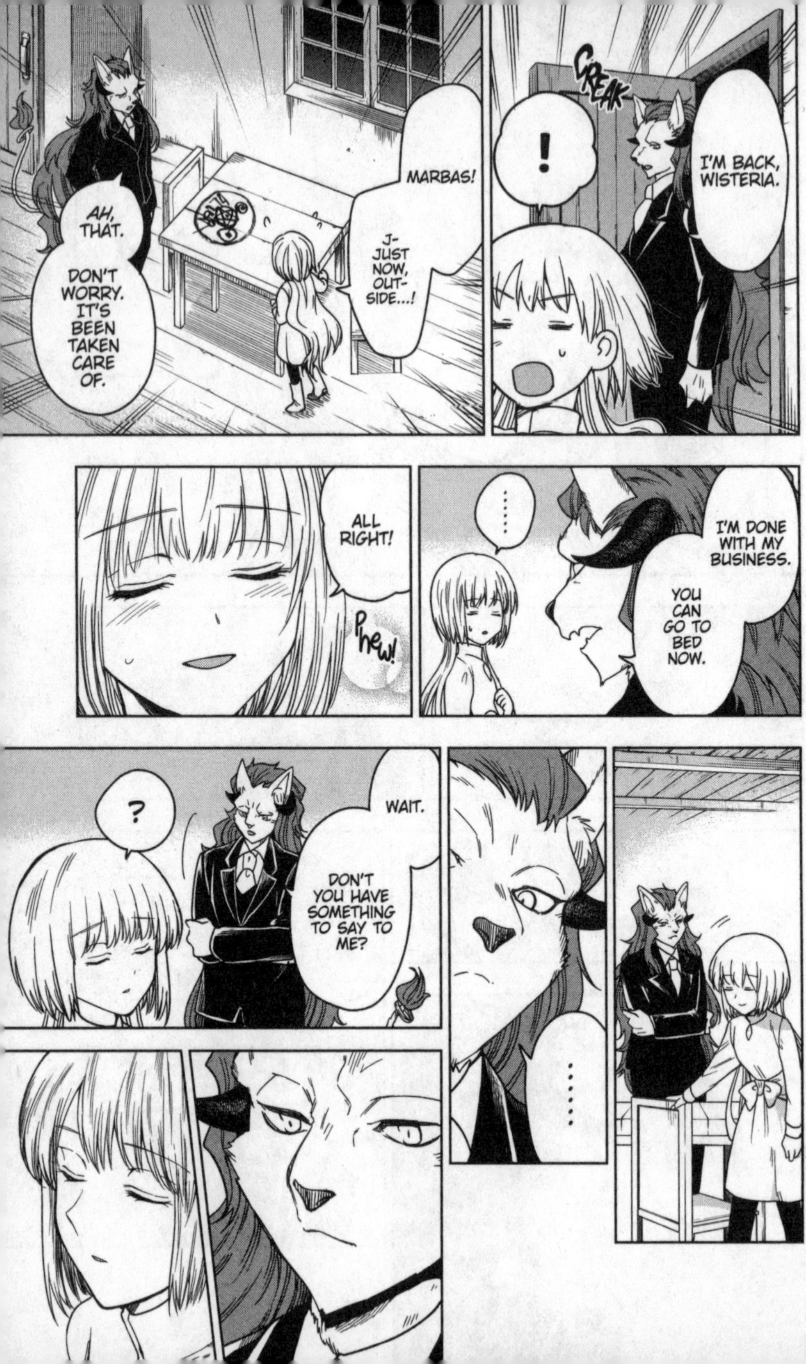
CREAK
I'M BACK, WISTERIA.
!
MARBAS!
J-JUST NOW, OUTSIDE...!
AH, THAT.
DON'T WORRY. IT'S BEEN TAKEN CARE OF.
I'M DONE WITH MY BUSINESS.
YOU CAN GO TO BED NOW.
......
ALL RIGHT!
Phew!
......
WAIT.
DON'T YOU HAVE SOMETHING TO SAY TO ME?
?

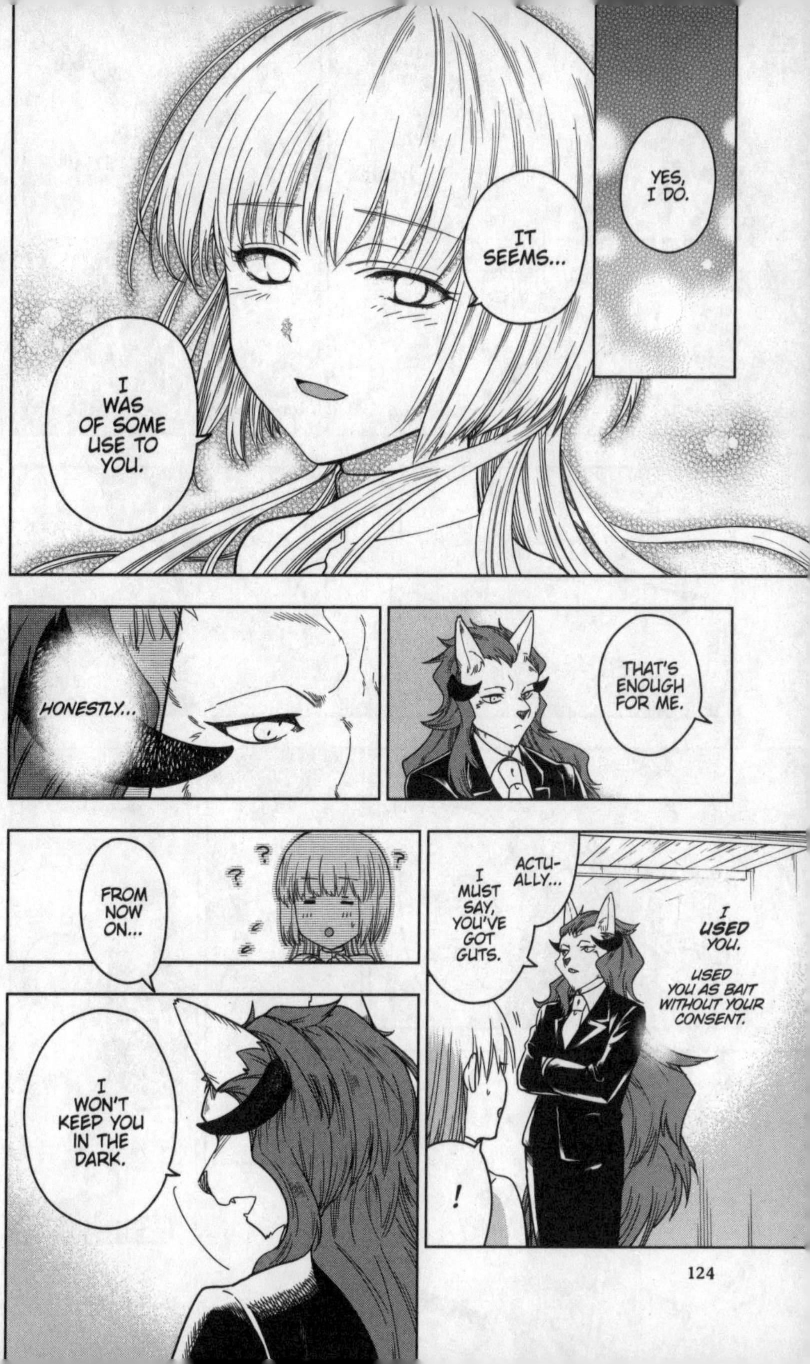
YES, I DO.
IT SEEMS...
I WAS OF SOME USE TO YOU.
THAT'S ENOUGH FOR ME.
HONESTLY...
ACTU-ALLY...
I MUST SAY, YOU'VE GOT GUTS.
I USED YOU.
USED YOU AS BAIT WITHOUT YOUR CONSENT.
!
? ? ?
FROM NOW ON...
I WON'T KEEP YOU IN THE DARK.

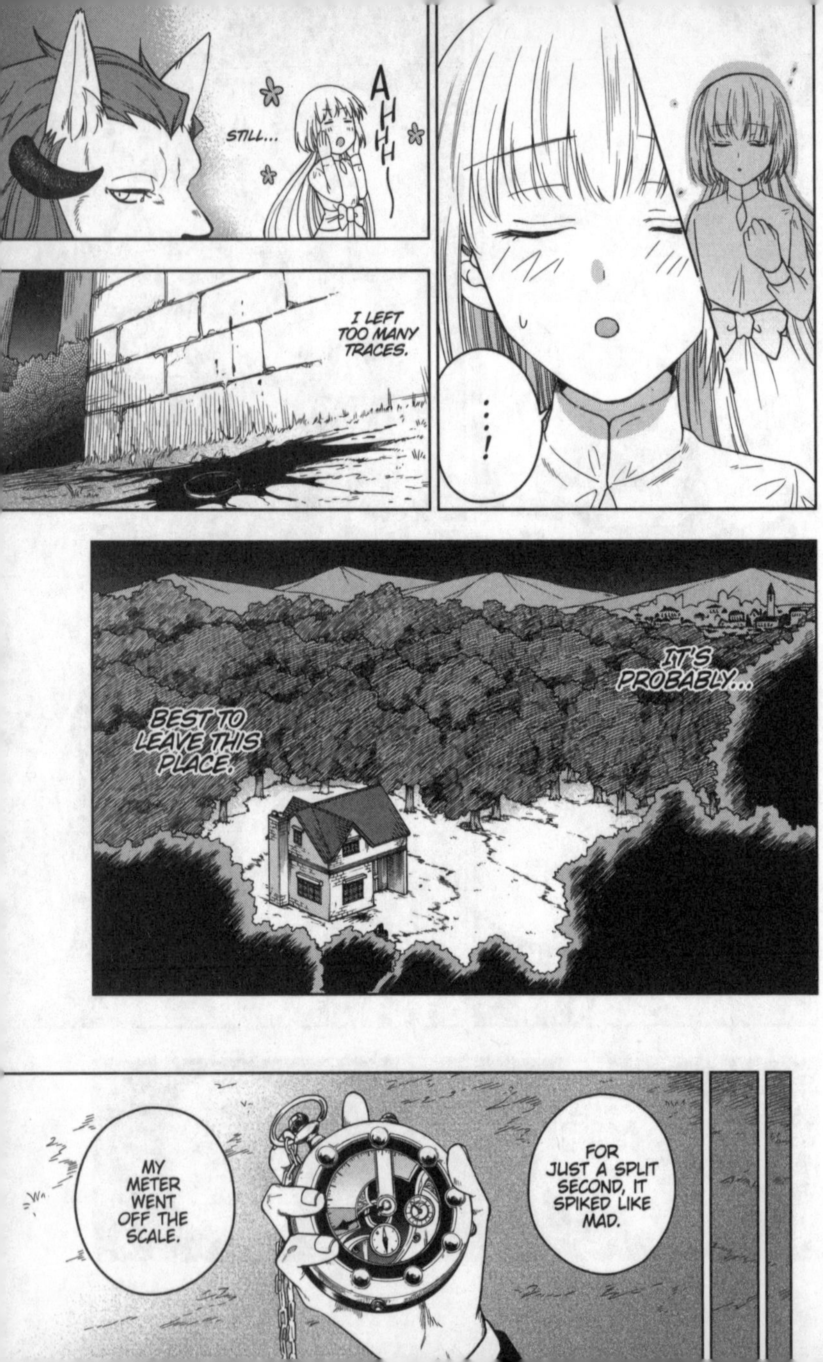
...!
AHHH
STILL...
I LEFT TOO MANY TRACES.
IT'S PROBABLY...
BEST TO LEAVE THIS PLACE.
FOR JUST A SPLIT SECOND, IT SPIKED LIKE MAD.
MY METER WENT OFF THE SCALE.

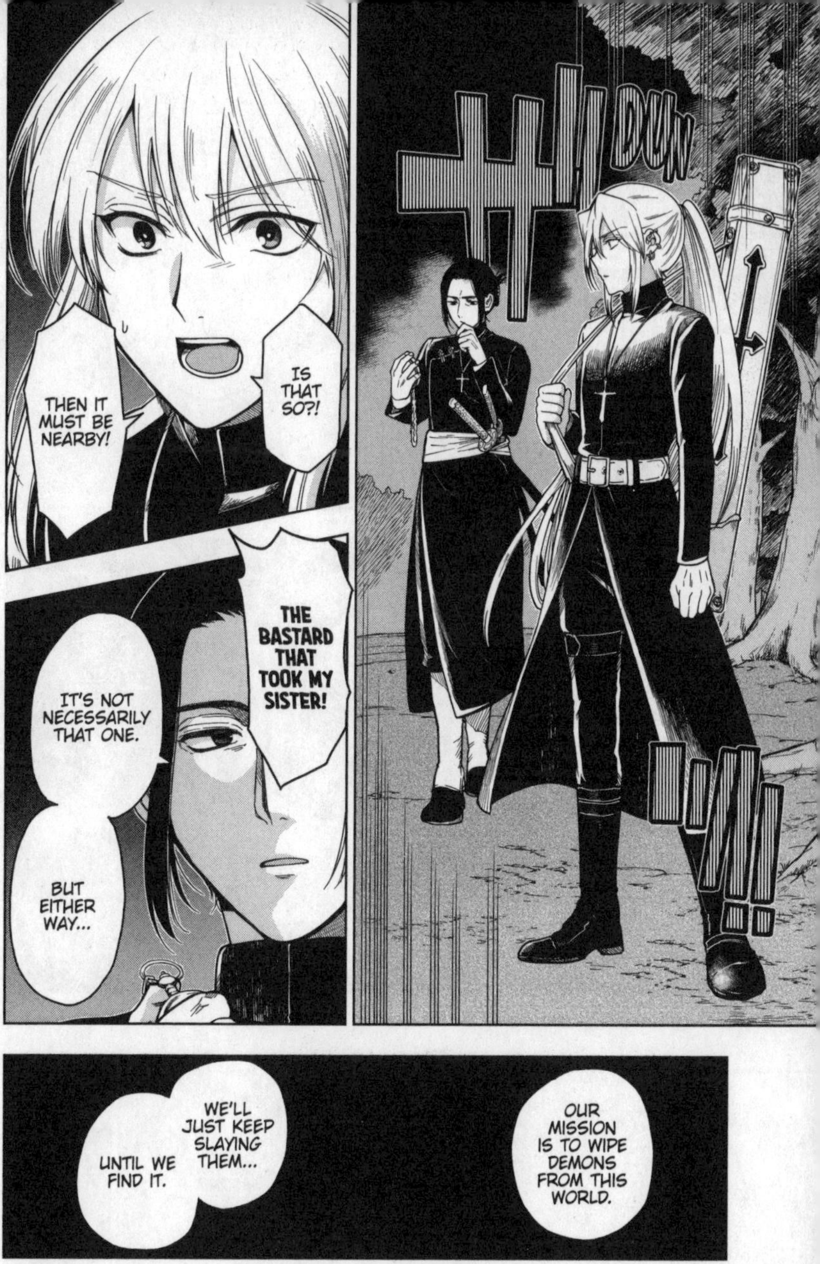

DUN
IS THAT SO?!
THEN IT MUST BE NEARBY!
THE BASTARD THAT TOOK MY SISTER!
IT'S NOT NECESSARILY THAT ONE.
BUT EITHER WAY...
OUR MISSION IS TO WIPE DEMONS FROM THIS WORLD.
WE'LL JUST KEEP SLAYING THEM...
UNTIL WE FIND IT.

⚜Night 4⚜ The Encounter

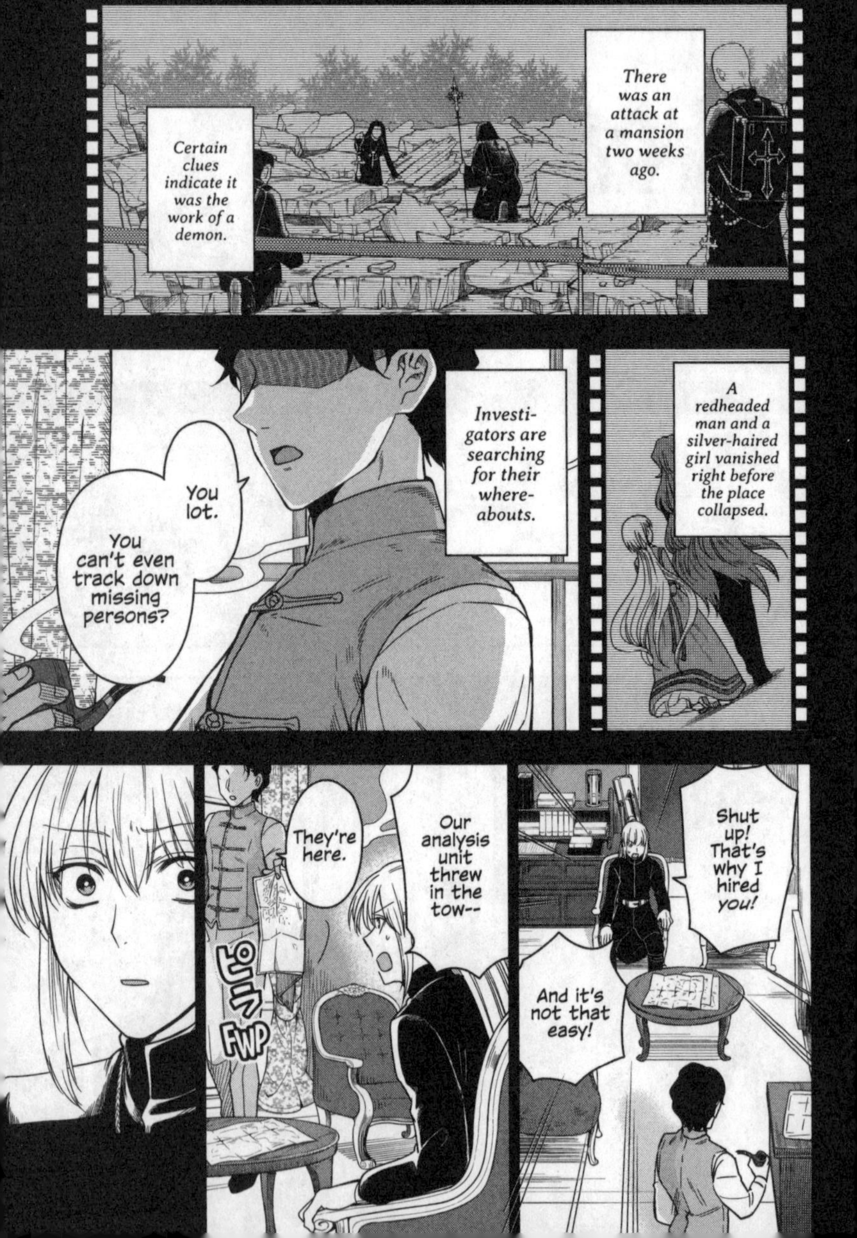
There was an attack at a mansion two weeks ago.
Certain clues indicate it was the work of a demon.
A redheaded man and a silver-haired girl vanished right before the place collapsed.
Investigators are searching for their whereabouts.
You lot.
You can't even track down missing persons?
Shut up! That's why I hired you!
And it's not that easy!
Our analysis unit threw in the tow--
They're here.
FWP

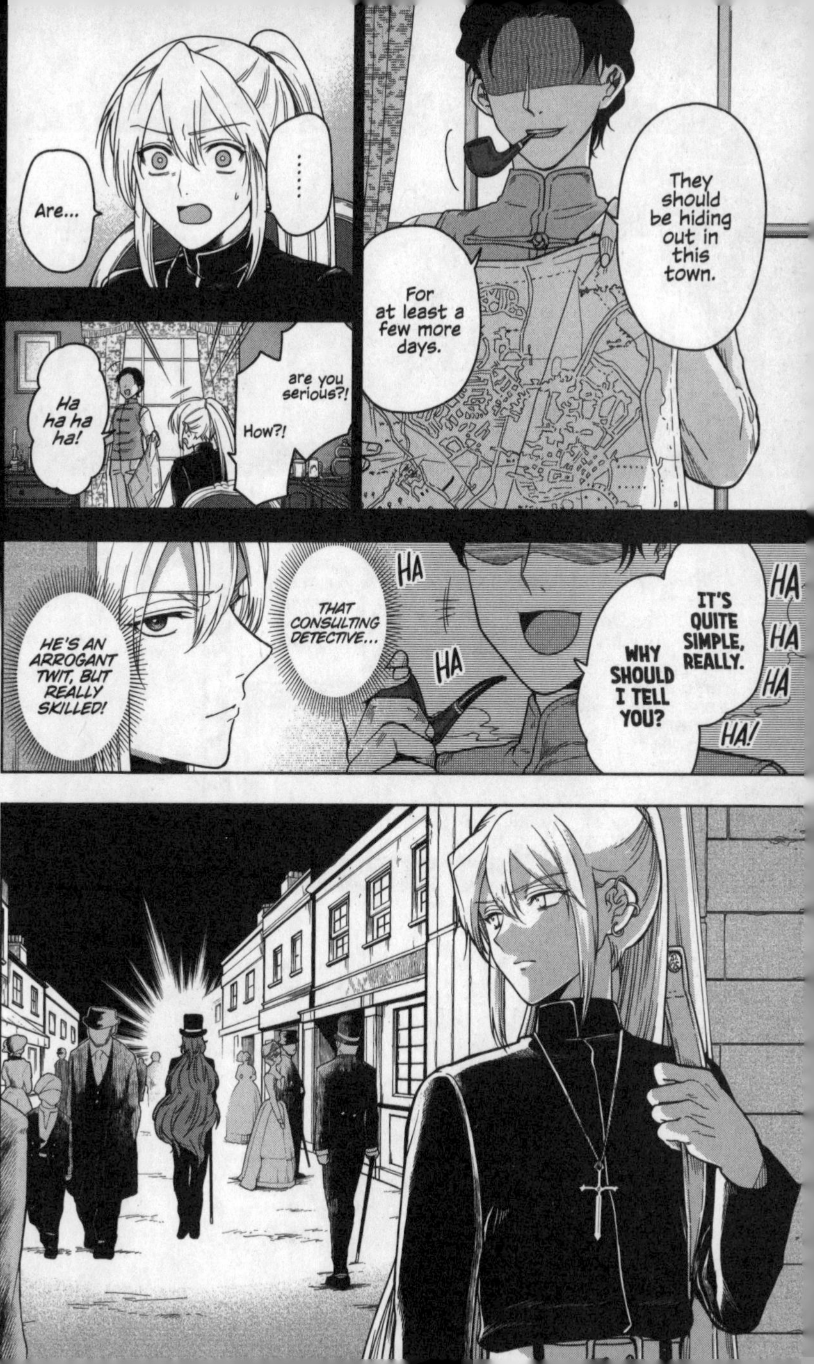
They should be hiding out in this town.
For at least a few more days.
......
Are...
are you serious?!
How?!
Ha ha ha ha!
HA HA HA HA!
IT'S QUITE SIMPLE, REALLY.
WHY SHOULD I TELL YOU?
HA
HA
THAT CONSULTING DETECTIVE...
HE'S AN ARROGANT TWIT, BUT REALLY SKILLED!

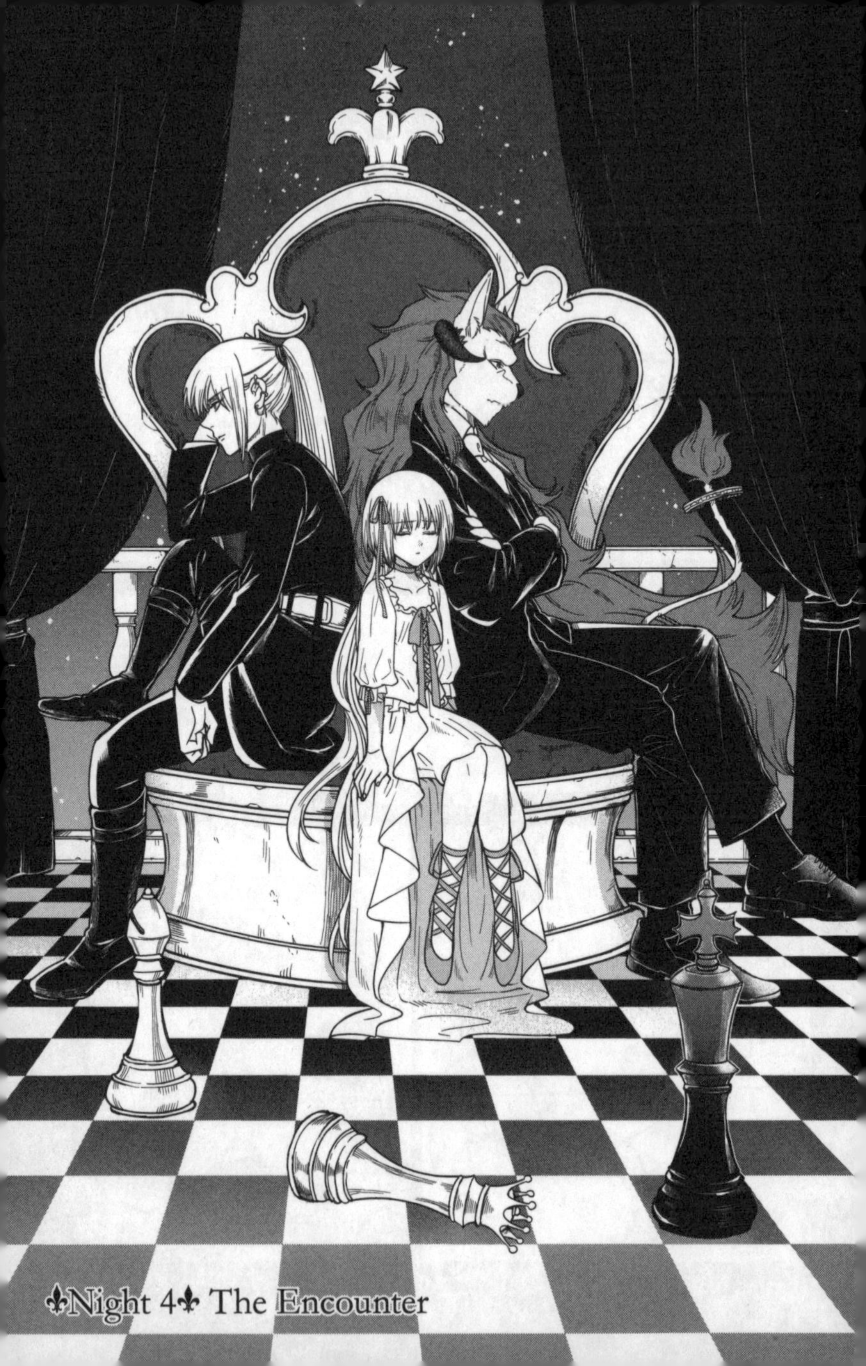

Night 4 The Encounter

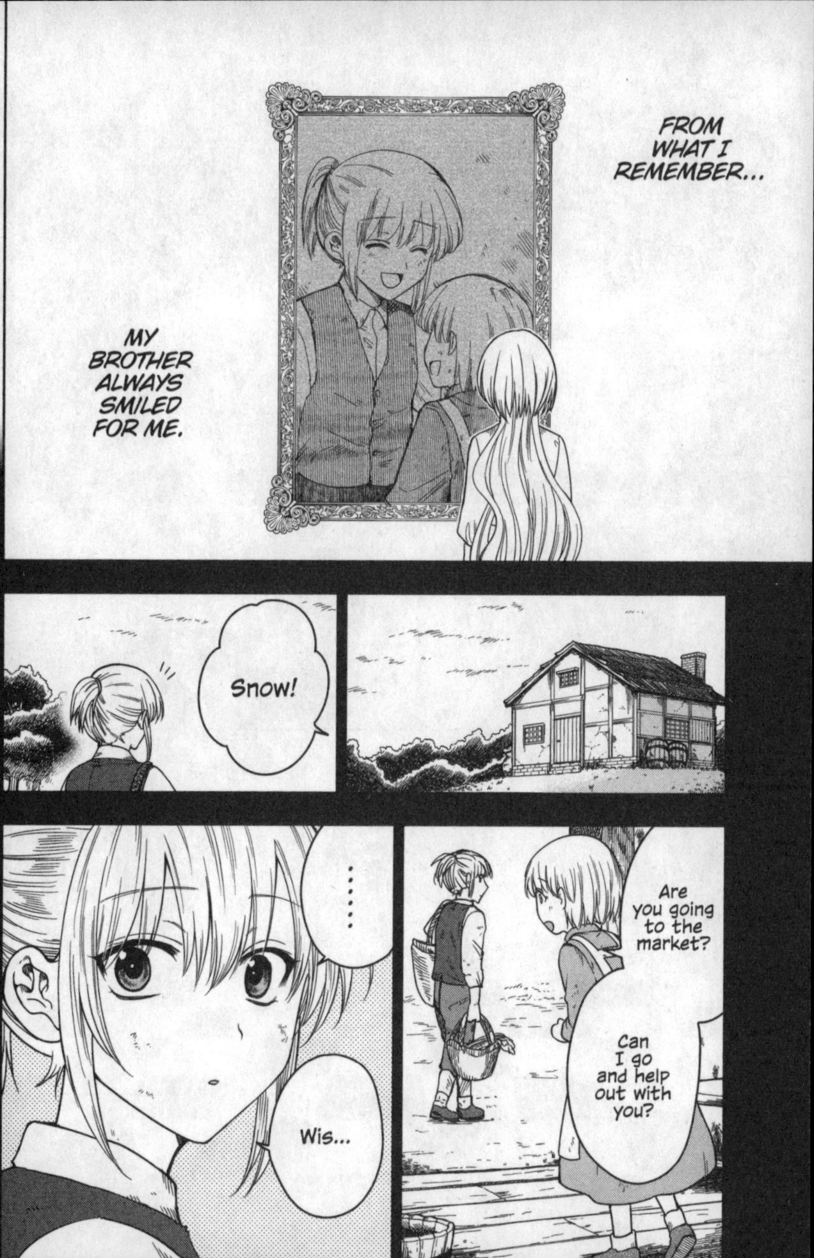
FROM WHAT I REMEMBER...
MY BROTHER ALWAYS SMILED FOR ME.
Snow!
Are you going to the market?
Can I go and help out with you?
......
Wis...

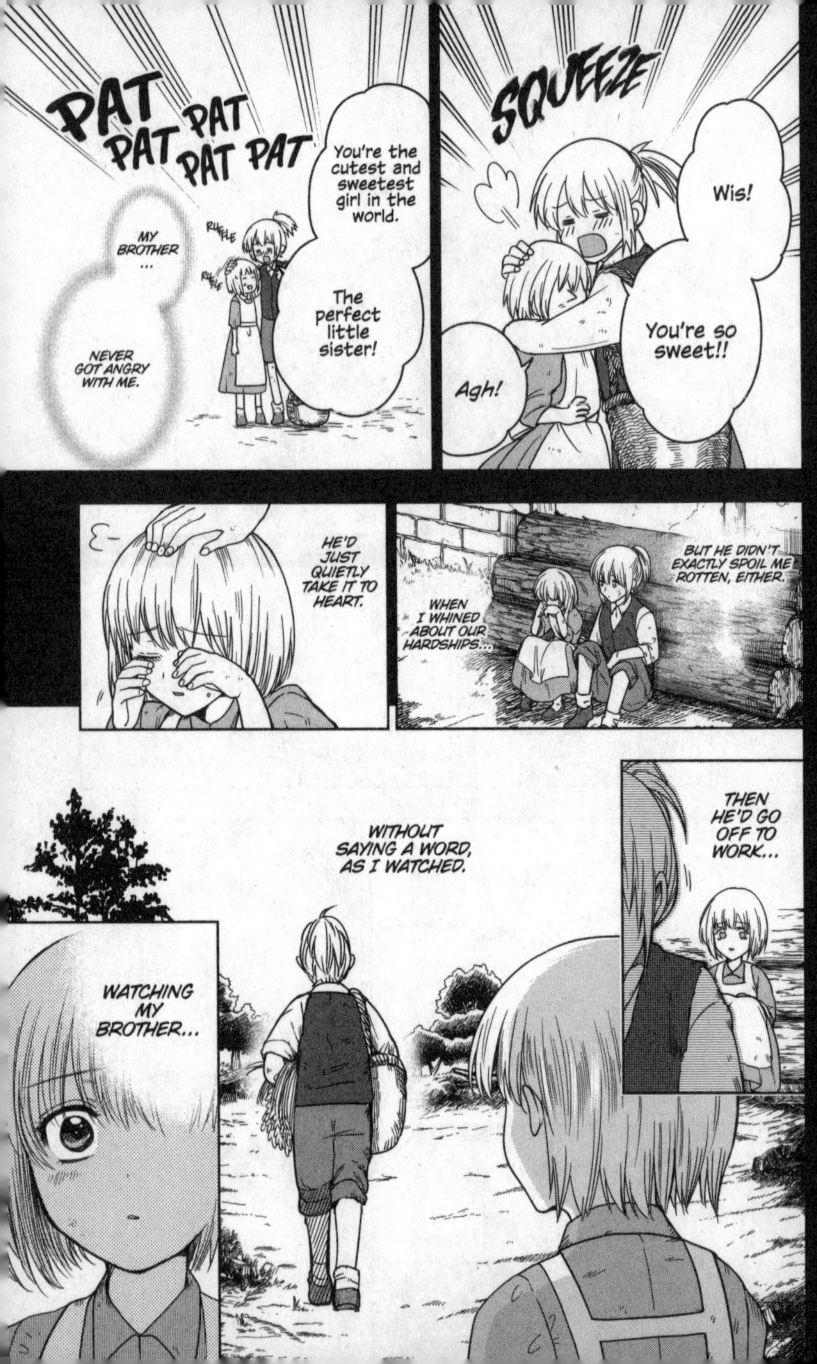
SQUEEZE
Wis!
You're so sweet!!
Agh!
PAT PAT PAT PAT PAT
You're the cutest and sweetest girl in the world.
The perfect little sister!
MY BROTHER ...
NEVER GOT ANGRY WITH ME.
BUT HE DIDN'T EXACTLY SPOIL ME ROTTEN, EITHER.
WHEN I WHINED ABOUT OUR HARDSHIPS...
HE'D JUST QUIETLY TAKE IT TO HEART.
THEN HE'D GO OFF TO WORK...
WITHOUT SAYING A WORD, AS I WATCHED.
WATCHING MY BROTHER...

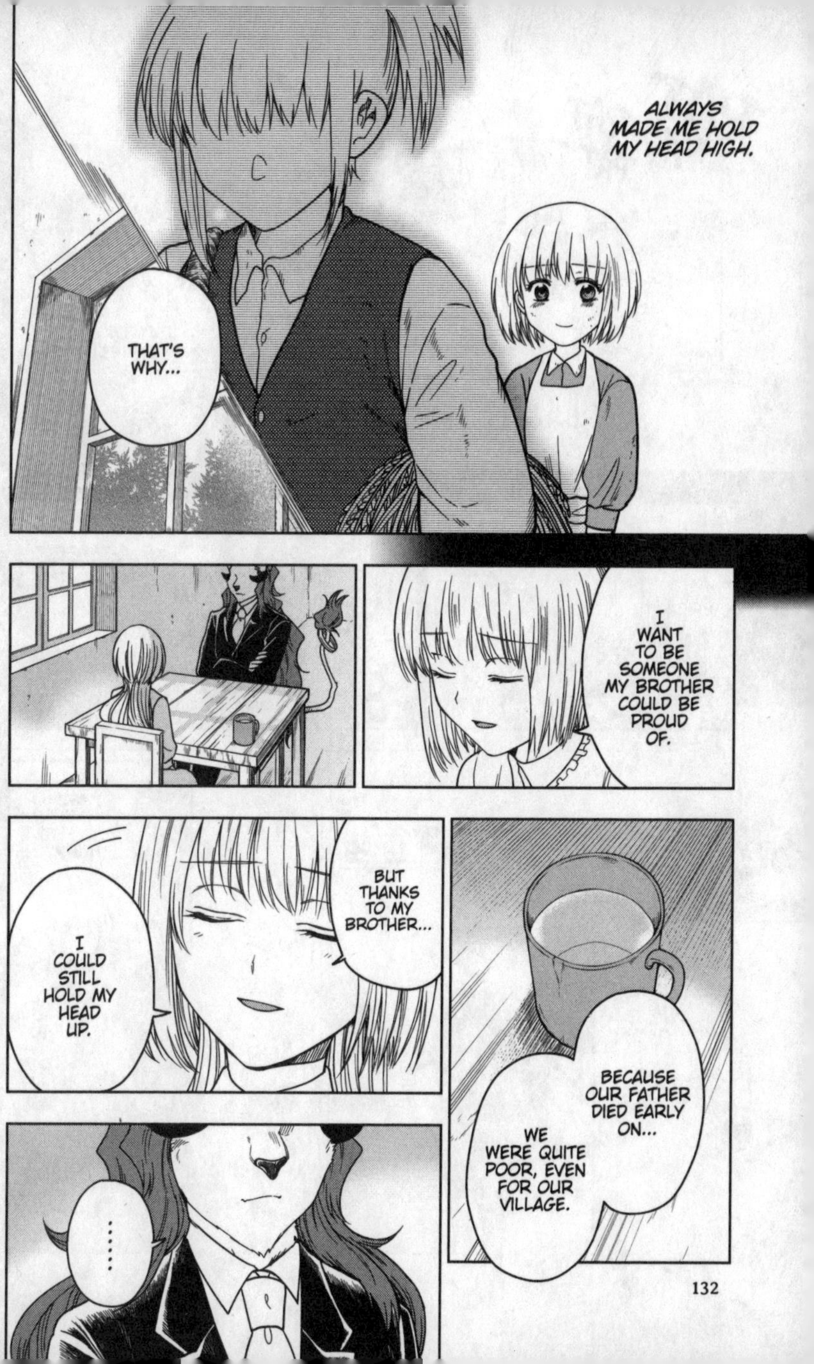
ALWAYS MADE ME HOLD MY HEAD HIGH.
THAT'S WHY...
I WANT TO BE SOMEONE MY BROTHER COULD BE PROUD OF.
BECAUSE OUR FATHER DIED EARLY ON...
WE WERE QUITE POOR, EVEN FOR OUR VILLAGE.
BUT THANKS TO MY BROTHER...
I COULD STILL HOLD MY HEAD UP.
......

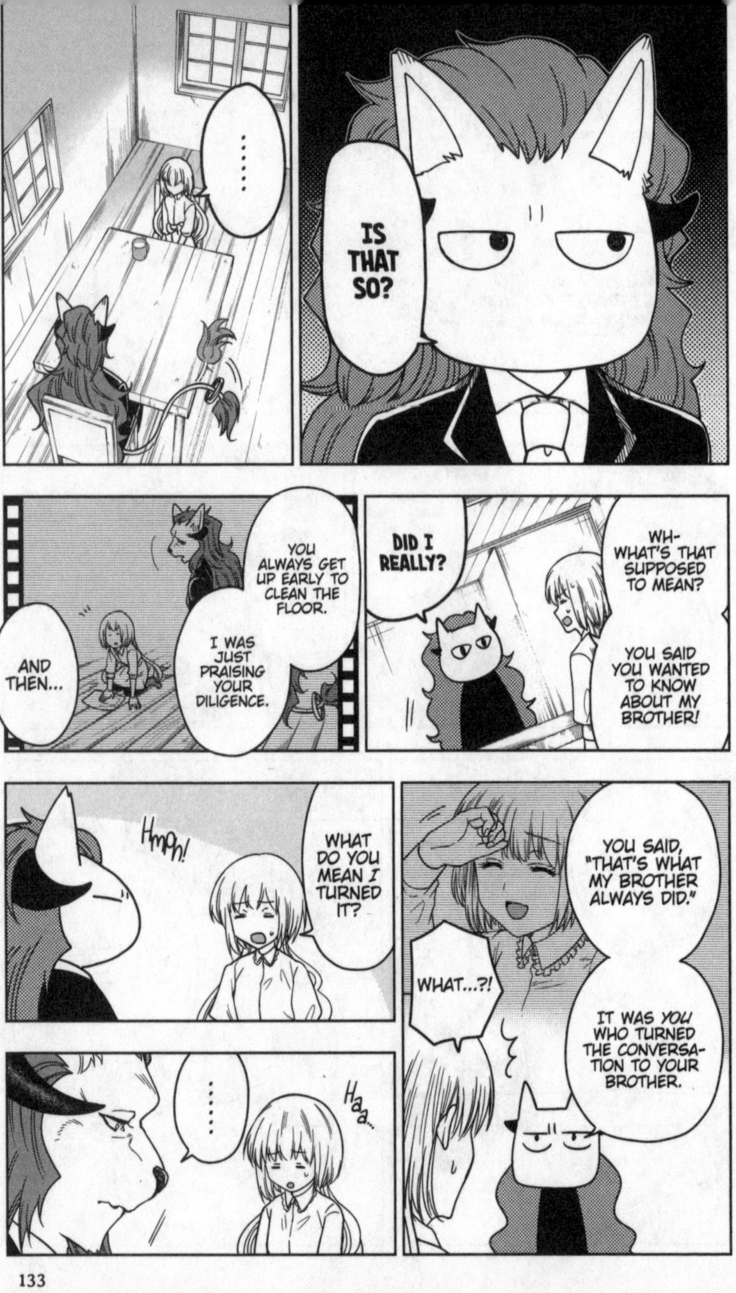
IS THAT SO?
......
WH-WHAT'S THAT SUPPOSED TO MEAN?
YOU SAID YOU WANTED TO KNOW ABOUT MY BROTHER!
DID I REALLY?
YOU ALWAYS GET UP EARLY TO CLEAN THE FLOOR.
I WAS JUST PRAISING YOUR DILIGENCE.
AND THEN...
YOU SAID, "THAT'S WHAT MY BROTHER ALWAYS DID."
WHAT...?!
IT WAS *YOU* WHO TURNED THE CONVERSA-TION TO YOUR BROTHER.
WHAT DO YOU MEAN *I* TURNED IT?
Hmph!
......
Haa...

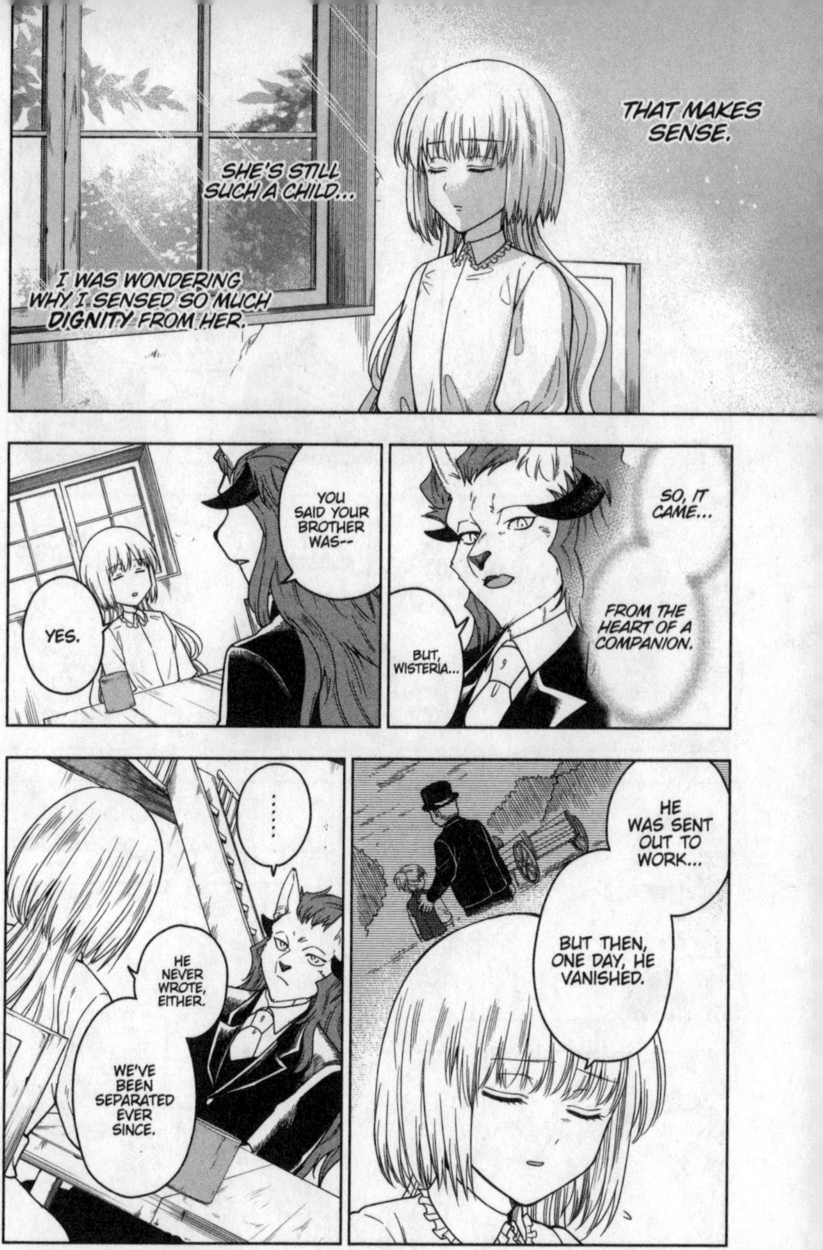
THAT MAKES SENSE.
SHE'S STILL SUCH A CHILD...
I WAS WONDERING WHY I SENSED SO MUCH DIGNITY FROM HER.
SO, IT CAME...
FROM THE HEART OF A COMPANION.
BUT, WISTERIA...
YOU SAID YOUR BROTHER WAS--
YES.
HE WAS SENT OUT TO WORK...
BUT THEN, ONE DAY, HE VANISHED.
......
HE NEVER WROTE, EITHER.
WE'VE BEEN SEPARATED EVER SINCE.

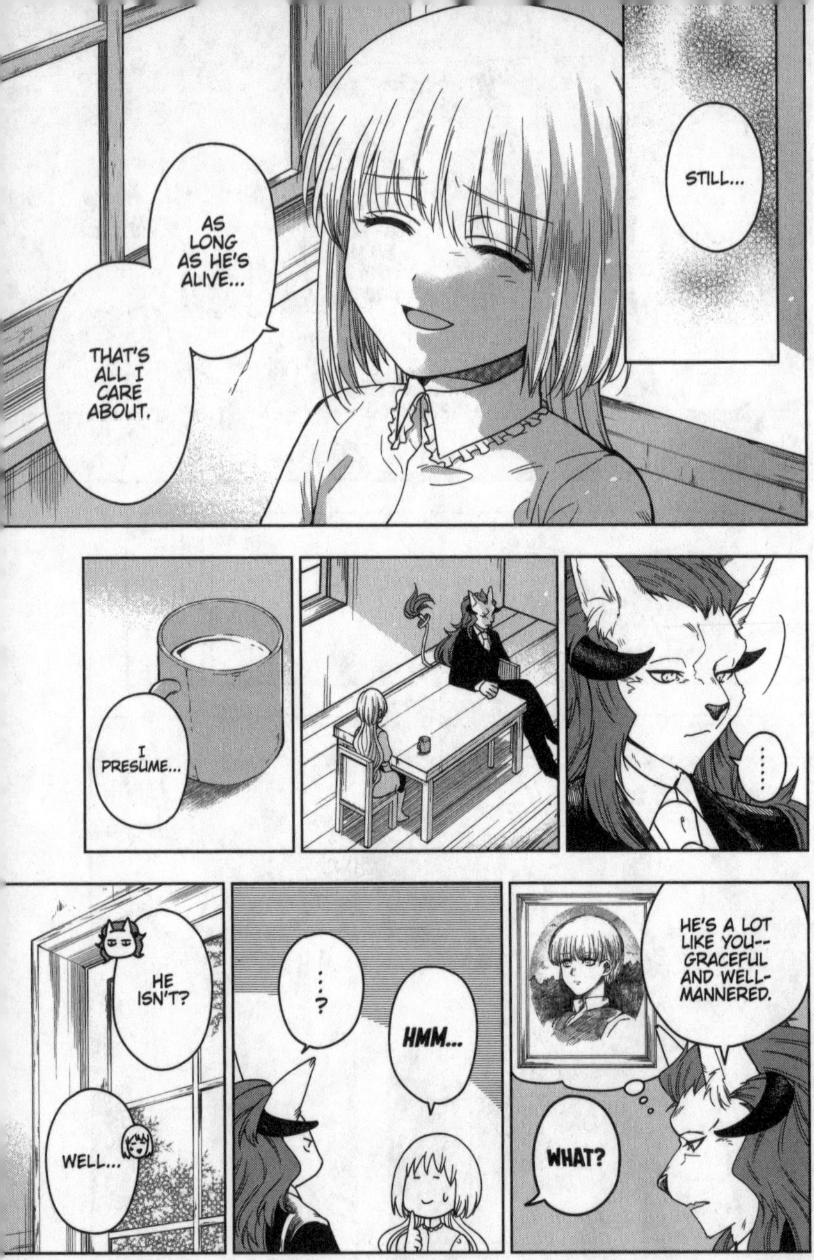
STILL...
AS LONG AS HE'S ALIVE...
THAT'S ALL I CARE ABOUT.
......
I PRESUME...
HE'S A LOT LIKE YOU-- GRACEFUL AND WELL-MANNERED.
WHAT?
...?
HMM...
HE ISN'T?
WELL...

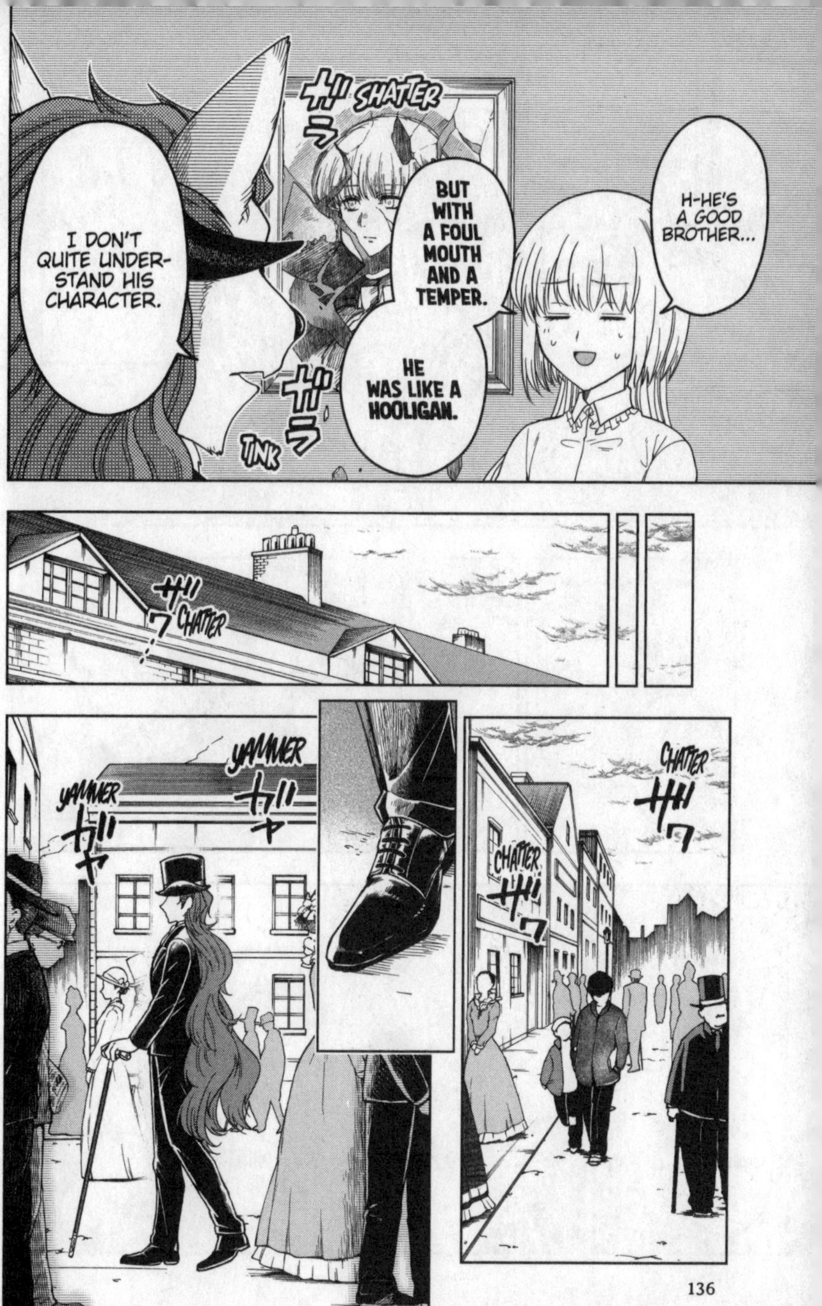
SHATTER
H-HE'S A GOOD BROTHER...
BUT WITH A FOUL MOUTH AND A TEMPER.
HE WAS LIKE A HOOLIGAN.
TINK
I DON'T QUITE UNDER-STAND HIS CHARACTER.
CHATTER
CHATTER
CHATTER
YAMMER
YAMMER

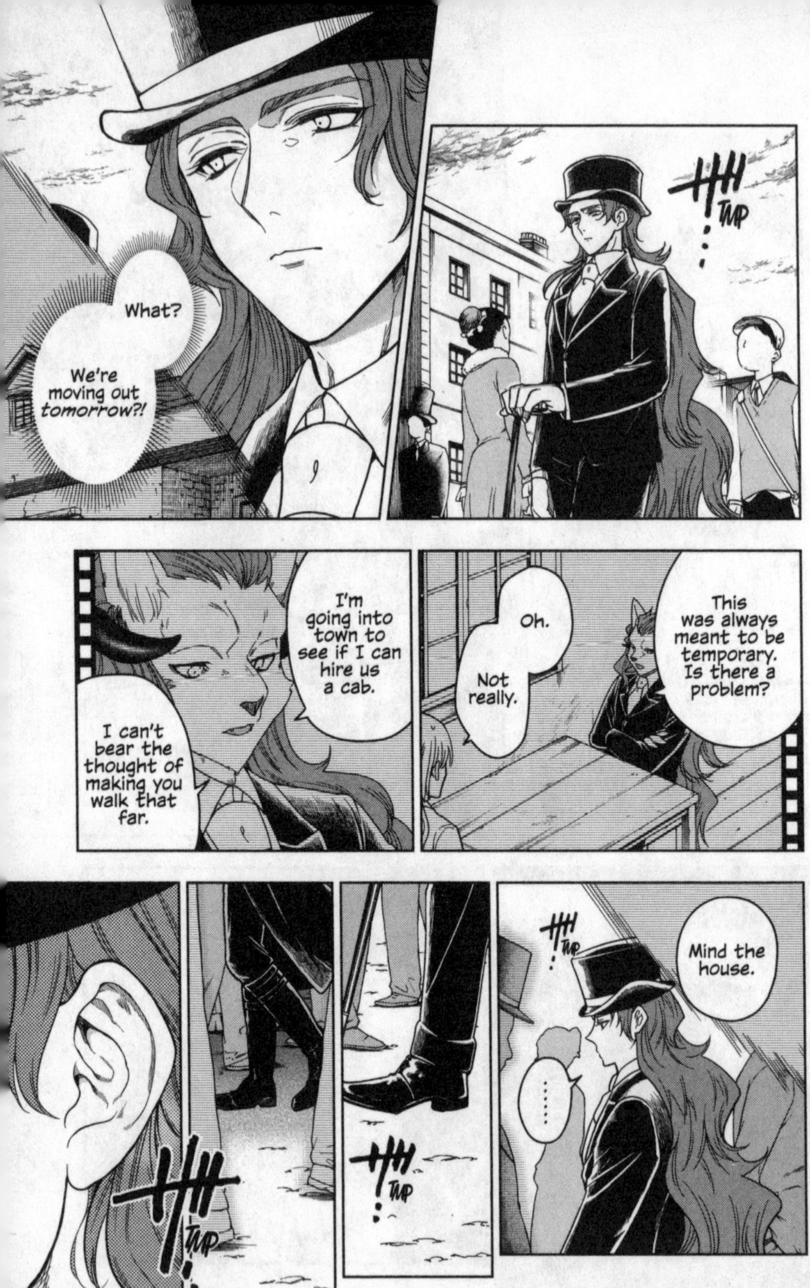
TMP
What?
We're moving out *tomorrow*?!
This was always meant to be temporary. Is there a problem?
Oh.
Not really.
I'm going into town to see if I can hire us a cab.
I can't bear the thought of making you walk that far.
Mind the house.
......
TMP
TMP
TMP

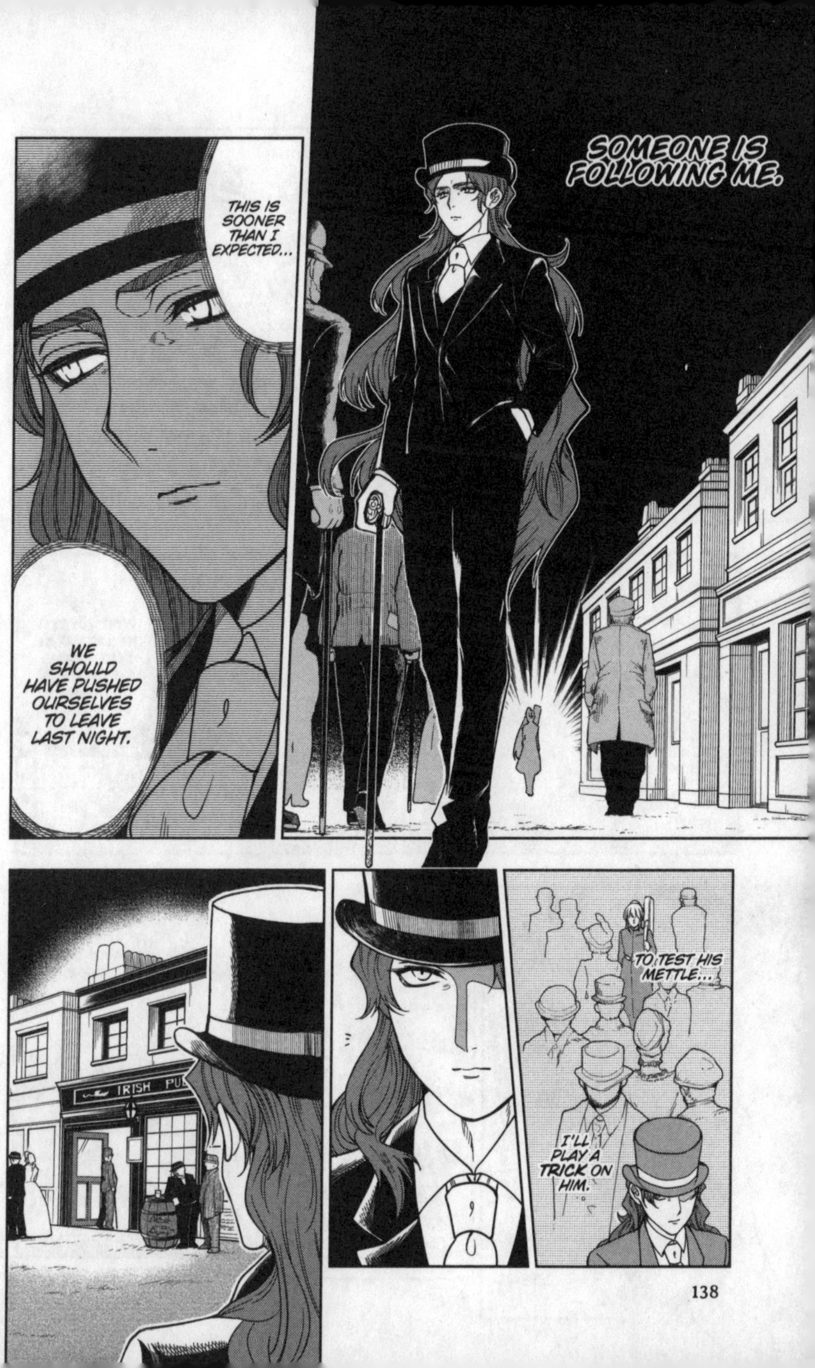
SOMEONE IS FOLLOWING ME.
THIS IS SOONER THAN I EXPECTED...
WE SHOULD HAVE PUSHED OURSELVES TO LEAVE LAST NIGHT.
TO TEST HIS METTLE...
I'LL PLAY A TRICK ON HIM.
IRISH PU

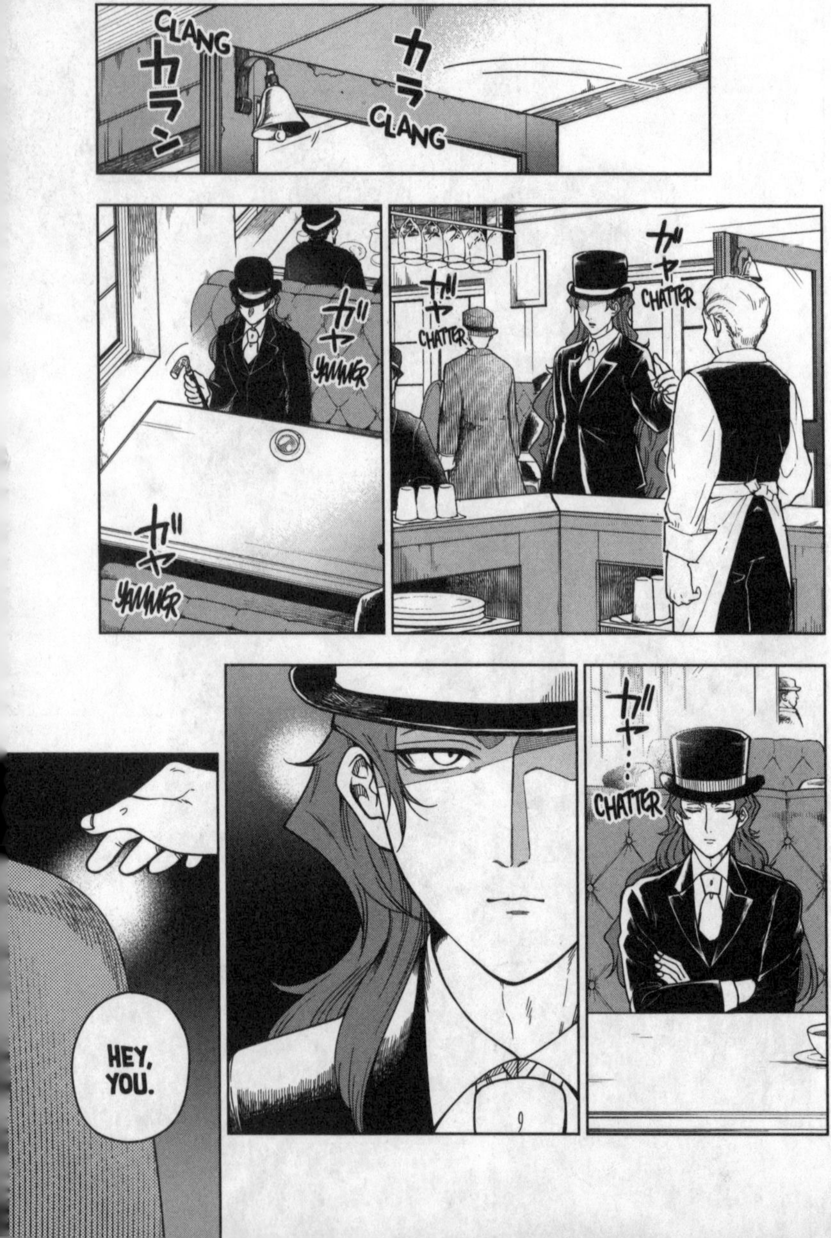
カラ
CLANG
CLANG
カラン
ガヤ
CHATTER
ガヤ
CHATTER
ガヤ
YAMMER
ガヤ
YAMMER
ガヤ…
CHATTER
HEY, YOU.

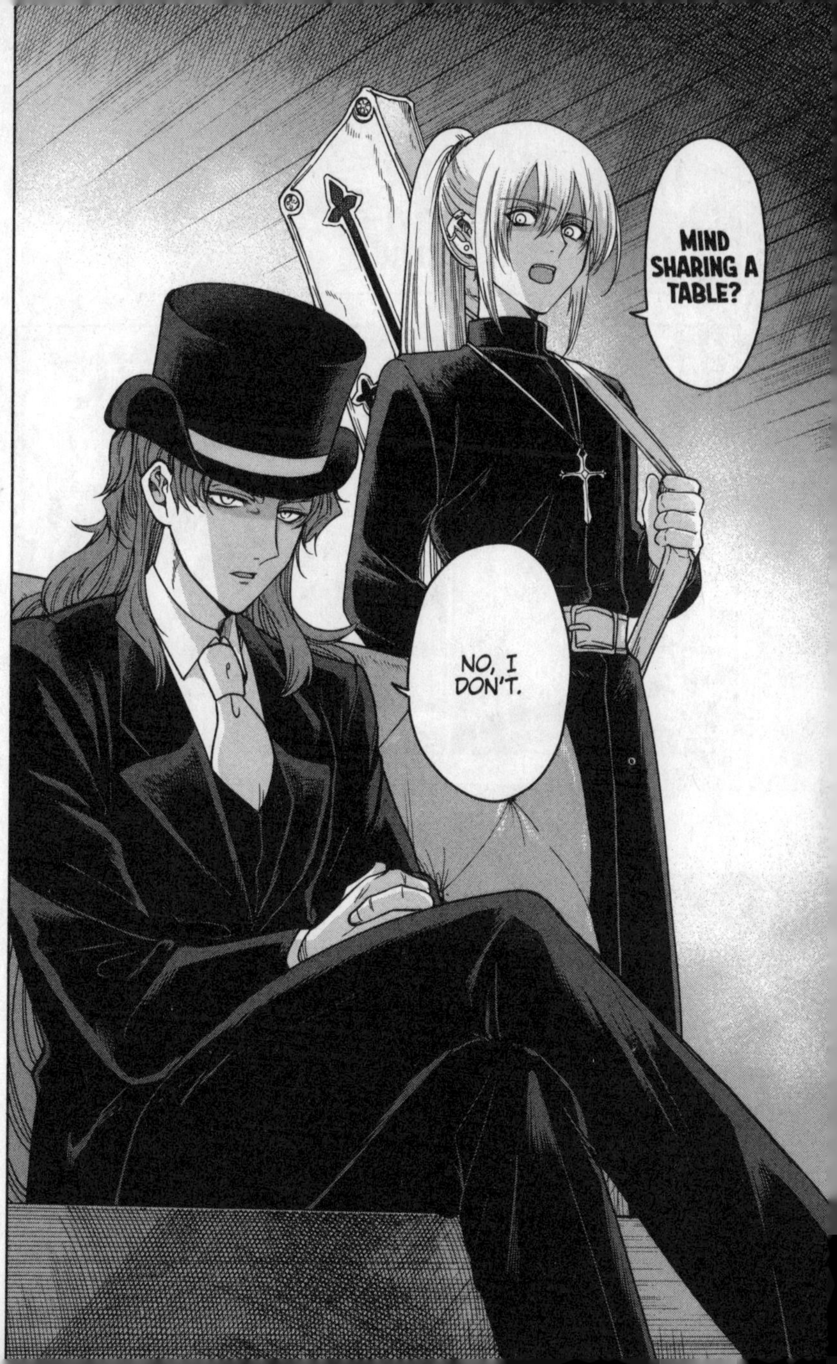
MIND SHARING A TABLE?
NO, I DON'T.

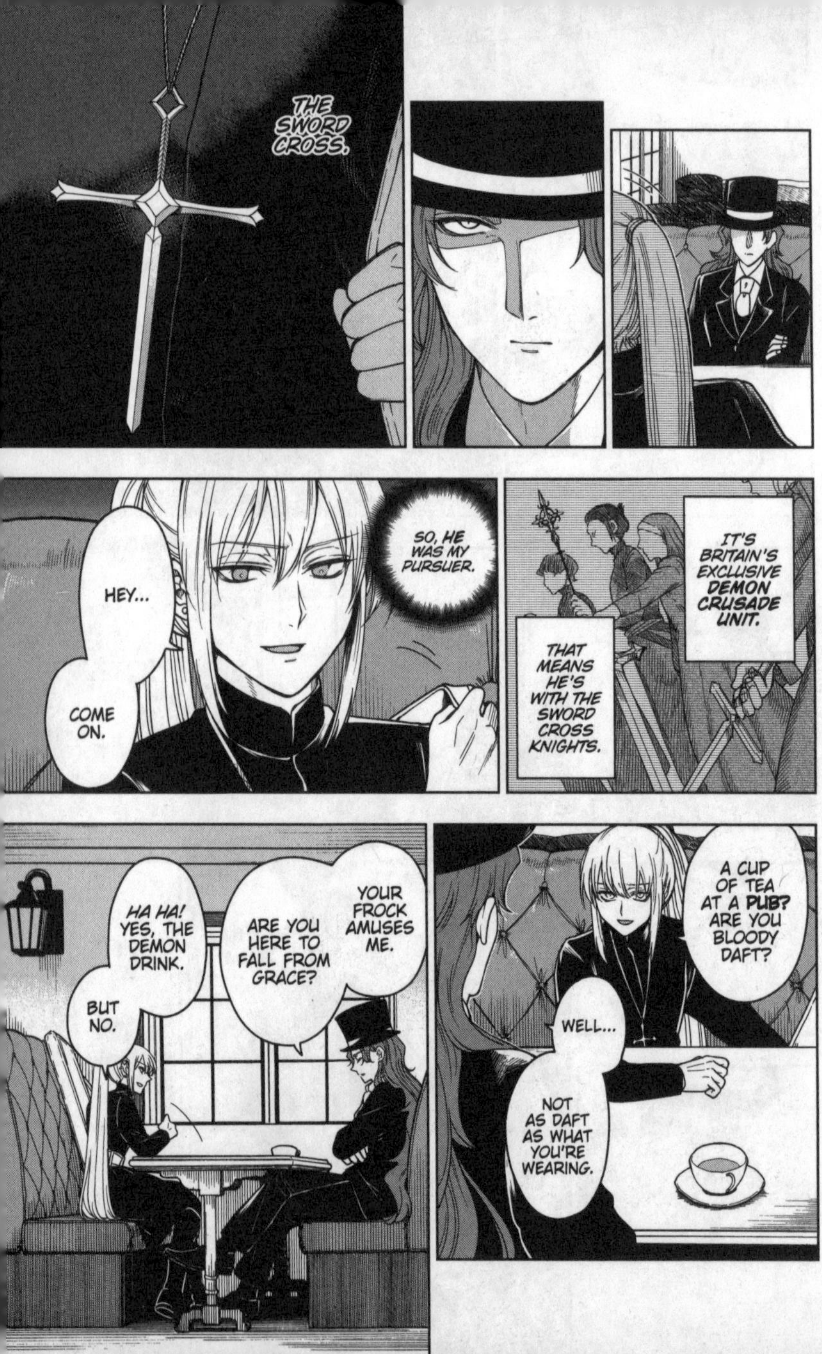
THE SWORD CROSS.
IT'S BRITAIN'S EXCLUSIVE DEMON CRUSADE UNIT.
THAT MEANS HE'S WITH THE SWORD CROSS KNIGHTS.
SO, HE WAS MY PURSUER.
HEY...
COME ON.
A CUP OF TEA AT A PUB? ARE YOU BLOODY DAFT?
WELL...
NOT AS DAFT AS WHAT YOU'RE WEARING.
YOUR FROCK AMUSES ME.
ARE YOU HERE TO FALL FROM GRACE?
HA HA! YES, THE DEMON DRINK.
BUT NO.

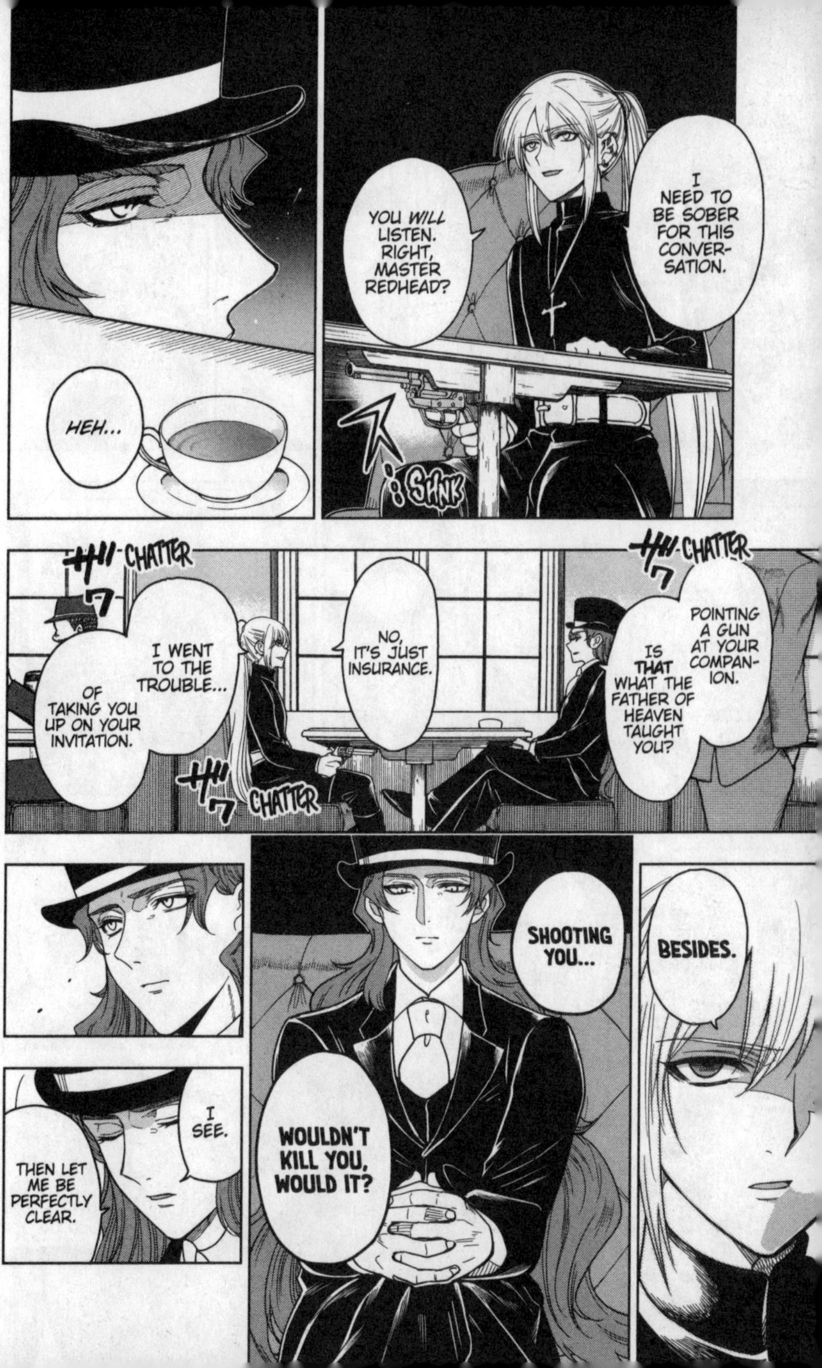
I NEED TO BE SOBER FOR THIS CONVERSATION.
YOU *WILL* LISTEN. RIGHT, MASTER REDHEAD?
SHNK
HEH...
CHATTER
POINTING A GUN AT YOUR COMPANION.
IS **THAT** WHAT THE FATHER OF HEAVEN TAUGHT YOU?
NO, IT'S JUST INSURANCE.
CHATTER
I WENT TO THE TROUBLE...
OF TAKING YOU UP ON YOUR INVITATION.
CHATTER
BESIDES.
SHOOTING YOU...
WOULDN'T KILL YOU, WOULD IT?
I SEE.
THEN LET ME BE PERFECTLY CLEAR.

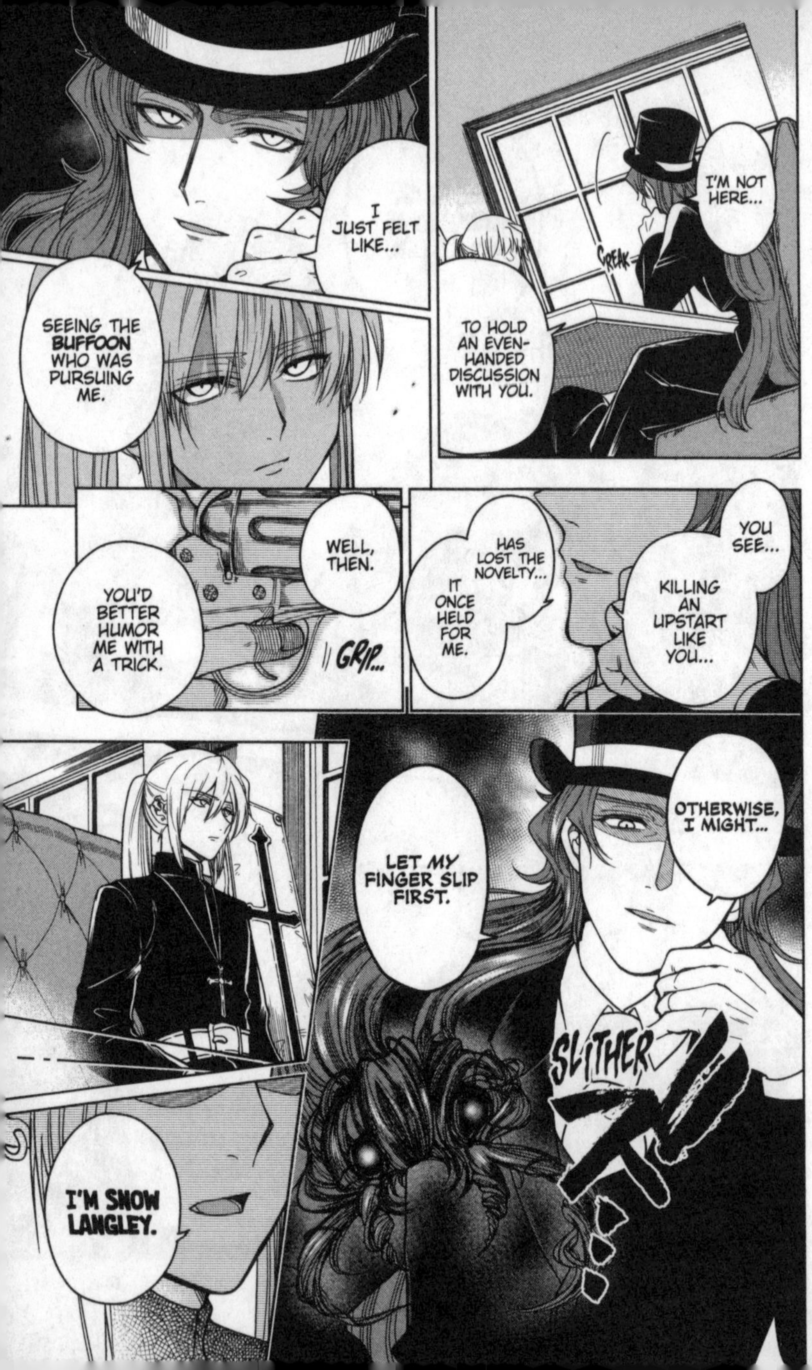
I'M NOT HERE...
CREAK
TO HOLD AN EVEN-HANDED DISCUSSION WITH YOU.
I JUST FELT LIKE...
SEEING THE BUFFOON WHO WAS PURSUING ME.
YOU SEE...
KILLING AN UPSTART LIKE YOU...
HAS LOST THE NOVELTY...
IT ONCE HELD FOR ME.
WELL, THEN.
GRIP...
YOU'D BETTER HUMOR ME WITH A TRICK.
OTHERWISE, I MIGHT...
LET MY FINGER SLIP FIRST.
SLITHER
I'M SNOW LANGLEY.

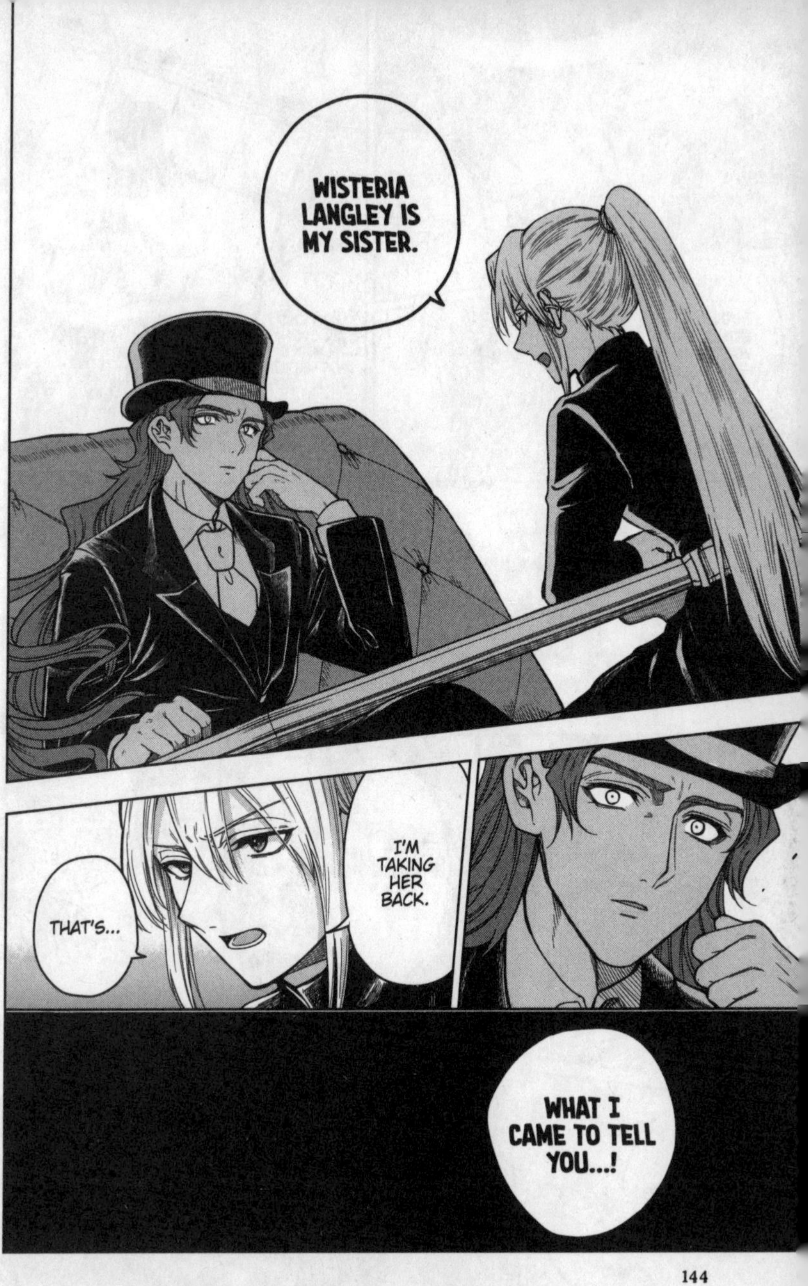
WISTERIA LANGLEY IS MY SISTER.
I'M TAKING HER BACK.
THAT'S...
WHAT I CAME TO TELL YOU...!

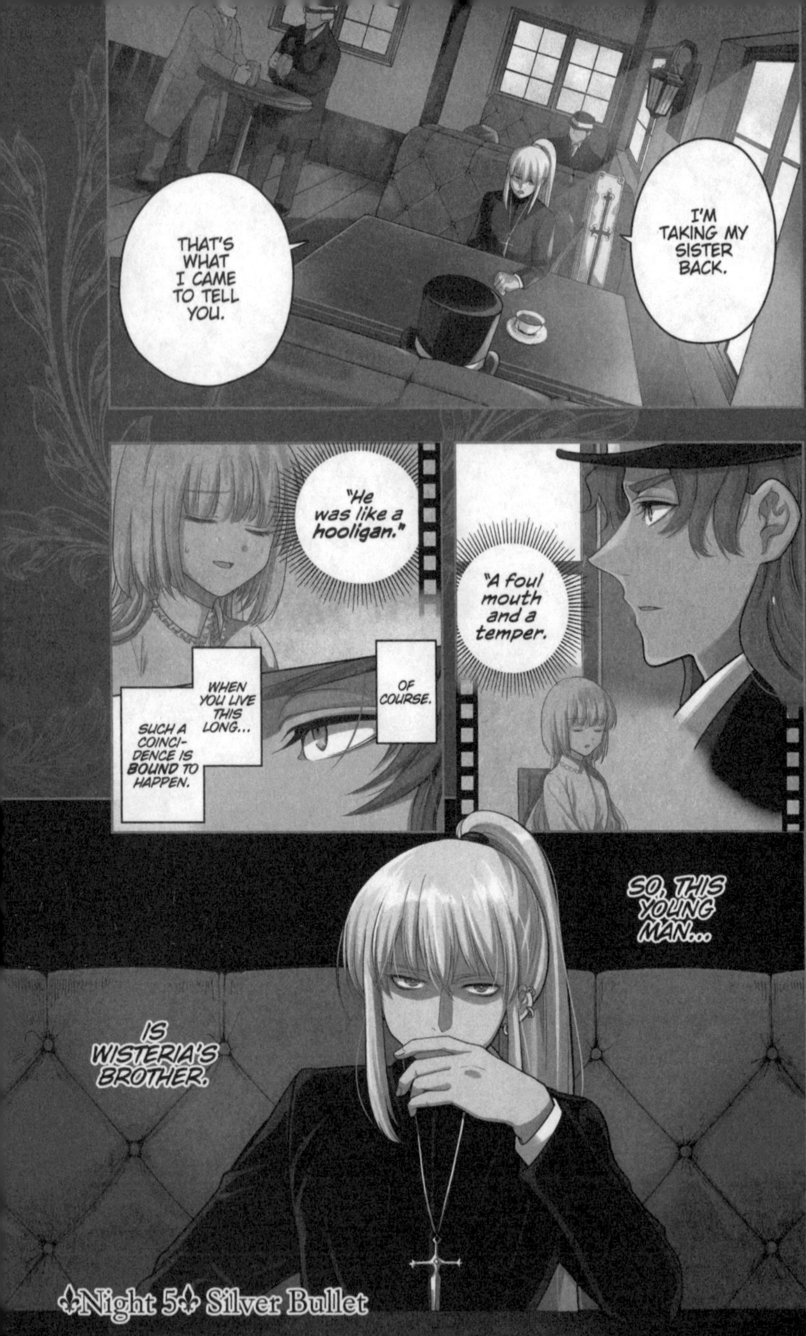
I'M TAKING MY SISTER BACK.
THAT'S WHAT I CAME TO TELL YOU.
"A foul mouth and a temper.
"He was like a hooligan."
OF COURSE.
WHEN YOU LIVE THIS LONG...
SUCH A COINCI-DENCE IS BOUND TO HAPPEN.
SO, THIS YOUNG MAN...
IS WISTERIA'S BROTHER.
Night 5 Silver Bullet

Night 5 Silver Bullet

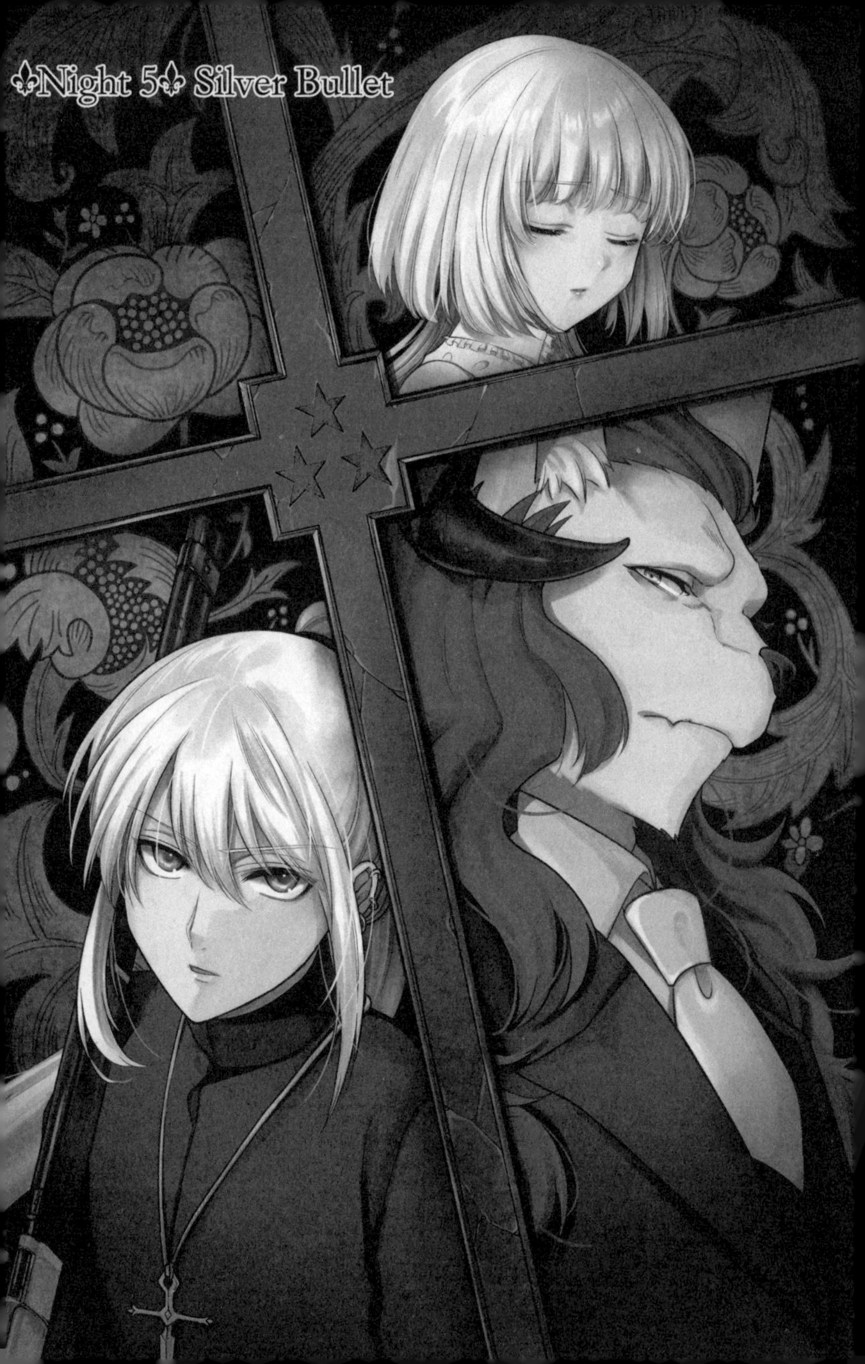

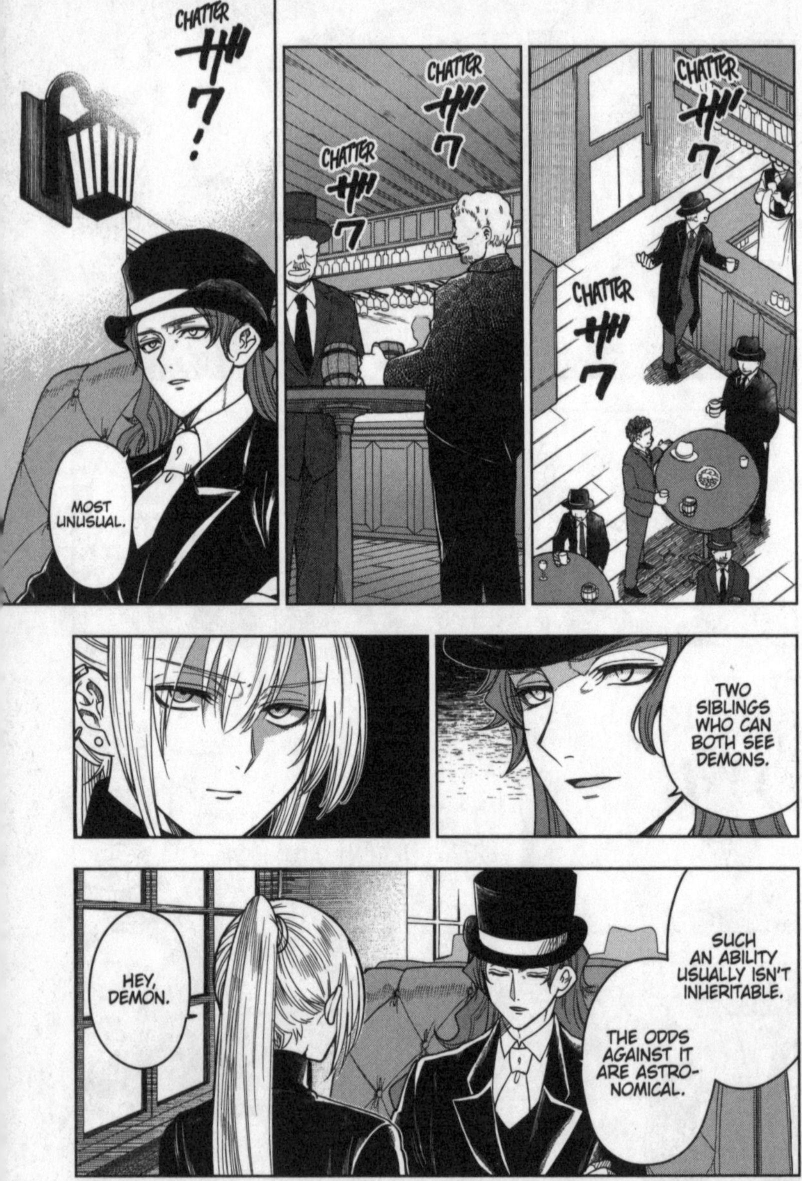
CHATTER
CHATTER
CHATTER
CHATTER
CHATTER
MOST UNUSUAL.
TWO SIBLINGS WHO CAN BOTH SEE DEMONS.
SUCH AN ABILITY USUALLY ISN'T INHERITABLE.
THE ODDS AGAINST IT ARE ASTRO-NOMICAL.
HEY, DEMON.

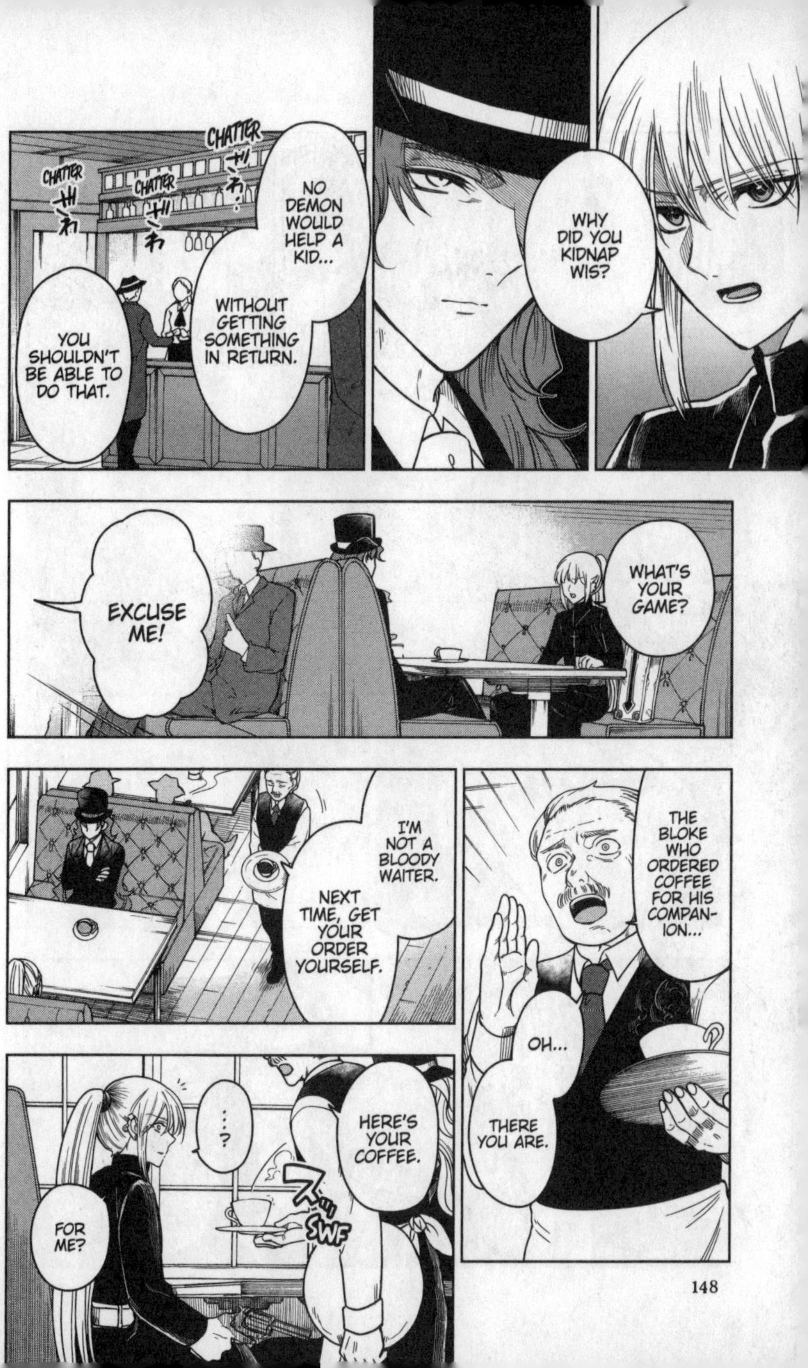
WHY DID YOU KIDNAP WIS?
CHATTER
CHATTER
CHATTER
NO DEMON WOULD HELP A KID...
WITHOUT GETTING SOMETHING IN RETURN.
YOU SHOULDN'T BE ABLE TO DO THAT.
WHAT'S YOUR GAME?
EXCUSE ME!
THE BLOKE WHO ORDERED COFFEE FOR HIS COMPANION...
OH...
THERE YOU ARE.
I'M NOT A BLOODY WAITER.
NEXT TIME, GET YOUR ORDER YOURSELF.
HERE'S YOUR COFFEE.
SWF
...?
FOR ME?

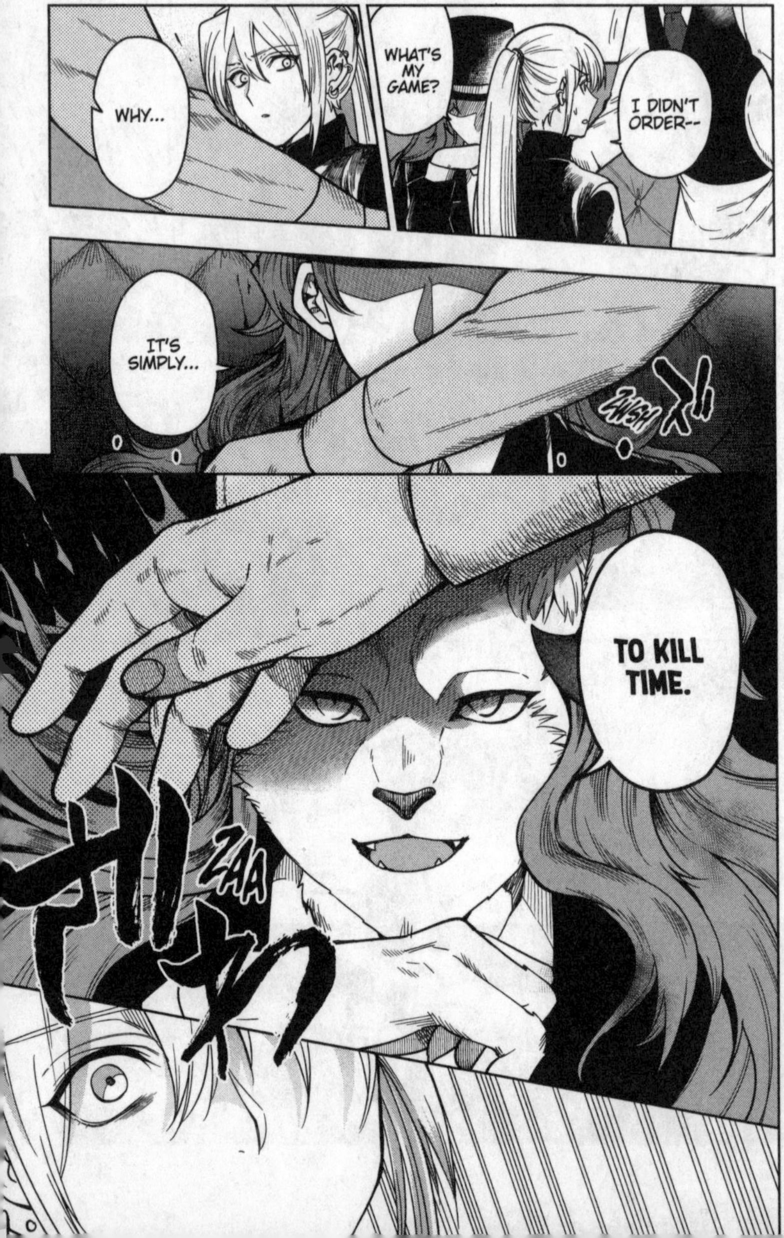
I DIDN'T ORDER--
WHAT'S MY GAME?
WHY...
IT'S SIMPLY...
ZWSH
TO KILL TIME.
ZAA

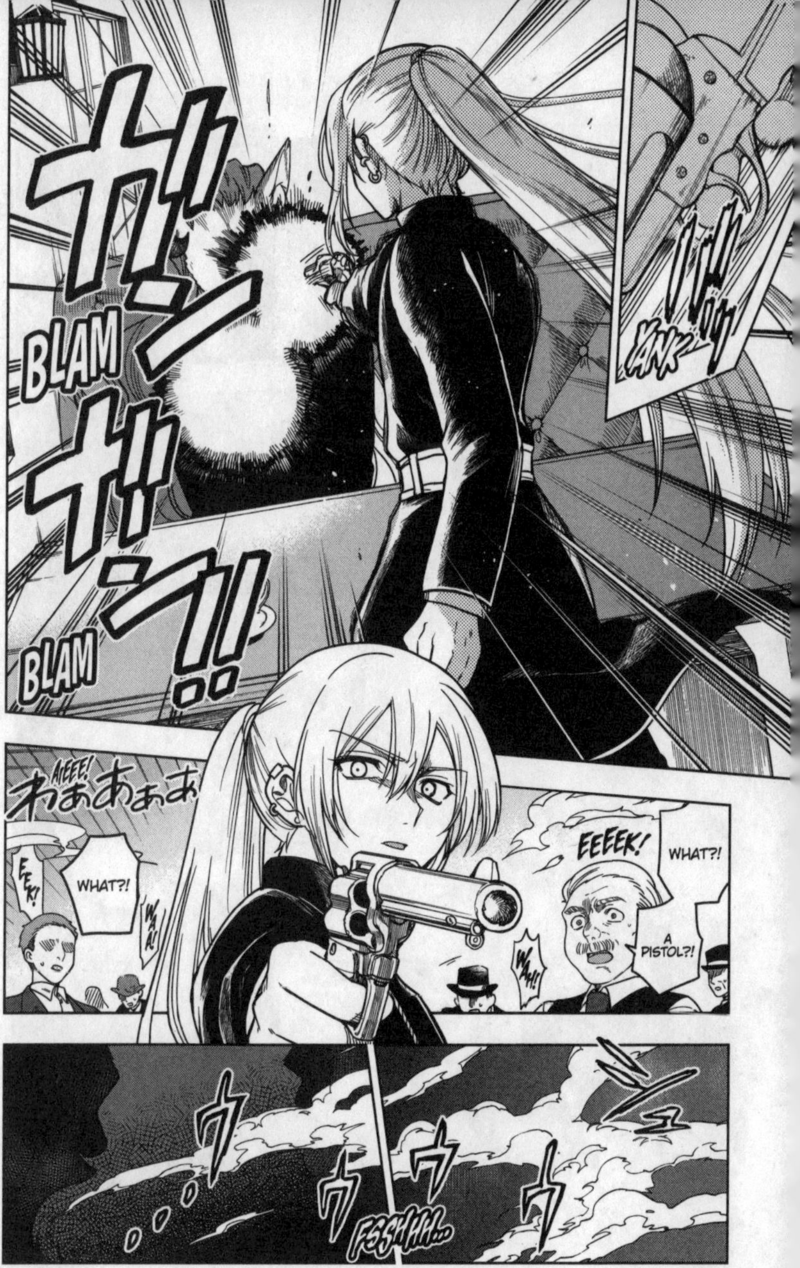
YANK
BLAM
BLAM
EEEEK!
WHAT?!
A PISTOL?!
WAH!
WAA!
WHAT?!
EEK!
AIEEE!
FSSHHH...

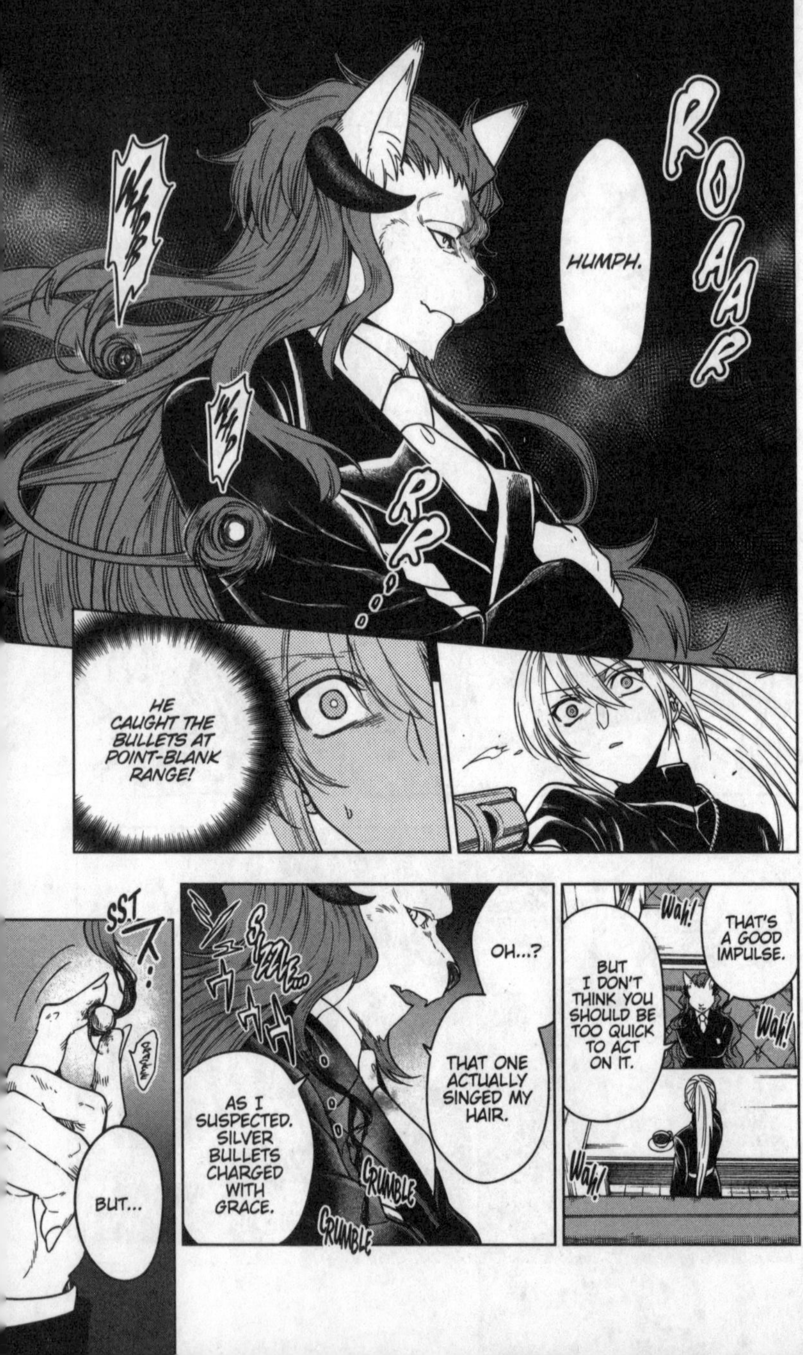
ROAAR
HUMPH.
RR...
HE CAUGHT THE BULLETS AT POINT-BLANK RANGE!
THAT'S A GOOD IMPULSE.
Wah!
BUT I DON'T THINK YOU SHOULD BE TOO QUICK TO ACT ON IT.
Wah!
Wah!
OH...?
SIZZLE...
THAT ONE ACTUALLY SINGED MY HAIR.
AS I SUSPECTED. SILVER BULLETS CHARGED WITH GRACE.
CRUMBLE
CRUMBLE
SST
BUT...

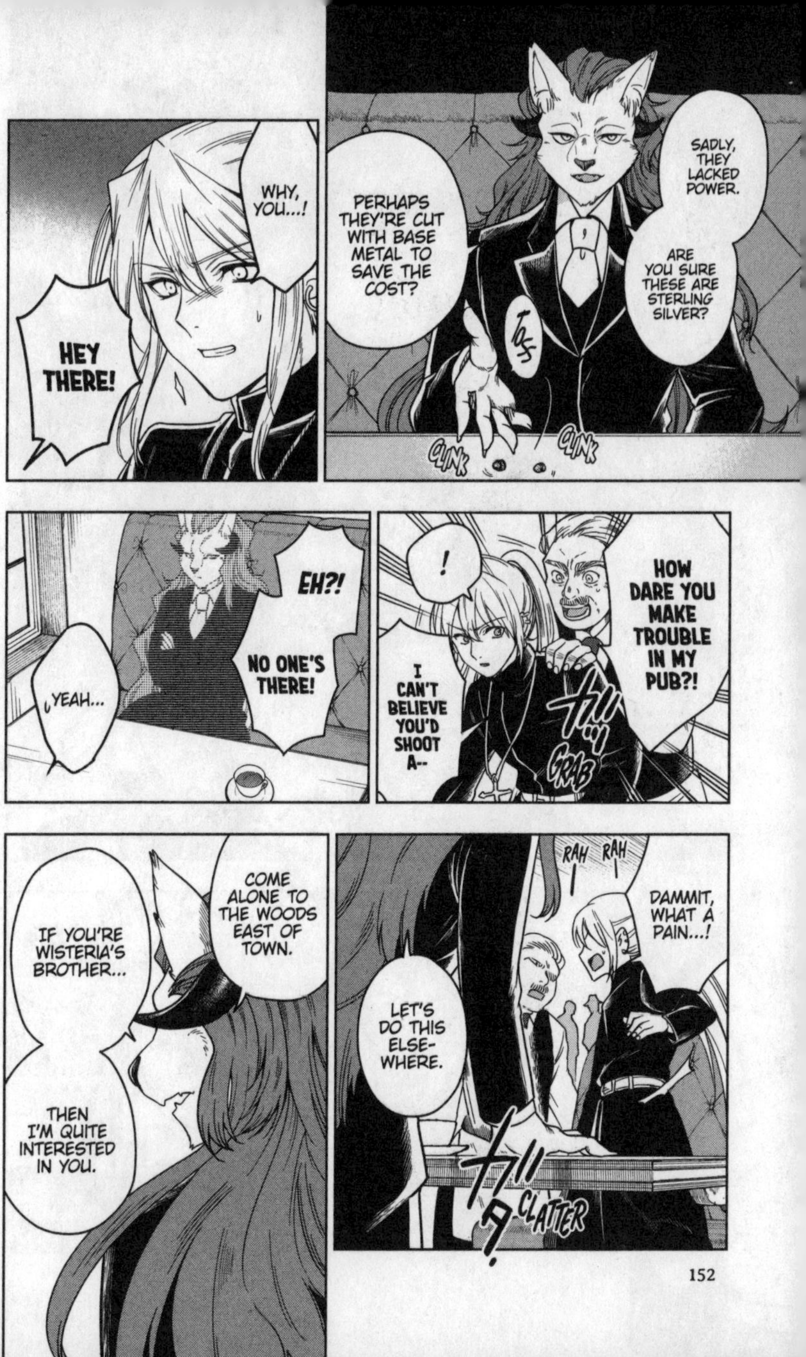
SADLY, THEY LACKED POWER.
ARE YOU SURE THESE ARE STERLING SILVER?
PERHAPS THEY'RE CUT WITH BASE METAL TO SAVE THE COST?
CLINK
CLINK
WHY, YOU...!
HEY THERE!
HOW DARE YOU MAKE TROUBLE IN MY PUB?!
!
I CAN'T BELIEVE YOU'D SHOOT A--
GRAB
EH?!
NO ONE'S THERE!
YEAH...
RAH RAH
DAMMIT, WHAT A PAIN...!
LET'S DO THIS ELSE-WHERE.
CLATTER
COME ALONE TO THE WOODS EAST OF TOWN.
IF YOU'RE WISTERIA'S BROTHER...
THEN I'M QUITE INTERESTED IN YOU.

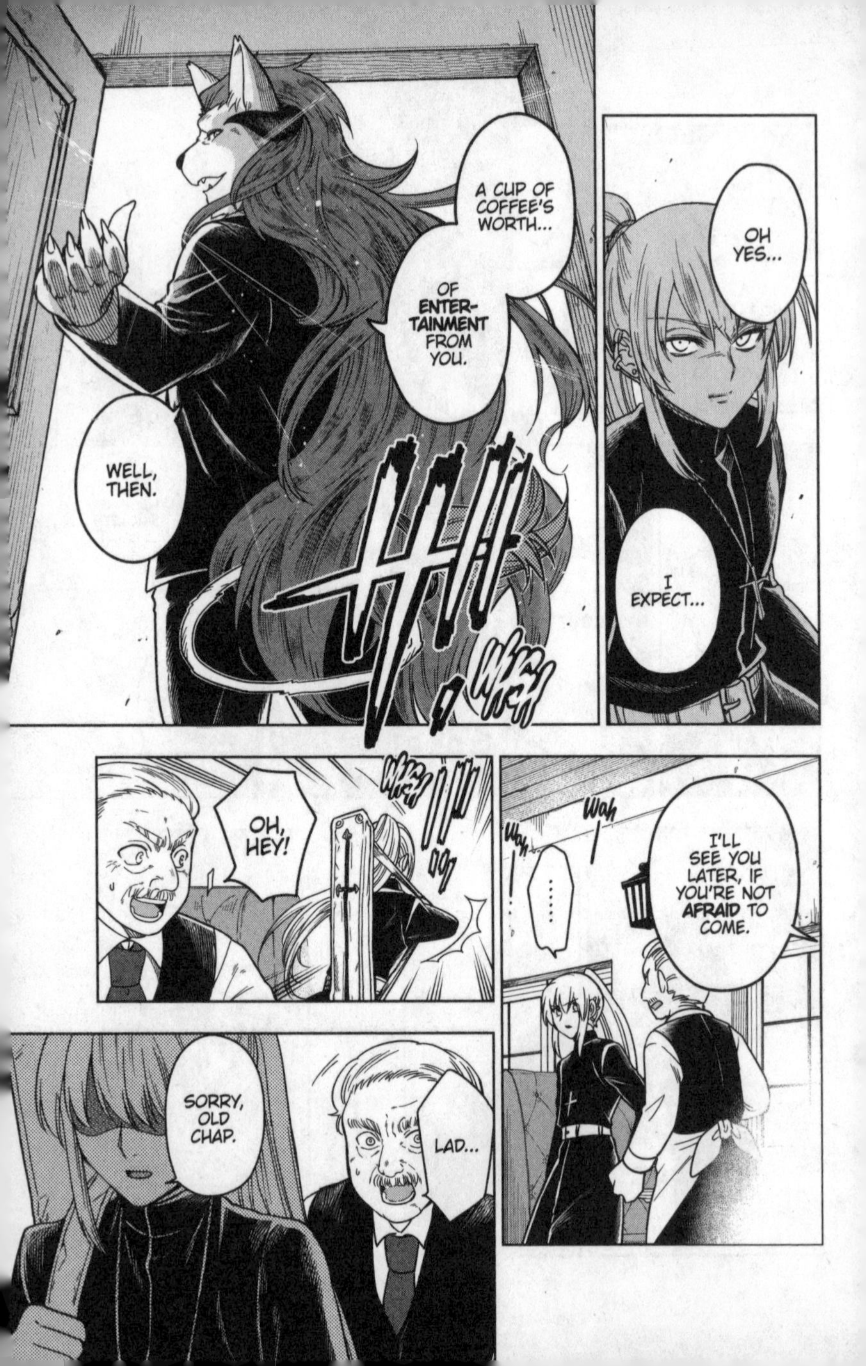
OH YES...
I EXPECT...
A CUP OF COFFEE'S WORTH...
OF ENTERTAINMENT FROM YOU.
WELL, THEN.
I'LL SEE YOU LATER, IF YOU'RE NOT **AFRAID** TO COME.
Wah!
Wah!
......
OH, HEY!
LAD...
SORRY, OLD CHAP.

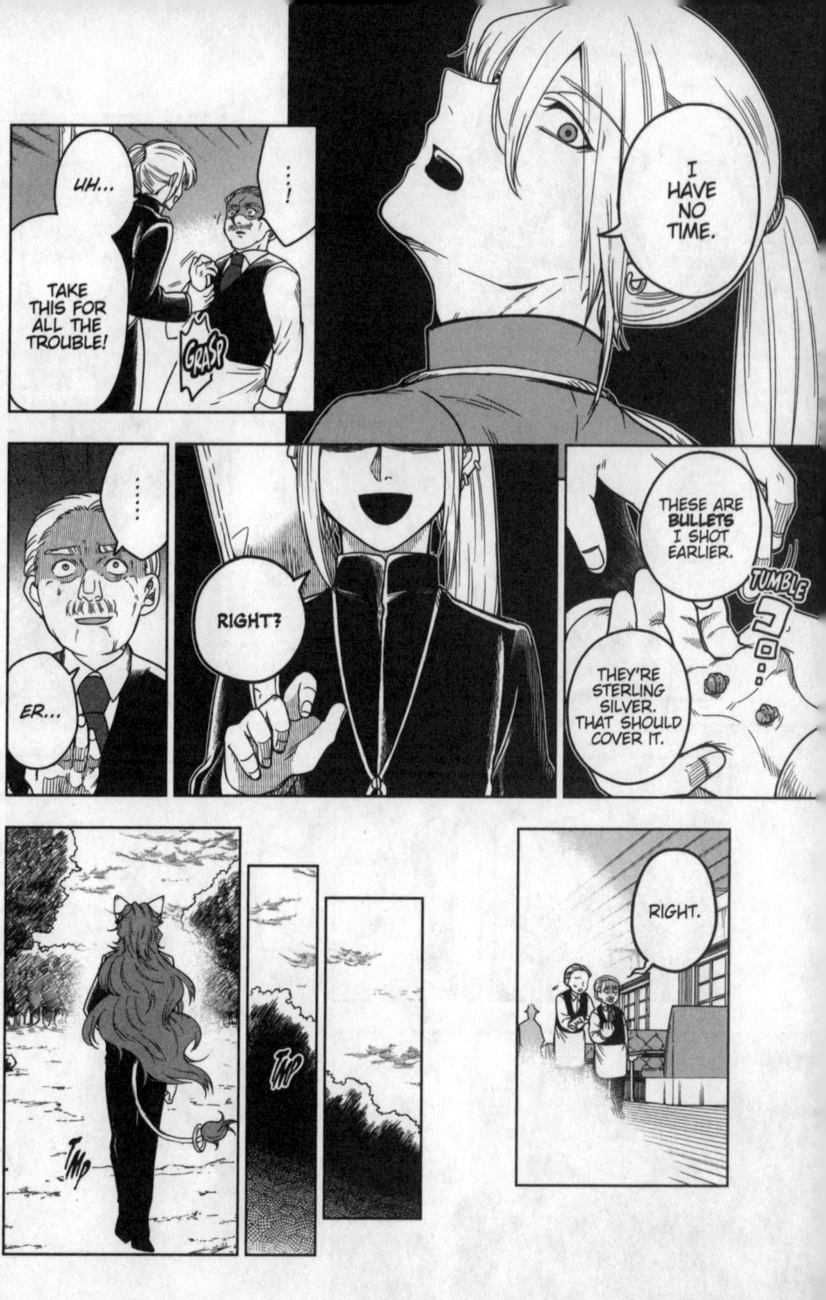
I HAVE NO TIME.
...!
UH...
TAKE THIS FOR ALL THE TROUBLE!
GRASP
THESE ARE BULLETS I SHOT EARLIER.
TUMBLE
THEY'RE STERLING SILVER. THAT SHOULD COVER IT.
RIGHT?
......
ER...
RIGHT.
TMP
TMP

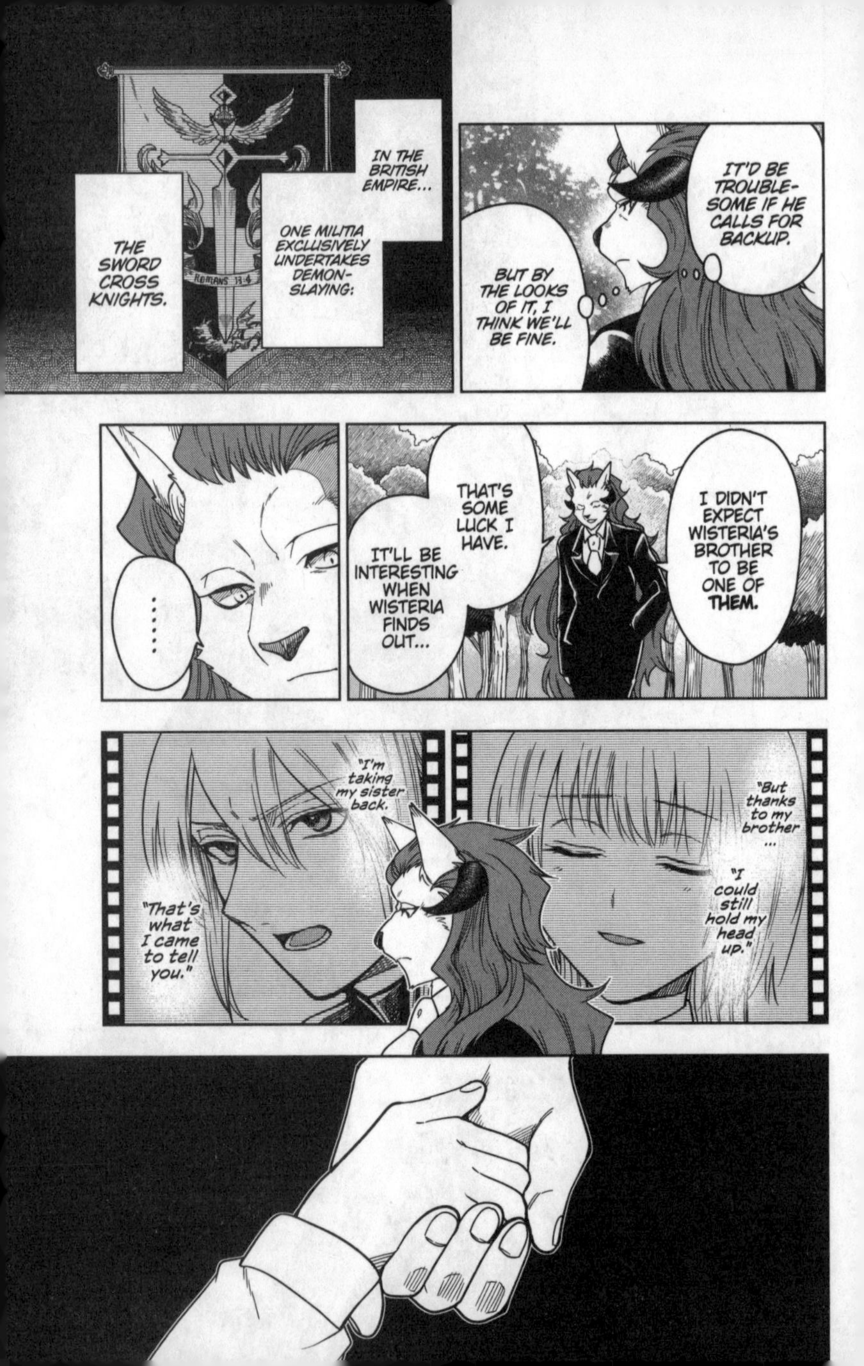
IT'D BE TROUBLESOME IF HE CALLS FOR BACKUP.
BUT BY THE LOOKS OF IT, I THINK WE'LL BE FINE.
IN THE BRITISH EMPIRE...
ONE MILITIA EXCLUSIVELY UNDERTAKES DEMON-SLAYING:
ROMANS 13:4
THE SWORD CROSS KNIGHTS.
I DIDN'T EXPECT WISTERIA'S BROTHER TO BE ONE OF **THEM.**
THAT'S SOME LUCK I HAVE.
IT'LL BE INTERESTING WHEN WISTERIA FINDS OUT...
......
"But thanks to my brother...
"I could still hold my head up."
"I'm taking my sister back.
"That's what I came to tell you."

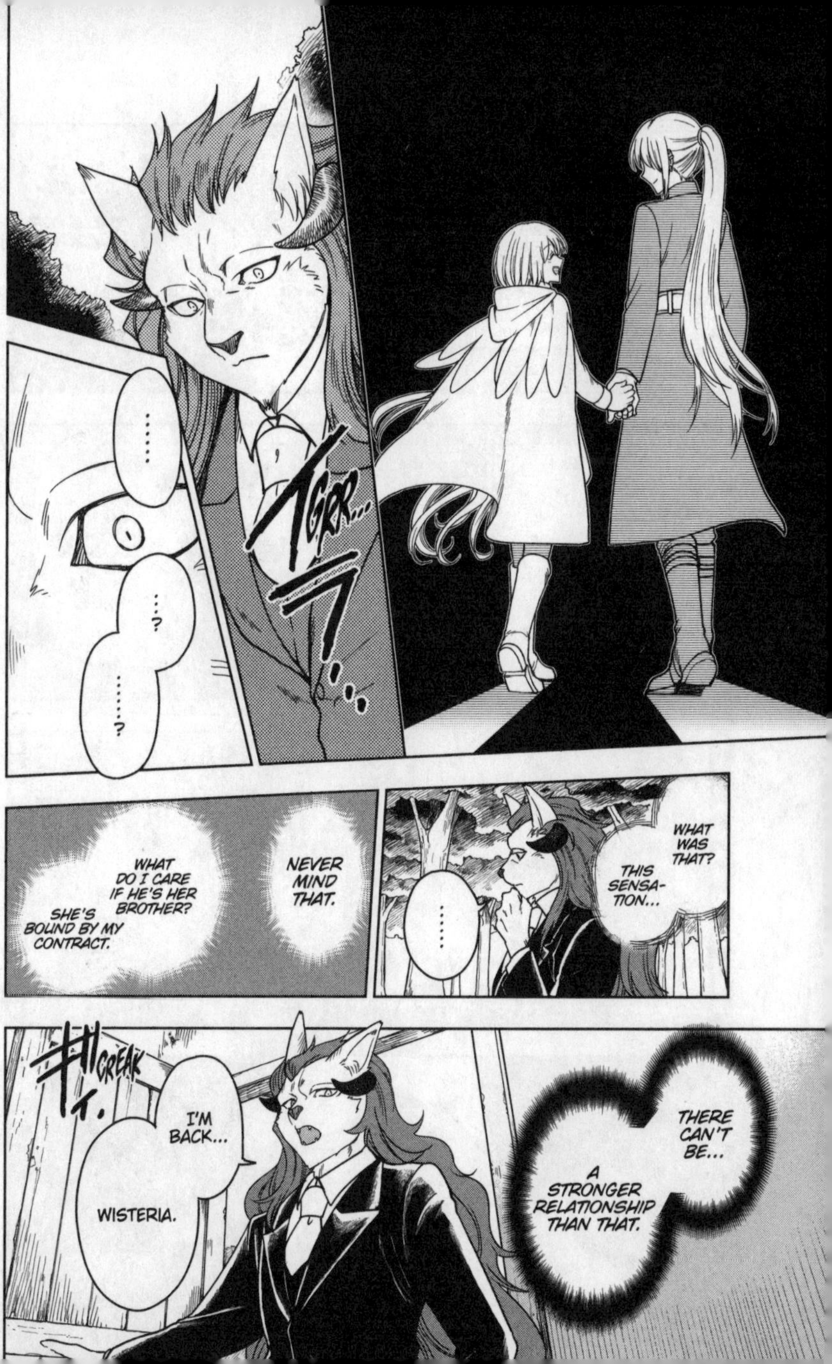
GRR...
......
...?
......?
WHAT WAS THAT?
THIS SENSATION...
......
NEVER MIND THAT.
WHAT DO I CARE IF HE'S HER BROTHER?
SHE'S BOUND BY MY CONTRACT.
THERE CAN'T BE...
A STRONGER RELATIONSHIP THAN THAT.
CREAK
I'M BACK...
WISTERIA.

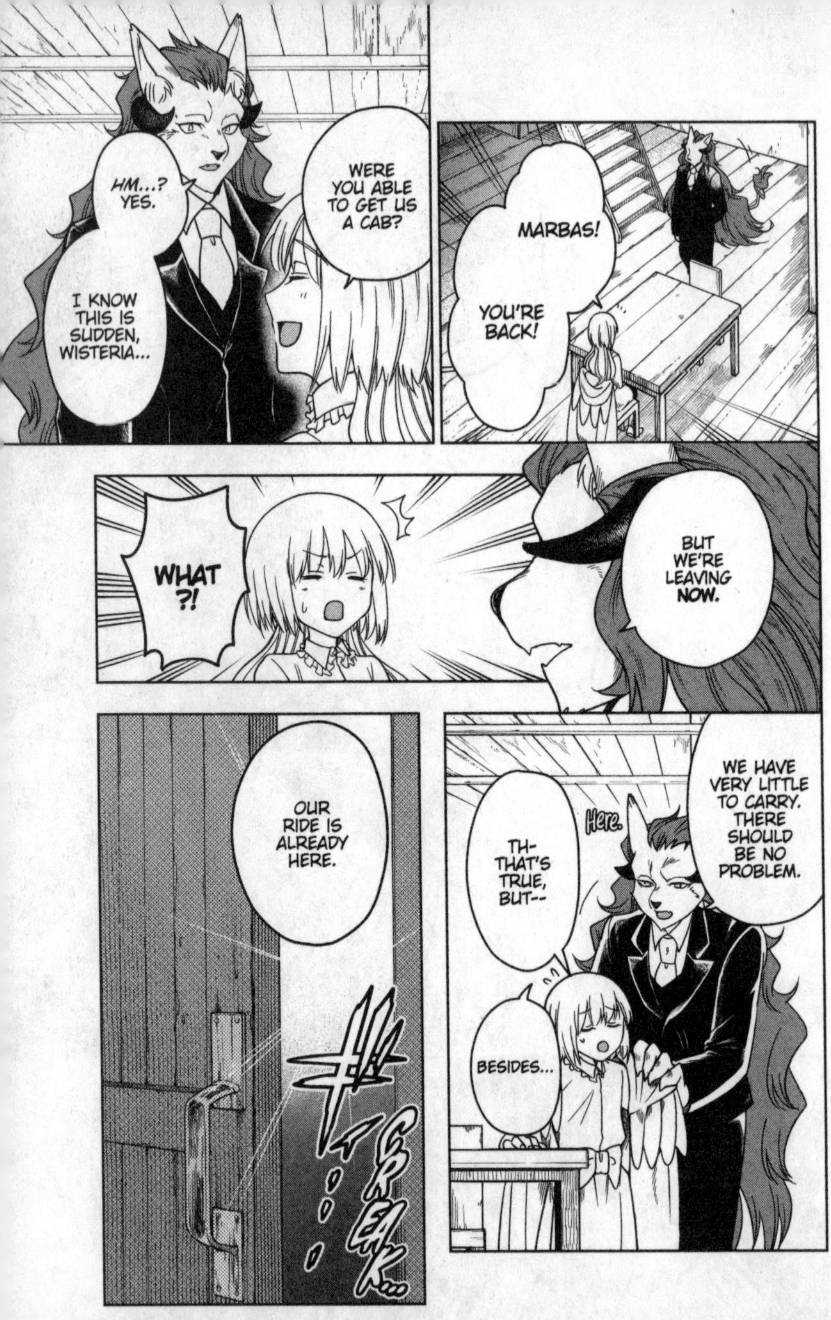
MARBAS!
YOU'RE BACK!
WERE YOU ABLE TO GET US A CAB?
HM...? YES.
I KNOW THIS IS SUDDEN, WISTERIA...
BUT WE'RE LEAVING NOW.
WHAT?!
WE HAVE VERY LITTLE TO CARRY. THERE SHOULD BE NO PROBLEM.
Here.
TH-THAT'S TRUE, BUT--
BESIDES...
OUR RIDE IS ALREADY HERE.
CREAK...

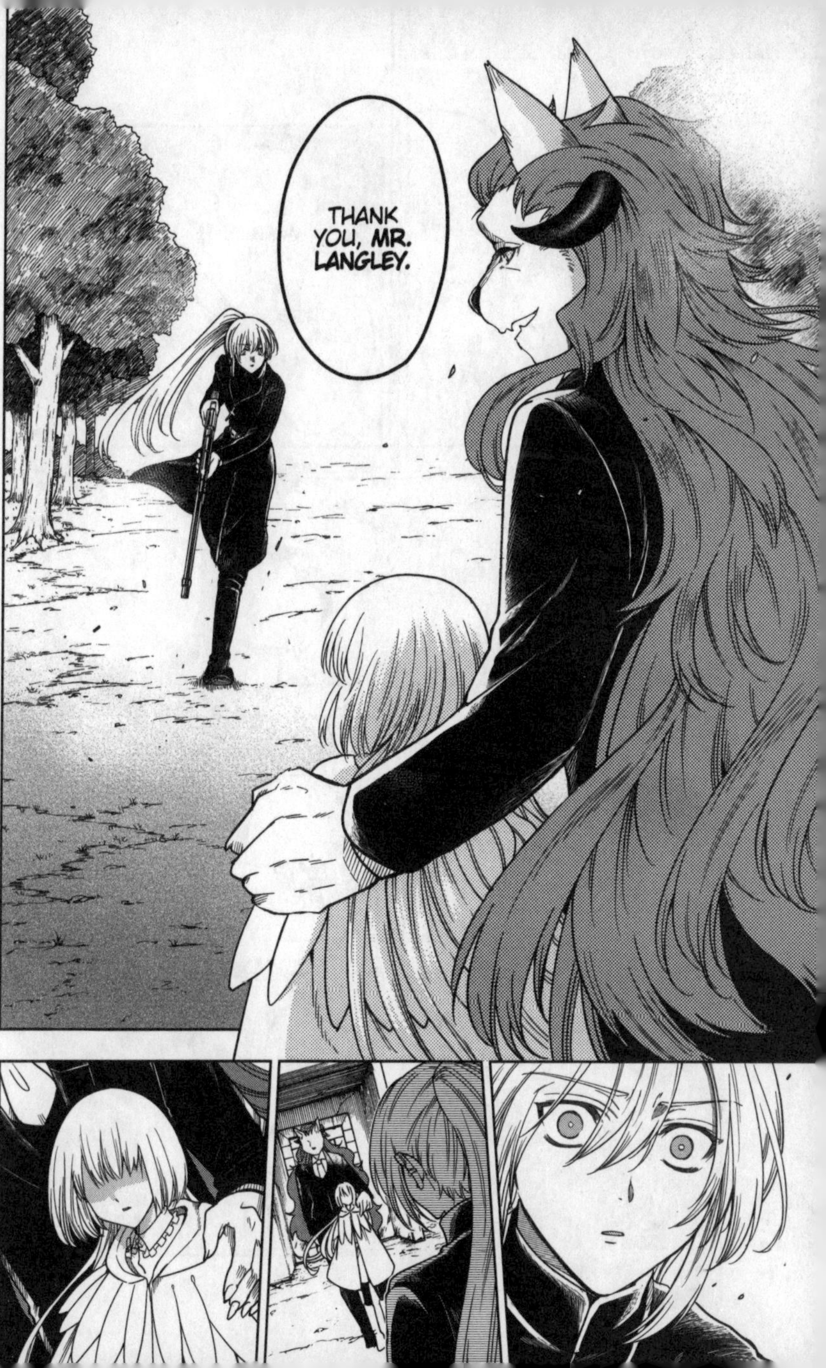
THANK YOU, MR. LANGLEY.

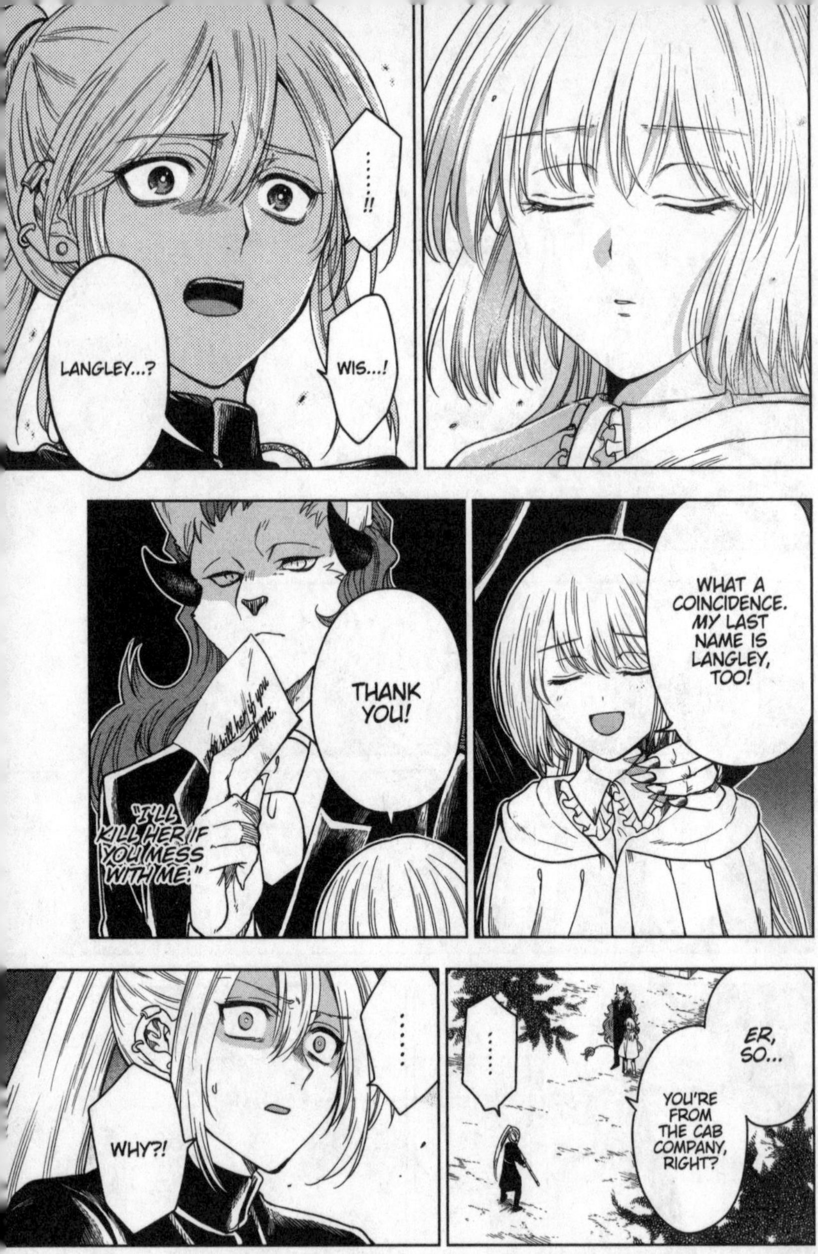
......!!
WIS...!
LANGLEY...?
WHAT A COINCIDENCE. MY LAST NAME IS LANGLEY, TOO!
THANK YOU!
"I'LL KILL HER IF YOU MESS WITH ME."
......
ER, SO...
YOU'RE FROM THE CAB COMPANY, RIGHT?
......
WHY?!

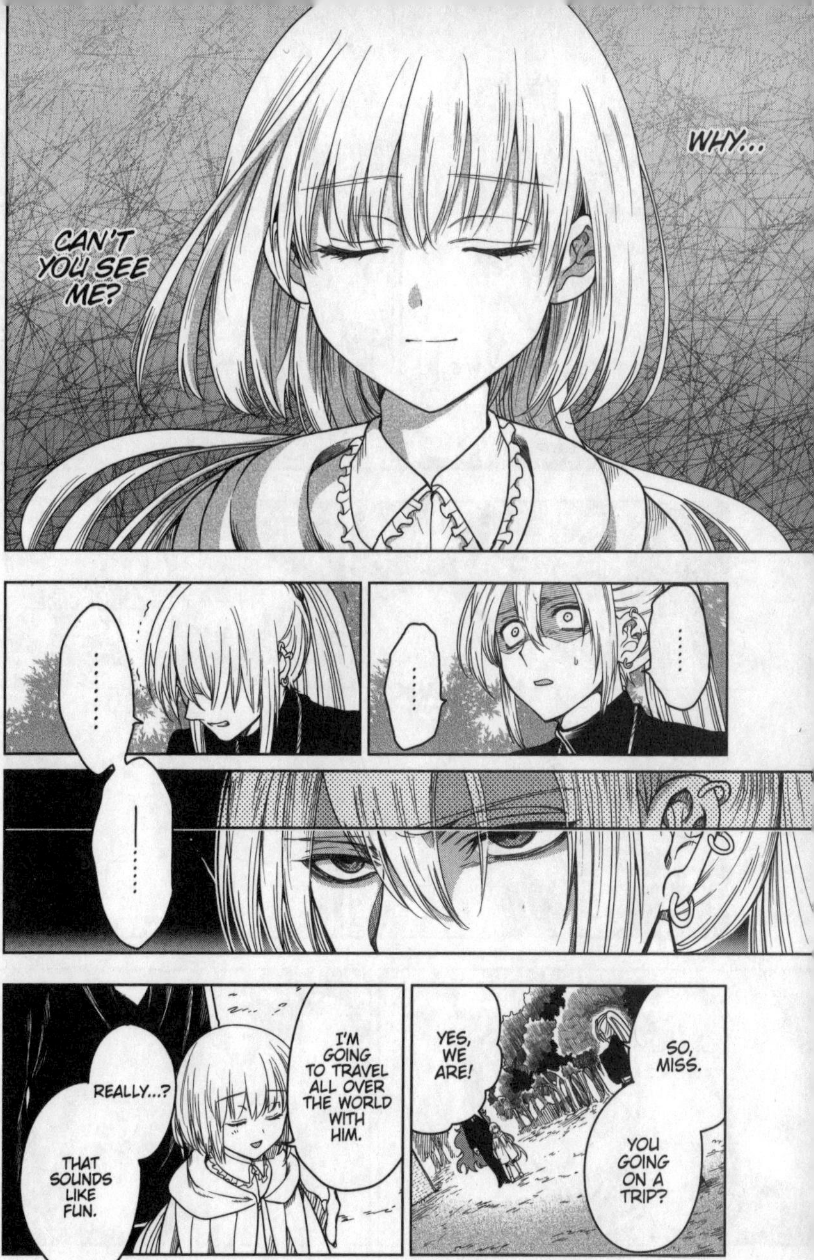
WHY...
CAN'T YOU SEE ME?
......
......
......
—......
SO, MISS.
YOU GOING ON A TRIP?
YES, WE ARE!
I'M GOING TO TRAVEL ALL OVER THE WORLD WITH HIM.
REALLY...?
THAT SOUNDS LIKE FUN.

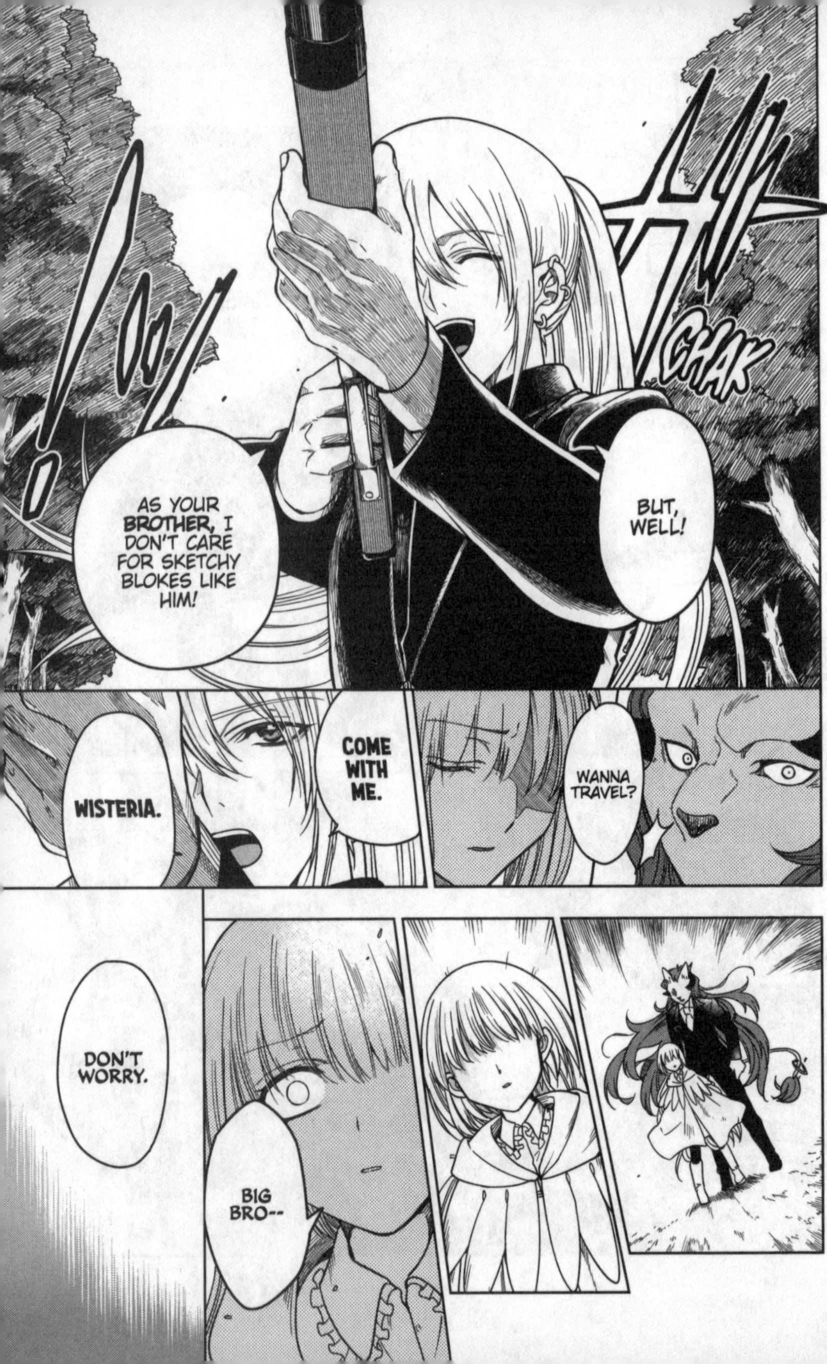
CHAK
BUT, WELL!
AS YOUR BROTHER, I DON'T CARE FOR SKETCHY BLOKES LIKE HIM!
WANNA TRAVEL?
COME WITH ME.
WISTERIA.
BIG BRO--
DON'T WORRY.

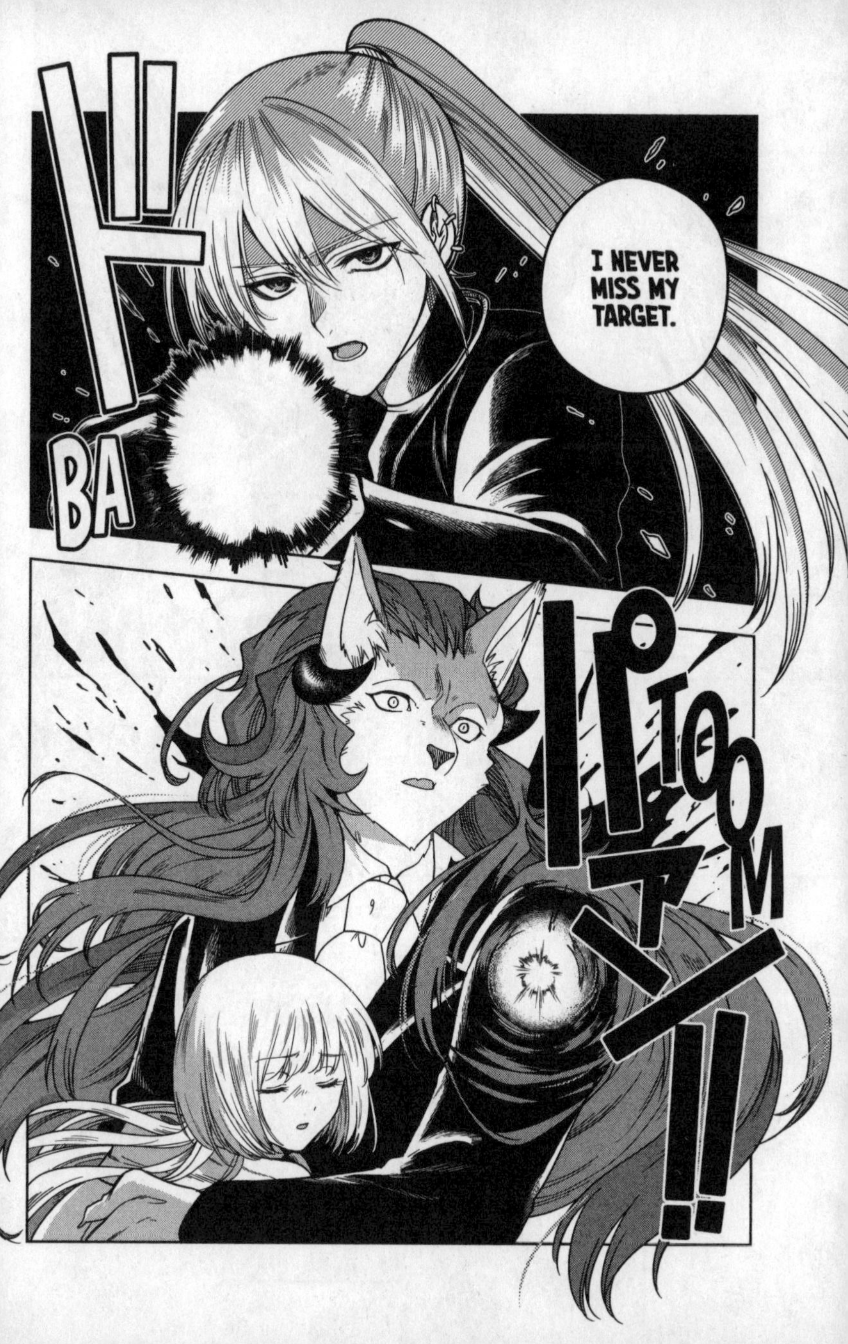
I NEVER MISS MY TARGET.
BA
TOOOM

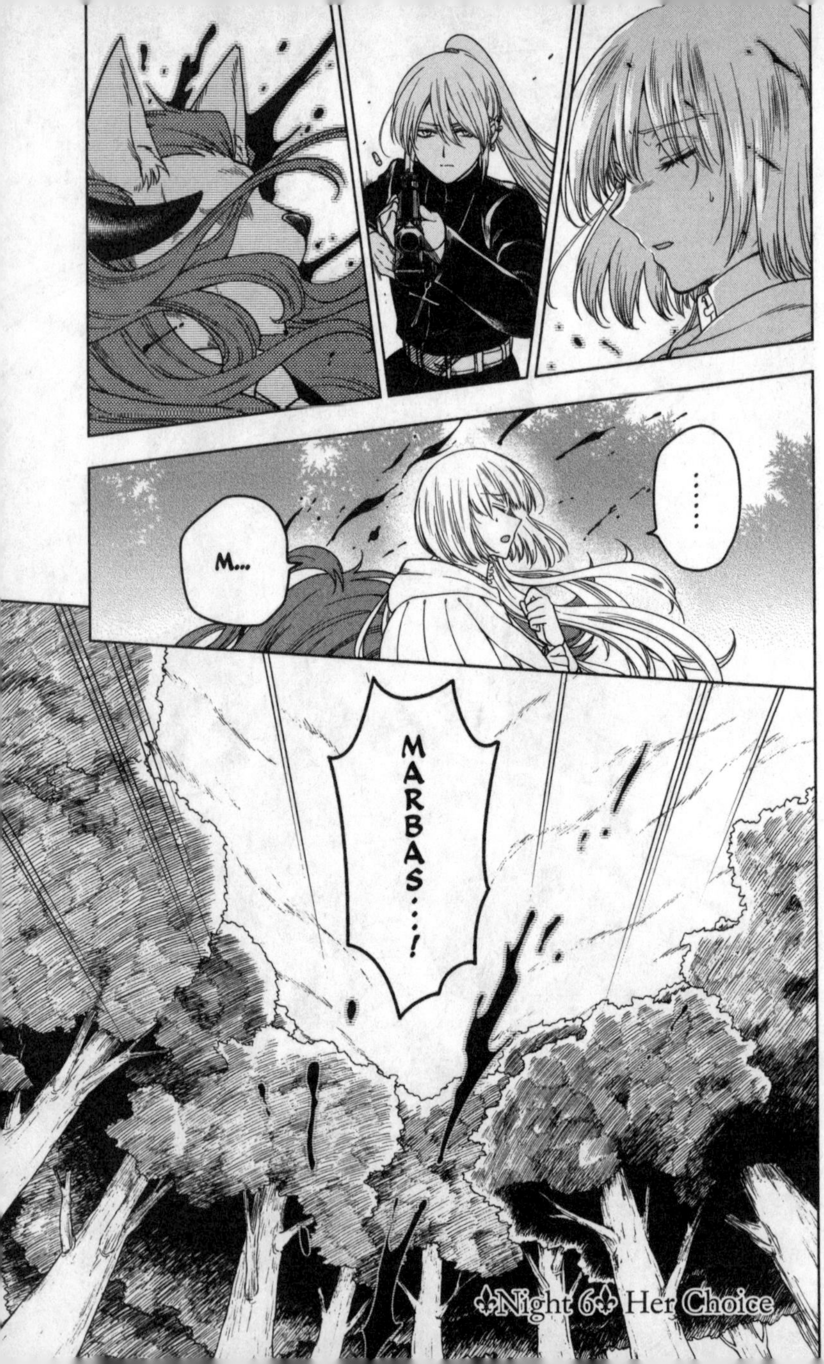
……
M…
MARBAS…!
Night 6 Her Choice

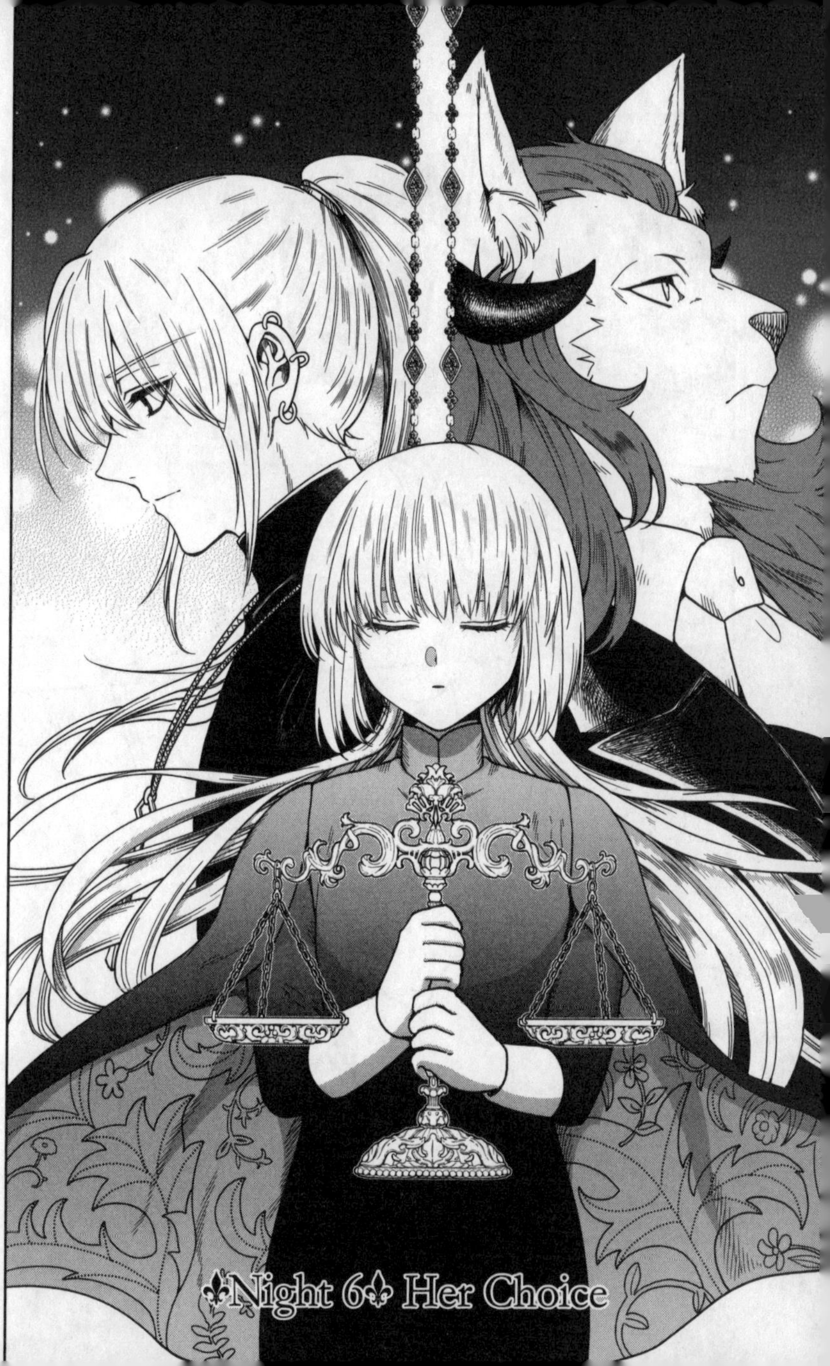
Night 6 Her Choice

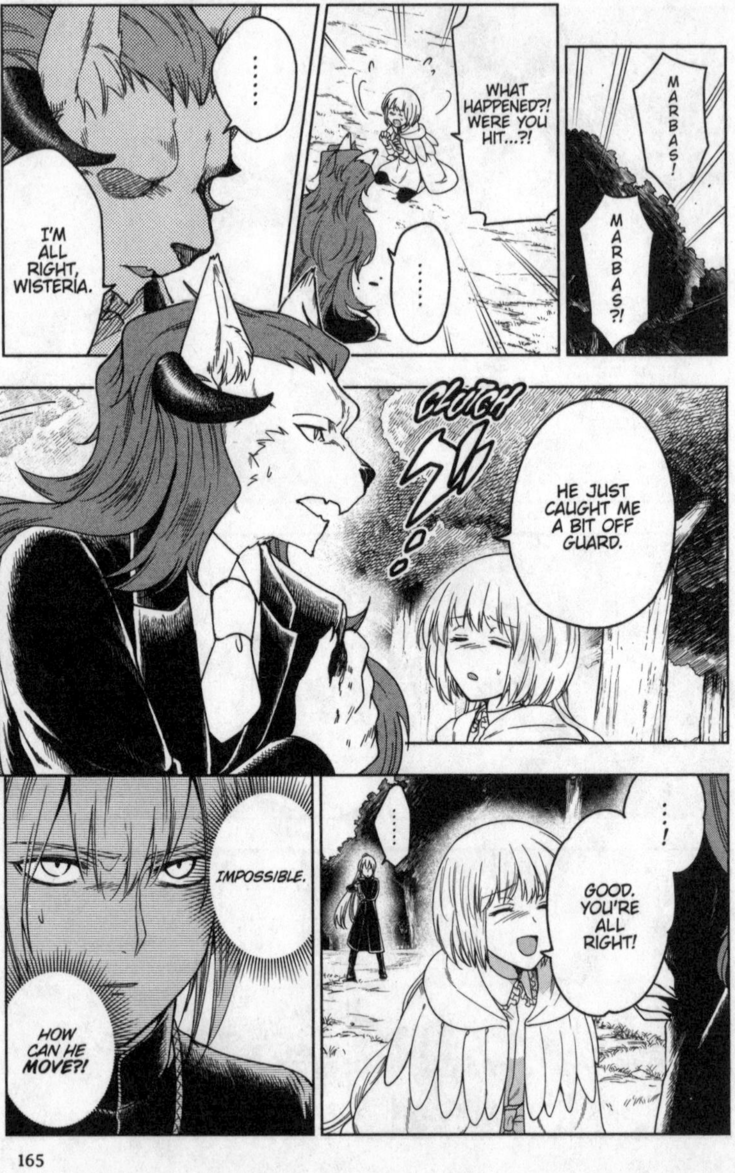
MARBAS!
MARBAS?!
WHAT HAPPENED?! WERE YOU HIT...?!
......
......
I'M ALL RIGHT, WISTERIA.
CLUTCH
HE JUST CAUGHT ME A BIT OFF GUARD.
...!
GOOD. YOU'RE ALL RIGHT!
......
IMPOSSIBLE.
HOW CAN HE MOVE?!

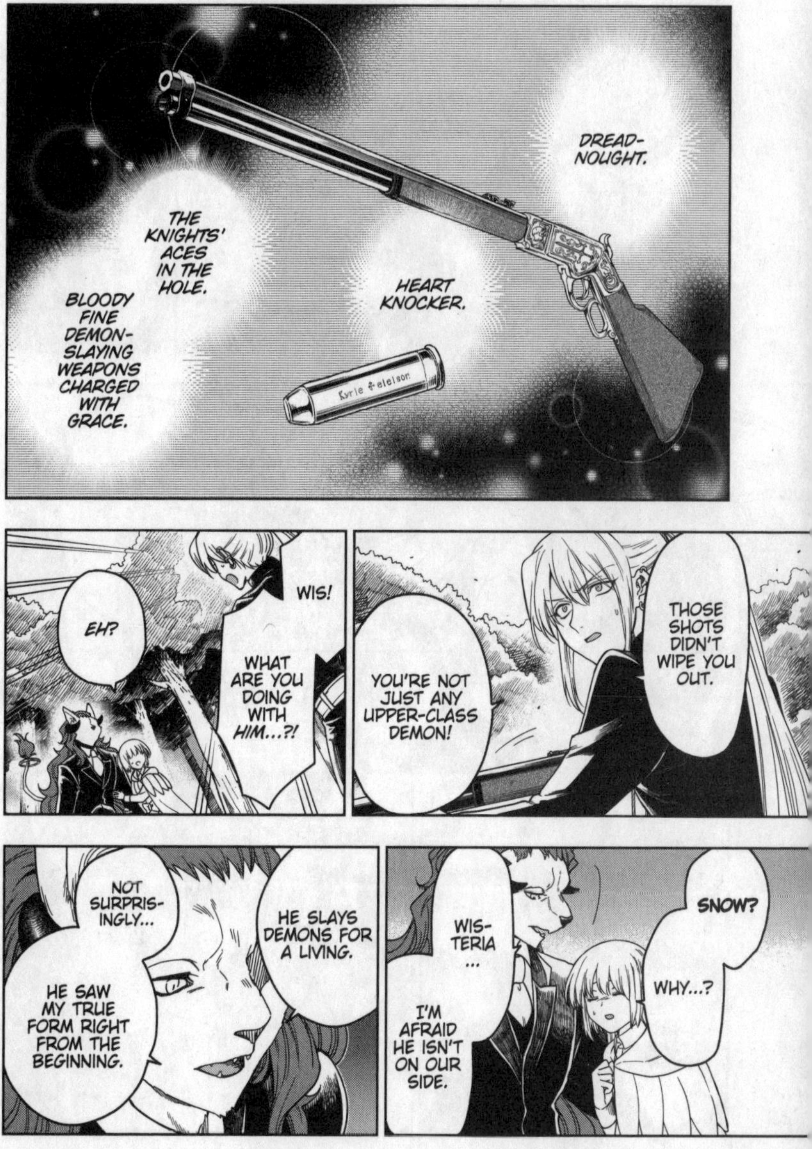
DREAD-NOUGHT.
HEART KNOCKER.
Kyrie eleison
THE KNIGHTS' ACES IN THE HOLE.
BLOODY FINE DEMON-SLAYING WEAPONS CHARGED WITH GRACE.
THOSE SHOTS DIDN'T WIPE YOU OUT.
YOU'RE NOT JUST ANY UPPER-CLASS DEMON!
WIS!
WHAT ARE YOU DOING WITH HIM...?!
EH?
SNOW?
WHY...?
WIS-TERIA...
I'M AFRAID HE ISN'T ON OUR SIDE.
HE SLAYS DEMONS FOR A LIVING.
NOT SURPRIS-INGLY...
HE SAW MY TRUE FORM RIGHT FROM THE BEGINNING.

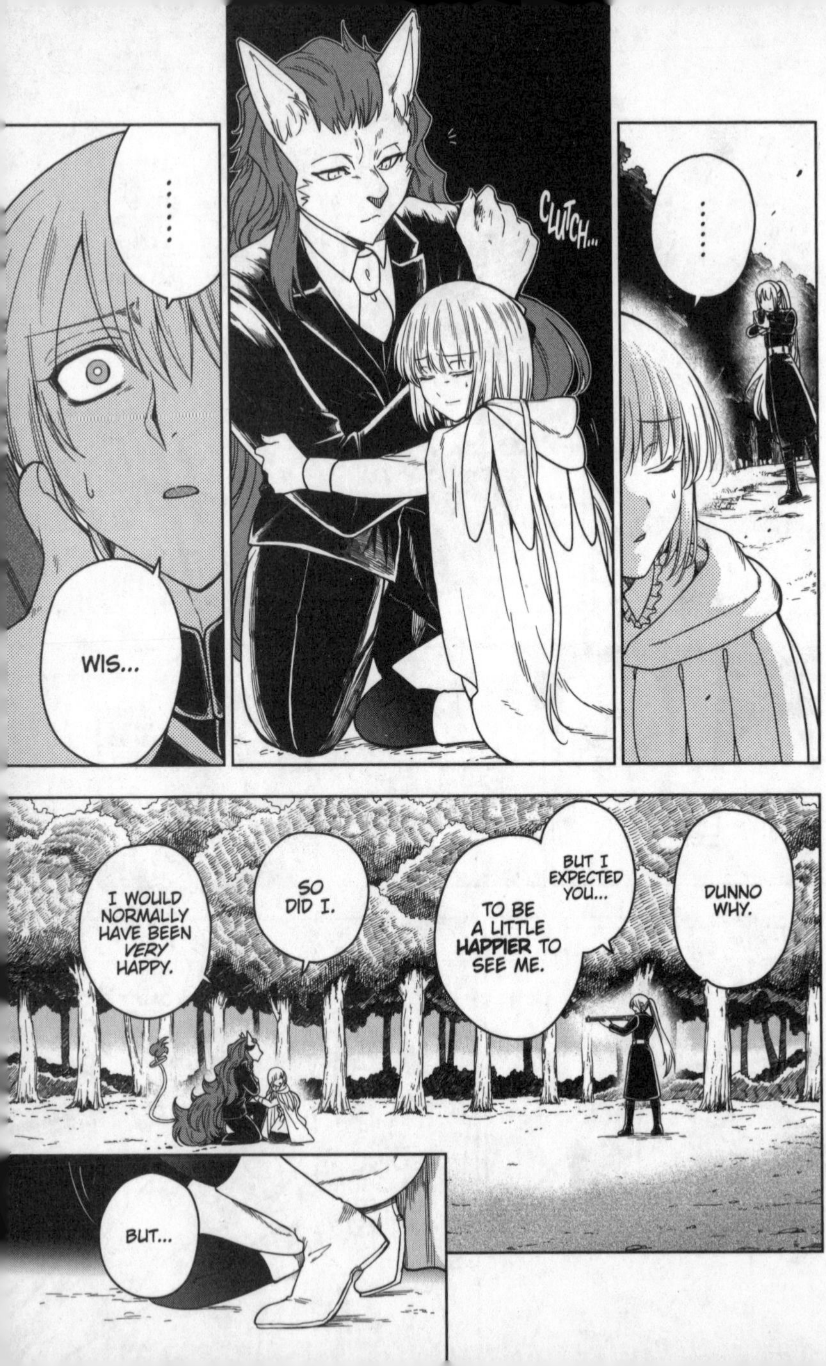
......
CLUTCH...
......
WIS...
DUNNO WHY.
BUT I EXPECTED YOU...
TO BE A LITTLE HAPPIER TO SEE ME.
SO DID I.
I WOULD NORMALLY HAVE BEEN VERY HAPPY.
BUT...

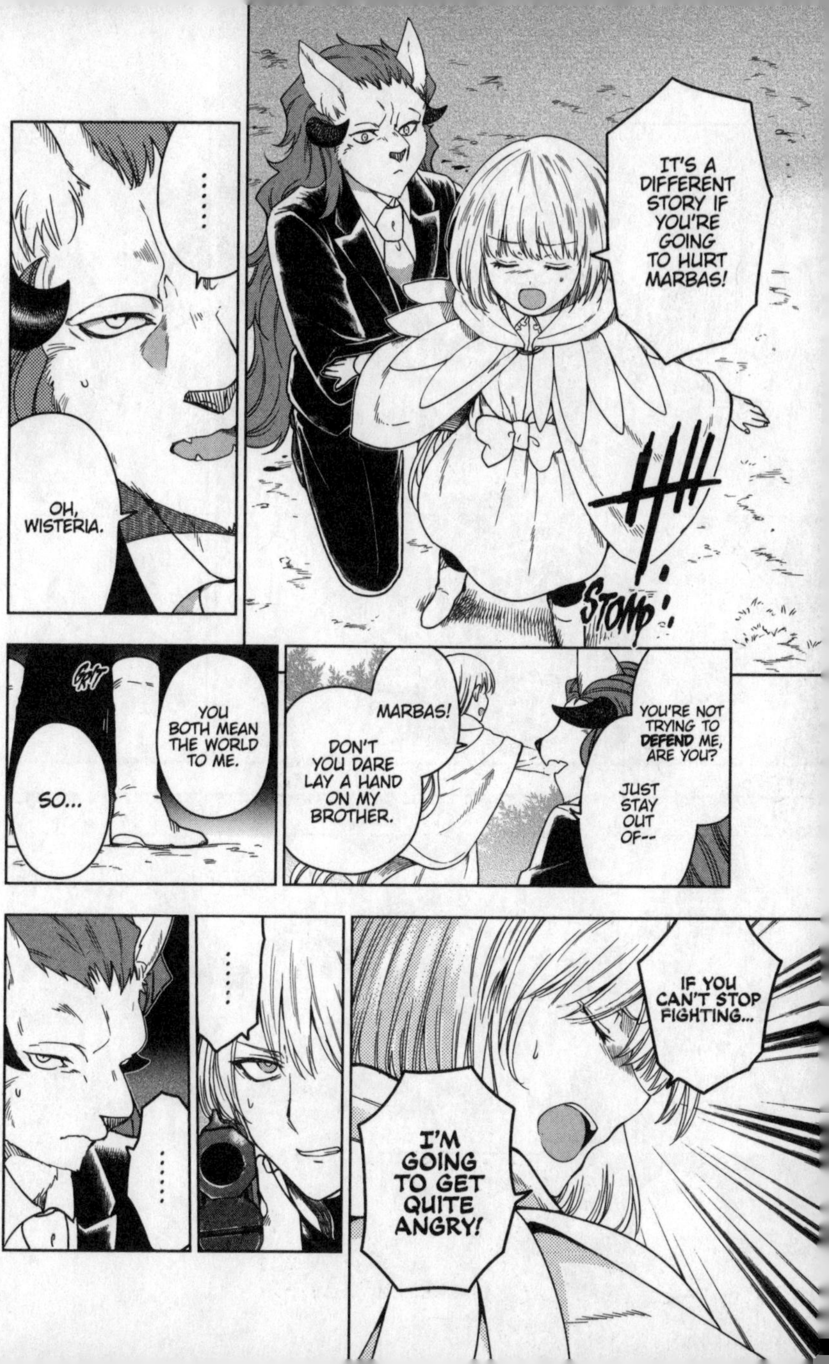
IT'S A DIFFERENT STORY IF YOU'RE GOING TO HURT MARBAS!
STOMP
......
OH, WISTERIA.
YOU'RE NOT TRYING TO DEFEND ME, ARE YOU?
JUST STAY OUT OF--
MARBAS!
DON'T YOU DARE LAY A HAND ON MY BROTHER.
YOU BOTH MEAN THE WORLD TO ME.
SO...
IF YOU CAN'T STOP FIGHTING...
I'M GOING TO GET QUITE ANGRY!
......
......

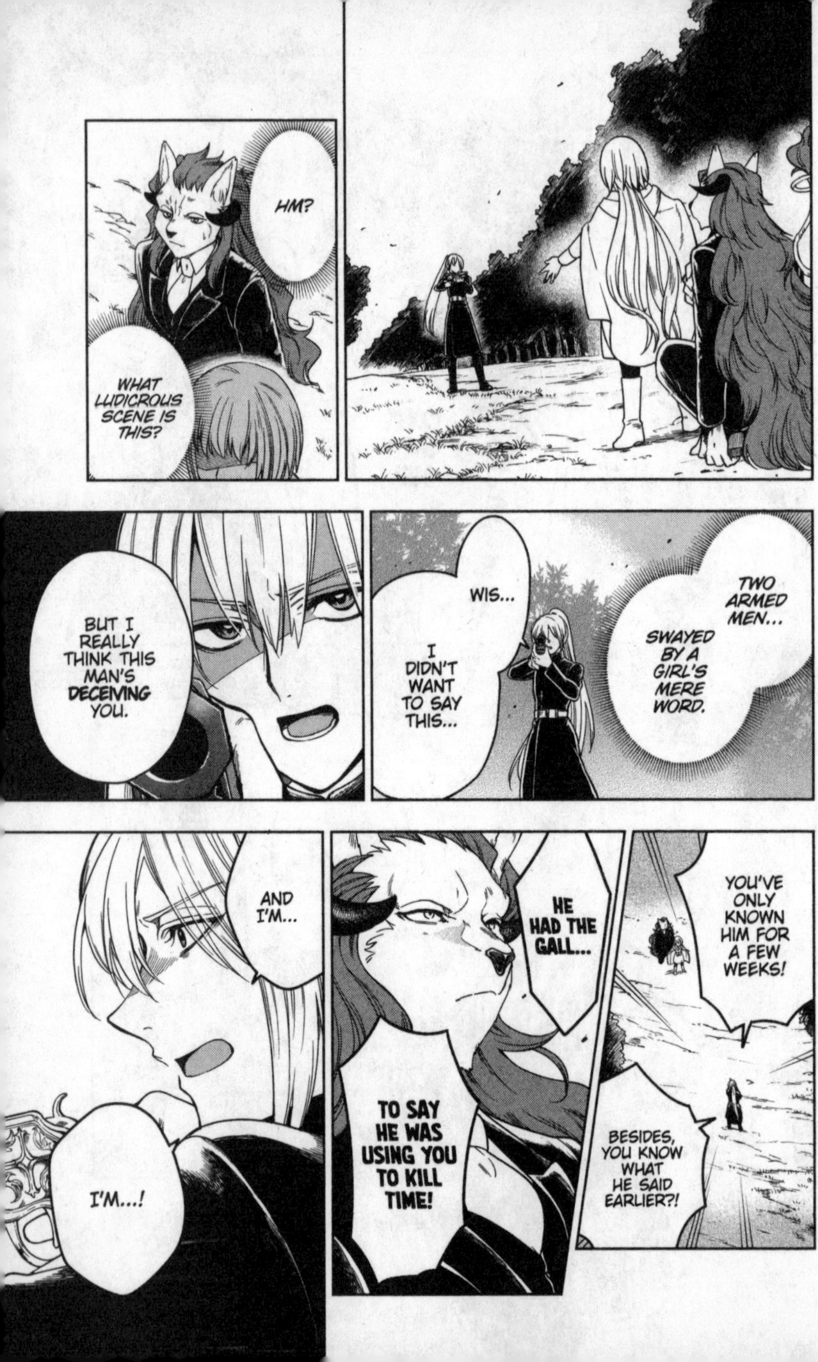
HM?
WHAT LUDICROUS SCENE IS THIS?
TWO ARMED MEN...
SWAYED BY A GIRL'S MERE WORD.
WIS...
I DIDN'T WANT TO SAY THIS...
BUT I REALLY THINK THIS MAN'S DECEIVING YOU.
YOU'VE ONLY KNOWN HIM FOR A FEW WEEKS!
BESIDES, YOU KNOW WHAT HE SAID EARLIER?!
HE HAD THE GALL...
TO SAY HE WAS USING YOU TO KILL TIME!
AND I'M...
I'M...!

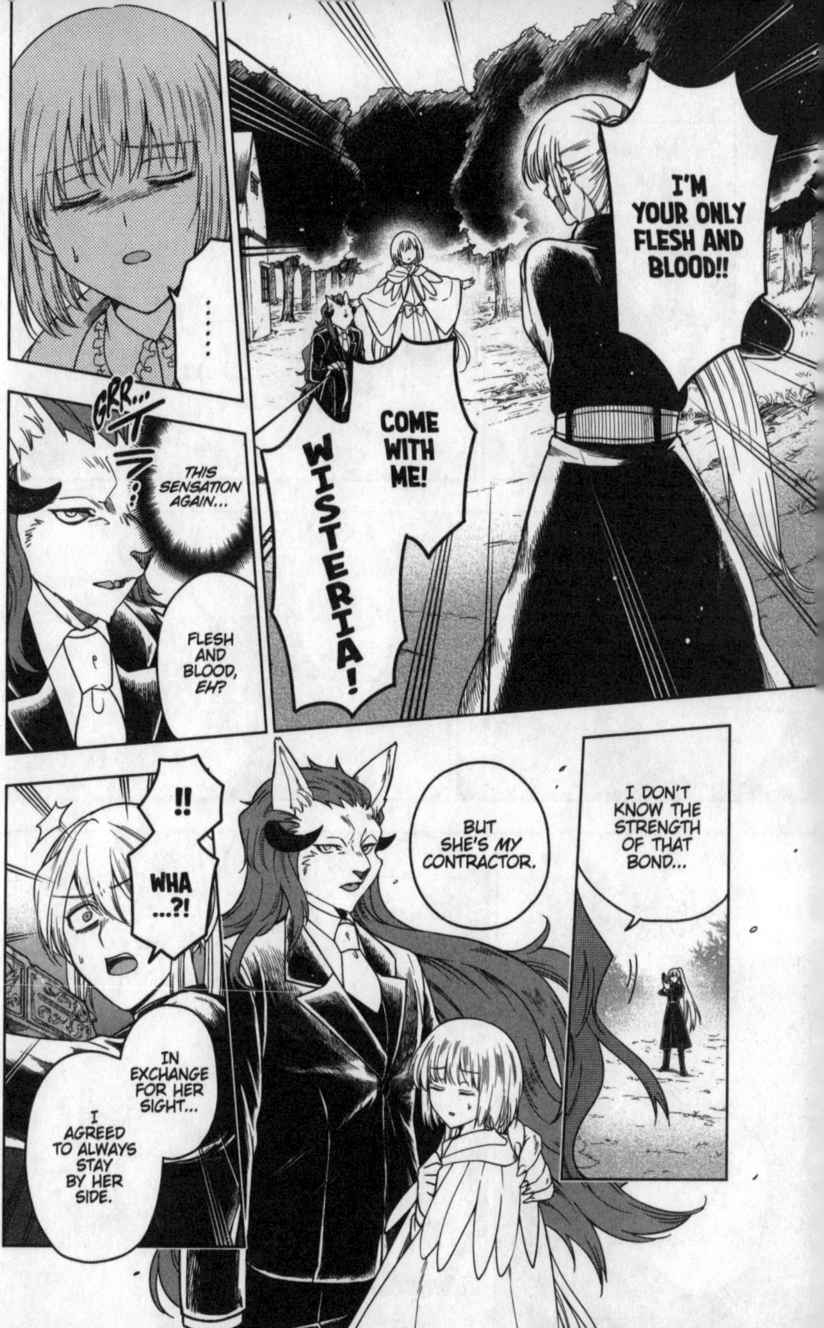

I'M YOUR ONLY FLESH AND BLOOD!!
COME WITH ME!
WISTERIA!
......
GRR...
THIS SENSATION AGAIN...
FLESH AND BLOOD, EH?
I DON'T KNOW THE STRENGTH OF THAT BOND...
BUT SHE'S *MY* CONTRACTOR.
!!
WHA...?!
IN EXCHANGE FOR HER SIGHT...
I AGREED TO ALWAYS STAY BY HER SIDE.

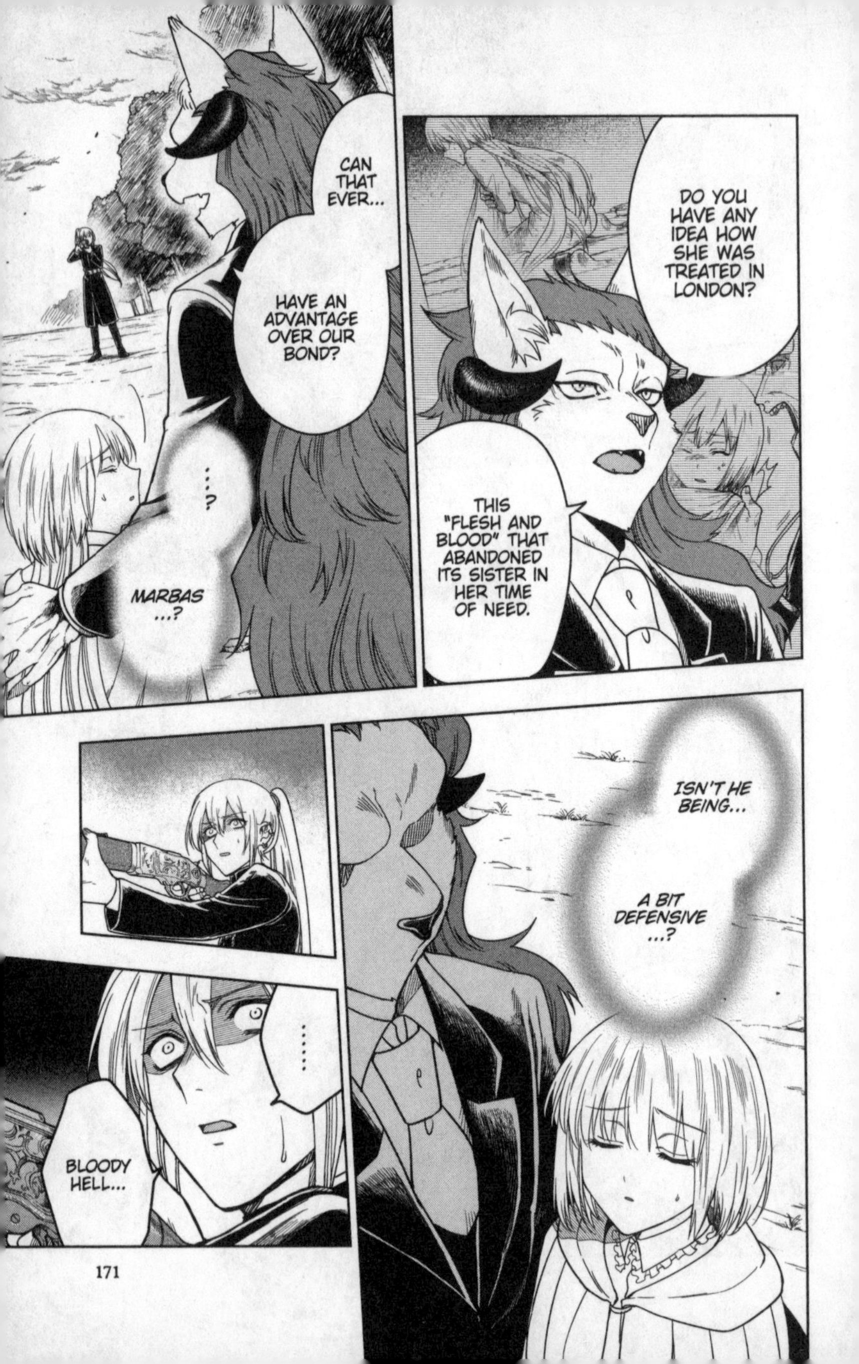
DO YOU HAVE ANY IDEA HOW SHE WAS TREATED IN LONDON?
THIS "FLESH AND BLOOD" THAT ABANDONED ITS SISTER IN HER TIME OF NEED.
CAN THAT EVER...
HAVE AN ADVANTAGE OVER OUR BOND?
...?
MARBAS ...?
ISN'T HE BEING...
A BIT DEFENSIVE ...?
......
BLOODY HELL...

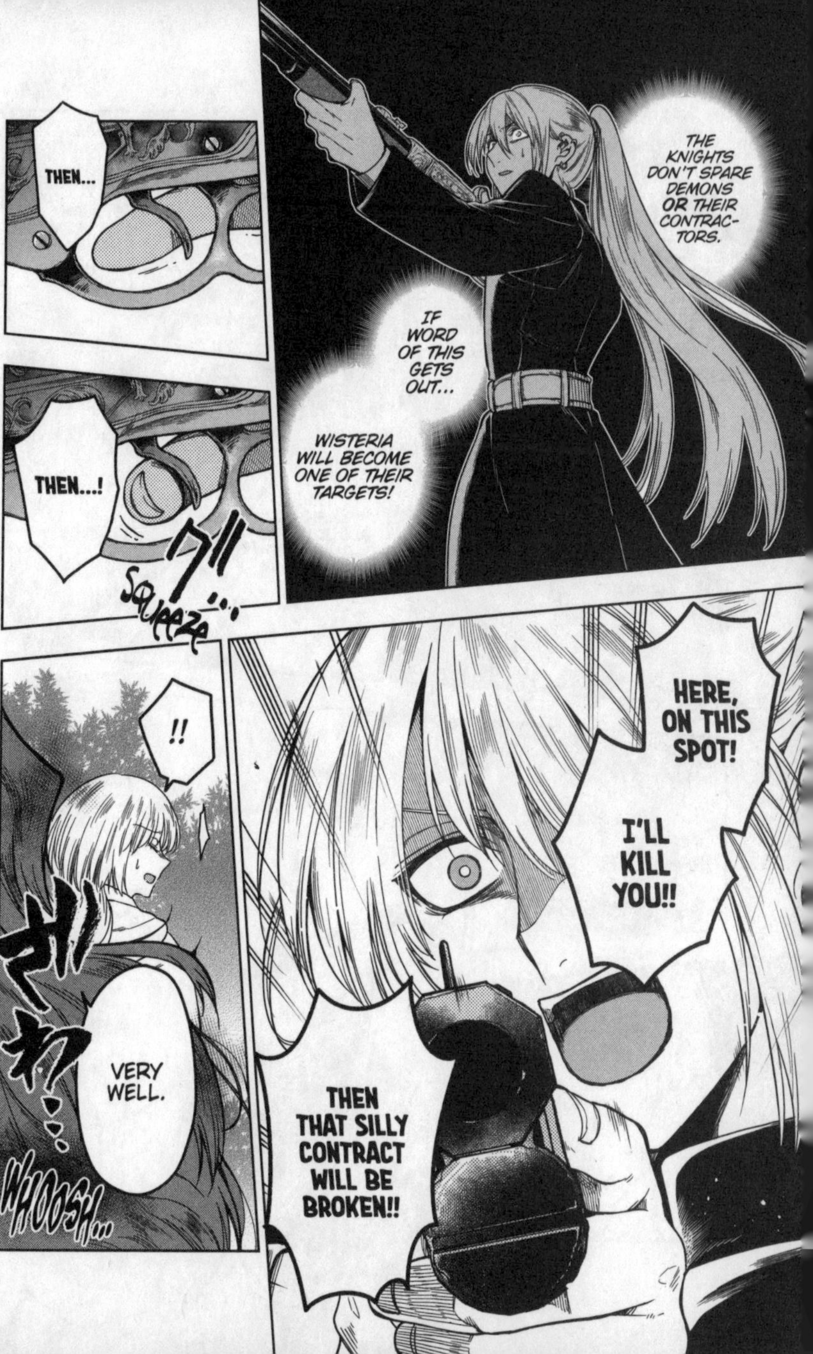
THE KNIGHTS DON'T SPARE DEMONS OR THEIR CONTRACTORS.
IF WORD OF THIS GETS OUT...
WISTERIA WILL BECOME ONE OF THEIR TARGETS!
THEN...
THEN...!
SQUEEZE...
HERE, ON THIS SPOT!
I'LL KILL YOU!!
THEN THAT SILLY CONTRACT WILL BE BROKEN!!
!!
VERY WELL.
WHOOSH...

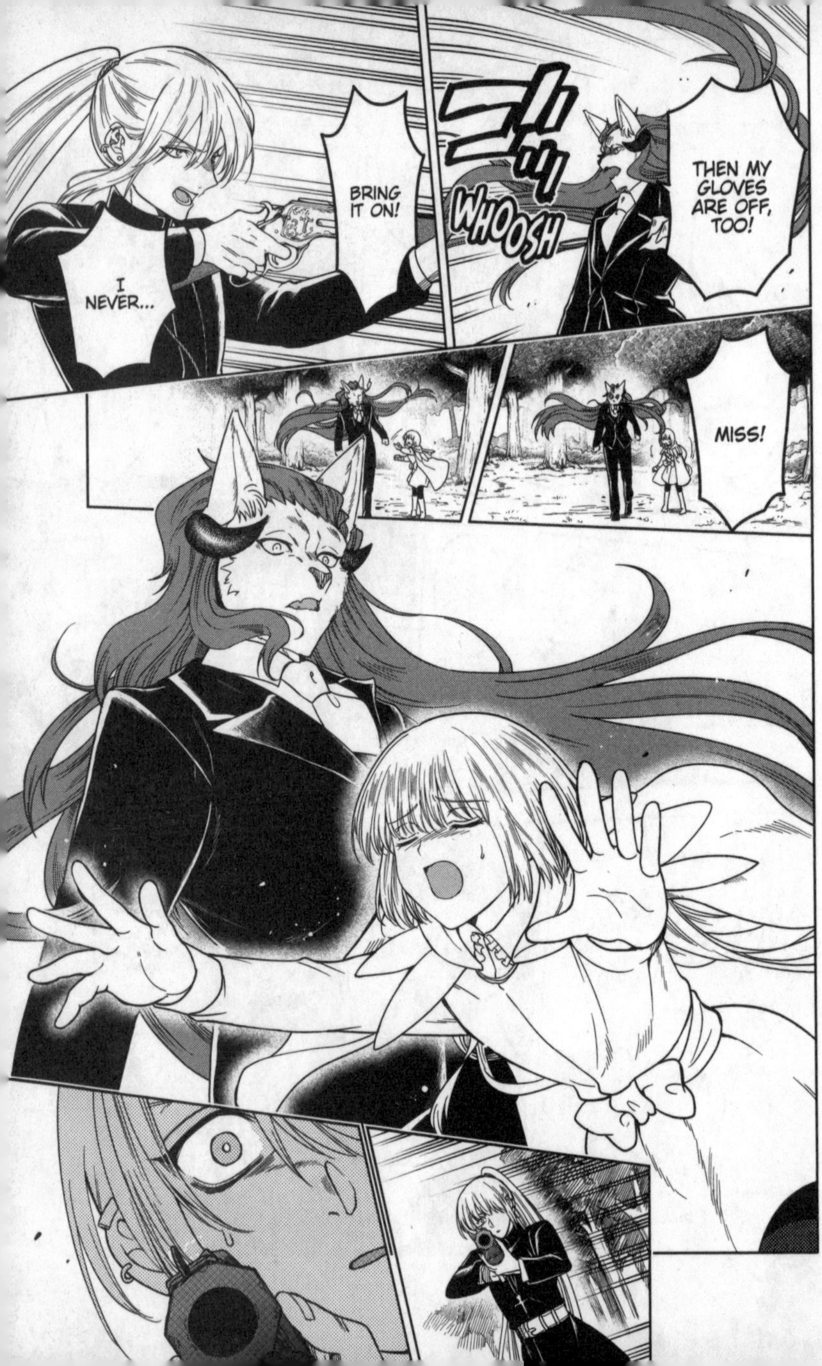
THEN MY GLOVES ARE OFF, TOO!
WHOOSH
BRING IT ON!
I NEVER...
MISS!

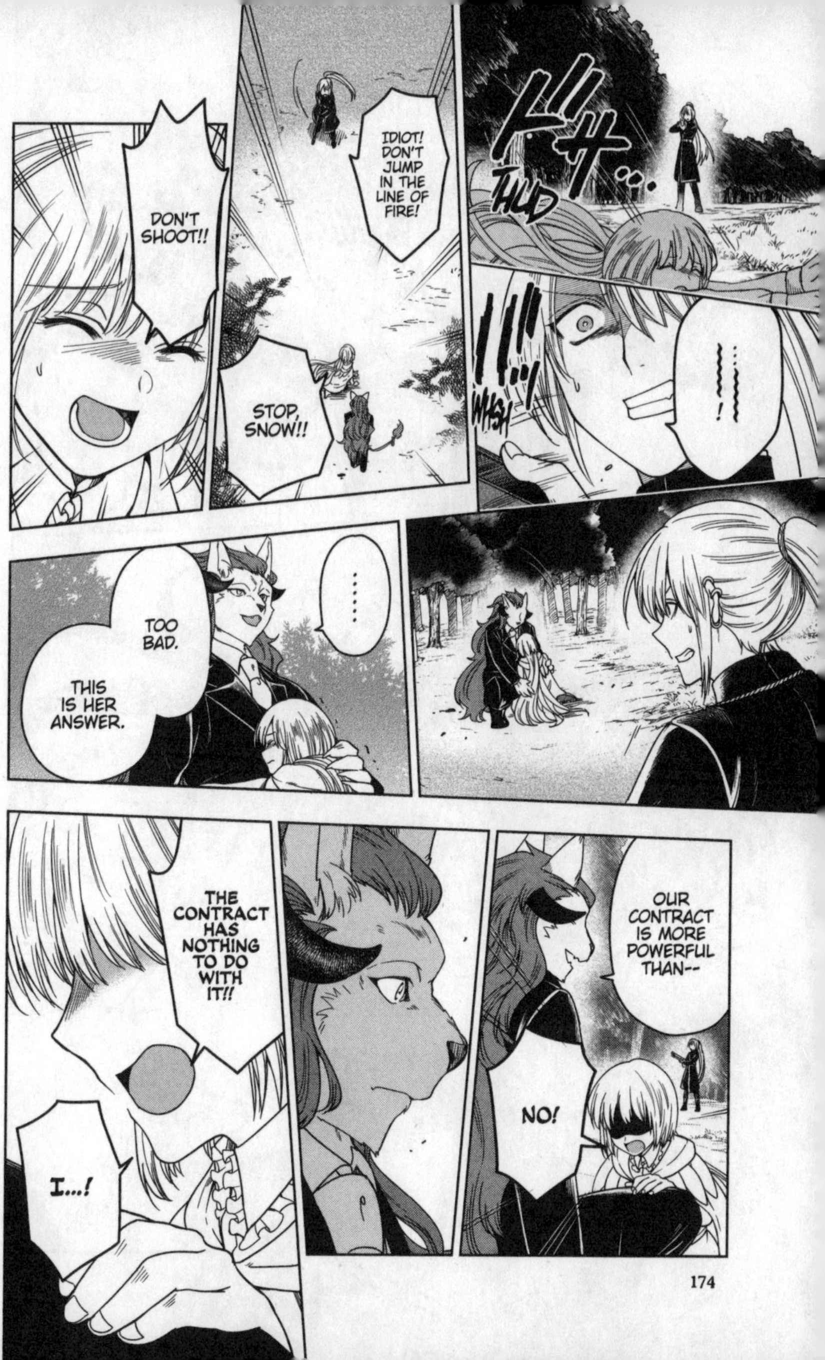
THUD
WHSH
......!
IDIOT! DON'T JUMP IN THE LINE OF FIRE!
STOP, SNOW!!
DON'T SHOOT!!
......
TOO BAD.
THIS IS HER ANSWER.
OUR CONTRACT IS MORE POWERFUL THAN--
NO!
THE CONTRACT HAS NOTHING TO DO WITH IT!!
I...!

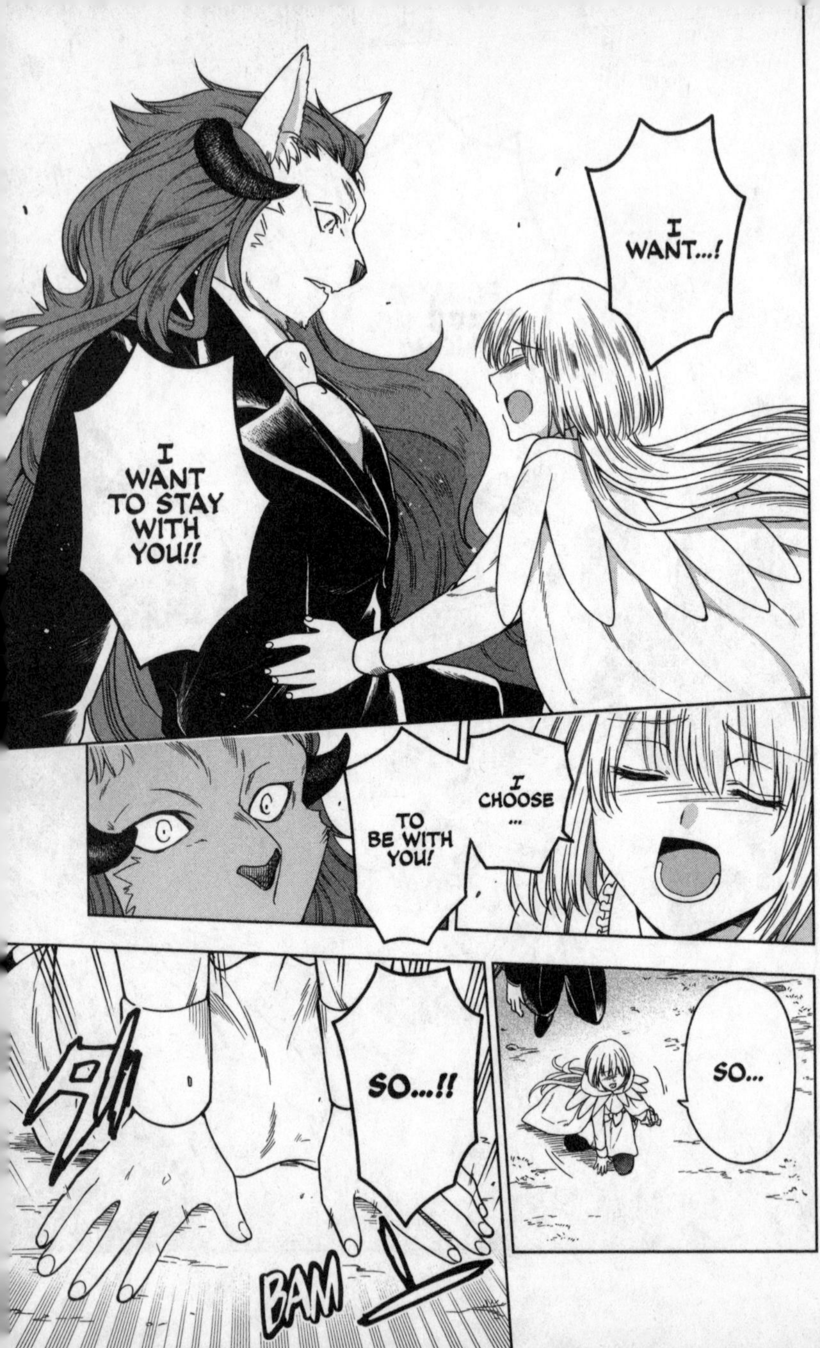
I WANT...!
I WANT TO STAY WITH YOU!!
I CHOOSE ...
TO BE WITH YOU!
SO...
SO...!!
BAM

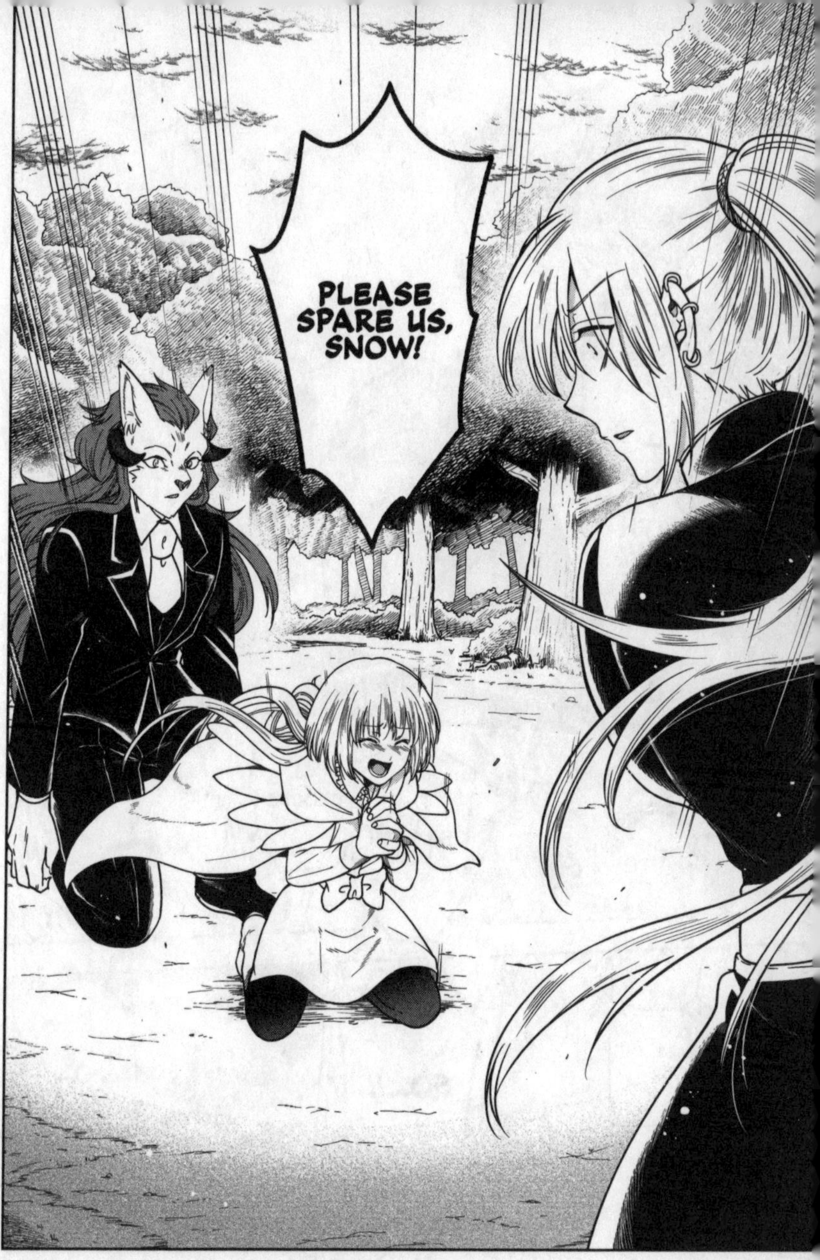
PLEASE SPARE US, SNOW!

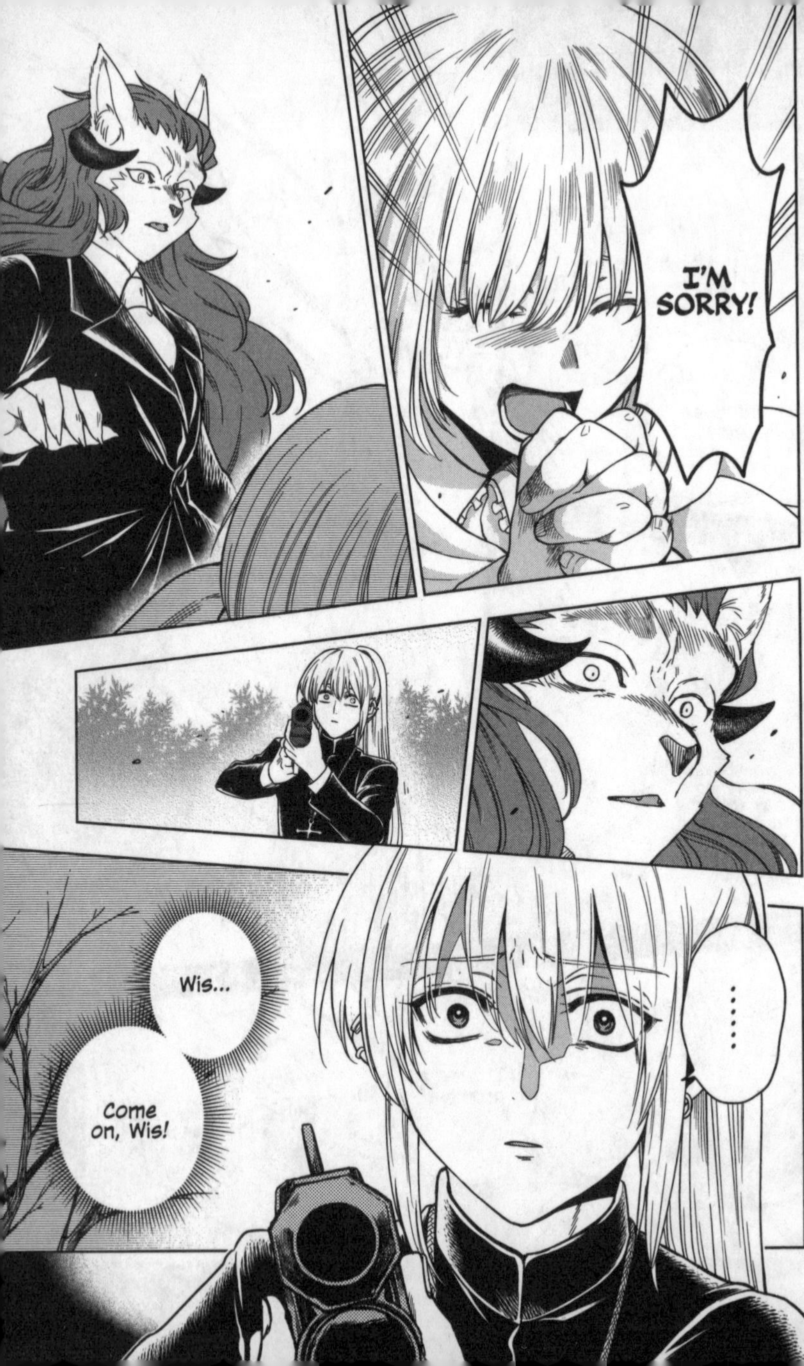
I'M SORRY!
......
Wis...
Come on, Wis!

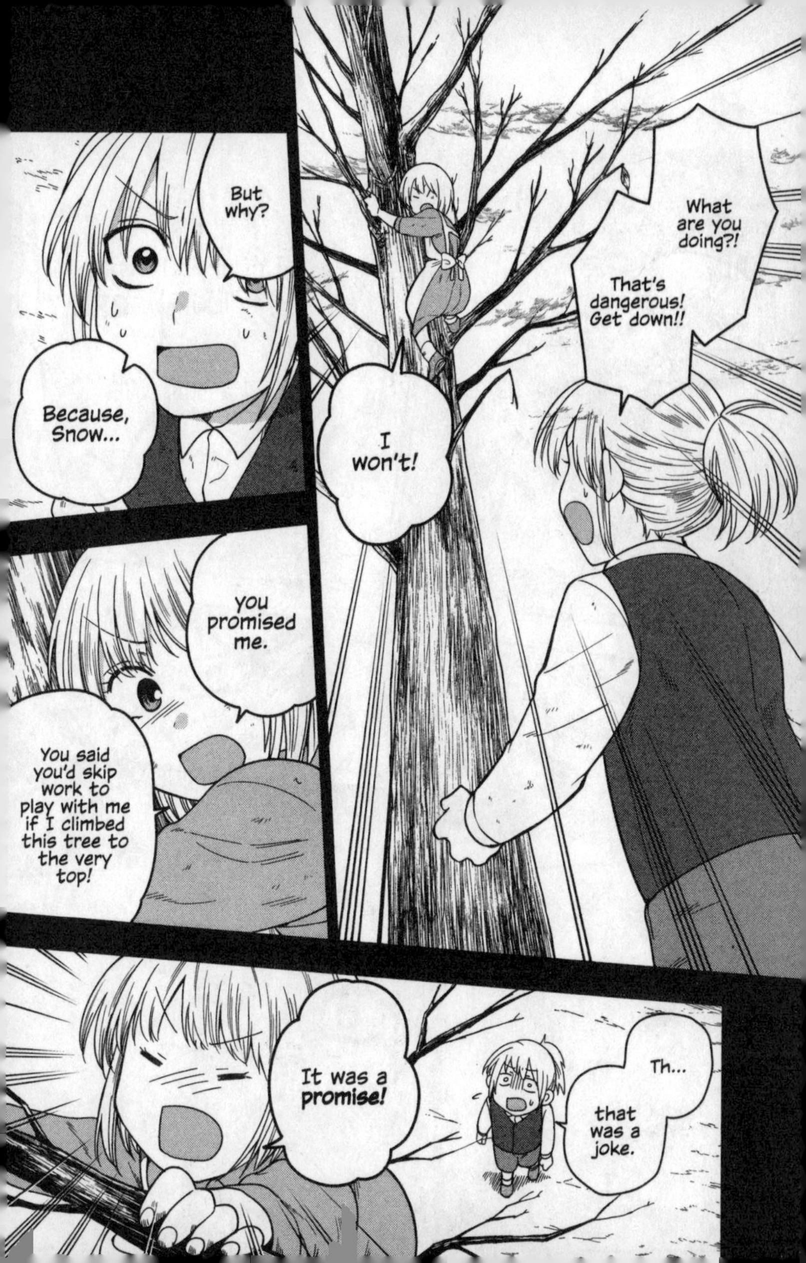
What are you doing?!
That's dangerous! Get down!!
I won't!
But why?
Because, Snow...
you promised me.
You said you'd skip work to play with me if I climbed this tree to the very top!
Th...
that was a joke.
It was a **promise!**

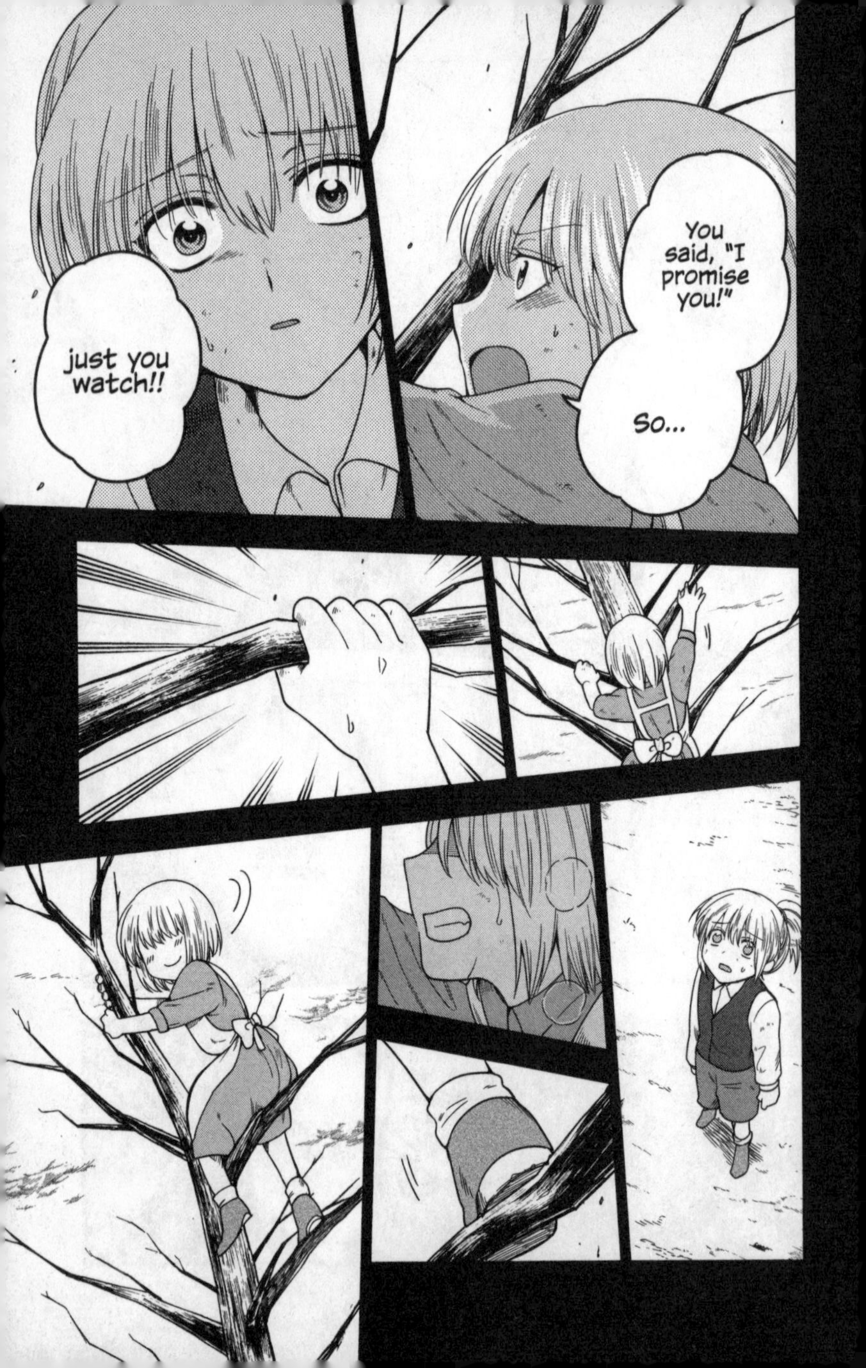
You said, "I promise you!"
So...
just you watch!!

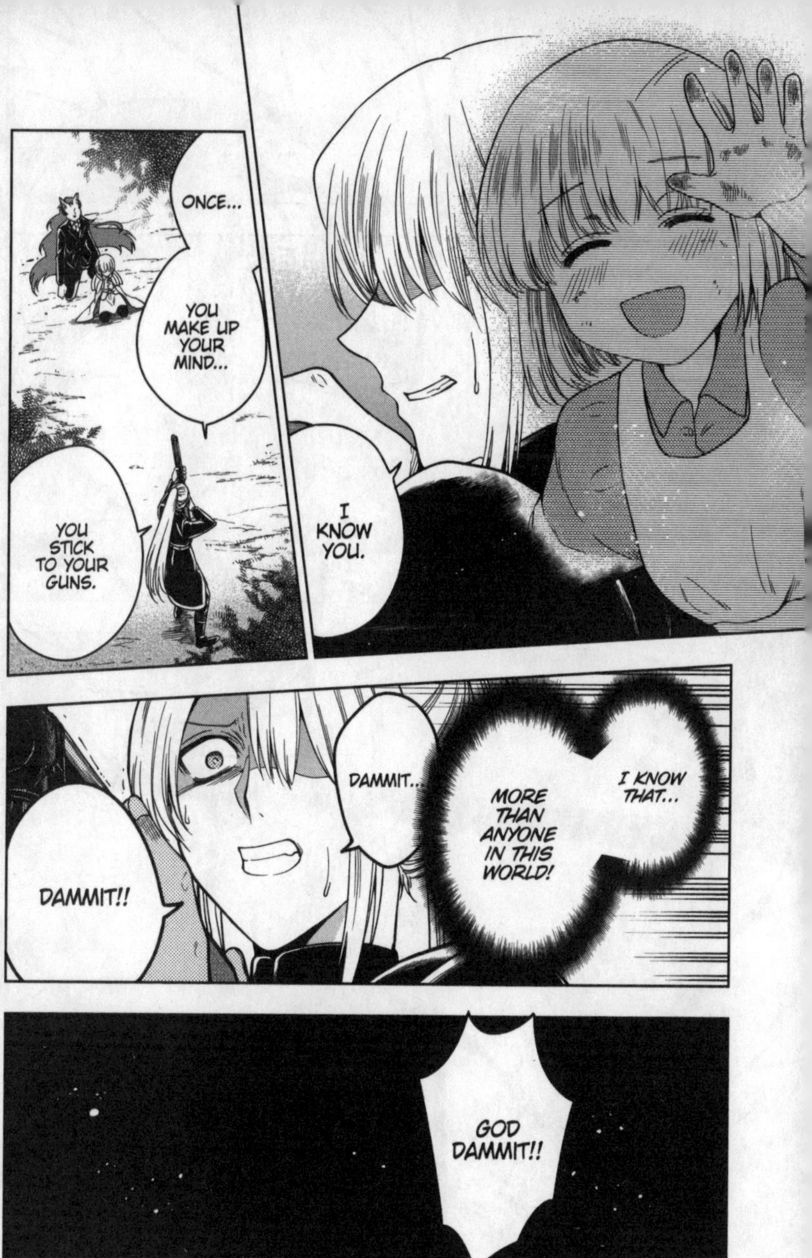
I KNOW YOU.
ONCE...
YOU MAKE UP YOUR MIND...
YOU STICK TO YOUR GUNS.
I KNOW THAT...
MORE THAN ANYONE IN THIS WORLD!
DAMMIT..
DAMMIT!!
GOD DAMMIT!!

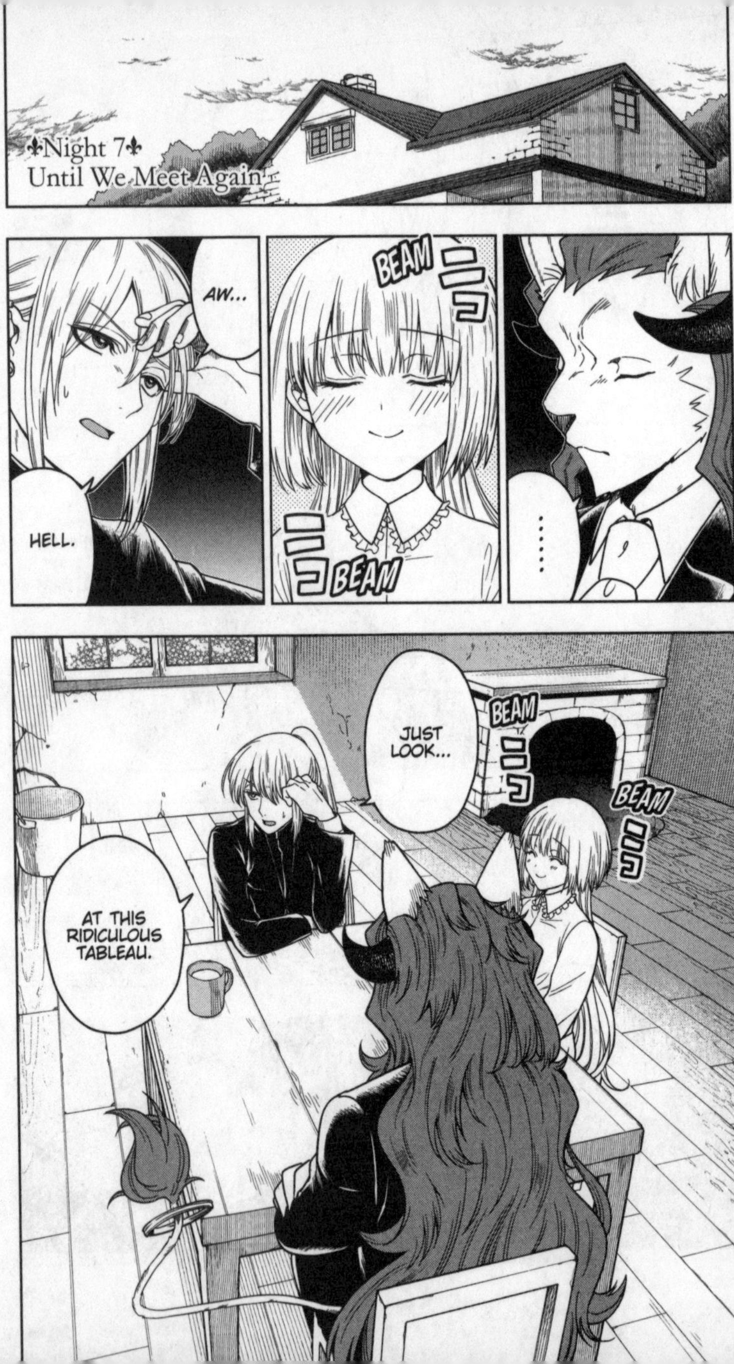

✦Night 7✦
Until We Meet Again
......
BEAM
ニコ
BEAM
ニコ
AW...
HELL.
BEAM
ニコ
BEAM
ニコ
JUST LOOK...
AT THIS RIDICULOUS TABLEAU.

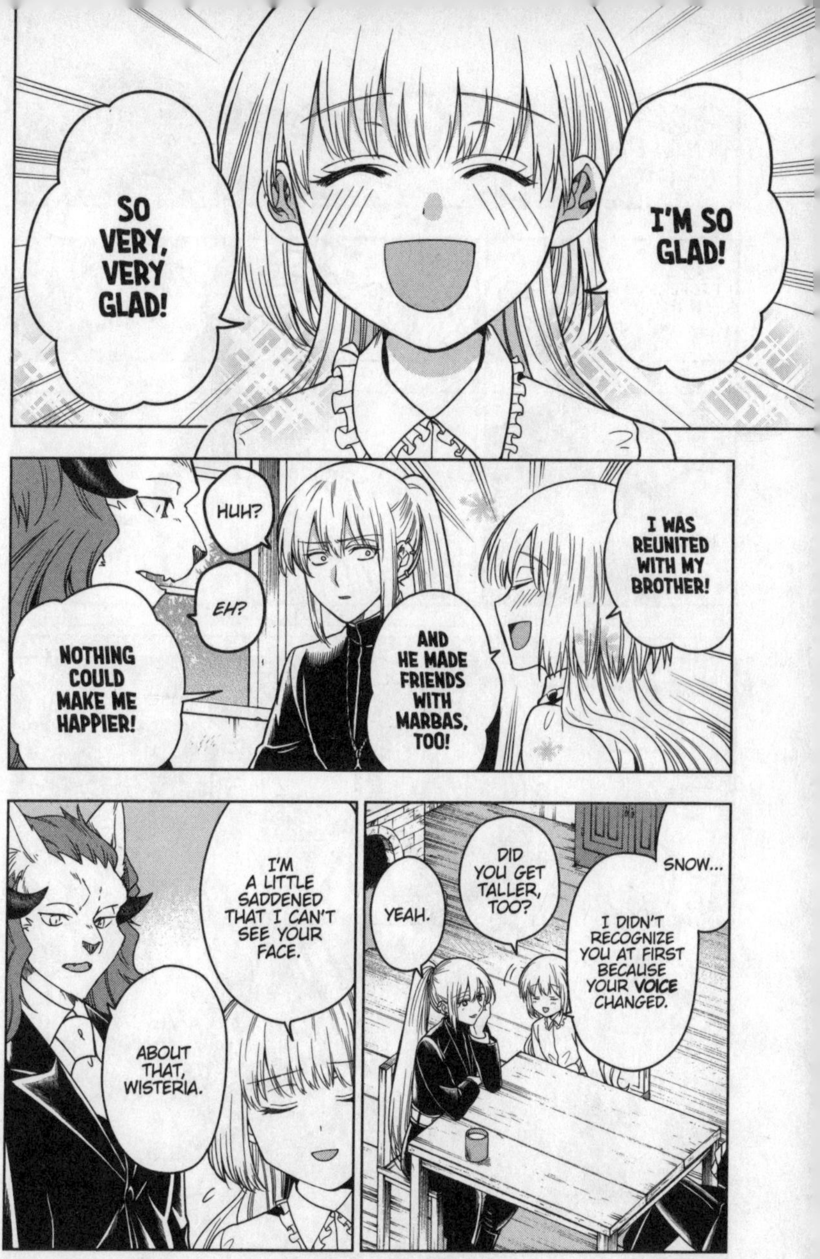
I'M SO GLAD!
SO VERY, VERY GLAD!
I WAS REUNITED WITH MY BROTHER!
AND HE MADE FRIENDS WITH MARBAS, TOO!
NOTHING COULD MAKE ME HAPPIER!
HUH?
EH?
SNOW...
I DIDN'T RECOGNIZE YOU AT FIRST BECAUSE YOUR VOICE CHANGED.
DID YOU GET TALLER, TOO?
YEAH.
I'M A LITTLE SADDENED THAT I CAN'T SEE YOUR FACE.
ABOUT THAT, WISTERIA.

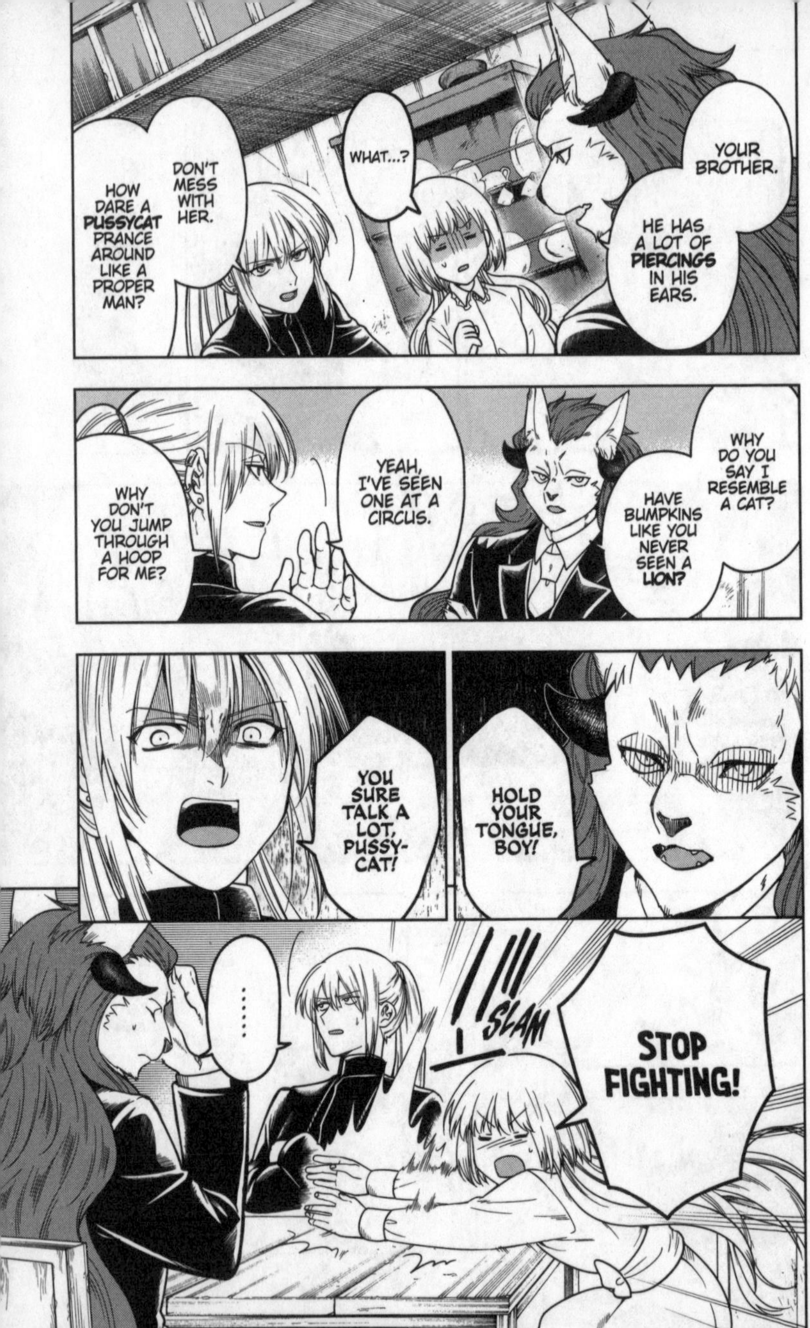
YOUR BROTHER.
HE HAS A LOT OF PIERCINGS IN HIS EARS.
WHAT...?
DON'T MESS WITH HER.
HOW DARE A PUSSYCAT PRANCE AROUND LIKE A PROPER MAN?
WHY DO YOU SAY I RESEMBLE A CAT?
HAVE BUMPKINS LIKE YOU NEVER SEEN A LION?
YEAH, I'VE SEEN ONE AT A CIRCUS.
WHY DON'T YOU JUMP THROUGH A HOOP FOR ME?
HOLD YOUR TONGUE, BOY!
YOU SURE TALK A LOT, PUSSY-CAT!
STOP FIGHTING!
SLAM
......

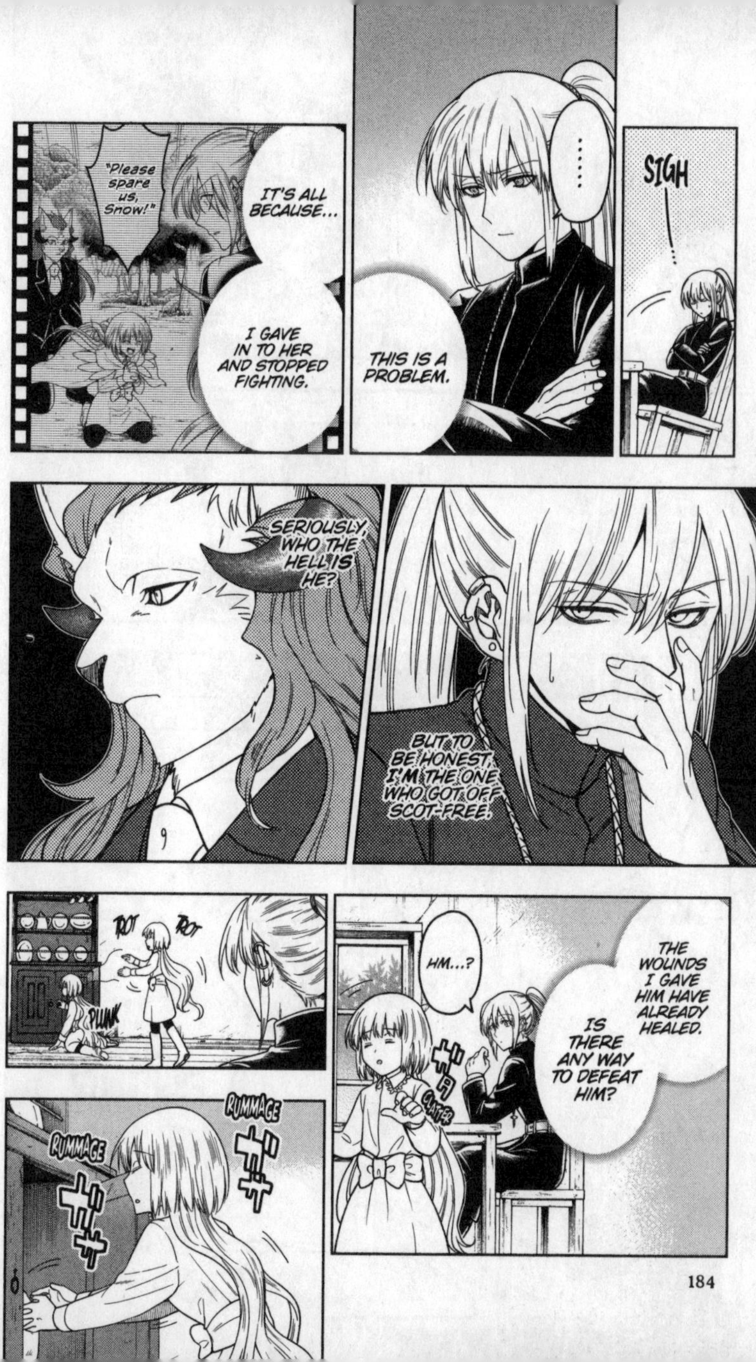
SIGH
......
THIS IS A PROBLEM.
IT'S ALL BECAUSE...
"Please spare us, Snow!"
I GAVE IN TO HER AND STOPPED FIGHTING.
BUT TO BE HONEST, I'M THE ONE WHO GOT OFF SCOT-FREE.
SERIOUSLY, WHO THE HELL IS HE?
THE WOUNDS I GAVE HIM HAVE ALREADY HEALED.
IS THERE ANY WAY TO DEFEAT HIM?
HM...?
CLATTER
TROT
TROT
PLUNK
RUMMAGE
RUMMAGE

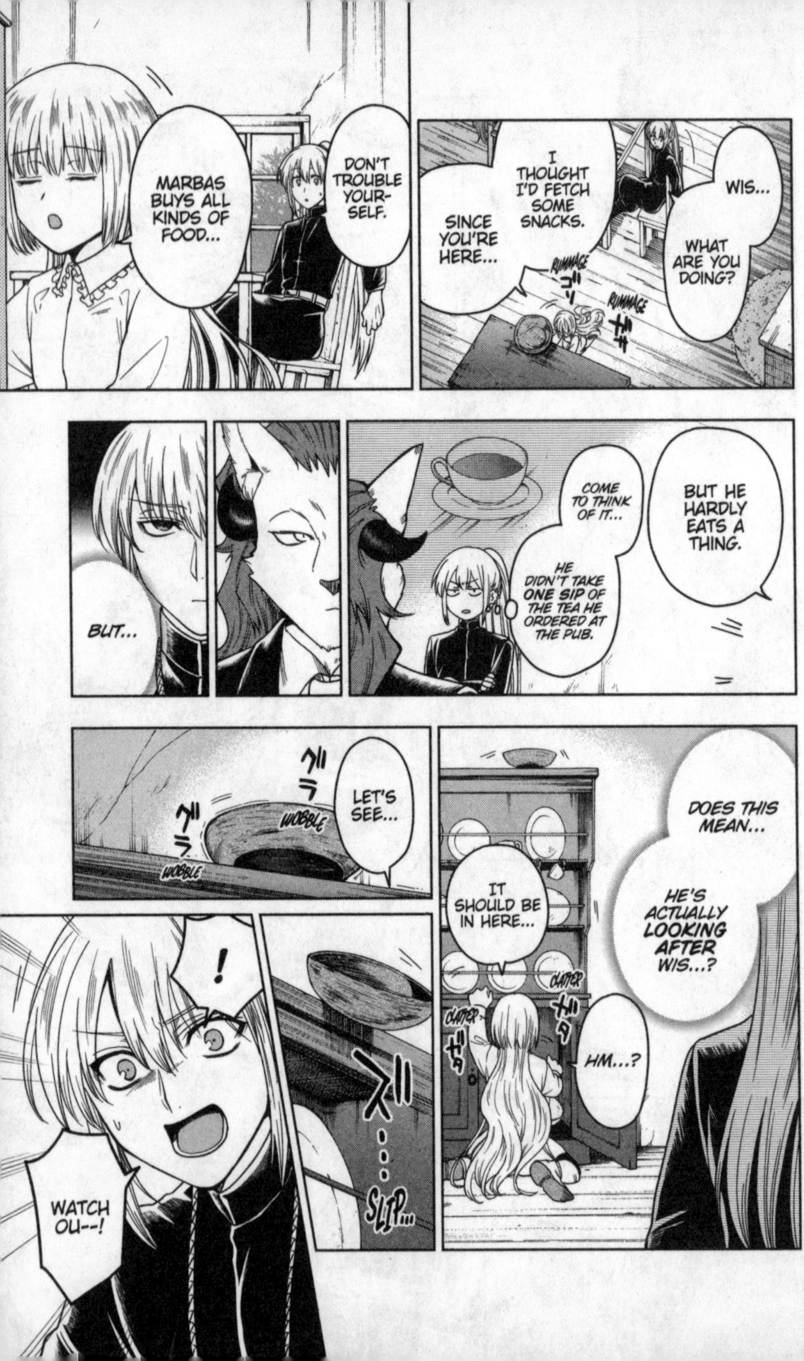
WIS...
WHAT ARE YOU DOING?
I THOUGHT I'D FETCH SOME SNACKS.
SINCE YOU'RE HERE...
RUMMAGE
RUMMAGE
DON'T TROUBLE YOURSELF.
MARBAS BUYS ALL KINDS OF FOOD...
BUT HE HARDLY EATS A THING.
COME TO THINK OF IT...
HE DIDN'T TAKE ONE SIP OF THE TEA HE ORDERED AT THE PUB.
BUT...
DOES THIS MEAN...
HE'S ACTUALLY LOOKING AFTER WIS...?
IT SHOULD BE IN HERE...
CLATTER
CLATTER
HM...?
LET'S SEE...
WOBBLE
WOBBLE
!
SLIP...
WATCH OU--!

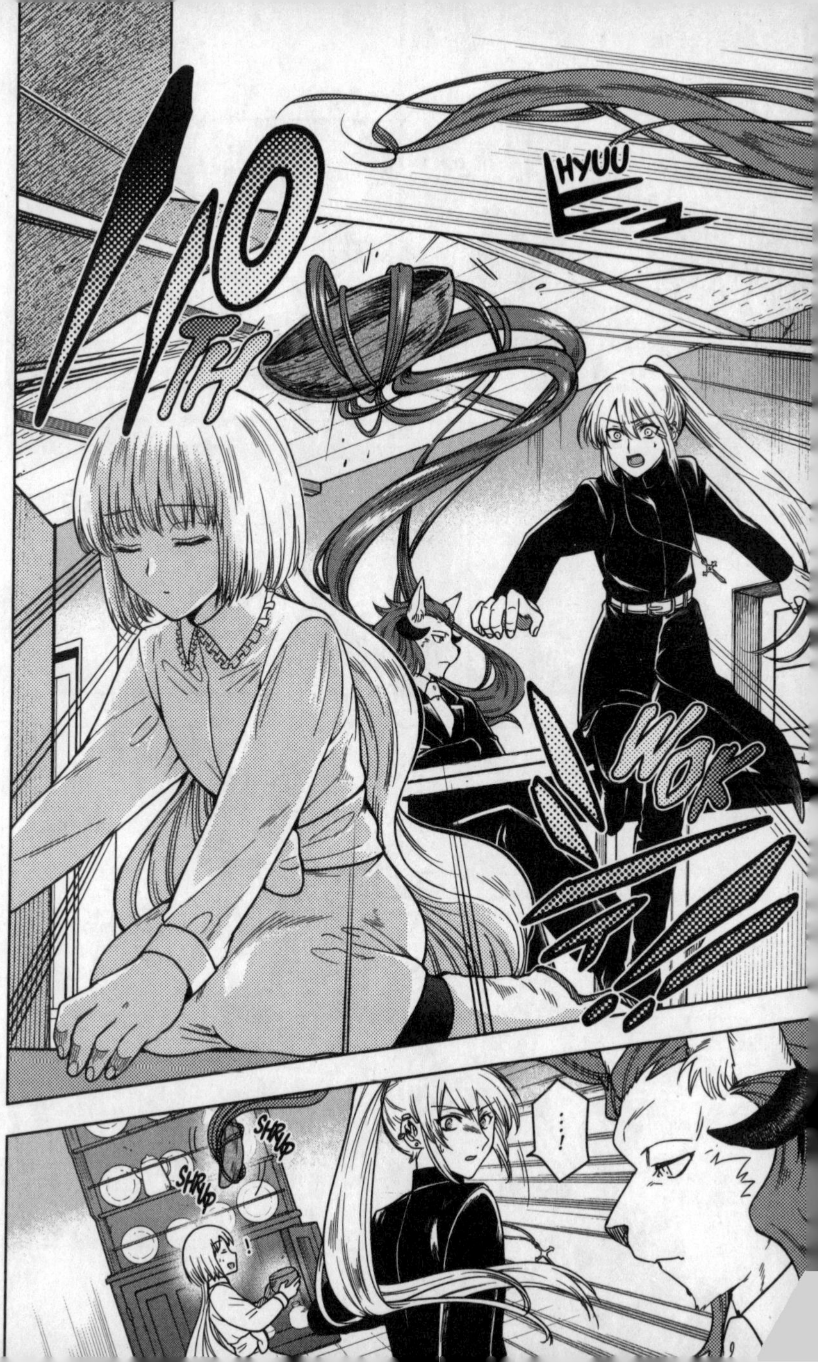
HYUU
WOTH
WOK
...!
SHRUP
SHRUP
!

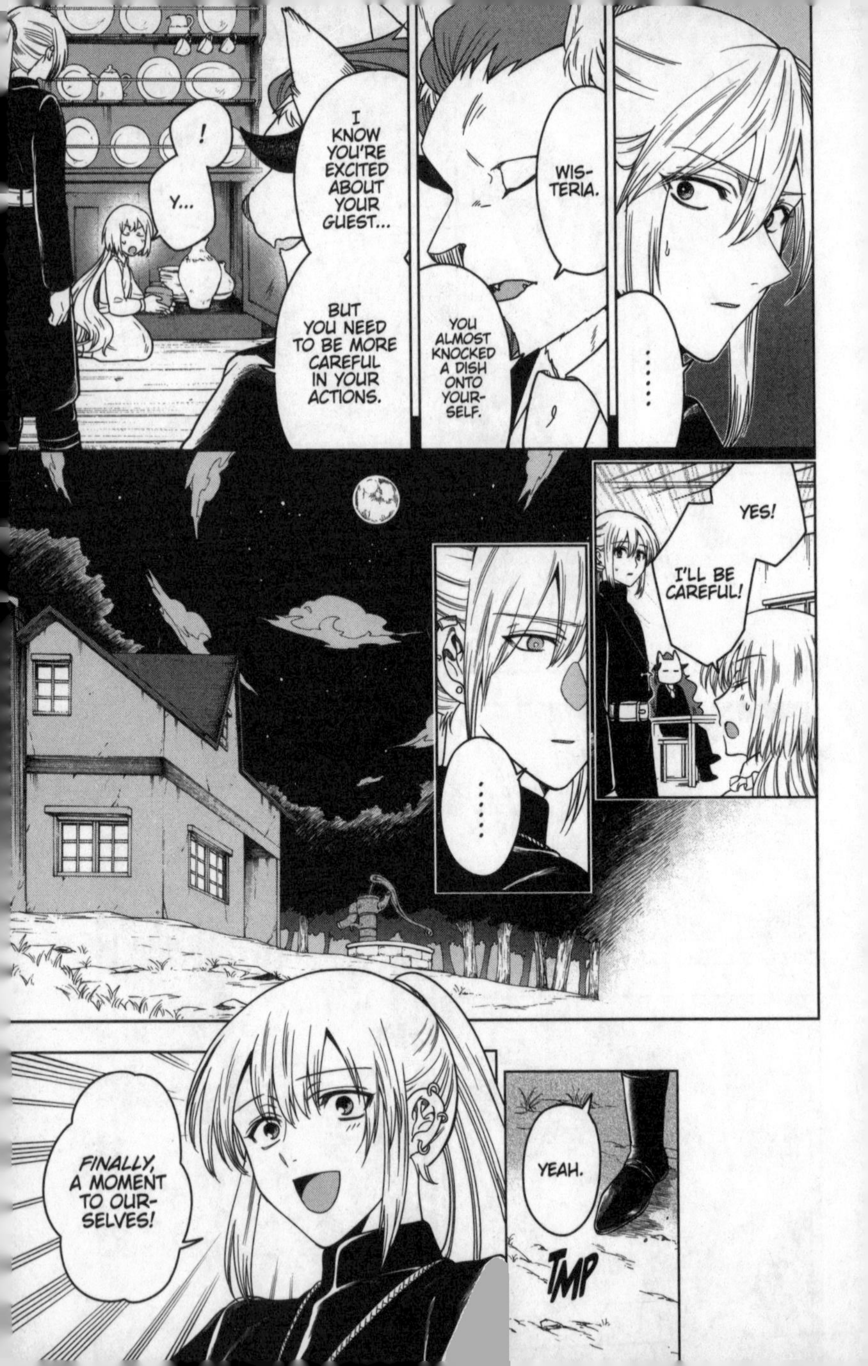
......
WIS-TERIA.
YOU ALMOST KNOCKED A DISH ONTO YOUR-SELF.
I KNOW YOU'RE EXCITED ABOUT YOUR GUEST...
BUT YOU NEED TO BE MORE CAREFUL IN YOUR ACTIONS.
!
Y...
YES!
I'LL BE CAREFUL!
......
YEAH.
TMP
FINALLY, A MOMENT TO OUR-SELVES!

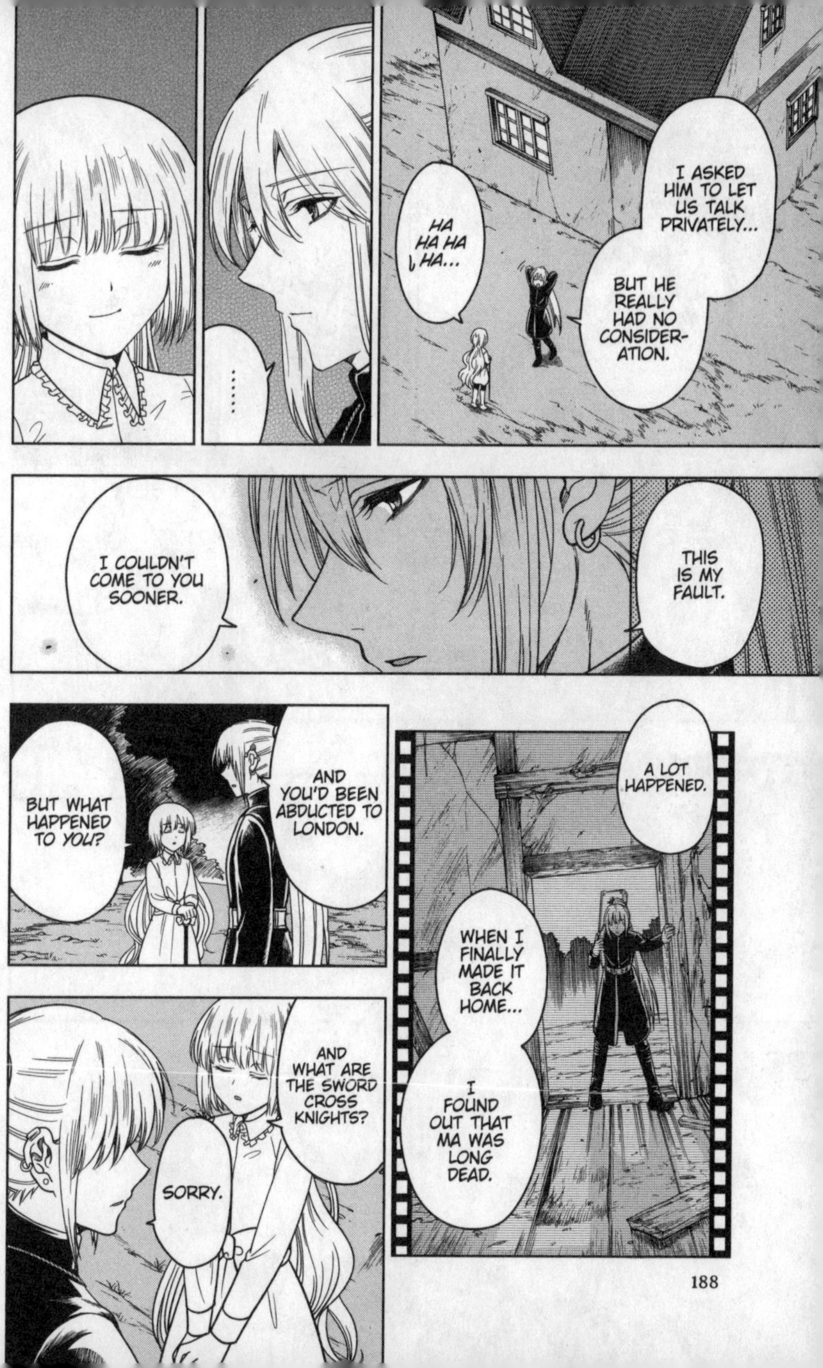
I ASKED HIM TO LET US TALK PRIVATELY...
BUT HE REALLY HAD NO CONSIDERATION.
HA HA HA HA...
......
THIS IS MY FAULT.
I COULDN'T COME TO YOU SOONER.
AND YOU'D BEEN ABDUCTED TO LONDON.
BUT WHAT HAPPENED TO YOU?
A LOT HAPPENED.
WHEN I FINALLY MADE IT BACK HOME...
I FOUND OUT THAT MA WAS LONG DEAD.
AND WHAT ARE THE SWORD CROSS KNIGHTS?
SORRY.

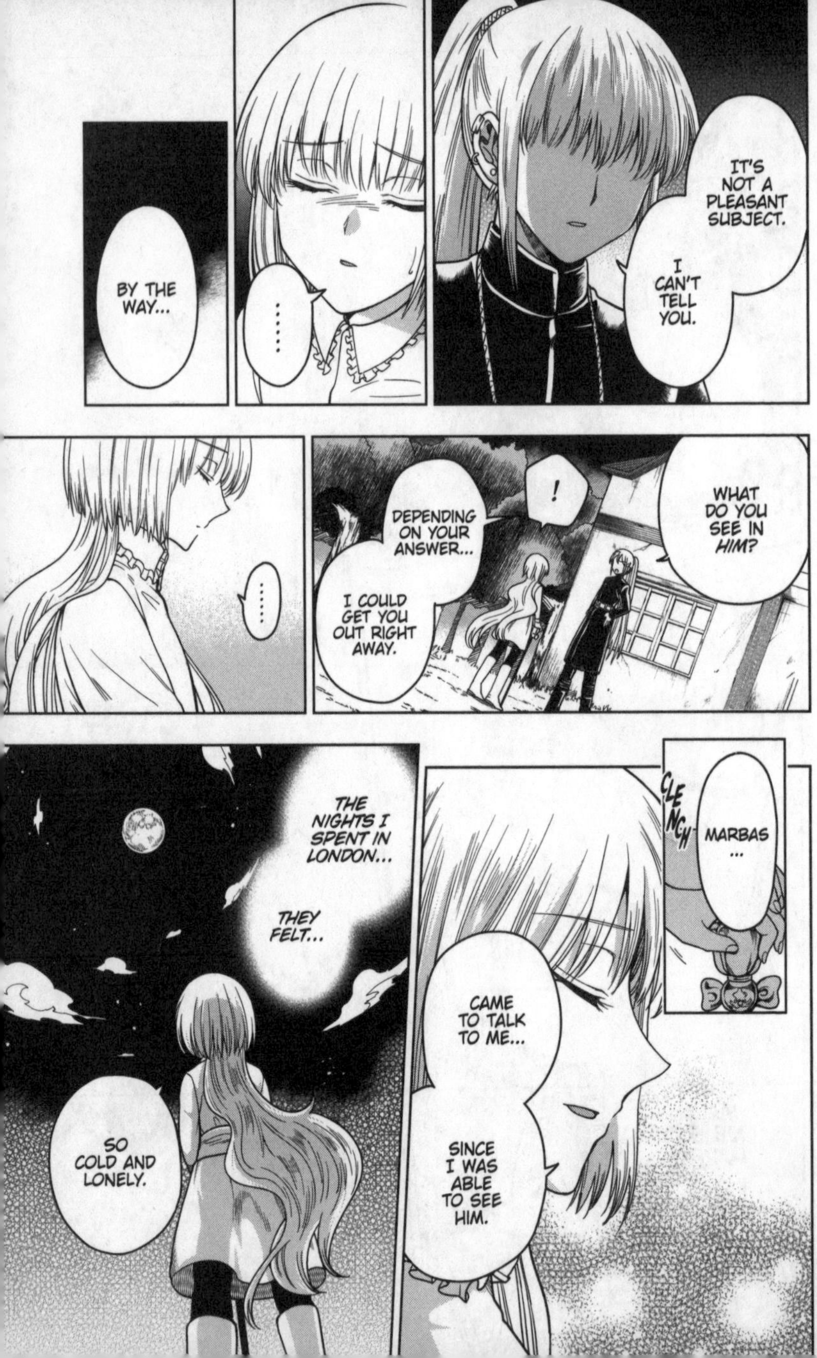
IT'S NOT A PLEASANT SUBJECT.
I CAN'T TELL YOU.
......
BY THE WAY...
WHAT DO YOU SEE IN HIM?
!
DEPENDING ON YOUR ANSWER...
I COULD GET YOU OUT RIGHT AWAY.
......
CLENCH
MARBAS ...
CAME TO TALK TO ME...
SINCE I WAS ABLE TO SEE HIM.
THE NIGHTS I SPENT IN LONDON...
THEY FELT...
SO COLD AND LONELY.

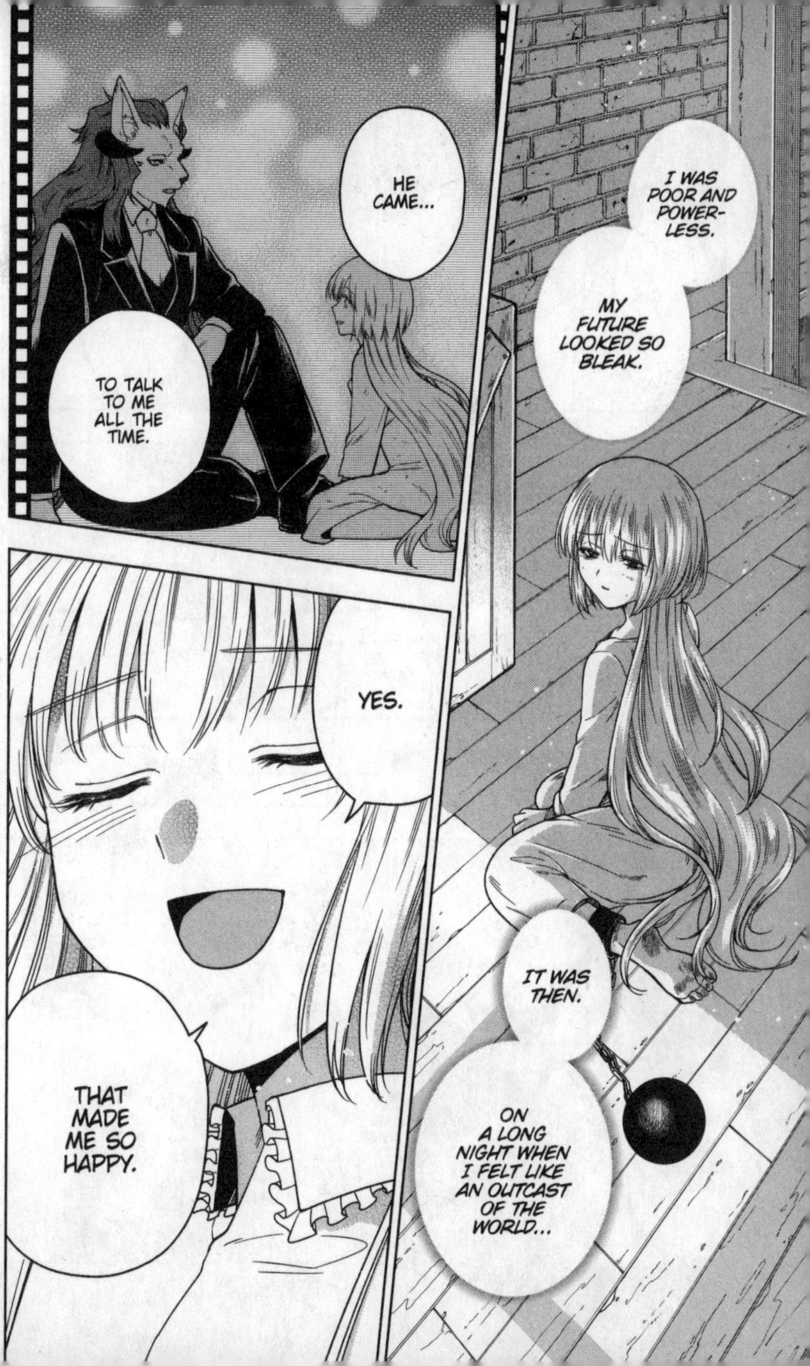
I WAS POOR AND POWER-LESS.
MY FUTURE LOOKED SO BLEAK.
IT WAS THEN.
ON A LONG NIGHT WHEN I FELT LIKE AN OUTCAST OF THE WORLD...
HE CAME...
TO TALK TO ME ALL THE TIME.
YES.
THAT MADE ME SO HAPPY.

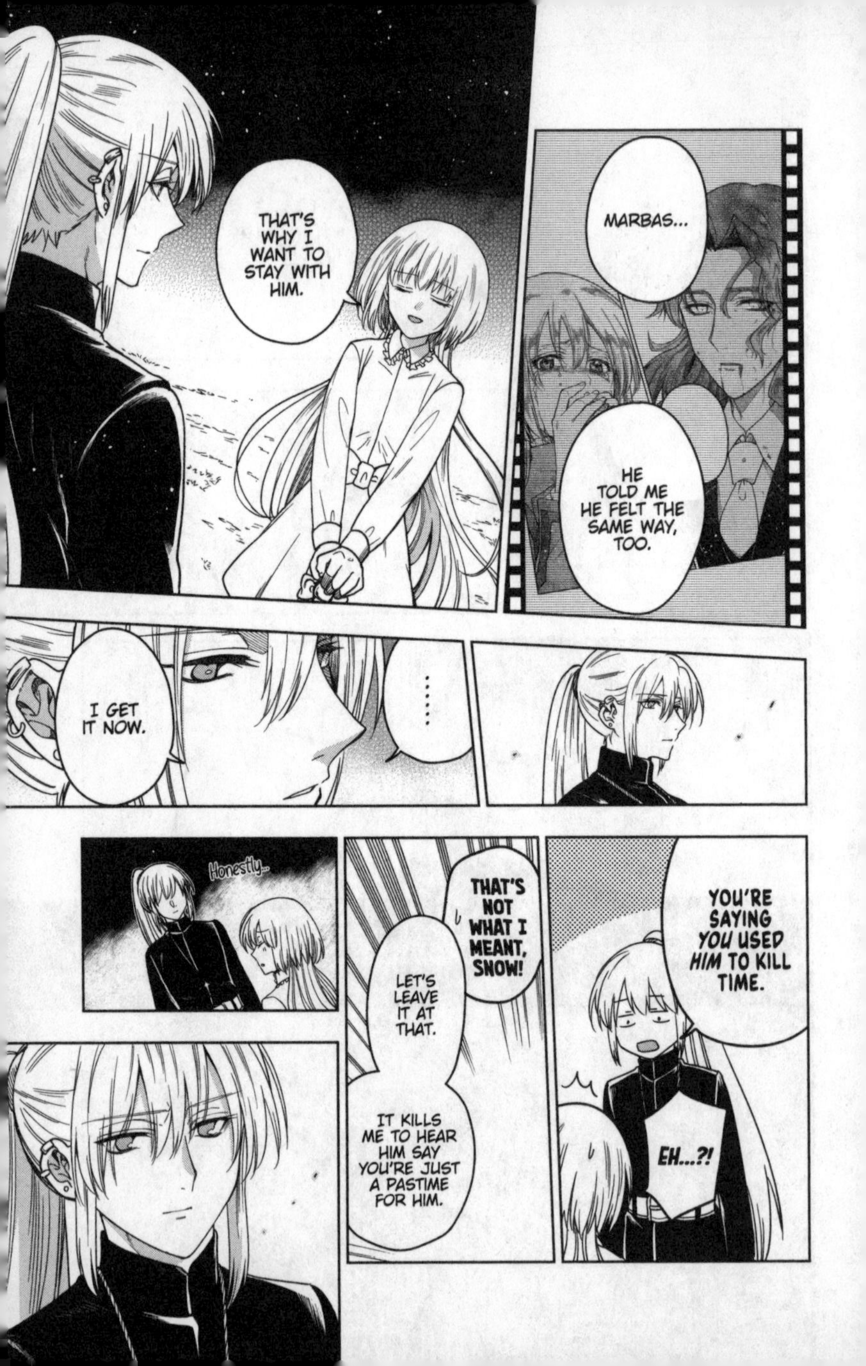
MARBAS...
HE TOLD ME HE FELT THE SAME WAY, TOO.
THAT'S WHY I WANT TO STAY WITH HIM.
......
I GET IT NOW.
YOU'RE SAYING *YOU* USED HIM TO KILL TIME.
EH...?!
THAT'S NOT WHAT I MEANT, SNOW!
LET'S LEAVE IT AT THAT.
IT KILLS ME TO HEAR HIM SAY YOU'RE JUST A PASTIME FOR HIM.
Honestly...

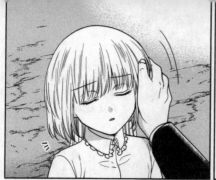

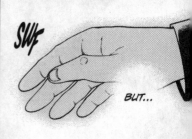

SWF

BUT...

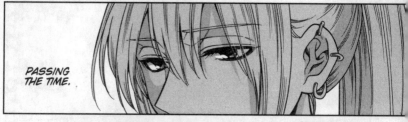

PASSING
THE TIME.

THAT WAS...

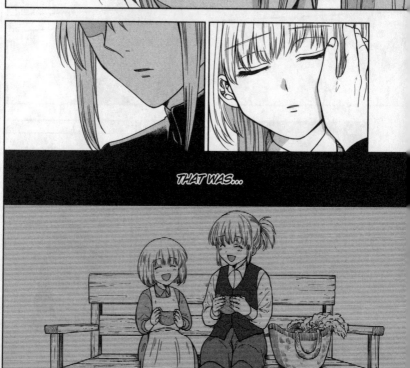

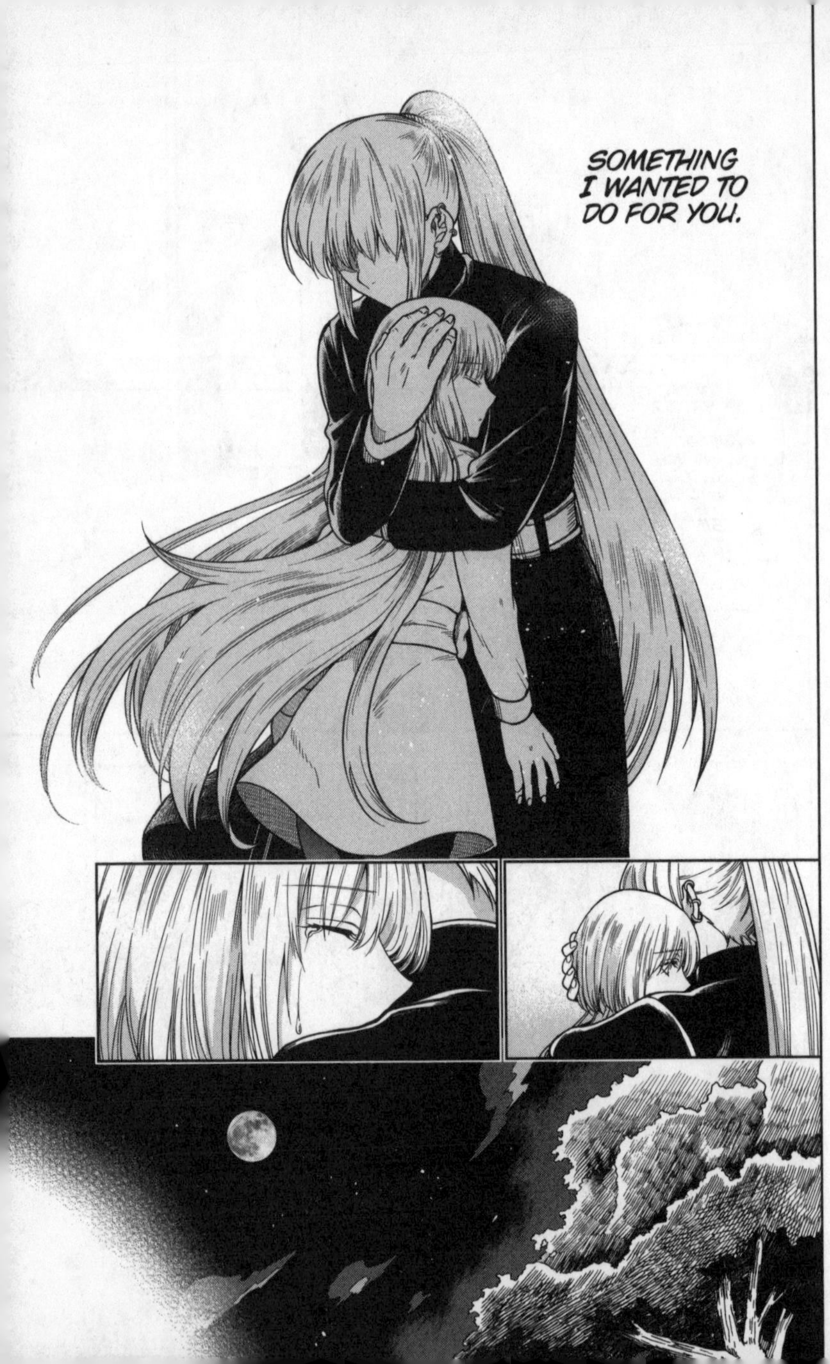
SOMETHING I WANTED TO DO FOR YOU.

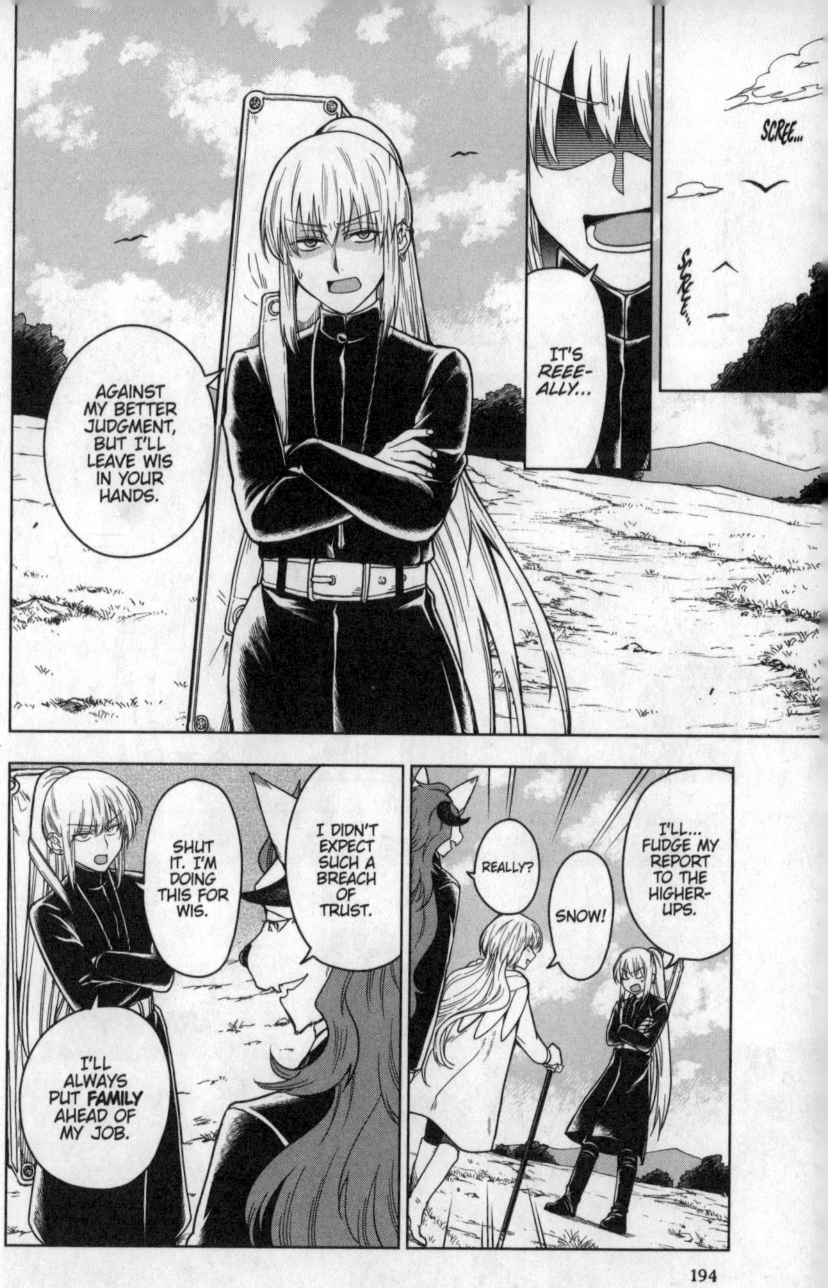
SCREE...
IT'S REEE-ALLY...
AGAINST MY BETTER JUDGMENT, BUT I'LL LEAVE WIS IN YOUR HANDS.
I'LL... FUDGE MY REPORT TO THE HIGHER-UPS.
SNOW!
REALLY?
I DIDN'T EXPECT SUCH A BREACH OF TRUST.
SHUT IT. I'M DOING THIS FOR WIS.
I'LL ALWAYS PUT **FAMILY** AHEAD OF MY JOB.

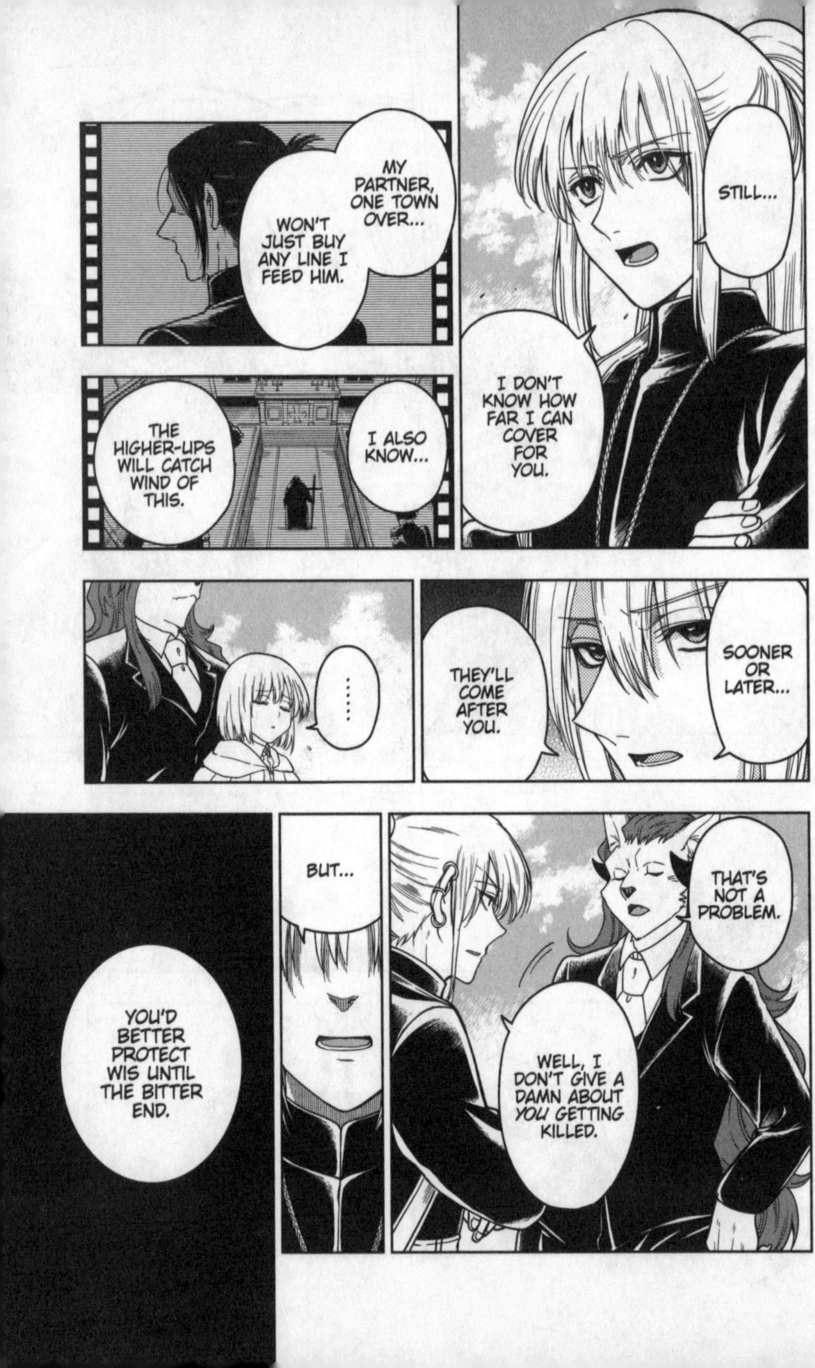
STILL...
I DON'T KNOW HOW FAR I CAN COVER FOR YOU.
MY PARTNER, ONE TOWN OVER...
WON'T JUST BUY ANY LINE I FEED HIM.
I ALSO KNOW...
THE HIGHER-UPS WILL CATCH WIND OF THIS.
SOONER OR LATER...
THEY'LL COME AFTER YOU.
......
THAT'S NOT A PROBLEM.
WELL, I DON'T GIVE A DAMN ABOUT *YOU* GETTING KILLED.
BUT...
YOU'D BETTER PROTECT WIS UNTIL THE BITTER END.

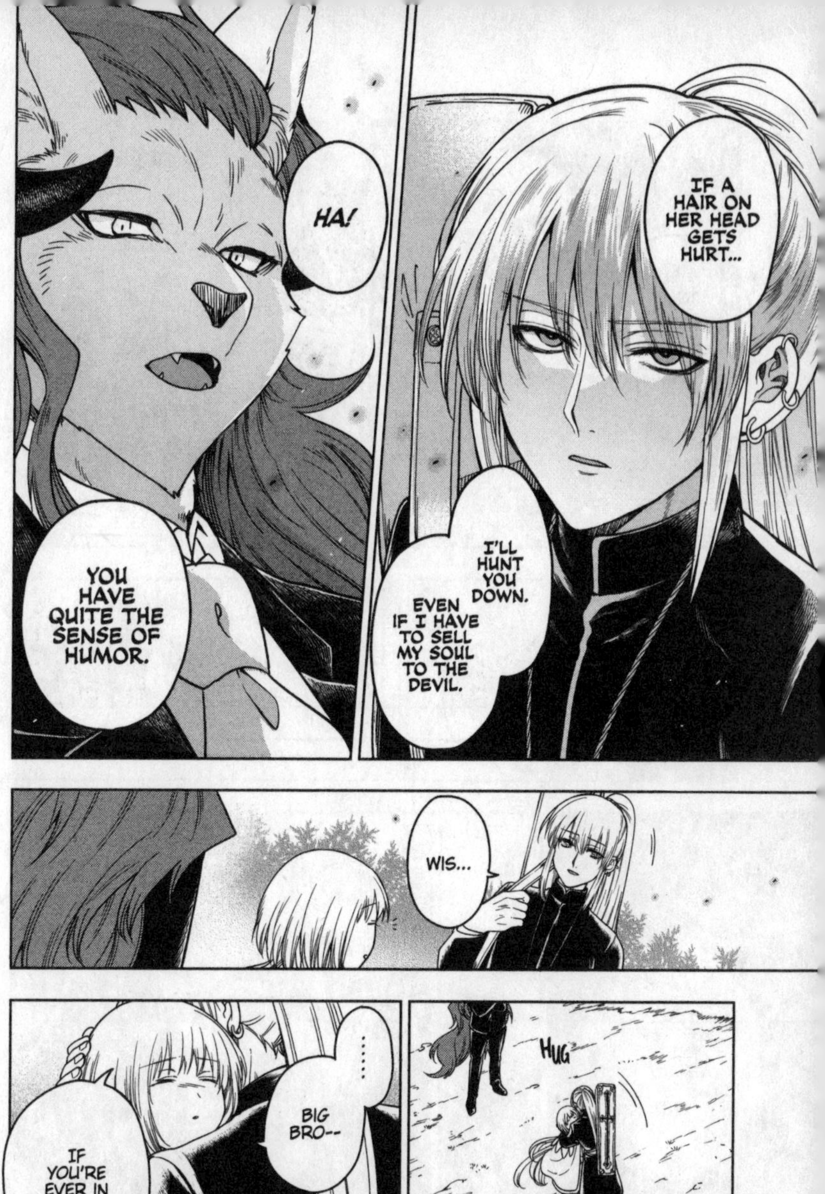
IF A HAIR ON HER HEAD GETS HURT...
I'LL HUNT YOU DOWN.
EVEN IF I HAVE TO SELL MY SOUL TO THE DEVIL.
HA!
YOU HAVE QUITE THE SENSE OF HUMOR.
WIS...
HUG
......
......
BIG BRO--
IF YOU'RE EVER IN TROUBLE...

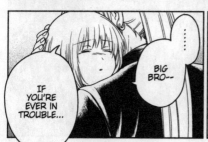

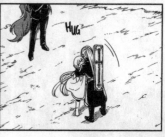

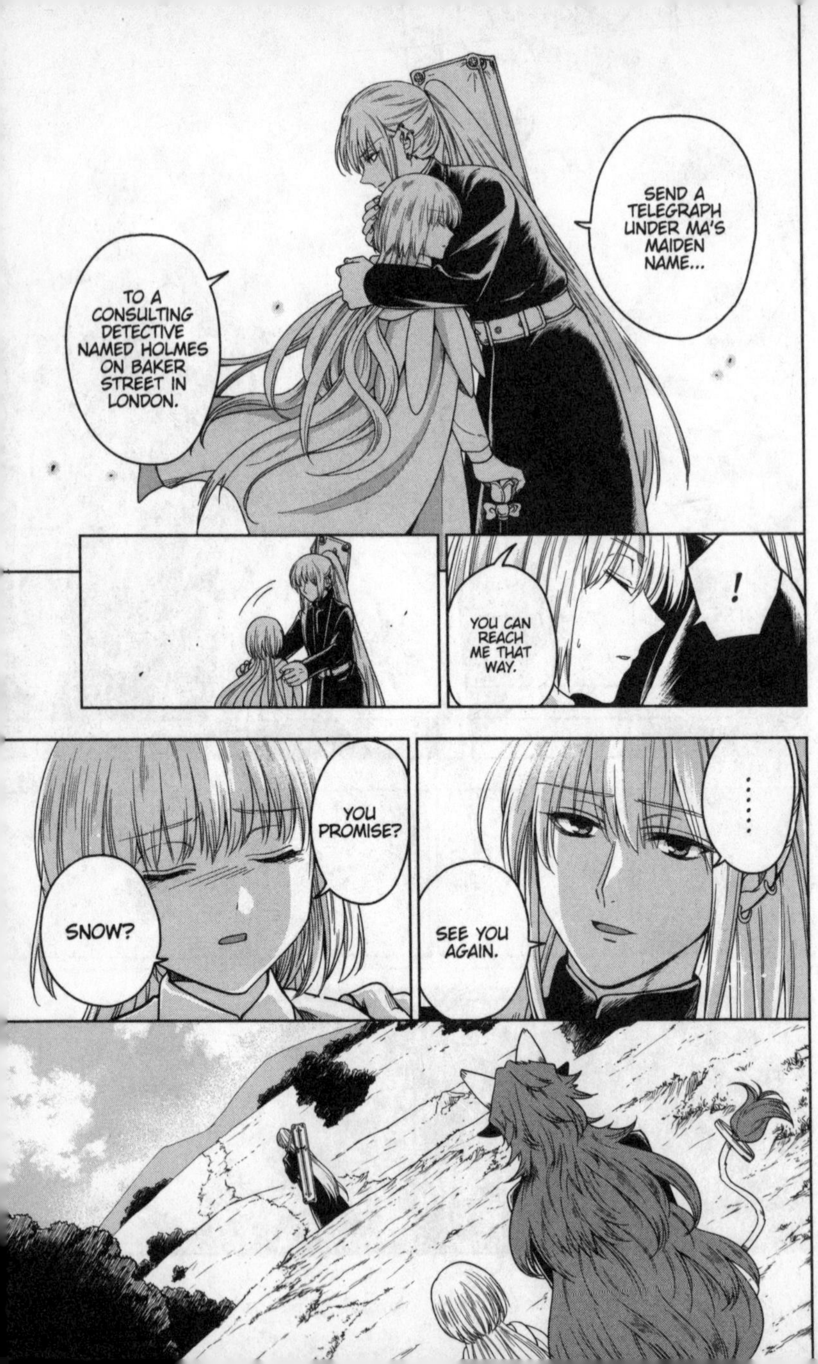
SEND A TELEGRAPH UNDER MA'S MAIDEN NAME...
TO A CONSULTING DETECTIVE NAMED HOLMES ON BAKER STREET IN LONDON.
!
YOU CAN REACH ME THAT WAY.
......
SEE YOU AGAIN.
YOU PROMISE?
SNOW?

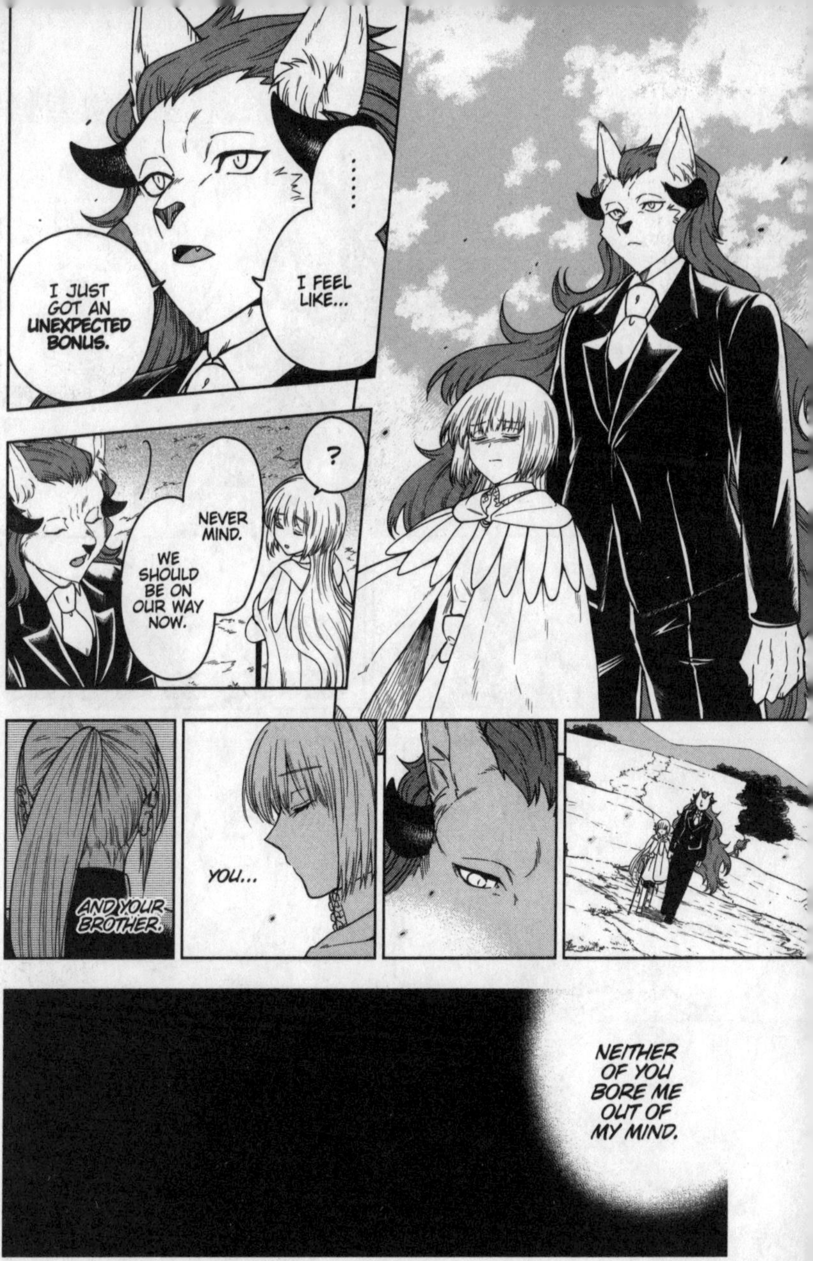
......
I FEEL LIKE...
I JUST GOT AN UNEXPECTED BONUS.
?
NEVER MIND.
WE SHOULD BE ON OUR WAY NOW.
YOU...
AND YOUR BROTHER.
NEITHER OF YOU BORE ME OUT OF MY MIND.

The Tale of the Outcasts Volume 1 • The End

The Tale of the Outcasts Volume 1

<Special Thanks>

Chihiro Makiguchi
Sanshi Fujita
Ugebeso Hatsumaru
Suzuka Takahashi
Michiru Mizuta
Akihisa Maki
Hirorin
Zakuro Mizuhara

<Editors>

Shiotani-san
Ogura-san

<Cover Design>

Arai-san

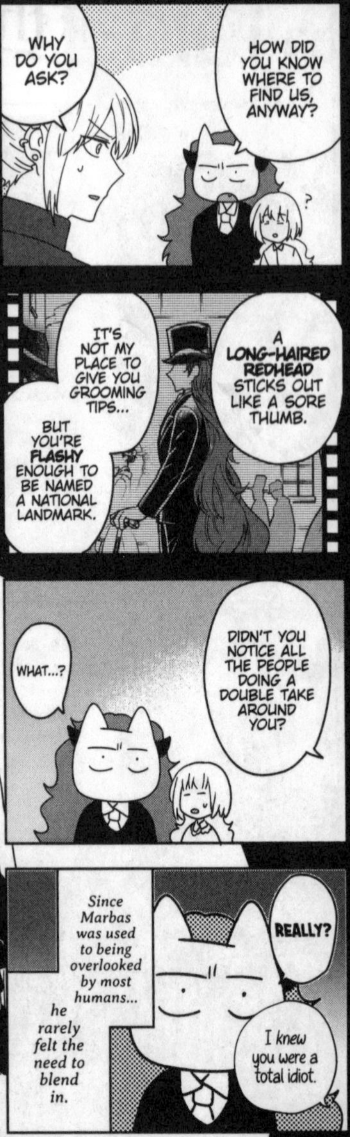

HOW DID YOU KNOW WHERE TO FIND US, ANYWAY?
WHY DO YOU ASK?
?
A LONG-HAIRED REDHEAD STICKS OUT LIKE A SORE THUMB.
IT'S NOT MY PLACE TO GIVE YOU GROOMING TIPS...
BUT YOU'RE FLASHY ENOUGH TO BE NAMED A NATIONAL LANDMARK.
DIDN'T YOU NOTICE ALL THE PEOPLE DOING A DOUBLE TAKE AROUND YOU?
WHAT...?
REALLY?
I knew you were a total idiot.
Since Marbas was used to being overlooked by most humans...
he rarely felt the need to blend in.

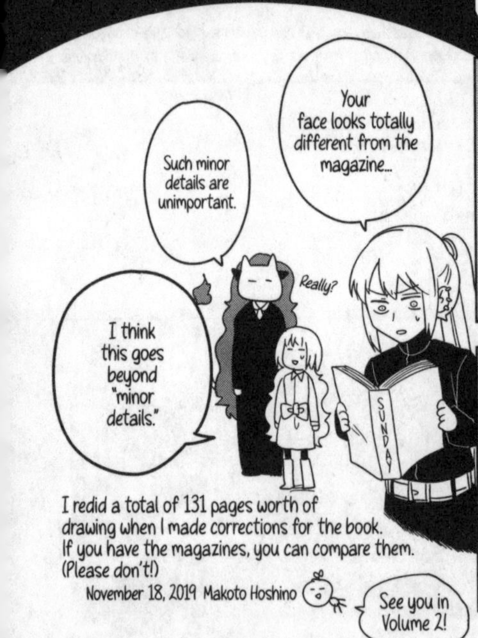

Your face looks totally different from the magazine...
Such minor details are unimportant.
Really?
I think this goes beyond "minor details."
SUNDAY
I redid a total of 131 pages worth of drawing when I made corrections for the book.
If you have the magazines, you can compare them.
(Please don't!)
November 18, 2019 Makoto Hoshino
See you in Volume 2!

SEVEN SEAS ENTERTAINMENT PRESENTS

The Tale of

story and art by MAKOTO HOSHINO

TRANSLATION
Elina Ishikawa

ADAPTATION
Ysabet Reinhardt MacFarlane

LETTERING
Brendon Hull

COVER DESIGN
Hanase Qi

PROOFREADER
Dayna Abel

EDITOR
Shanti Whitesides

COPY EDITOR
Dawn Davis

PREPRESS TECHNICIAN
Rhiannon Rasmussen-Silverstein

PRODUCTION ASSOCIATE
Christa Miesner

PRODUCTION MANAGER
Lissa Pattillo

MANAGING EDITOR
Julie Davis

ASSOCIATE PUBLISHER
Adam Arnold

PUBLISHER
Jason DeAngelis

NOKEMONO-TACHI NO YORU Vol.1
by Makoto HOSHINO
© 2019 Makoto HOSHINO
All rights reserved.
Original Japanese edition published by SHOGAKUKAN.
English translation rights in the United States of America, Canada, and the United
Kingdom arranged with SHOGAKUKAN through Tuttle-Mori Agency, Inc.

Seven Seas press and purchase enquiries can be sent to Marketing Manager Lianne
Sentar at press@gomanga.com. Information regarding the distribution and purchase of
digital editions is available from Digital Manager CK Russell at digital@gomanga.com.

Seven Seas and the Seven Seas logo are trademarks of
Seven Seas Entertainment. All rights reserved.

ISBN: 978-1-64827-115-1
Printed in Canada
First Printing: June 2021
10 9 8 7 6 5 4 3 2 1

//// READING DIRECTIONS ////

This book reads from *right to left*,
Japanese style. If this is your first time
reading manga, you start reading from
the top right panel on each page and
take it from there. If you get lost, just
follow the numbered diagram here.
It may seem backwards at first,
but you'll get the hang of it! Have fun!!

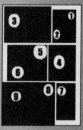

Follow us online: www.SevenSeasEntertainment.com